Tori hung up the phone and looked up as Sikes intercepted the young woman walking through. He flashed his most seductive smile and she shook her head. Any woman was fair game as far as Sikes was concerned. She was about to turn away when the woman walked purposefully to the Lieutenant's office.

Surely to God this was not her new partner. She leaned back in her chair and studied the woman. She would have called the blond woman petite, but she was a bit too tall for that. She looked almost slight in the blazer that hung loosely from her shoulders. She watched until the woman walked into the Lieutenant's office, then slid her eyes to Sikes.

"Back off, Hunter. She's out of your league," Sikes said from across the room with a laugh.

Tori gave him a humorless smile. "She looks like she might have a brain cell or two. I think she's obviously out of *your* league, Sikes."

The other detectives laughed and John Sikes took his seat.

"Good one, Hunter."

Visit

Bella Books

at

BellaBooks.com


or call our toll-free number

1-800-729-4992

# HUNTER'S WAY

CRIME SCENE — KEEP OUT

## GERRI HILL

Bella
BOOKS

2005

**Bella Books, Inc.**
P.O. Box 10543
Tallahassee, FL 32302

Printed in the United States of America on acid-free paper
First Edition

Editor: Anna Chinappi
Cover designer: Sandy Knowles

**ISBN 1-59493-018-X**

# Chapter One

"Hunter, get in here."

Tori glanced at Lieutenant Malone, then tossed the file she had been scanning onto her desk. She ignored the curious stares of the other detectives as she walked calmly into his office.

"Shut the door," he said.

She did and sat down quietly in front of him, waiting. His bald head glistened under the fluorescent lights and she silently watched him as he rubbed his bare forehead. Finally, he looked up from a thick file, locking glances with her. She looked down and realized that the file he had been looking at was her own.

"You've been with me seven years, Tori."

"Yes, sir."

He took his glasses off and tossed them on top of the file, then leaned back in his chair.

"You've had six partners."

She sighed and rolled her eyes to the ceiling. Not this again.

"Wasn't it only a few months ago that we went over this?" she asked.

"Yes. And at that time, you'd only had five partners."

"You cannot possibly blame me for Dickhead's two broken legs," she exclaimed.

"Detective Kaplan will most likely be on desk duty the rest of his career." Then he sighed. "Dickhead?"

"You didn't have to work with him every day," she said dryly. "He was a prick."

"If witnesses hadn't verified that you'd jumped out first, I'd be the first to think you'd pushed him out of the goddamn window."

"Oh, please. If I'd wanted to get rid of him that badly, I'd have just shot him."

He let a ghost of a smile cross his face, laughing outright when he met her eyes.

"Tori, you know I let you get away with more shit than anyone else in this squad. You're my best detective and you know it. Hell, everyone knows it. But this thing with partners, it's got to stop."

"Stan, is it my fault they get injured?"

"Injured?" He grabbed her file and flipped through the pages. "Two were killed in the line of duty, Hunter. One is on permanent disability. Two quit the force. And now Kaplan. Desk duty because he'll walk with a limp the rest of his life."

She looked away. She wanted to feel remorse. She really did. But she'd not had a relationship with any of them. They had not liked her and she had not liked them. They never clicked, never formed the bond necessary to be partners. They had not trusted each other. And that makes for the worst of partners.

"You can't blame me for this. I tried to tell you with every one of them that it wasn't working. None of them could get past the fact that I'm a woman," she said.

"I know you did, and I know they weren't right for you. But I don't always get to make the decisions. You're too much of a maverick, Hunter. You don't follow rules. I find it amazing that it hasn't caught up with you yet."

2

She glared at him. She'd heard this speech numerous times before. It always preceded his announcement that she would be getting a new partner.

"So who is he this time? Some burnout from Central?"

Lieutenant Malone shuffled through papers on his desk and put his glasses back on.

"Detective Kennedy. From Assault."

"And?"

"And she's been assigned to us."

"*She?*" Tori sat up straight in her chair. "A woman? You're pairing me with a woman?" She leaned her elbows on his desk. "Stan? A goddamn *woman?*"

"What's wrong with that? You're a woman."

She rose quickly, pacing across his office. A woman? Some bimbo from Assault? Jesus!

"She won't last a day," Tori threatened. "And you know it."

"She will last a day, Tori." Malone stood, too, and pointed his finger at her. "Because if she doesn't, they'll ship you out to foot patrol in Central. Or they'll put you behind a desk in CIU. Hell, Hunter, even the Chief called me."

"The Chief? Christ, I didn't think he knew my name."

"I mean it, Hunter. Make this work. I don't want to lose you, but I can't protect you forever. In case you haven't noticed, no one wants to work with you."

Tori shoved her hands in her pockets, her dark eyes piercing his. A woman. Well, this ought to be fun.

"Take her under your wing, Tori. Show her the ropes. It might do you good to have a female partner. You'll be the only one shooting off testosterone that way."

"Very funny."

3

# Chapter Two

Samantha Kennedy smoothed her blazer over neatly pressed slacks one more time before entering the squad room. Walking confidently to the Sergeant's desk, she stood patiently as he finished typing a report. Finally, he looked up.

"Yeah?"

"I'm Detective Kennedy. Lieutenant Malone is expecting me," she said.

"Through there." He pointed. "Name's on the door."

"Thank you," she said politely, but he had gone back to his typing, dismissing her.

She walked into the large room, easily sidestepping two uniformed officers who nearly bumped into her. She glanced around, noticing that most of the desks were empty. A phone rang insistently and she wondered why no one picked it up. Her eyes finally landed on a handsome young man with blue eyes who flashed her a grin. She nodded at him and continued on, her eyes scanning the offices for Lieutenant Malone's name.

"Need some help?"

She turned. The blue-eyed man was standing, his eyes traveling up her body and resting on her breasts. God, could he be less subtle?

"Hey, eyes are up here," she said slowly, pointing to her face. When he finally looked up, she asked, "I'm looking for Lieutenant Malone."

"Two doors down. Right there," he said, pointing with one well-manicured hand. Then he walked over. "I'm Detective Sikes. John. Is there something I can help you with?"

Samantha looked him over, much as he had done her. Then she smiled.

"No, thanks."

She knocked once on the Lieutenant's door, then entered.


Tori hung up the phone and looked up as Sikes intercepted the young woman walking through. He flashed his most seductive smile and she shook her head. Any woman was fair game as far as Sikes was concerned. She was about to turn away when the woman walked purposefully to the Lieutenant's office.

Surely to God this was not her new partner. She leaned back in her chair and studied the woman. She would have called the blond woman petite, but she was a bit too tall for that. She looked almost slight in the blazer that hung loosely from her shoulders. She watched until the woman walked into the Lieutenant's office, then slid her eyes to Sikes.

"Back off, Hunter. She's out of your league," Sikes said from across the room with a laugh.

Tori gave him a humorless smile. "She looks like she might have a brain cell or two. I think she's obviously out of *your* league, Sikes."

The other detectives laughed and John Sikes took his seat.

"Good one, Hunter."

Tori looked up and caught the laughing eyes of Tony Ramirez. He was really her only friend on the squad, if she would even call him that. She often wondered why Malone didn't partner her up with him. They got along well and on the few occasions they had worked together, he had never once treated her as anything other than his equal.

She looked around the room at the other detectives. Matthew Donaldson had come up with her in the Academy. He probably knew her better than anyone here, but he avoided her like the plague. She was the only woman and he was the only African-American. He knew all about discrimination. Apparently he thought it only involved skin color, not gender.

Then there was Richard Adams. A fifty-two-year-old who was strictly old-school. Women had no place on the force, and they certainly had no place among the detectives. He took every opportunity to belittle her. But what he and the others didn't understand was that she simply didn't care whether they liked her or not. She did her job.

She finally glanced at John Sikes. Even she had to admit he was handsome. Blond and blue-eyed, he used his looks to get witnesses to talk time and again. Unfortunately, that was his best quality as a detective. He, most of all, despised Tori. Not because she was a woman. Sikes was probably the only one here who could work with a woman. No, he disliked her because she was gay.

She shrugged, then went back to her files. None of it mattered. She had the best conviction rate among them all and she never rested until her cases were solved. Night after night, they would all go home to their lives and their families and she would stay, poring over reports again and again. But then, it wasn't like she had someone to go home to.


"Lieutenant Malone?"

"Yes, come in. You must be Kennedy."

"Yes, sir."

Stan observed the woman who walked into his office and took a seat in front of his desk. He hadn't known what to expect, but he assumed it would be someone older, more seasoned. Not the young blonde sitting before him now. She was attractive. Her blond hair reached just to the collar of her blazer, and she nervously brushed it away from her face. Oh, Hunter would eat her alive. He gave it two days before the woman came running scared to him, asking for a new partner. Then green eyes met his own and he smiled. She returned the smile and his old heart did a flip-flop. She was beautiful.

He cleared his throat and picked up the file he'd been given yesterday. He'd barely glanced through it.

"I understand you requested this move," he started. "Your Lieutenant said they had you earmarked for CIU."

"CIU doesn't really appeal to me," Samantha said. "More desk work than anything."

"A stepping-stone to the FBI," Malone countered. "We've lost some good men that way."

She smiled. "Yes, but I'm a woman."

Stan felt his face flush. "Figure of speech."

"Yes, sir."

"So, you've been with the Assault Division four years. You have a good record, your Lieutenant spoke highly of you. Why the change?"

"Every Lieutenant and Captain I've met comes from Homicide. Not Assault."

He smiled. "So, you have higher aspirations than just a lowly detective, huh?"

"I spent three years on the East Side, three in Central. I was honored when they requested me at Assault. But after four years, I watched men come and go, moving on to Homicide, CIU, Tactical. They skipped right over me. Please don't take this the wrong way, but as a woman, I understand if you want to move up higher in the chain, you have to do things twice as well as the men. Where better than Homicide?"

Stan Malone grinned, then laughed. Well, looked like he'd just found Tori Hunter the perfect partner. A woman with ambition.

7

She raised her eyebrows. "Funny?"

"No, no. I'm laughing at myself, not at you." He patted the thick file on his desk. "I take it you don't know anything about your new partner?"

"No, sir. But please don't tell me he's some old-timer who can't stand to work with women."

"Oh, no. Detective Hunter. He's a she."

"Hunter?"

"Heard of her?"

Samantha had heard the stories. She was a nutcase, by most accounts. *Great. Just great.*

"I've heard some," she said. "Didn't her partner get killed a few years ago?"

"She's my best detective. Somewhat of a rogue. It's hard to keep her on a tight leash. But you can learn a lot from her. If she'll let you."

"If she'll *let* me?"

"She likes to work alone. Damn near lives here. Her partners go home, she stays here, cleans up the case. They come back the next day, it's all done. Most men can't take that. She rarely listens to advice from her partners, just does her own thing. They either follow her or get lost in the chase. Two have been killed in the line of duty. Everyone wanted to blame Hunter. But in both instances, they decided not to follow her lead. She came out unscathed and got her man. They ended up dead by simply making the wrong decision.

"Two actually quit the force after working with her. Another was injured when a car ran over him. Permanent disability. And Kaplan, your predecessor, jumped out of a two-story window and broke both legs."

"Why in the world did he jump?"

"He was following her."

Samantha's eyebrows shot up. "*She* jumped out of a two-story window?"

"Yes." Then he grinned. "Just like the movies. Jumped to the fire escape, swung down the railing, bounced off the trash Dumpster and caught the perp."

"Great," she murmured. Definitely a nutcase.

He stood, motioning her to do the same.

"Let me introduce you around. A couple of things, but you'll find out soon enough yourself: Adams is old-school. You're a woman and he won't give you the time of day. And Sikes, he fancies himself a ladies' man. He *will* give you the time of day. Every day. But there's no love lost between them and Hunter. In fact, Ramirez is the only one that gets on well with Hunter. A mild case of hero worship or a crush or something." He stopped before opening his door. "Don't you dare tell either of them I said that."

"No, sir."

He motioned her out the door, then followed, stopping in the middle of the squad room.

"Listen up, people."

All heads popped up except Tori's. She continued with her phone conversation, ignoring the Lieutenant and the young woman.

"Detective Kennedy's been assigned to us from Assault. She'll be replacing Kaplan."

He pointed around the room and Samantha followed his introductions.

"Richard Adams and Matthew Donaldson. John Sikes and Tony Ramirez over there. Sergeant Fisk out front there. And Tori Hunter. That's our team."

Samantha nodded at them, murmuring hellos, her eyes finally landing on the woman who would be her new partner, landing on her profile anyway. The woman had yet to look her way.

"Make her feel at home." Then, to Samantha, "Come on. I'll introduce you personally."

Tori hung up the phone just as Malone walked over.

"Hunter, this is Detective Kennedy. She's been assigned to you. Try to play nice," he said with just a hint of a threat.

Tori looked over the blond woman in front of her, with her

9

pressed slacks and neat jacket. No jewelry, save the watch and ear-rings. Hesitant green eyes peered back at her, then the woman offered her hand.

"Nice to meet you, Detective Hunter," she said pleasantly.

"Yeah. A real pleasure," she said dryly. The woman looked like an attorney, not a cop. She wondered if she'd ever done fieldwork or just sat behind a desk. "That's yours," she said, pointing to the desk butting up against her own. At least the woman would be nicer to look at than Kaplan's old sour puss.

Samantha looked quickly at Lieutenant Malone, who smiled apologetically and squeezed her shoulder.

"You'll be fine," he said quietly, then left them alone.

Samantha looked back to the other woman, who had already picked up the phone again. Great. Just great. She hates me already, she thought.

"Sit down."

She stared at the woman, who had the phone cradled against her shoulder, and took the file she handed her. She sat, her eyes still on the dark-haired woman.

"Yeah, this is Hunter. I need the lab results." A pause. "You said it would be this morning." Another pause. "It's goddamn nine o'clock! That *is* morning."

Samantha raised her eyebrows.

"Fine. If you meant noon, then say noon." Tori slammed the phone down. "Idiots," she murmured.

Samantha watched, her apprehension growing with each passing second. She should have stayed in Assault. She should have requested CIU.

"Teenage girl found in a trash Dumpster on the East Side. Jane Doe," Tori said, pointing to the file she'd handed Kennedy. "Hooker, most likely. Consensus is a john killed her. But I don't think so."

"If a john killed her, why would he go to all the trouble of dumping her body? Why not leave it?"

10

Tori looked up, startled. That was her theory as well.

"Maybe if he left her at the scene, there would be too much evidence that would point to him," Tori said.

"Motels that rent by the hour? Come on. You could get hundreds of prints."

Tori nodded.

"Okay. Her pimp?"

"That would be logical, but we can't find anyone who recognizes her."

"Then maybe she's not from East Dallas," Samantha said. "Downtown?"

"Probably. There's a small area on the West End and Little Mexico. That's about it."

"She was black. I doubt she worked Little Mexico," Samantha said.

Tori leaned back and studied the other woman. She looked young.

"How long have you been a detective?"

"Five years. Why?"

"You barely look thirty," Tori said.

"Thirty-four, but does it matter?"

"Of course it matters. No one takes a woman seriously, especially when she looks like she's fresh out of college."

"Why, thank you. I knew there was a compliment in there somewhere," Samantha said sarcastically.

Tori Hunter stood and grabbed her coffee cup and walked away. Samantha stared after her. She was taller than Samantha, but only by a few inches. Short dark hair, dark eyes. She wouldn't call her boyish, she was too attractive for that. Definitely moody. Why the sudden change? Did she answer one of the questions wrong?

"Don't worry about her, honey. She's just being her usual bitchy self," John Sikes told her as he walked over.

"Excuse me?"

"Hunter," he explained.

11

"No. *Honey?* Were you talking to me?"

He flashed her a charming smile and sat on the corner of her desk.

"Sorry. No offense." He stuck out his hand. "John Sikes, at your service," he said.

She took his hand, then dropped it quickly as he squeezed.

"No offense, John, but I'd appreciate it if you didn't call me *honey*. I'll try to refrain from calling you names as well."

He laughed and she smiled at him. He really was attractive, she had to admit.

"So, you're stuck with Hunter. Sorry about that. I wish you luck."

"I'm sure I'll be fine," she said.

"Well, if you need anything . . . *anything* at all, you just let me know."

"Thanks. I'll keep that in mind."

Tori came back with two steaming cups of coffee and set one on Samantha's desk. She flicked her eyes to Sikes.

"Don't you have work to do?"

"Just introducing myself, Hunter. Don't get excited."

"Trust me, you don't excite me."

He laughed again, then pulled himself off of Samantha's desk, ignoring Tori. "So, Samantha, you want to maybe get dinner some night? I can fill you in on all the local gossip," he offered.

"No thanks. I'm involved with someone. I doubt he'd appreciate that," she said.

He shrugged. "You never know. Offer is always open," he said as he walked away.

"Stay away from him," Tori said. "He's a jerk."

Samantha smiled. Yes, she agreed.

"Does anyone here like you?" she asked.

"No."

"Why?"

"I don't bullshit, I don't play games."

"That doesn't mean you can't be friends with the people you work with," Samantha said.

"Friends? With those guys?" Tori leaned forward. "Adams hates me because I'm a woman. He could care less about my job performance. I'm just a woman. Donaldson, his partner, follows his lead, even though Adams barely tolerates him because he's black. Ramirez is the only one who shows me even the slightest consideration and because of that, he has to listen to ridicule from the others, especially Sikes, his partner."

"That can't all be because you're a woman."

"No, not just because I'm a woman. Because I'm a woman and I'm better at the job than they are."

"Oh. Well, it's good to know you're not in the least conceited," Samantha said with a smile.

"Why are you here?"

"Excuse me?"

"Did they ask you or did you volunteer?"

"I requested a transfer months ago. I don't know what you're talking about."

Tori nodded and sipped from her coffee. "So, you have a boyfriend?"

"Yes. Why?"

Tori shrugged. "It'll make it easier on you. Sikes will only hit on you every other day. Adams will at least think there's hope you'll get married and pregnant and get out of his territory."

"You paint a very bleak picture of this office, Hunter. I've worked around men my whole career. I've never had a problem with them. I doubt I will here, either. I do a good job."

Tori shrugged again. She was probably right. She was straight and attractive. She was no threat to them. Unlike herself.

"I'm going to go down to Central and show our girl's picture around. Maybe she's been hauled in before. Want to come?"

"As opposed to staying here and being leered at by Sikes?"

# Chapter Three

It was after six when Samantha walked into her apartment and collapsed on her sofa. It had been a mentally trying day and she was exhausted. She glanced over at the phone. Three messages. Kicking off her shoes, she stretched out, hitting her voice mail as she lay down.

*"It's me, sweetheart. I wanted to see if you were up to dinner. Can't wait to hear about your first day. Call me when you get in."*

She nodded, waiting for the beep.

*"It's me. So how did it go? If you can sneak away from Robert one night, why don't we get dinner. It's been awhile."*

She nodded again, mentally making a note to call Amy later.

*"Sorry, Samantha, can't do dinner tonight after all. I've got a late meeting. I'll call you when I'm done. Maybe I can swing by."*

She shook her head. She was too tired. She was actually thankful Robert had a meeting. She pushed off the sofa, taking her clothes off as she headed to the bathroom. A long, hot shower helped revive her somewhat. Unfortunately, her refrigerator didn't miraculously contain dinner. Sorting through the frozen meals in her freezer, she grabbed one and popped it in the microwave. Her refrigerator did, however, contain a bottle of wine.

She took a glass and the entire bottle into the living room, settling into her recliner.

"Ahh," she murmured as she put her feet up. She grabbed the phone, and with her thumb, punched out Amy's number.

"It's me," she said when her best friend answered.

"Well, hello, Detective. How'd it go?"

Samantha smiled and sipped from her wine.

"I survived . . . barely," she said. "I'm afraid it's dangerously close to a mental ward, but I survived."

"That bad, huh?"

"I've never in my life seen so many egos and that much testosterone in one place before."

Amy laughed. "I told you to stay put. The boys in Homicide don't mess around with little girls."

"My partner's a woman," Samantha said.

"You're kidding? What? They lump you both together so you won't get in the way?"

"You may have heard of her. Tori Hunter."

"Jesus Christ! She's the nut that jumped out of the two-story building. We're defending the guy she nabbed," Amy said.

"Yes, that's her. So, you got the case?"

"No, Michaels does. It's a dead end, though. He's going to plea."

"She's supposedly very good at her job," Samantha said. "She doesn't exactly fare too well with partners, though. I'm not sure we're going to get along."

"Oh, you'll do fine. Everyone likes you."

"Yes. But not everyone likes her. It's going to be difficult. She's moody as hell and she resents me being assigned to her."

"I'm sure you'll win her over. Where's Robert?"

"Meeting. Thankfully. I was too tired for dinner. In fact, I'm too tired for company, period."

"So how are things going with you guys?"

"Okay."

"Okay? You've been seeing him for two years. When are you going to talk marriage?"

"Marriage? I don't think we're at that stage, Amy." In fact, she knew she wasn't. Robert had hinted they might move in together, but she'd balked. She liked her privacy and her time alone. He didn't really understand but he didn't push. Not much, anyway.

"He's a good guy, Samantha. You could do a lot worse."

"Yes, I know. He's a sweetheart. I'm just not ready to get married."

"You think it'll interfere with your career?"

"Well, there's that," she said. "He hates it now when I'm out nights. Can you imagine if we were married?"

"And working Homicide, you'll be out nights more often," Amy said.

"Most likely. So, how are you doing? Still seeing Eric?" Samantha asked, thankful to change the subject.

"Yes. I wish I could say I'm in love with him, but I'm not. He's just so damn attractive. I keep thinking it'll come," she said with a laugh.

Samantha shook her head. Amy had always been swayed by a pretty face. In that, Samantha was lucky. Robert was handsome and she was . . . well, she loved him. Was she in love with him? Maybe. At least she thought she should be.

They really had a great relationship. They rarely argued. When they did, it was usually over cases. He was a defense attorney. Thankfully, they had never worked the same case.

She was asleep on the sofa when he called later that evening. He wanted to come over.

"Robert, I'm really exhausted. Can we hook up tomorrow?" she asked.

"Of course. How did it go today?"

"It went . . . okay," she said. "It'll be different, that's for sure," she said around a yawn. "I'm sorry," she murmured.

"That's okay. Go back to sleep. I'll talk to you tomorrow."

She wanted to burrow deeper into the sofa, but she made herself get up and into bed.

# Chapter Four

Samantha felt refreshed when her alarm went off at six. She showered quickly, deciding to grab coffee on the way. She wanted to be early. For some reason, she felt the need to beat Tori Hunter to work.

It was a sunny morning and warm for March. Of course, that was relative. March in Dallas was either hinting at summer or hanging on to winter. Spring lasted but a few weeks.

She was early enough to beat traffic and she stopped at a coffeehouse on the corner of Commerce and Oakland. She eyed the pastries before deciding on a croissant. Ham and cheese filled, but still better than a pastry, she reasoned. She ate while she drove the two blocks to the station. She was early. The lot was only half full.

But her good mood vanished when she saw Tori Hunter sitting at her desk, phone already tucked on her shoulder. The same as it was when she'd left last evening. Damn, did the woman even go home?

"Morning," she said.

"Uh-huh." Tori glanced up briefly, then away. "It's Hunter. I want to go over the lab reports. I'll be down in a half-hour." A pause. "Yes, I know what time it is. Do *you*?" She hung up. "Idiots."

"Well, off to another fine start," Samantha murmured. She pulled out her chair and sat looking at her new partner, wondering what was on the agenda today. The lab reports, obviously. She'd left after five and they hadn't received them yet. Apparently, Tori had gotten her hands on them somehow.

"Seems our girl was busy before she died. Four different semen types," Tori said.

"When did you get the report?"

"Last night," she said absently. "You want to come or do you want to stay here and settle in?"

Samantha waited until Tori Hunter looked up.

"Are you always this difficult to work with?"

"Yes."

"No wonder Kaplan jumped. He was probably wishing it was four stories instead of two."

"Very funny. Are you coming?"

"Yes, Hunter, I'm coming. Christ, did you even go home?"

"No."

"Did you sleep?"

Tori turned and faced Samantha.

"Whether I slept or not and where is none of your business." She turned and left without another word.

"Lovely. I've landed in hell."

The trip to the lab was made in silence and Samantha kept her hands locked together in her lap, staring straight ahead as they crept along in traffic. *Couldn't wait a half-hour and let the traffic die, no. Had to leave right then. Had to have us stuck together in this god-damn car.*

"So, do your friends call you Sam?"

"Excuse me?" It was the first words they had spoken since they left the squad room.

18

"Sam? Do they call you that?"

"Not if they expect me to answer them," Samantha said.

Tori nodded. "Sam it is, then."

"No. I detest that name."

"Sorry. Samantha is just too . . . formal."

"Formal? It's my name."

"I like Sam better," Tori said.

"Well, I don't. I forbid you to call me *Sam*."

"Forbid?" Tori laughed. "You're not serious, are you?"

*I hate her.*

It seemed like hours later before they walked into the lab. Samantha noticed that no one greeted them. In fact, they avoided them. *Great. I'm partnered with a psycho whom no one can stand.* She thought it amazing that Hunter got any cooperation at all in the department.

"Jackson. Good morning," Tori said, walking up to an older man and touching hands with him briefly. "This is Sam Kennedy, my new partner," she said, motioning to Samantha.

"It's Samantha," she said through clenched teeth as she shook the doctor's hand.

"Nice to meet you, Detective. I'm Arthur Jackson." He took a stick of gum from his lab coat and folded it into thirds before sticking it in his mouth. "My staff tells me you've been badgering them, Hunter. What's the problem?"

"No problem. Just six hours late on lab reports," she said. "I got impatient."

He laughed. "You get impatient when we're an hour late. I can't imagine your attitude after six." He walked down the hall and they followed. "Your Jane Doe was a popular gal, Detective. I'm guessing she's sixteen, maybe seventeen. Hard to tell. Life on the street ages you quickly."

"Her street name was Lorraine," Tori said. "She's fairly new on the streets, they tell me."

Samantha stared, wondering how in the world Tori had gotten this information. And why the hell hadn't she told her.

"I'm going to guess she's from New Orleans," Dr. Jackson said. "She has a tattoo on her right arm. Mardi Gras type of thing. We traced it. Some sort of gang symbol down there. Sara's running a report for you."

"Thanks. Now, what about the semen?"

Dr. Jackson held the door open to his office and they preceded him, each taking a seat in front of his desk.

"Four types. You'd think they'd be smart enough to use condoms." He flipped open a file on his desk. "Two were from semen in the rectum. The only sign of violence was strangulation. No recent bruises. There were two old fractures. Wrist and tibia. That's it."

"You run the semen through? No DNA matches?"

"None."

"Drugs?"

"Clean."

"Not much to go on, Doc."

"No. There's not."

Samantha sat and listened to their exchange, still seething because Tori apparently had been working last night while she was sleeping peacefully in her bed.

Tori's cell phone interrupted her thoughts. She watched as Tori pulled it off the clip on her jeans.

"Hunter."

*"Got another hooker. Dumpster over in Central."*

Samantha saw the frown, the tightening of lips.

"Great. Thanks, Fisk." Tori looked briefly at Samantha, then folded her cell phone. "Got another body, Jackson." She stood, then turned back. "I'm looking for a semen match."

Samantha hurried after Tori as she nearly ran down the hallway. She hated not knowing what the hell was going on. When they were on the road again, Samantha turned to her.

"What's up?"

"They found another body."

"Yes. I heard. Thank you. But I want to know what's going on," she said.

20

Tori shrugged. "You know as much as I do."

"Bullshit! How do you know her street name was Lorraine?"

"I asked."

"You asked who?"

"Hookers."

"Goddamn it, Hunter! I'm supposed to be your partner. Not some puppy dog that just follows you around during daylight hours and goes home. If you were going out last night, why didn't you tell me? I could have gone with you."

"You'd already put in nine hours, Detective. You were tired. You have a boyfriend waiting. There was no reason for you to hang around the back alleys at midnight asking about a dead hooker."

"What the hell does that have to do with anything? If you're working, I should be working. You could have at least asked me," she said.

"I work at odd hours. I doubt you'd be able to keep up," Tori said lightly.

"Try me," Samantha challenged. "You're not going to run me off, Hunter. So unless you shoot me or push me out of a two-story building, I'm going to be here. I *want* to be here." *God, did I just say that?*

"Why do you think I'm trying to run you off?"

Samantha stared at her. "You've hardly been friendly. Hell, you've barely been tolerable. You don't share shit with me. You go off on your own like some cowboy. Do you even know what the word *partner* means?"

"Look, this is my case. I've been on my own for two months since Kaplan . . . fell." She nearly laughed. She could still picture him dangling from the railing, yelling for her to wait.

"Well, this is *our* case now and why the hell are you smiling?"

"Sorry. Thinking about Kaplan," Tori said.

"He fell out of a two-story window. That makes you smile?"

"He was twenty pounds overweight. I told him to go down and take the stairs," she said. "But he couldn't let me win. Couldn't let me catch the guy without him."

"So he jumped?"

21

"Jumped? No, he tried to hang himself from the fire escape," she said. "He was up there doing chin-ups, trying to climb back up."

Samantha didn't know Kaplan, but the visual she got made her smile.

"So, where are we going?"

"Central. Why don't you call Fisk and get the address."

Twenty minutes later, they were in the downtown warehouse district. Samantha recognized one of the uniformed men from her days at Central. Paul Stanton. He'd asked her out nearly once a week for the first year.

"Hey, Paul, how's it going?"

"Samantha? What are you doing here? I thought you were with Assault."

"I'm with Homicide now. Did you find her?"

"No. Someone called it in. By the time we got here, there was already a crowd. Got a woman over there that can identify her," he said, pointing to an elderly lady talking to another officer.

"Thanks, Paul."

Tori watched the exchange silently, noting the friendly smile Samantha gave Stanton. Well, they definitely had different methods. She nodded as Sam headed off. She went in the opposite direction, to the Dumpster.

"What do we have?" she asked as she peered inside.

"What you see is what you get, Hunter."

Tori glanced up quickly, then took a step forward. "I see what I see. I asked what you had?" she said quietly, her piercing stare pinning him in place.

"Working girl, most likely. Teenager. Dumped last night, probably. The guy in the bookstore found her when he was taking out trash."

"Why do you think she was dumped last night?"

He shrugged.

"Who's here from the Medical Examiner?"

"Spencer."

22

"Where is she?"

"Back in the van," he said.

Tori walked over to the van and knocked once on the outside panel. The back door swung open and Rita Spencer stepped out. Their eyes met and there was an uncomfortable silence. There was always an uncomfortable silence, ever since the one night they'd spent together nearly a year ago. Tori shoved her hands in her pockets and waited for Rita to speak.

"Figured this was your case, Hunter. Sara said you'd been raising hell at the lab yesterday over the other one."

Tori nodded. "How are you?"

"Great. You?"

"Wonderful," Tori said dryly. "What you got?"

"Appears to be the same MO. The only bruising I can see is around the neck. We'll have to wait until we open her up, of course. But I'd say you've got a serial."

"Yeah. Wonderful."

Rita motioned with her head to Samantha as she walked toward them. "Who's your partner?"

Tori waited just a second until Samantha joined them. "Sam Kennedy. Rita Spencer," she said.

"It's Samantha," she said, shaking hands with the other woman. "Same as before?"

"Most likely."

Samantha nodded, then looked at Tori. "Mrs. Perez says her name is Crystal. Says she comes into the bakery every morning when they open. Seven," she said in response to Tori's raised eyebrows. "She doesn't know where she lives. She walks north when she leaves."

Tori nodded. They had nothing. Well, except the fact that the girl wasn't dumped last night. Tori had seen her at one. She turned without a word and walked away.

23

# Chapter Five

Tori drove through the city, all four windows of her Explorer down. The air was cool. Once the sun had set, the springlike temperatures had disappeared. She didn't care. She was too damn tired. She bypassed her small apartment in South Dallas and headed to Fort Worth. She needed to rest. She'd had only a few hours' sleep each night for the past week. Taking the Loop, she headed west, out of town, toward Eagle Mountain Lake. She hadn't been to her boat in three weeks, since the first murder. But tonight, she needed the peace and quiet that the lake offered.

The marina was deserted by the time she got there. She punched in her code and walked through the gate, her footsteps quiet as the water rippled silently around the piers. She walked to the end, where her boat was docked, pausing to stare up at the twinkling stars before boarding. Flipping on the pier light, she slid open the glass door, leaving it cracked to let in fresh air. She grabbed a beer, drinking nearly half before heading to the tiny shower. She stood under the slow stream of hot water and closing her eyes, she tried to relax.

Later, she pulled a lawn chair out on the deck and sat, watching the stars overhead and listening as the water splashed gently against her boat. She reached for the bottle of wine that sat next to her chair and she refilled her glass, setting it back down without looking.

Two dead girls. No clues. She tipped her head back. Probably going to be more dead girls. Hell of a way for her new partner to get her feet wet.

She lifted one corner of her mouth in a smile. Samantha Kennedy. Well, she was definitely the prettiest partner she'd ever had. And after two days, Tori knew she wasn't going to run her off. Probably just as well. She'd had a lot worse. At least the woman was willing to follow her lead and not buck her at every turn. Again she grinned. Well, it wasn't like she'd given her a choice. She did, however, suspect that Samantha Kennedy had a temper. That could be fun.

"I'm just tired, Robert. I'm sorry," Samantha murmured as she rolled onto her side. She just didn't have the energy to make love. She'd barely made it through dinner.

"It's okay, sweetheart. It's just that we haven't seen much of each other this week. I miss you."

"Me, too. We'll have the weekend, Robert."

She felt him nod, and she closed her eyes. Sleep claimed her immediately.

# Chapter Six

Tori sipped her coffee and watched as Sam made her way through the squad room. Pressed navy pants today, she noted. Matching blazer. It made her green eyes look blue.

"Exactly what time do you get to work?" Samantha asked. She tossed her purse on her desk and grabbed her coffee cup.

"Early."

"It's seven-thirty," she said as she walked away.

"Earlier than that," Tori murmured.

Samantha came back and pulled out her chair, grimacing at the taste of the coffee. She should have stopped on the way.

"Please tell me you didn't drive around the streets again last night," Samantha said.

"No. I was tired," Tori said. She snatched up the phone. "It's Hunter. Jackson in yet?" She stared at Sam, then nodded. "We'll be over at nine."

"They already have lab results?"

"They will."

"Are you thinking serial?"

"Yes. This girl, Crystal, I spoke with her the night she died," Tori said quietly.

"You what?"

"I saw her on the street. It was nearly two. I showed her our Jane Doe. She knew her as Lorraine."

"Why are you just now sharing this?" Samantha demanded.

"What difference does it make?"

Samantha slammed her fist on her desk, causing the papers to fly around her. "We're partners," she said slowly. "I know you don't know the definition of that word, Hunter. You can't just drop information like that in casual conversation. They think she was dumped during the night. You knew all along that wasn't true," she accused. "I spent half the day trying to find out who she was with *before* midnight!"

"I'm sure the ME will give a time of death. And it'll be after two."

Samantha stared at Tori with flashing green eyes.

"Morning, ladies."

Tori turned to Malone, away from the angry green eyes of her partner.

"Morning, Lieutenant."

Samantha shoved her chair away, walking purposefully behind Lieutenant Malone, following him into his office.

"Kennedy? What's up?" he asked as he hung his jacket on the coat rack.

"She's impossible," Samantha said, slamming the door behind her. "Impossible!"

"Ah. Third day. You've done good. I expected you in here yesterday," he said. "Sit. What's the problem?"

"What's the problem? She's insane," she said. "Psychotic."

He nodded.

"She keeps things from me, she goes out at all hours of the night, she barely speaks to me."

He nodded again.

"She's impossible to work with. No wonder Kaplan jumped. I'd have jumped, too."

Malone laughed, then stifled it as angry green eyes shot his way.

"Please tell me it'll get better," Samantha said quietly. "It's almost as if she doesn't want anyone to like her, Lieutenant. She goes out of her way to antagonize people. And one minute she's nice, the next a total bitch. It's like we almost connect, then she goes off and does something to intentionally piss me off!"

"Calm down, Kennedy."

"I am calm!"

"Look, I told you she was . . . difficult. She has her own rules. But they are effective. Would I like six detectives like her? No, of course not. And if not for departmental rules, I'd let her work alone. She can handle herself out there. She knows the streets. I don't envy you, Detective. But like it or not, she's your partner."

"Why doesn't she want anyone to like her?" Samantha asked quietly.

Malone stared at her. Samantha Kennedy had been with Hunter two days and had already figured out what the others hadn't in years. Tori Hunter was abrasive. Not by nature, he knew. But by design. It had taken him four years to figure that out. And one night in a quiet downtown bar, Tori Hunter had bared her soul to him. He hadn't been able to look at her the same since.

Malone glanced out his windows, finding Tori's chair empty. It really wasn't his place to tell Samantha Kennedy about Tori's past, but he thought this time, maybe he'd found someone who could stick by Tori. Samantha Kennedy wasn't in competition with Tori, unlike other partners.

"What I'm about to tell you doesn't leave this room, Detective," he said.

Samantha nodded.

"Tori's father was on the force. A detective, too. When she was twelve, one night at dinnertime, a man broke in. He tied them all to chairs in their dining room. Mother, father, two brothers and a

28

sister. And her. One by one, he killed them. Tori was the last alive. He held the gun to her head but didn't shoot. He never spoke a word. He just left. Left her tied to her chair with her dead family all around her. The case was never solved."

"Oh my God," Samantha whispered.

"She has all the files, all the old data. She still works the case, I'm sure, although she won't admit to it. It eats at her. She doesn't have anyone in her life, Kennedy. No family, no friends that I know of. Just this job and old memories. And she's reckless beyond words because deep down, she doesn't care if she lives or dies. So she makes her own rules and lives by them."

"I'm sorry," she murmured.

"She's angry, Samantha. Angry at life. So if she takes it out on you, it's not personal."

Samantha nodded. Jesus, now what? How could she possibly be annoyed at the woman?

"If she ever finds out I told you that, it'll be hell to pay. No one knows. That was twenty-five years ago."

"How *did she* survive? I mean, mentally?"

Malone smiled. "Some would say she didn't. She's a very strong woman. Apparently, she was a very strong girl. She lived with her aunt down in Houston after that. Came back up here after college. She's managed. She's a good cop. I think that's why she won't let a case rest until it's solved. I've seen her work twenty-four hours straight on numerous occasions. But then, I don't think she sleeps much, anyway. She said she still has nightmares."

"I can't believe she opened up that much to you. She barely speaks to me and then, only when I ask questions."

He nodded. "I got her drunk one night in a downtown dive. I think she was embarrassed by it. She wouldn't speak to me for a week afterward."

"I won't ever bring it up, Lieutenant. But thank you for telling me. Her . . . attitude at least makes more sense now."

Samantha was still visibly shaken as she walked back to her desk. She couldn't even begin to comprehend the pain a twelve-year-old girl felt after seeing her family murdered. After nearly being a victim herself, only to be left behind, alone.

Tori Hunter's chair was empty and Samantha noticed the scribbled note on her own desk.

*"Gone to lab."*

"Great," she murmured.

"Good morning, Detective Kennedy."

Samantha turned as John Sikes made his way over to her. His light blue shirt accented his eyes and he flashed her a charming smile. For some reason, it did nothing for her.

"Morning, Sikes."

"Where's your partner?"

"She went to the lab."

"Taking off without you already? Get used to it." He again sat on the corner of her desk and sipped from his coffee. "So, has she hit on you yet?" he asked casually.

"Excuse me?"

"As pretty as you are, I figured she'd try the first day. Donaldson said she'd wait a week, at least."

"What are you talking about, Sikes?"

"Come on. She's a lesbo. A dyke." He bent closer to her. "I told her you were way out of her league, though. You have nothing to worry about."

Samantha leaned back, away from him. She didn't know what to say. Actually, the thought that Tori might be a lesbian had not even crossed her mind. She'd been too busy being angry with her to be curious about her personal life. But then, so much more made sense now. The guys didn't just hate her because she was a woman. It was because she was a gay woman. An attractive gay woman who wouldn't give them the time of day.

"Sikes, why do I get the feeling that you're the one hitting on me? I mean, I thought you were the one who was gay," she said with a smile.

He jumped off the desk, nearly spilling his coffee.

"What the hell? I'm not a goddamn fag! Where'd you get that?"

She smiled at him. "There's nothing wrong with it if you are," she said.

"Well, I'm not!"

She shrugged. "It's just the way you dress, you know. So neat. Everything matching perfectly."

His retort died as Malone stuck his head out of his office.

"Sikes, Ramirez, got a domestic over near Fair Park. Murder-suicide. A detective from Family Violence is already on the scene."

"Yes, sir. Right on it," Ramirez said. "Come on, Sikes."

John looked back at Samantha. "We'll finish this later."

"Sure."

Samantha was left alone in the squad room with Donaldson and Adams. Neither of them looked her way. She noticed that theirs were the only two desks that didn't butt up against each other. Instead, they sat at an angle. Most likely, so they wouldn't have to stare at each other all day. She shook her head. Talk about a dysfunctional squad, this was it. She found it amazing they were as successful as they were. She had never heard rumors that there were problems in Homicide. In fact, she'd heard nothing but praise for the division and Lieutenant Malone. Of course, they probably kept everything in-house. Once they left the building, everyone put on happy faces and worked as a team. And wasn't that how it was with Hunter? Both days, out in public, she'd treated her as her partner. Well, sort of. At least she hadn't totally ignored her.

It was only a short time later that Hunter walked in, strode past their desks without speaking and went for coffee. Samantha sighed. She got up and followed Tori.

"Want some?"

"No thanks. Did you find out anything?"

"Got a semen match. Of course, little good it does us. We already figured it was the same perp."

"So, we need to find out who Crystal worked for," Samantha said.

"She worked for Ramon Blackmon. I'll go out tonight and see if I can find some of his girls. See if I can find him," she said.

"*We'll* go out," Samantha corrected.

Tori stared at her and shrugged. "Suit yourself." She moved to walk away, but Samantha grabbed her arm.

"Can we talk?"

"Sure."

"In private?"

Tori looked around, then motioned toward the ladies' room. Samantha followed.

"What's up?" Tori asked when the door had shut.

"Why didn't you tell me?"

"Tell you what? That I was going to the lab? You were in with the Lieutenant. I figured you were requesting a new partner, anyway."

"No. Why didn't you tell me that you're gay," she said.

Tori smiled. "Why would I tell you? I don't recall you telling me you were straight," she said. "Besides, are you blind?" she asked, pointing to herself.

"It just never occurred to me. I wouldn't want to just assume . . . because you look . . ."

"What? Butch?"

"I wasn't going to say that," Samantha murmured. She looked at Tori, really looked at her for the first time. She was attractive, in an androgynous sort of way. Her dark hair was short, neat. High cheekbones, smooth tan skin, full lips, long eyelashes that framed dark, intense eyes. Eyelashes that most women would envy. No, she would never use *butch* to describe this woman. But she was powerful. Tall, fit. No wonder the guys felt threatened by her.

"Look, you're not a homophobe, are you? I've already worked with my quota," Tori said.

"I just think you could have told me so I didn't have to hear it from Sikes."

"It's not really your business, is it? I don't bring my personal life into the squad room. I would hope you'd do the same and not subject me to stories about you and your boyfriend."

"Don't you think we could work together better as partners if we shared a little about our lives and attempted to be friends?" Samantha asked, ignoring her comment.

32

"I'm not your friend. And you're not mine. We work together. After that, you go home to your boyfriend and you have another life. It's separate from this."

"Who do you go home to?" Samantha asked quietly.

"I don't go home."

They stared facing each other, dark eyes locked on green.

"Why is it so hard for you to talk to me? Why won't you even attempt to have a friendly relationship with me?"

"You ever think that maybe I don't like you? Maybe I don't want to have a friendly relationship with you. We work together. That's it. And when you go home at night, you'll be glad to be rid of me."

Tori turned and walked away, leaving a seething Samantha Kennedy staring after her.

"Yeah. I'm glad to be rid of you, all right," she said loudly as the door closed. "Bitch," she murmured through clenched teeth.

She looked at herself in the floor-length mirror, then raised her leg, executing the best sidekick she'd ever done.


Tori jumped at the sound of breaking glass. Even Donaldson and Adams stood up. She kept walking, ignoring Lieutenant Malone as he came out of his office.

"What the hell was that?"

Tori shrugged. "Apparently, she's got a temper."

They all stared as Samantha walked out of the ladies' room and brushed past Tori. She sat down and picked up the file on their Jane Doe. Then she looked up, seeing all eyes on her.

"What?"

They all shrugged and went back to their desks. Tori looked at Malone with raised eyebrows, and he shrugged, too.

# Chapter Seven

"She's impossible, Amy," Samantha explained. She looked up as the waiter brought their drinks. "Thanks." Then she turned back to Amy. "Antagonistic, rude. I think she practices being a bitch, and she enjoys it."

"So you really broke the mirror?"

"God, I was so embarrassed. I don't know what came over me. Well, I do know. She just . . . drives me crazy! If I didn't think she'd hurt me, I'd have tackled her and beat the shit out of her."

Amy laughed. "I've never seen you this upset before. Why are you letting her get to you?"

"Because we have to work together. I've always been able to be friends with my partners. Maybe not always close friends. And it's not like we hung out after work or anything. We would always go home to our separate lives. But we talked. We shared things. Just normal conversation, you know. With her, it's all work and even then, it's like pulling teeth to get anything out of her."

"Why don't you go to her Lieutenant?"

"I'm not going to run and tattle and complain that she's not playing nice. Besides, he knows how she is. Everyone knows how she is."

"You've been there a week. How are you going to make a month or even a year?"

"I can't. Not like this. I keep thinking, if I try to be nice to her, she'll come around. God, she calls me Sam. Can you believe that?"

"And you let her?"

"I've asked her not to. She ignores me."

"Well, I don't envy you. What does Robert say about it?"

"I've not really told him. He just thinks it's the stress of a new job. We've seen each other only once this week."

Amy raised her eyebrows. "Everything okay?"

"Yes, fine. I'm just tired when I get home. We're going to spend the weekend together."

"Samantha, don't let this new position screw up your relationship with Robert."

"I'm not, Amy. Don't worry."

And truthfully, she wondered if subconsciously, she was thankful for her new position. She'd enjoyed being away from Robert this week.


Tori drove down the dark streets, her wipers keeping pace with the steady drizzle that had been falling all day. The Saturday night crowd was thin, no doubt the weather dampening many plans. She saw two girls huddled together on a corner and she pulled over, lowering her window as they approached.

"Evening, ladies," she said. She flashed her badge and they rolled their eyes.

"We ain't doing nothing wrong," one said. "Just standing here visiting."

"I'm not looking to bust you." She held up the two pictures of Lorraine and Crystal. "Know them?"

They looked at each other, then back at her.

"Know they're dead," the blonde said.

"Know who they work for?"

"No," they said quickly.

"Ramon Blackmon?"

"Never heard of him."

Tori smiled. "Oh, come on. This is his area. I want to talk to him."

"Hey, man, he didn't do this."

"I don't think he did. I'm looking for johns," she said.

"You know how it works, officer. We don't take names. Not like they give a real one, anyway."

Tori nodded. They were scared, she could tell that. But they weren't talking. She pulled out her card and handed it to the blonde.

"Call me if you hear something, okay? Streets aren't safe for you girls right now. You need to be careful who you pick up," she said.

"So what's new?"

# Chapter Eight

Samantha was late. She'd spent the weekend at Robert's but had planned on going home Sunday. He'd talked her into staying. She'd barely had time to run home and shower, then she caught the morning traffic. Now it was eight-fifteen and she hurried into the squad room, tossing a quick "good morning" to Sergeant Fisk as she passed by.

"Sorry I'm late," she said to Tori as she pulled out her chair.

"No problem."

"Did you have a good weekend?" she asked. She'd told herself she was going to attempt to get along with Hunter. And she was determined to draw her partner out. Whatever the consequences.

"It was lovely," Tori said dryly. "You?"

Samantha was startled by the question.

"Yes. Caught up on sleep," she offered.

"Is that why you're late? Slept in?"

Samantha smiled. "No. I was at Robert's. Had to swing by my apartment this morning."

Tori nodded. She would make an effort. She had spent all day Sunday on her boat. She had fished and relaxed. And she told herself that she was being too hard on Samantha. What would it hurt to open up a little?

"The boyfriend. Is it serious?"

Samantha stared. Tori was actually asking a personal question. Whatever in the world was wrong with her?

"Not marriage serious," she said, leaning forward. "What's wrong with you?"

"Excuse me?"

"Body snatchers?"

Tori smiled. "Yes. Don't worry. They'll return my evil twin by afternoon."

"Hunter, Kennedy. In here."

They both looked up as Malone stuck his head out of his office. They looked back at each other and shrugged.

"What's up?" Tori asked as she took one of the chairs in front of his desk.

"How's your Jane Doe?"

"Dead end. No one's talking. Can't find Ramon Blackmon. As far as I know, he's just a name."

"And the girls?"

"No ID. No priors."

"Okay. CIU is requesting bodies. They got another terrorist alert. Oil and gas this time. There's an old gas pipeline company east of the city. It's spread over about twenty acres. It's one of three that aren't in use right now. They need a hand checking them out. I've sent Donaldson and Adams out to Mesquite. You guys run by there, make sure everything's quiet."

"It's not like we don't have a case, Lieutenant," Tori said. "Can't the local sheriff do it?"

"Your case is a dead end, Hunter. You said so yourself. Besides, Sikes and Ramirez are both out. It'll just take an hour to drive out there. Make sure nothing's going on, no vehicles, no activity. Report to CIU and head back. Simple."

"If it's so simple, why aren't they doing it?"

"Because they've got their hands full with the ones that are active, Hunter. That's obviously the most likely target. But we all know that the ones that are shut down still have tons of shit underground. It's not like they secure the area when they close up shop."

"Four thousand cops on the force and it falls to Homicide?"

"Give me a break, Hunter. I'm just following orders."

"Come on, Tori. It'll be fun. Give us a chance to talk," Samantha said.

"Fun? Talk?" She followed Samantha out the door. "Sam, just because we had a little chat this morning, doesn't really change anything. I'm still a bitch."

"Oh, I don't doubt that for a minute. And I'd hardly call that a chat."

Tori allowed a smile to touch her face, one she kept hidden from Samantha. She rapped her knuckles on the counter. "Fisk? Lieutenant's sending us to damn near Terrell. You got a Lexus or something gassed up and ready to go?"

"Sure, Hunter. Why don't you just take the Mercedes?" He grabbed keys off the rack and tossed them to her. "213. Bring it back in one piece."

Samantha watched this exchange with eyes wide. She'd never seen Tori tease with anyone before. And especially Fisk. If there was anyone in the office that intimidated her, it was this giant of a man.

The Mercedes ended up being a drab beige Ford. Standard issue. No perks. Samantha didn't even suggest that she drive. She went obediently to the passenger's side.

Tori maneuvered them through downtown and to the interstate in silence. They were several miles away when the silence got to Samantha.

"Where do you live?"

Tori glanced at her then back at the road.

"Why?"

"Just curious. Just making conversation," she said.

"I have a tiny apartment on the south side of Dallas. Near Oak

Cliff. Don't go there much, though. I have a boat, a cabin cruiser, on Eagle Mountain Lake. That's more home, but I don't make it out there too much, either."

"So, I was right. You don't sleep." *Oak Cliff? Good Lord, why would a cop live near Oak Cliff?*

"I didn't say that."

"Okay. You just don't sleep in your own bed. Nothing wrong with that."

"Like you didn't sleep in your own bed this weekend?"

"So, is there someone special?" Samantha asked, ignoring Tori's own question.

"Special?"

"You know, a girlfriend," Samantha prompted.

Tori laughed. "No girlfriend, no one special."

"One-night stands? Every night?"

"If I had the energy," she murmured. "No, downstairs in the gym, there's a cot in the locker room."

"I see. No wonder you beat me to work each morning." Samantha glanced at her. "Does Malone know?"

"Of course. Who do you think put the cot down there?"

Samantha hesitated, then turned to Tori again. "Why don't you go home?"

Tori tightened her hands on the wheel. If this had been last week, she'd have told her to mind her own fucking business. But this was a new week and Tori was making an effort.

"You were right. I don't sleep much," Tori finally said. "I stay up here late. I usually go to the gym to work out anyway. I don't see the point of driving home when it's after midnight just to turn around and drive back."

Samantha wanted to ask more questions, but she dared not. She saw the grip Tori had on the wheel, saw the frown that creased her forehead. She thought she would change the subject.

"How will we know if anything is out of the ordinary? I mean, it's not like we know what a shut-down gas pipeline is supposed to look like. Do we?"

Tori shrugged. "Maybe there'll be all kinds of activity and we can call the boys at CIU to come to our rescue."

"Somehow, I can't see you doing that," Samantha said.

Malone had been right. It took them only an hour to reach the area. They had to stop at a convenience store for directions, and now they drove down the tiny country road, past hay meadows and crop fields. They saw the towers of the old plant from a mile away. Tori slowed her speed and they pulled to a stop at the locked gate. They got out and stood in front of the car, scanning the buildings for any activity, listening for noise.

"What do you see?" Tori asked.

"Nothing."

"Look in front of the gate."

"There's nothing. No tracks."

"No. Not there. But look up ahead, about fifteen, twenty yards," she said, pointing.

There, in the dirt, looked like fresh tire tracks. But not by the gate. Then Samantha looked closer. The dirt looked almost as if it had been brushed, obscuring the tracks.

"Oh shit," she murmured.

"Come on."

Tori turned the car around, then parked on the side of the road.

"What are you doing?"

"We're going to have a look," Tori said.

"Shouldn't we just call it in?"

"Call what in? Tire tracks? So they can send in a SWAT team and find out there's nothing here? We would never hear the end of it."

Tori was already walking back down the road. Samantha jogged to catch up. She was afraid she was about to see Tori Hunter in action. And she wasn't sure she was prepared for it.

"How are we going to get in?"

"Climb the fence."

"There's barbed wire at the top," Samantha pointed out.

"Yes, there is."

Samantha kept her mouth shut. It was pointless to ask questions. She followed along silently, stopping when Tori did about twenty yards from the gate. She watched as Tori scanned the area, then followed her across the ditch to the fence.

"Take your jacket off," Tori instructed.

"My jacket?"

"We need something to wrap around the wire."

"My *jacket?* Do you know how much this jacket cost?"

Tori stood with her hands on her hips and stared at Samantha. She finally held out her hand.

Samantha took off the jacket. She watched as Tori climbed the ten-foot fence, dangling from the side with one arm as she wound the jacket around the barbed wire with the other. Then she swung her leg over, sitting across the wire.

"Damn," she hissed. Even with jeans, the barbs stuck her. She pulled her leg free, then dropped to the ground on the other side.

Samantha stared at her. She looked down at her own slacks and loafers, then back at Tori's jeans and sneakers.

"Come on, Sam," Tori said impatiently.

"You seriously expect me to do that?"

"Climb up, swing your legs over, jump down. How hard is it?"

Samantha closed her mouth. She refused to complain. So she ripped her pants? So her jacket was ruined? By God, she was following Tori Hunter over the goddamn fence!

Easier said than done. She got to the top but didn't have the strength to pull herself over.

"Jesus Christ," Tori mumbled. She climbed back up and reached over, grabbing Samantha by the thigh and pulling one leg over.

"Ouch . . . damn, Hunter. You're ripping my leg off. Will you watch it?" She teetered on the top, her eyes squeezed closed as she felt her flesh ripping from the barbs. Tori moved along the fence, reaching over again to grab her other leg.

"Will you come on?"

"I hate you. You know that, don't you?"

Tori ignored her, instead pulling her leg free of the barbs and nearly pushing her to the ground. She landed on her ass. Tori dropped down beside her, a grin on her face.

"That was great."

"If you tell *anyone* what just happened, I'll shoot you," Samantha threatened.

Tori laughed, then reached out a hand and pulled Samantha to her feet. Jogging the rest of the way to the first building, they walked quietly along the side to the door. They paused and listened. Nothing. She tried the handle, but it was locked. They walked down to the windows and peered inside. It was dark, but they saw no movement.

"Come on. Let's go around back," Tori said quietly.

They rounded the corner, then stopped, both pressing themselves against the side. Three trucks were parked in the back and several men stood around them.

"Now seems like a good time to call it in," Samantha whispered.

"Yeah, you're right." Tori grabbed her cell phone, never taking her eyes off the men. She punched out the number without looking. "Fisk? Tell Malone to send the troops. Yes." She looked behind them. "Oh shit!" She folded her cell phone as two men approached them from behind. She grabbed Samantha's hand and started running toward the towers. Shouts, then gunfire followed them.

They slipped behind one tower, pausing to get their bearings. It was at least two hundred yards to the woods and another fence. Between them and that lay ground wells.

"Come on, Sam. Run!"

"Don't call me *Sam*!"

Tori passed by two wells before stopping. At the third, she grabbed the metal ladder and lowered herself down.

"Come on," she yelled.

"Oh, shit," Samantha murmured. But she followed Tori down the hole. "Do I *even* want to know what's down here?"

"No."

They crawled down the ladder nearly thirty feet before the

rungs ran out. Tori felt for a ledge and found one. A tiny one, barely a foot wide. She stepped gingerly onto it, guiding Samantha down beside her. They both pressed back against the damp wall. Up above, they heard shouts.

"They don't know which well we went into," Tori said quietly.

"Great. Is now a good time to tell you that I'm claustrophobic?"

"No." Tori turned, facing Samantha, then stepped around her, straddling her body with both legs as she struggled to stay on the tiny ledge.

"Do we really know each other well enough for this?" Samantha whispered as she felt Tori's body pressed up tight against her own.

"You wish," Tori chuckled, then reached around her to grab the ladder. She put her hand at Samantha's waist and pushed off, hanging on to the ladder with both hands.

"Stay here."

"Like I'm going somewhere," Samantha whispered. She couldn't see a foot in front of her and she was afraid to look up, afraid she would see them looking back at her.

Tori grabbed the ladder tightly and went down, hanging by her arms until she hit water.

"Shit."

She lowered herself into the cold, rank water until she touched the bottom. The water was to her shoulders.

"What the hell are you doing?"

"There's always a tunnel. The water has to go somewhere."

"A *tunnel*? Are you out of your *mind*?"

"They're going to get lights. They're going to shine it down here and find us and then they are going to shoot us. So yes, I'm hoping there's a goddamn tunnel!"

Tori took a deep breath, then disappeared under the water. She felt along the side, finally finding the opening she was looking for. She swam into it, then up into the air pocket, breathing hard. She had no idea where the tunnel ended up, but it was better than being sitting ducks in the well. She took a breath, then went back the way she'd come, breaking water right at Samantha's feet.

44

"Come on. I found it," she said.

"No. I can't," Samantha insisted.

"Yes, you can. Now get in here."

The voices were louder. Soon, they would be caught.

"Sam, *now*," Tori hissed, grabbing Samantha's foot and nearly dragging her over the side.

They splashed together into the water, Samantha clutching Tori hard around the shoulders.

"I hate this. I really *fucking* hate this."

"It's not too bad from where I'm standing," Tori murmured as two frantic hands moved over her shoulders.

"Is that supposed to be funny?" But Samantha didn't release her grip.

"Hold your breath," Tori instructed. "I'll guide you through. There's an air pocket in the tunnel. You'll be fine."

"If we make it out of here alive, I'll shoot you myself," Samantha said through clenched teeth.

"On three."

They both took deep breaths, silently counting. Then Tori disappeared under water, pulling Samantha with her. Samantha thought for sure her lungs would burst, then Tori pushed her up and she banged her head on the top of the tunnel, gasping for breath.

"I hate you, have I told you that?" she gasped. "You damn near gave me a concussion."

"You did great."

"Uh-huh. Now what?"

"Now we see where the tunnel goes."

"See? I can't even see you," Samantha said.

"We'll feel our way. These ground wells have to empty somewhere. A holding tank or something."

"What are these things, anyway?"

"Probably where they dump the wastewater."

"Do I want to know?"

"No, you don't."

"You don't think there're like . . . rats or something in here, do you?"

45

"No. No rats. Maybe snakes," Tori said.

"Snakes?" Samantha hissed, again grabbing onto Tori, nearly climbing her back.

"I'm teasing. Come on."

They inched along the tunnel, keeping their heads above the water in the air pocket. Samantha held tightly to Tori's waist as Tori felt along the sides of the tunnel. They came to a junction with another tunnel and stopped. Closing her eyes, Tori tried to imagine the direction. The tunnel they entered would have been on the north side of the well. Most of the other wells were to the east. Logic would make the tunnel to the west the drain tunnel.

"What do you think?" Samantha asked.

"We go left," Tori said.

Samantha nodded. She wasn't going to argue. She never released her hold on Tori's waist. The water level lowered considerably as they walked on and she slipped down once, nearly pulling Tori with her.

"Hang on," Tori said. She turned around and gripped Sam's arms, pulling her up. "You okay?"

"Just peachy," Samantha murmured.

"You really should wear sensible shoes," Tori teased.

"These shoes are perfectly sensible for the city. Had I known we were going to go *swimming* this afternoon, I'd have dressed appropriately."

"Okay . . . I'm trying to picture you in a bikini."

"I haven't worn a bikini in ten years."

"Okay. A one-piece Speedo then," Tori said as they continued walking up the tunnel. The water was only at their waists now. "A dark green one. You know, your eyes."

Samantha grinned. One-piece Speedo? She hadn't been swimming in years, either.

"Hey, look," Tori said.

Samantha looked around Tori and laughed. Daylight!

"Oh, thank God," she said.

"Thank God? I'm the one that dragged you through this tunnel," Tori said.

"Yes. You're the one that dragged me *into* this tunnel."

"Better than getting shot."

"Definitely."

The tunnel was level and Samantha finally released her hold on Tori as they made their way to the tunnel's entrance. But up ahead, a creature lurked and Samantha grabbed hold of Tori once again.

"What the hell is that?" she whispered.

"Too big for a rat. Maybe a nutria," Tori said.

"A what?"

"Nutria. A big, hairy water rat," Tori explained.

Samantha tried to climb on her back.

"What the hell are you doing?"

"Shoot it!"

"I will not."

"Then I will. Get out of my way."

"Sam, it lives here. This is his home. We're not going to shoot it. Besides, don't you think that would call attention to us?"

"I *know* you don't expect me to walk *past* it," she said.

"Stay here."

"Gladly."

Samantha looked behind her, envisioning hundreds of the hairy creatures coming at her from the tunnel. She shivered. Tori walked closer to the creature, clapping her hands as she went. It finally crawled out toward the entrance and disappeared.

"All clear," she called.

"Are you sure?"

"Yes. Now come on."

Samantha walked hesitantly toward Tori, her eyes never leaving the entrance, watching for the rat to reappear.

"It's okay, Sam. I doubt they attack."

"I'm not even going to ask how you knew what it was," she said.

"I lived down in the Houston area for a while, on the bayou. They used to come out right before dark," she said.

Samantha stared. This was the first bit of personal information Tori had shared with her.

"I like to think they're more like a beaver than a rat," Tori continued.

"Well that makes all the difference," Samantha said. "Why didn't you say so to begin with?"

"And miss out on you climbing up my back?"

Samantha smiled. "I probably would have climbed up anyway."

They both stood at the entrance to the tunnel. Samantha rolled her eyes. They were thirty feet up. She wondered where the rat had gone.

"Damn. They dump this shit right into the creek," Tori said, pointing. "Can you believe that?"

"We'll play environmental cop later, Tori. How the hell do we get out of here?"

Tori gripped the sides of the tunnel, looking up. They were on the side of the creek bed. It was probably only ten feet up to the top, but there were no footholds. Concrete had been poured. She turned and looked down. A few tree roots protruded but not much else.

"Wonder how deep it is?"

"Deep? The creek? I *know* you're not suggesting we jump," Samantha said.

"Just in case we fall," Tori said. "Come on."

"Come on where?"

"We're going to try to climb down." She was already sitting on the tunnel floor, legs dangling over the sides.

"Are you insane?"

"It's been mentioned," she said lightly. "Sit down here," she said, pointing beside her.

"I'm not really crazy about heights," Samantha murmured. "Is now a good time to tell you that?"

"I'll go first. If you start to fall, I'll catch you."

"Oh, well that makes me feel better."

They sat side by side, both peering over the edge. Then they looked at each other and smiled, then laughed.

"Been a hell of a day, huh?"

"Oh, yeah," Samantha said. "And it ain't over yet."

"Creek beds are usually pretty soft. You know, mud and all."

"In case I fall?"

"Yeah."

"I thought you were going to catch me?"

"In case I don't."

Samantha watched as Tori turned around and gripped the edge of the tunnel, lowering herself. She grabbed a root, then slipped as it pulled from the earth. She dropped five feet before stopping.

"You're not allergic to poison ivy, are you?" Tori called up.

"I don't know."

"Well, you'll know in a couple of days." Tori continued to climb down, finally looking back as Samantha still sat on the edge. "Come on, Sam. You can't stay up there."

"You could use your cell phone and call for help," she suggested.

"Well, besides the fact that it's been under water for a while now, can you imagine what the guys would say about that? No way. I'd rather get shot."

"I'd rather get rescued by helicopter," Samantha murmured. Then she took a deep breath and attempted to follow Tori down. Unfortunately, the tree root didn't hold. She slid and bumped her way down the embankment, landing with a thud in the water, face first. It was waist deep.

Tori tried in vain to grab her as she slid past. Without thinking, she jumped the last twenty feet, landing just beyond Sam in deeper water. She grabbed for her.

"Are you okay?"

"As soon as I find my *gun*, I will be. I'm going to shoot you," Samantha hissed.

Tori laughed, then reached out and brushed at the mud covering Sam's face. She laughed harder.

Samantha stood up straight, then dove at Tori, tackling her and landing them both in the water again. They came up sputtering. They stood in waist-high water, staring at each other as mud and water ran down their faces. Tori grinned and Sam did the same. Then they laughed, hard laughs that shook them both.

"Wonder where the hell we are," Samantha finally said.

Tori looked at her watch. It had been two hours.

"Wonder where the cavalry is?"

The words had barely left her mouth when gunfire was heard. They both looked up, listening.

"Come on," Tori said. She grabbed Sam's hand and pulled her out of the water.

They waded through the creek to the other side. Samantha had only one shoe. They took only a few steps before the gunfire stopped.

"That didn't take long," Tori said. She walked over and was helping Sam along when the explosion hit. Tori took them to the ground, instinctively covering Sam's body with her own. The earth beneath them shook, then another smaller explosion sounded.

"Are you okay?"

Samantha considered the question. She was soaking wet and covered with mud and water. Her clothes were ruined and she'd lost a shoe. And now, the not unpleasant weight of another woman covered her body. Was she okay? Yes, she'd just had the time of her life.

"You weigh a ton," Samantha said and heard Tori chuckle, then felt her move away. They sat up, looking back to the tunnel they had come from. Smoke was seeping out.

"Damn."

Sam nodded, glancing once at Tori. They were sitting side by side, soaked head to toe. It was obvious Tori wore no bra . . . her shirt clung to her. For some unknown reason, Sam couldn't pull her eyes away. Then a shoulder nudged her own.

"Come on. They'll be looking for us."

Samantha blinked and looked up, meeting Tori's eyes. Then she smiled and reached out, brushing at the mud covering Tori's face.

"I don't think that's going to help." Tori stood and offered a hand to Sam, who took it willingly.

# Chapter Nine

"You could have been killed," Robert said for the third time. "I can't believe I was listening to it on the news all day and you were right in the middle of it." He brought over a hot cup of tea and Samantha reached for it.

"I'm fine, I told you. A few bumps and bruises is all." She sat in the corner of her sofa, wrapped up in a thick robe sipping her tea. After being wet all day, it had taken her hours to get warm.

"So, are you going to stay?" he asked hesitantly.

"Stay? Stay where?"

"With Homicide? With your partner?"

She set her cup down and stared at him. "Robert, what are you asking?"

"I just think maybe this is more than you bargained for," he said.

"Well, yes it is. We were helping out CIU. You remember, you thought CIU would be the perfect place for me," she reminded him. "And yes I'm staying." She leaned forward. "Robert, in all my years on the force, this is the most fun I've ever had."

"Fun?"

"Yes, fun. It was exhilarating. And you know what? There wasn't a single moment that I felt like we were in danger. Well, we were in danger, but I mean grave danger. She was amazing, totally amazing. Whatever she suggested we do, I trusted her. And she was right. She got us out of there."

"She got you *in* there," he said. "I've heard stories about her. She's dangerous."

"She's not dangerous. We were just doing our job, Robert."

"You could have been killed."

"Will you stop with that? I could be killed every time I go out."

"I just worry about you, honey." He sat down beside her and rubbed her thigh. "I don't know what I'd do if I ever lost you."

"Oh, Robert." She leaned forward and kissed him. "I'm fine. Exhausted, but fine."

"You want me to stay with you tonight?" he asked quietly.

She shook her head. "No. I'm going to go to bed and crash. I wouldn't be great company."

"I hate to leave you. You know, if we lived together, I wouldn't have to leave," he said, moving over to kiss her again.

She wanted to tell him that even though they didn't live together, he still didn't *have* to leave. But she wanted him to leave. She wanted to be alone. Like she said, she was exhausted. The ordeal today and the endless questioning by CIU had lasted for hours.

"I just want to get some rest, Robert. Maybe tomorrow, I'll get away early and cook dinner for you. How does that sound?"

He put his arm around her and pulled her close, kissing her forehead.

"That sounds great."

Later, as she crawled under the covers alone, she wondered what Tori was doing. She wished she had her phone number. Surely, she wasn't at the station on the cot tonight. Surely she went

52

home. Samantha lay back, her eyes wide open. Her new partner was most likely alone, with no one worrying over her well-being or bringing her a hot cup of tea. No one to fuss over her almost being killed. The thought saddened her. She hated to think of Tori being alone. Not after a day like today.

And why was she alone? Samantha didn't know anything about the gay lifestyle, but Tori was attractive. In fact, she was . . . gorgeous, with a body to go with it. Why didn't she have someone?

But Samantha knew the answer. Tori didn't want someone.


Tori flipped on the lights to her tiny apartment and looked around. She hadn't been there in nearly a week. She tossed her keys on the counter, opened the fridge and stared inside. Two beers and a carton of milk that had soured, nothing else. She slammed the door and opened a cabinet, taking out a bottle of scotch. She grabbed a large glass and filled it nearly to the top, then moved to her lone chair, a recliner.

"Hell of a day," she murmured to the empty room.

# Chapter Ten

"Well, well, hero for a day," Sikes said as he walked over to Samantha and patted her shoulder. "Good job, Kennedy."

"Thanks, Sikes. All in a day's work," she said lightly.

"You looked great on the news, all wet with your hair slicked back," he continued, taking his usual perch on the corner of her desk.

"I didn't think you noticed things like that, Sikes."

He stood up quickly. "I told you, I'm not gay! I don't know where you got that from, but it better stop here."

She only smiled at him and nodded.

Tony Ramirez walked over then, sticking out his hand and shaking Samantha's.

"You guys were great," he said. "Good plug for Homicide. Can't believe Hunter did that."

"Well, CIU was acting like they busted the whole thing on their own," she said. She actually couldn't believe it either. When the

TV crew had asked how long she'd been with CIU, Tori had laughed. "We're with Homicide, not CIU. They were too busy to check out this dead-end lead, so they had us run out here. Hell of a dead end, huh?"

"You should have heard Fisk when he was telling the story. *'Tell Malone to send the troops. Oh shit!'*" Ramirez said, mimicking Tori.

Samantha laughed. That was only the beginning of their ordeal.

"Where is Hunter, anyway?" she asked.

"Haven't seen her."

"It's eight-thirty," Samantha said. "She's always here before me."

He shrugged. "She's probably out working already." Then he handed her something warm wrapped in foil. He laid an identical one on Tori's desk. "My mother made these. Tori loves them. Chorizo and eggs."

"Thanks, Tony. That was sweet of you."

She unwrapped hers, finding a warm tortilla rolled inside, bulging with eggs and Mexican sausage. She took a bite and moaned. Wonderful.

But it was another half hour before Tori walked in, looking like she'd hardly slept at all. She walked past Samantha's desk and straight to the coffee.

"Are you okay?" Samantha asked when Tori returned.

"Uh-huh," she said, sipping from the hot liquid. She looked at the foil on her desk and grinned. Tony's mother had no doubt cooked for her again.

"Where have you been?"

Tori raised her eyebrows.

"What? I can't ask that? I would think after yesterday, I could ask anything I damn well pleased."

Tori grinned. "That's what you think, huh?"

"Yes, that's what I think."

"Okay, fair enough. I was at my boat. I overslept," she said.

"Why don't I believe you?" She lowered her voice. "You look like you hardly slept at all, Tori."

"Oh, but I did. I went to my apartment first. There was nothing there but a bottle of scotch. About midnight, I went out and got something to eat, then drove to my boat. I fell asleep about four. Got caught in traffic."

Samantha stared at her. Four? She was asleep by ten. She was about to comment when the Lieutenant called for them.

"You two want to come in here?"

Tori sighed, then pushed away from her desk. She was used to existing on only a few hours' sleep each night but for some reason, she couldn't shake it this morning.

"Well, you had quite a day, Detectives," he said. "Congratulations. You made the department proud."

They both looked at him, saying nothing.

"CIU's got their panties in a wad, though. Press ate up your interview last night, Hunter."

She shrugged.

"I just wanted to tell you that you did a good job. Glad you made it back in one piece." He looked from Hunter to Kennedy, then back. Kennedy looked rested. Hunter looked like shit. "I guess it's back to your Jane Doe. The lab called this morning, Hunter. Fisk has the info. They found some matching fibers."

"Great. We'll check it out."

They got up to leave but Malone called Tori back.

"Hunter . . . a word?"

Samantha glanced at them both, then shut the door behind her. Tori sat back down, waiting.

"You okay?"

"I'm fine, Lieutenant."

He nodded. "How are things going with Kennedy?"

"Fine."

"Think it might work out?"

She nodded, then grinned. "I think it might work out. She was a real trouper out there yesterday. Only threatened to shoot me a couple of times."

"Go easy on this one, Hunter. She could be good for you."

"I think you may be right."

56

"How do you feel about letting me work out with you?" Samantha asked later as they drove toward Central.

"In the gym?"

"I realized yesterday that my upper body strength is a little lacking," she admitted.

"Maybe. But it'll cut into your time. I usually work out later in the evening, but we can arrange to go right after work a few days a week." Tori glanced at her quickly. "Don't you want to check with your boyfriend first?"

"Why would I need to do that?"

"Like I said, it'll cut into your time."

"Yes, but it's my time. Not his."

As soon as the words left her mouth, Samantha heard them echoing in her brain. Robert would be upset. Not mad. He didn't get mad. But it would take away from their time together and lately, that time had been stretched thin. Well, he would understand. Her job was important to her, just as his was to him. He had late nights, too. She always understood when he had a meeting after hours or had a case to prepare. She didn't complain. He would be just as understanding.


"Three nights a week? But Samantha, we hardly see each other as it is. And look at you. I hardly think you need to go to the gym," he said.

"I could barely climb that fence, Robert. Yes, I need to go to the gym. I'm not in great shape."

"I beg to differ. I think you have a great shape."

She smiled at him and handed him his plate.

"Thank you. But you know what I mean."

"Well, hopefully, you won't be climbing fences too often. Don't you think you're overreacting?"

They sat across from each other at her small table and she watched silently as he poured wine. Was she overreacting? It was just that Tori was in such good shape. Samantha didn't want to hold her back, didn't want Tori to feel like she had to help her over and through obstacles if they arose. Samantha should be able to keep up. And besides, if they worked out together, it would give her more time with her partner. More time to get to know her. Samantha suspected the Tori Hunter everyone knew was nothing like the Tori Hunter she had glimpsed that day in the tunnel. Tori had never lost her cool, had never gotten impatient with Samantha. In fact, she had been teasing, had acted like it was all a game. Maybe that's why Samantha had not really felt like they were in danger. Tori had simply taken charge and gotten them out of there. And it had been fun.

And Samantha wanted more of it.

# Chapter Eleven

"You're killing me," Samantha complained as she attempted to lift the weights one more time.

"Two more."

"Two? You said one."

"I lied."

Samantha pushed up, straining. Was this really her idea? What had she been thinking? She took a deep breath, finally pushing the weights over her head.

"Great," Tori said, taking the bar from Sam. "Now, leg press."

Sam stood up, shaking her arms at her sides.

"You better hope I don't have to draw my weapon tomorrow," she said.

"Why's that?"

"Because I doubt I'll be able to lift my arms."

"Tomorrow will be fine. It'll be the next day," Tori said. She walked over to the leg press and pointed. "Sit."

Samantha did as she was told, lying back and bending her knees, resting her feet against the plate. She watched as Tori adjusted the weight.

"Try that."

She did. It moved only a few inches. Tori lightened it and Sam tried again. This time, she was able to extend her legs. With effort.

"Great. Ten."

"Why don't I believe you?" Sam murmured as she pushed down on the plate.

Tori watched, surprised at the thigh muscles that were well defined. She reached out a hand and touched Sam's leg lightly, feeling the muscles move under her hand.

"You jog?" she asked.

Sam was conscious of the hand that rested against her thigh as she breathed hard to finish the set. "Used to. But not in a couple of years. I make do with a stationary bike now."

"Better than nothing. Your legs look like they're in good shape."

"Thanks." For some reason, that made her feel better. Then she leaned up. "Why aren't you working out?"

"I'll do it later tonight. I promised I'd help you," she said.

"Can't we do both? I hate that you're just standing around watching me."

Tori raised her eyebrows. "Could be worse," she teased. "I could be stuck watching Sikes or somebody."

Samantha grinned. She loved it when Tori was relaxed and teasing. "Why don't you work out now with me? Then I'll treat you to dinner," Sam offered.

"Dinner?"

"Yes. I doubt you'll take the time to eat if you're planning on working out later. Come on, we'll get a burger or something."

Tori stared. She hadn't been asked out to dinner in so long, she hardly knew how to respond. Who knew? Apparently, Sam liked her. So she nodded.

Samantha flashed her a smile and reached out and squeezed her arm.

"Thanks."

"That doesn't mean you're getting off lightly," Tori said. She took the machine next to Sam. Leg curls. She stretched out on her stomach and hooked her ankles beneath the bar. She closed her eyes and took a breath, then curled her legs behind her in a steady rhythm, counting silently to herself.

Samantha stared at the legs stretched out beside her, calf muscles bulging with each repetition. She looked at her own thin legs, wondering if she'd ever have that much definition.

"Come on, Sam. Another set," Tori said beside her.

"Yeah, yeah," she mumbled.

They moved through the various weight machines, Tori helping Sam reacquaint herself with them. It had been years since she'd been in a gym. She actually felt invigorated by the exercise. She followed Tori's instructions, not at all self-conscious as she struggled through some of the weights. But later, in the locker room, shyness overtook her as she undressed only a few lockers down from Tori. Tori apparently didn't have a shy bone in her body. She stripped where she stood, walking naked into the shower.

"Good God," Sam murmured as she watched Tori walk away. The woman was a goddess, sculpted body head to toe. She looked down at her own body, still clad in sports bra and shorts. She certainly wasn't embarrassed by her body. In fact, Robert said on numerous occasions that she had a wonderful body. It just wasn't as defined as Tori's. Well, that's why she was here, she told herself. She slipped off her bra and shorts and grabbed a towel, walking quickly into a shower stall.

Tori was already dressed when she walked out. She was bending over tying her shoes, and she glanced once at Samantha, then away.

"I'll wait outside for you," she said.

"Okay. I'll just be a sec," Samantha said.

She dropped her towel as soon as Tori left, dressing quickly. She pulled on jeans and a sweatshirt, ran a brush through her damp hair and shoved everything into her gym bag. She found Tori sitting on a weight bench when she walked out.

"Better?" Tori asked.

Samantha smiled. "I feel great. Thank you."

Tori stood and shoved both hands in her pockets, waiting.

"How about Albert's over on Pearl?" Sam asked. "It's casual enough."

"Sure. I'll follow you."

Samantha was conscious of the Explorer behind her and she looked up several times in her mirror. She was nervous and she couldn't imagine why. Maybe because she hadn't told Robert. Then she glanced at her cell phone, which was off. She could call him, but she doubted it would be a short conversation. No, she would talk to him afterward.

Albert's was crowded for a weeknight and they had to sit at the bar until a table opened up. They both ordered a beer, then rested their arms casually on the bar top.

"Oh God, that is so good," Sam said after her first long drink.

"Mmm," Tori agreed.

"Thank you for doing this. The workout and dinner," Sam explained. "I really want us to be friends, Tori. I think it'll make it so much easier to work together."

"Is that right?"

"Yes." Samantha leaned her elbows on the table and looked at Tori. "You have to admit, this is much better than arguing and bickering or just plain not talking. Right?"

Tori smiled and nodded.

"I'm serious. You scared the hell out of me that first week, you know."

"Did I?" She shrugged. "I don't know why. I was just being me."

"Were you?" Sam asked. "Who are you being now?"

Tori flicked her gaze at Sam then went back to her beer, draining half of it in one swallow.

"It was like you wanted so badly for me *not* to like you," Sam continued. "I can't for the life of me figure out why."

"No one likes me, Sam."

"I like you."

"Why?"

Samantha shrugged, then smiled.

"Is it safe to tell you that I had more fun with you the other day than I've had in my whole life?"

"In the tunnel?" Tori asked with raised eyebrows.

"Yeah. The tunnel."

"Fun? You threatened to shoot me several times," Tori reminded her.

"Oh, I know. At the time, it seemed like a good idea," Samantha said with a laugh. "In fact, when I think about the water, I imagine it being a pretty aqua blue! Most likely, it was the color of coffee."

"Most likely."

"I mean, we were being chased and shot at and then you tried to drown me. Then there was the man-eating rat. Not to mention the thirty-foot drop into the creek."

"Don't forget the explosion."

Samantha laughed. "Yes. The only good thing is I'm not allergic to poison ivy."

It was Tori's turn to laugh. "I don't think you were there long enough to find out. You should have seen your face as you were falling."

"You should have seen your face when I dunked you under the water," Sam shot back.

Tori smiled and nodded. Yes, it had been fun. They could have been killed, but it was fun. And she couldn't remember the last time she'd had fun.

# Chapter Twelve

Sam watched Tori pull away, then followed her onto the street. It was late. After ten. Robert would be furious. But she shrugged. She'd make it up to him. She had been enjoying herself too much to call an end to the evening. Tori had opened up. Not much, but some. She'd talked mostly about her boat. In fact, she'd invited Samantha—and Robert—to join her some weekend. That surprised Sam. She doubted Tori ever invited anyone to do anything with her. She didn't mention one word about her childhood or family, and Samantha didn't ask. If Tori wanted to share, she would. Samantha was just thankful they were talking at all. It would make working together so much easier.

Finally, she could put it off no longer. She turned on her cell phone. The insistent beeping told her she had messages. Four of them. She grabbed it and flipped through caller ID. All from Robert. She didn't bother listening to them. She punched out his number, waiting only one ring before he answered.

"Are you okay?" he asked quickly.

"Of course."

"Where are you?"

"I'm just leaving Albert's," she said.

"Albert's? What were you doing at Albert's?"

"We grabbed a burger after our workout. I'm sorry, I didn't have a chance to call you," she said, allowing herself that one small lie.

"I've been worried. I expected you home hours ago."

*Home?*

"Robert, I told you I was going to work out. I didn't think you'd be waiting for me."

"I thought you'd be through by seven, at the latest. I waited for you. I thought we could have dinner together," he said.

She groaned silently. She should have called him.

"I'm sorry," she said again. "Do you want me to come over?"

"That would be nice. Even nicer if you'd pick me up something to eat."

She nodded. "Okay. A burger?"

"Chicken sandwich would be better."

"Okay. I'll be there in about fifteen, twenty minutes," she said. She was tired and wanted nothing more than to go home and crawl into bed—alone. But she felt guilty for not calling Robert. She would go to him tonight, but she was not sorry she'd spent the evening with Tori Hunter.

# Chapter Thirteen

Tori glanced up as the blond woman walked gingerly across the room. She set a tall cup on her desk and a matching one on Tori's, then bent slowly to her chair.

Tori grinned and reached for her coffee, pulling off the lid and sniffing. Cappuccino. Mmm.

"Thanks. I'm surprised you were able to lift two, though," Tori teased.

"Not one word," Samantha threatened.

"Got a little lactic acid buildup, do we?"

Sam glared at her. "I couldn't get off the toilet this morning, thank you," Samantha said. "My thighs refused to cooperate."

Tori laughed, causing several heads to turn their way. Even Adams and Donaldson looked up.

"You should've gotten on the stationary bike this morning, loosened up a little."

"Are you kidding?"

"Maybe you should've had Robert give you a massage," Tori suggested. "I hear that helps."

Samantha only grunted. Robert was still a little peeved at her. Not so peeved that he didn't want to sleep with her last night, but peeved enough not to want to talk about her night at the gym. She, however, was too tired for even a little snuggling much less making love.

"Hunter?"

Tori looked up as Fisk walked over, taking the note from his hands.

"Got another body. Little Mexico this time."

Tori glanced at the paper and nodded.

"Thanks, Fisk. Come on, Sam. Time to play cop."

Samantha squeezed her eyes shut as she stood, letting out a small groan at the burning in her thighs.

"Need help?" Tori offered. "Want me to carry you?"

"This is all your fault," she said. "'One more set, Sam. One more set,'" she mimicked, following Tori out of the squad room.


They both slipped on gloves as they walked over to the Dumpster. The Medical Examiner was still standing over the victim, taking pictures.

"Same?" Tori asked Rita Spencer.

"Hardly. Take a look."

"Jesus," Samantha whispered and she gripped Tori's arm and squeezed hard.

Their girl was naked, covered in blood. Her stomach had been sliced open.

"There's a lot of blood," Tori said quietly. "Was she killed here?"

"Doubtful," Rita said. "The blood is all concentrated on the victim, a little where it seeped down here." She pointed into the trash bin. "They found a bloody footprint." She turned and pointed down the alleyway.

"I'll take a look," Samantha offered. Anything to avoid staring at the young girl.

"So, killed somewhere else and dumped. If there's this much blood here . . ."

"Yes, there'll be twice as much at the scene. I've bagged her hands. Broken nails. This one fought back. We might get a skin sample."

Tori shrugged. They already had DNA on a semen match on the first two. She stepped closer, looking around the Dumpster. There were drops of blood on the edge and a smear on the side.

"Any chance for prints?" she asked.

"No. The smear there is nothing. I'm sure he wore latex."

Tori reached in and brushed the matted hair away from the girl's face. Something wasn't right.

"Rita . . . no makeup," Tori said. She picked up the girl's arm, staring through the plastic bag Rita had put around her hand. "No painted nails."

"And?"

"I don't think she's a hooker."

"Tori, the print is from a sneaker," Samantha said as she walked back to them. She glanced once at the body, then back at Tori. "But, it's walking away, not *to* the Dumpster. Why would there be a bloody print there"—she pointed—"and not here?"

They all stepped back, looking on the ground around them. Tori calculated the print was a good twenty feet from the Dumpster. It was also going into the alley, not toward the street, where a car could be parked.

"How far does this alley go?" she asked one of the uniforms standing by.

"Three blocks. But there's a side entrance over there," he pointed. "It splits the bakery and the grocery store."

"Let's take a look."

Tori and Sam walked down the side alley, both looking at the ground for blood drops.

"Tori, a car would barely fit through here."

"Yes. Barely. Check the trash cans. Maybe we'll get a scratch."

Sam nodded, walking toward the street, checking the cans. Tori walked beside her, letting Sam take the lead. Most of the cans were dented.

"Green paint on this one," Sam said, pointing. "Could be anything, but it looks fresh."

"Yeah." Tori lifted the lid. The can was full. It smelled. "Great." She looked back at the two uniforms who were standing in the alley waiting. "Sam, what's that guy's name again?"

"Sanchez."

"Right." Tori motioned to the two guys. "Sanchez? Find out what store this belongs to. I want to take it. Send it to the lab. I want this paint."

"Yes, ma'am."

They squatted beside the trash can, looking at the small scrape of paint on the side.

"He drove in here," Tori said, "bumping the can as he tried to squeeze between it and the wall. Parked up there. Carried the body to the Dumpster. Laid her out like all the others, then walked back to his car, leaving the one footprint."

"Why just one?"

"And why that far from the Dumpster?"

"Maybe he left it on purpose," Samantha suggested.

"A clue? To tease us? Then we really have a sick bastard," Tori said.

"She was so much worse than the others," Sam said quietly. "Why?"

Tori shrugged. "Maybe she put up more of a fight. I don't think she was a hooker, Sam. Her face looked too clean. There was no makeup. Her nails were short, not painted."

"He could have cleaned her up."

"Why would he do that? The other two were made up. They looked the part. Not this one."

Sam shrugged. She didn't have an answer.

❧

They had barely walked into the squad room when Malone called them into his office. He shut the door behind them.

"Captain called. Wants to know if it's a serial for sure. If we think it is, we need to call in a profiler from CIU."

"The first two are definitely linked. Won't have lab reports until tomorrow."

"What does your gut say, Hunter?"

"This one is different. I'm not certain she was a hooker. The first two were. The first two were strangled. This one had her belly ripped open. The first two had clothes on. This one was naked," Tori stated.

"Copycat? Two murdered hookers has barely made the papers. I doubt a copycat," he said.

"No. She was laid out in the Dumpster like the others. But maybe our angle of hookers is wrong."

"What makes you think she wasn't a hooker?"

"She was just different."

"She had no makeup, Lieutenant," Samantha said. "Her nails were short, not long and painted like the others."

"Hardly conclusive. Come up with something. Two hookers slipped through the papers. Three? It'll make front page. Mayor's office will be calling. They'll want to send someone over for a report. I'll try and stall them for a few days."

"At least until we get the lab results. I want to sit in on the autopsy tomorrow, too."

"You want a profiler?"

"CIU? That ought to go over well," Hunter said.

"Maybe you should let Kennedy handle that part. I don't believe she pissed them off quite as much as you did."


Tori was still entering notes about their case when Sam tapped her on the arm. Tori looked up wearily.

"I'm going," Samantha said. "It's after six."

Tori nodded, then went back to her notes.

"I know you're tired. Why don't you give it a rest until tomorrow?" Sam suggested quietly.

Tori leaned back in her chair, watching Sam. Her pressed slacks were a little wrinkled now, but still neat. Her sleeves were rolled nearly to her elbows and her blond hair was in disarray. Tori knew it was from the numerous times Sam had run her hands through it during the day.

"I just want to make sure I get all the notes in the computer, while they're still fresh."

"Fresh? We've been going over this all day," Samantha said. "I suppose you'll be staying here tonight?"

"Probably."

"Will you at least get dinner?"

"Yeah. I'm on first-name basis with the pizza delivery guy."

"Okay. Then I won't worry about you."

"I'm not used to someone worrying about me," Tori said.

"Well, get used to it," Sam said as she walked away. Then she stopped. "I don't even have your phone number. If I need you for something, how will I get in touch with you?"

"There's just my cell."

"Yes. I don't even have that."

Tori pulled out her drawer and grabbed one of her cards. She scribbled her cell number on the back and handed it to Sam.

"Thank you. Now get some rest."

Tori nodded. "You, too."

"I wish. I promised Robert I'd go to a dinner party with him. That's the last thing I want to do." Then she paused. "I could stay here with you and work. Then I'd have an excuse not to go," she said hopefully.

"You don't want to stay here with me, Sam. Go and have a good time. At least you'll get dinner."

Samantha nodded. Then she smiled and walked away, knowing that Tori would spend many more hours right there at her desk. She made a mental note to invite Tori to dinner again tomorrow after their workout.

# Chapter Fourteen

Tori blindly grabbed for the last piece of pizza, and she scanned the computer again, going over the files for all three women. She was tired and her vision was blurry, but she didn't stop. It wasn't adding up. It was no longer about random hookers being murdered. She was convinced the third girl wasn't going to be lumped with the others.

She landed again on the tattoo that Lorraine had on her arm. She had already read the report Sara supplied. It was brief. The design dated back to the early 1900s as a symbol of the first black krewe that secretly participated in Mardi Gras. It was now used by local gang members in New Orleans. Not much. Maybe the Internet could provide more.

But an hour later, she was still surfing through yet another Web page of tattoos. So far, no match. She'd found other Mardi Gras masks that had been used as designs for tattoos, but not this one. This one was dark, evil looking. Sinister. No wonder a gang had adopted it. She had given up hope that she would find it but continued flipping through the Web pages. She very nearly skipped right over it when it popped up on her screen.

"I'll be damned," she murmured.

"You still here?"

She jumped. She hadn't heard Andy come in. He pushed the large trash bin in front of him, bending at Sikes's desk to collect the trash.

"It's late, Detective. I got your cot all ready."

"Thanks, Andy. But who could sleep with all that racket down there. What's going on?"

"They busted up some rave. Got teenagers running all over the station."

She nodded, then looked back at her printout.

"Hey. Come here a second, Andy."

"Sure thing, ma'am."

"Look at this." She pointed to the screen. "Does it match?" She held up the printout of their girl's tattoo.

"Well, let's see." He pulled his glasses out of his pocket and slipped them on, peering over her shoulder at the screen, then to the paper.

"Yup," he said. "Appears the same." Then he took the printout. "Except this here has that circle thing at the bottom."

"Let me see." She took the printout and squinted. Yes, at the bottom of their tattoo was a circle with a . . . damn, a female symbol. She looked back to the screen, then clicked on "variations." Four came up. One had the female symbol. She clicked on that.

"I'll be damned," she murmured as she read. "Thanks, Andy."

"Sure thing." He walked on, emptying wastebaskets as he went.


"You hardly said two words all night," Robert complained as they got ready for bed.

"I'm sorry. I'm just really, really tired," she said. She brushed

73

her teeth, then sidestepped him as she walked into his bedroom. She should have gone home. Damn, she should have stayed at the office with Tori. The dinner party had been unbearable. All she could think about was the case and the autopsy she would have to sit through in the morning. It had been years since she'd done an autopsy, and the last thing she wanted was to get squeamish in front of Tori.

"If you were that tired, we could have stayed home."

"Robert, these are your colleagues. You couldn't have stayed home." She pulled back the covers and crawled under, sighing heavily.

"I just wish you had, you know, enjoyed yourself."

"I got dinner," she said, echoing Tori's words. "That's all that mattered," she said quietly, rolling over and closing her eyes. She felt him crawl in beside her, felt his arm as he snaked it around her waist. She didn't move.

# Chapter Fifteen

Tori was in much the same position that Samantha had left her. Staring at her computer, one hand on the mouse, chin resting in the palm of the other hand. Sam walked over and set a cup of cappuccino in front of her.

"How can you possibly look so fresh and rested?"

"What do you mean?" Tori asked as she pulled the lid off the coffee. "Mmm, thanks."

"How late did you work?"

Tori shrugged. "Not late."

"Why don't I believe you?"

"I don't sleep much."

"You look like you got eight hours."

"You don't."

"Oh, thanks a lot."

"How did your dinner party go?"

"It was awful." Samantha sat down and pulled off her own lid, sipping quietly at her coffee. "I was so tired and the last thing I wanted was to be at a dinner party with defense lawyers telling war stories."

"Is that what he is?"

"Yes. And he loves it."

"Someone's got to do it," Tori said. She went back to her computer, flipping through the notes she'd made last night.

Samantha watched her. She really did look rested. Maybe she'd taken her advice and made an early night of it. She looked . . . well, fresh. Her dark hair was as neat as always. Her ever-present jeans were complemented this morning with a light blazer.

"You look nice," she said.

"Nice?"

"The jacket. What's the occasion?"

Tori grinned. "Ran out of clothes here. The T-shirt is dirty."

Samantha sighed and shook her head.

"When do you do laundry?"

"When I run out of clothes."

"So tonight?"

"No. I have a stash at my apartment."

"Can we do a workout?"

"Are you up to it?"

"Yes. I'm still sore, but I want to continue." She flexed her muscles. Yes, definitely sore. "Dinner?"

Tori raised her eyebrows.

"After our workout," Sam explained.

"Sure, if you've got time."

"I have time. Besides, I know I'll be starving. After this autopsy, I doubt I'll want to eat for the rest of the day."

"I guess at Assault you didn't have much occasion to witness an autopsy, huh?"

"It's been years," Sam admitted.

"You can skip it," Tori offered. She remembered the first time she'd done an autopsy with Kaplan. He'd barely left the room before losing his breakfast. She'd never let him live it down. She wondered why she was offering Sam an out now.

"I will not. We're partners. In everything."

They both looked up as Donaldson walked over. In the few weeks Samantha had been here, she'd hardly spoken to the guy.

"Kinda need some help, Hunter," he said hesitantly.

"What's up, Donaldson?"

"Gay bars? How well do you know them?"

Tori glared at him, narrowing her eyes.

"Black clubs? How well do you know them, Donaldson?"

"I'm just asking for some help here, Hunter."

She leaned back, glancing at Samantha, who nodded and gave her a slight smile.

"Okay. What do you want?"

"We have a transvestite. He was . . . damn near decapitated. His landlord found him this morning. We've got two club stamps on him." Donaldson looked at his notes. "One from Changes, the other from the Pink Lagoon."

"You and Adams got this case?"

He nodded.

"Well, I'll bet you're both going to be busting your ass trying to solve it."

"Just doing our job, Hunter. Do you know the clubs?" he asked..

"You would think Changes would be for the transgender crowd, but it's not. The Pink Lagoon caters mostly to them."

"Thanks."

"You and Adams going down there?"

He nodded.

"That ought to be fun," she drawled. "Wish we could come and watch." Then she leaned forward. "Be careful. Adams might get hit on," she teased. "Make sure he knows that they're really men under all those dresses."

Samantha covered the smile on her face as Donaldson's eyes widened.

"We'll manage, Hunter."

Tori shook her head, then grinned at Sam.

"Homophobic. Both of them. Trust me, that case will never get solved."

"Neither one of them have really spoken to me, you know. How long will it take before they accept me?"

"They're assholes. Don't worry about it."

"Is that your way of saying they won't ever accept me?"

"No. They'll warm up. You're pretty. You're straight. If you do a good job, they'll warm up. Well, Adams may not, but Donaldson will."

"It's because you're gay, right?"

"What?"

"That they treat you like this."

Tori grinned. "No. It's because I'm a bitch."

"I don't believe that."

"What? That I'm a bitch?"

"Well, if you'd asked me a couple of weeks ago . . ." Sam said. "But you put on a good front."

"Oh? And you think you've broken through? That you've seen the real me?"

"Yes."

Tori stared at her for the longest moment.

"I don't know what the real me is anymore," she said quietly.

"I think you do."

They stared at each other across the desks, then Tori nodded. Sam smiled.

"Come on. We've got an autopsy. I'll fill you in on what I found out last night."

Samantha pushed her chair back and grabbed her purse, following Tori.

"I knew you worked last night. Did you even eat?"

"Pizza." Then Tori tossed Sam the keys. "You drive."


"You really think she was gay?" Samantha asked as they walked into the lab. "She was a hooker. Is that possible?"

Tori stopped. "She was a hooker. That was her job. It wasn't making love, Sam. It was sex for money. When she wasn't working, yes, I think she was gay."

"I don't know, Tori. Just because the tattoo was a lesbian gang, that doesn't prove anything. She was a hooker."

"We'll follow up with that later. Let's see what turns up today."

Jackson had already started when they walked in. Samantha stood back, away from the body. A sheet still covered her torso.

"You're late," he said. "I've already done a prelim."

"Hope we didn't miss anything."

"Got your skin samples from under the nails," he said. "We got a hair, too, but no skin tag." He pulled back the sheet and Samantha gasped. "Sorry, Detective." He pointed at her neck. "Bruising around the neck, indicative of the others but that's not what killed her. The wounds at her midsection were not post-mortem."

"Time of death? Rita thought after midnight."

"Sounds right. Stomach was empty. What was left of it, anyway. She had been sodomized. Brutally. I found wood fibers in the rectum, there was hemorrhaging," he stated.

"I'm looking for a semen match," Tori said.

"Yes, I know. We'll have DNA this afternoon. I'll have the lab do a rush."

Samantha stared as they walked around the body. She watched Tori's impassive face, then Dr. Jackson's. They didn't seem affected at all. She was thankful she'd not taken the time for breakfast.

"There is bruising on her legs and arms. Look here." He pointed. "Her wrists were bound. We have rope fibers. Well, two," he said. "I'll match them with the ones we found on the second victim."

"What was she cut with?"

"My guess is a serrated kitchen knife or maybe a bread knife. The initial wound was here." He pointed. "Then the killer pulled up on the knife, up to her sternum. It lodged here." He showed Hunter. "I'll be able to get some markings off the bone. If you can find a knife, we can match it."

"Sam, take a look . . ." Tori stopped when she saw the whiteness of Samantha's face. She walked over quietly, standing in front of her, blocking the body. She waited until Sam met her eyes. "Why don't you get some air?"

"I'm fine."

"No, you're not. I'll finish up here. Get some air."

Sam swallowed, then turned and walked quickly from the room. Tori turned back to Jackson and shrugged.

"Sorry."

"It's okay. At least she didn't throw up all over the floor like Kaplan."

"Yeah. I was afraid it was about to come to that, though."

A half hour later, Tori found Samantha sitting on a bench outside in the sunshine. She walked over and sat beside her.

"You okay?"

Sam stared straight ahead, her anger returning.

"I wish you hadn't embarrassed me like that."

"I didn't mean to embarrass you, Sam. You were as white as a sheet."

Sam finally turned her head and looked at Tori. But Tori's eyes were warm, concerned. Her anger disappeared. Tori hadn't sent her out of the room to embarrass her in front of Dr. Jackson. She'd simply been concerned about her.

"I'm sorry. It'll take me a while to get used to that."

"Used to it? I don't think you ever get used to it." Tori leaned back and stretched her legs out. "You just have to separate it. It's no longer the body of a young girl. It's evidence to catch a killer."

"Did you find anything else?"

"Until we get DNA back, it's hard to believe it was the same killer. The first two bodies were clean, except for semen. This one . . . rope fibers, wood fibers, the knife wound . . . everything's different."

"Maybe he's just progressing."

"Yeah. Listen, Jackson is going to get the photos in the database as soon as he can. If we get a DNA match, I think you should set up a meeting with CIU for a profiler. I'll stay out of your way. Besides what happened last week, me and CIU go back a ways."

"Is there anybody in the department that you *haven't* pissed off?"

"I think I've pretty much made the rounds."

Tori's cell phone interrupted them.

*"Hunter, I think we may have an ID on your girl."* Fisk said.

"Which one?"

*"This one. Got a missing persons on a Rachel Anderson. Description fits. I've sent a unit over to her parents' house. You want me to bring them in?"*

"Let's get photos first and we'll take a look. We don't need to upset them if it's not her."

*"Roger that."*

"Come on, Sam," Tori said, already walking to the car. "Missing Persons got a possible match."


Tori watched through the glass window in one of the interrogation rooms as Sam spoke quietly with Mrs. Anderson. She had never been good with this part of the job. Too many memories crowding in. But Sam, she had a warmth about her. Tori watched as the woman reached out to Sam, clutching her arm. Tori looked away from the pain. Sam had just told her about her daughter. If it was left up to Tori, she would have just blurted out the news.

"Hunter?"

"Yeah?" She turned to face Malone.

"Mayor's office just called. They want to meet tomorrow. Have you read the paper?"

"No."

"Don't. We get ripped. Seems it's our fault they didn't report enough about the first two murders." He looked at Samantha. "Is that the mother?"

"Yes."

"You going to question her?"

"Yes. As soon as Sam thinks it's okay."

Malone nodded.

81

"So, she's working out okay? I've never seen you stand on the sidelines before," he said.

She shrugged. "She's better at this than I am."

"Okay. But be quick about it. We need to meet. Do you want me to bring in another team?"

"No."

"All right. But we're under the microscope with this one."

"I have a theory. I'll know more after we speak with the mother."

"Let me know."

Tori returned her gaze to Sam, watching as the mother dabbed at her eyes. She finally moved away from the glass and opened the door. Both women looked up at her.

"Mrs. Anderson, I'm Detective Hunter. I'm terribly sorry about your daughter," she said.

The woman only nodded, still dabbing at her eyes. Sam still clutched her hand.

"We have to ask you some questions," she said quietly. She pulled out a chair across from her, then looked quickly at Sam. Sam nodded. "There have been three young women killed. The first two were . . . prostitutes. We thought that was the pattern."

"Prostitutes? Surely you're not suggesting that my Rachel was . . ."

"No, of course not. We're trying to find a link between them. We think it's the same killer. Mrs. Anderson, was your daughter . . . gay?"

Mrs. Anderson raised teary eyes to Tori, then sobbed. She nodded.

"Yes. She . . . she told me about a year ago. I couldn't believe it. My husband, he still . . . can't accept it."

"I understand. I'm sorry." Tori looked at Sam again.

"Mrs. Anderson," Sam said. "Do you know if she was seeing someone? Do you know what clubs she frequented?"

Mrs. Anderson shook her head.

"We didn't talk about it," she said quietly. "We didn't want to know."

"Do you know who her friends were?"

82

Mrs. Anderson's eyes widened.

"Do you think one of them did this to her?"

"No, no. We're just trying to find out where she went, who she hung out with. Where she might have been the night she died," Tori said.

"She left the house about nine. She said she'd be home by midnight. She was rarely out later than that."

"Did she have a computer?" Sam asked.

"Yes, of course. She needed it for school."

"We're going to need her computer, Mrs. Anderson. What about a cell phone?"

"Yes, she had one."

"We found her car in a parking lot in Fair Park. There wasn't a cell phone. Did she have it with her?"

"Yes."

"Okay." Sam smiled gently at her, then glanced at Tori. "I think that's all for now. Do you want me to call your husband?"

"No. I should do it. But will you stay with me?"

"Of course. I'll stay until he comes."

"Will we . . . will we need to identify her?" she whispered.

"No."

Tori stood up, then touched Sam's shoulder.

"Can I have a word?"

Sam nodded. "I'll be right back, Mrs. Anderson."

They closed the door behind them, their eyes locking together. Tori saw a hint of tears in Sam's.

"Thank you for doing that. I know it was tough."

"It broke my heart."

"I know. I'm sorry."

Sam nodded, then folded her arms across her waist.

"So, not hookers. Lesbians?"

"Well, we have two of each, I think," Tori said. "If we can find out more about Crystal, then we can be sure. Malone wants to meet with us as soon as her husband gets here. Tomorrow, the mayor's office is visiting. They want a report."

"Okay. But I want to stay until the husband gets here."

"That's fine. I'll go write this up and give the lab a call, see if they have results back yet."

Sam nodded. She touched Tori's forearm as she walked past, squeezing gently. Tori's eyes followed the slim fingers as they wound themselves around her arm, then watched them slip away just as quickly. As she walked to her desk, her hand touched her skin where Sam's fingers had been.

It was different. She wasn't used to people touching her. Not like that. Not so casually as if it were second nature. Sam was obviously an affectionate person and touching was part of it. She should have known that from their time spent in the tunnel. Sam's hands had been on her for nearly two hours.

God, who would have thought she could ever tolerate this? She smiled as she opened up the file on her computer. She'd known Sam three weeks. And in three weeks' time, Sam had become more of a partner to her than all the others combined. Sam ignored her moods, ignored the rumors she'd heard about Tori, ignored the fact that she was gay. And if Tori wasn't careful, they would end up being good friends. When's the last time that happened?

She typed quickly, making the few notes of their conversation with Mrs. Anderson. Then she picked up the phone and dialed the lab. It had only been a few hours, but she would push.

"It's Hunter. Is Jackson around?"

"He's still in the lab."

"Can you page him? I need to know if you have anything yet. We got a positive ID on the victim," she said.

"We got it. Rachel Anderson. It'll be a couple of hours on the report. He's put a rush on it, Hunter."

"Call me as soon as you get it."

"Don't we always?"

"Sara, who are you kidding? If I didn't hound you to death, I'd have to wait days."

"Don't worry. We'll call, Hunter. The Mayor's office has already been checking on it."

"What? Why the hell did they call? It's not their fucking case," she exclaimed, her voice rising.

"Hey, the Mayor outranks you, okay?"

"Call me first," she growled. "I mean it." She slammed the phone down. "Idiots."

"That had to have been the lab," Samantha said as she pulled out her chair. "What's going on?"

"Mayor's office called them instead of us. You wouldn't think a few hookers getting whacked would stir up things quite so much," she said.

"I thought we decided it wasn't because they were hookers."

"They don't know that." Tori stood and grabbed the file and the reports she had printed out last night. "Come on. Let's go over it with Malone."

"You know, if you want to skip the workout tonight, I won't mind," Sam said as she followed Tori.

"What about your upper body?"

"What about it?"

Tori stopped and stared, her eyes moving slowly up from Sam's waist, pausing briefly at her breasts, then up to her face.

"Well, it looks fine to me. You're the one that thought it needed work."

Sam put her hands on her hips.

"Were you just checking me out?"

Tori grinned. "Of course not. I did that the first day."

Sam stood rooted to the spot as Tori walked into the Lieutenant's office.

"Kennedy? You going to join us or what?" Malone called.

She walked in, intentionally bumping Tori's arm as she sat down next to her. She was rewarded with a quick grin.

"Okay, let's hear what you have," he said.

"Jane Doe Number One. Street name Lorraine. Strangled. Left in Dumpster in East Dallas. Got DNA on four semen samples. No matches in the database. Jane Doe Number Two. Street name Crystal. Strangled. Left in Dumpster in the downtown area. Semen match from first Jane Doe. Now, Rachel Anderson. Left in Dumpster in Little Mexico." Tori glanced up. "Belly ripped open. She's the only one of the three that was naked. We got rope fibers and wood fibers. Rachel Anderson was bound. All three were sodomized." She looked at Malone. "Rachel Anderson wasn't a hooker. She was gay, according to her mother. The tattoo on Lorraine, it traced back to a gang symbol in New Orleans." She handed him the copy she'd found on the Internet last night. "The tattoo was altered. The symbol at the bottom indicates she was a lesbian, too."

"So you don't think someone's knocking off working girls?" he asked.

"No. I don't think it's random, either. We need to find out something about Crystal. Maybe she was a lesbian, too. That could be our angle."

Malone leaned forward. "They were hookers, Hunter. Forgive me for my ignorance, but are lesbians hookers?"

"Everybody's got to make a living, Lieutenant."

"Unless you get something on this Crystal, I don't think that's going to fly. Besides, you don't really know about Lorraine. Could just be a female thing, this tattoo. Could be, the whole thing is random and it's just a coincidence that two of them were hookers."

"We all know that serial killers don't do anything randomly. Something has to link them."

"Maybe just the fact that they are women," Samantha suggested.

"No. They're all young, under twenty. It's not random. If it were random, chances are one of them would have been older. Why three teenagers? There has to be a link," Tori said.

"Find out something about Crystal or verify that tattoo, Hunter. We meet tomorrow at ten. They'll probably send Jenkins," he said.

"Are you serious?"

"Most likely."

"Who is Jenkins?" Sam asked.

"Mayor's task force," Malone said. "He and Hunter aren't exactly kissing cousins."

"And who is?"

"Very funny," Hunter said dryly.

"What about the profiler? I think we should bring someone in."

"Yes. I'll meet with them," Samantha said.

Malone looked at Tori. "That okay?"

"Yeah."

"Okay. I'll call CIU. Get me something else, Hunter."

"We're working on it."

"What are we working on?" Samantha asked as they walked back to their desks.

"I'm going to hit some women's bars tonight, show our pictures around."

"I guess you mean *we're* going to hit some bars tonight," Sam corrected.

Tori stopped. "That's not necessary. I can do it."

"I'm sure you can. But you're not."

"Sam, there's no need for you to come along. I'm just going to show the pictures around, see if anyone knows them."

"Goddamn it, Hunter. We're partners. If you're going out, then I'm going out."

"You have . . . a life. You have someone. There's no need for both of us to be out at midnight."

"What the hell does that have to do with it?" she demanded. "We work together on this one. And don't throw up the fact that I *have* someone," Samantha said. "That's lame."

"Okay. Then how about the fact that you won't fit in? People are more likely to talk to me than to you."

"I've seen you talk to people. I don't think that will be true."

Sikes walked over and stood between them, grinning.

"You girls fighting again? Need a referee?"

"Get lost, Sikes," Tori said, glaring at him.

"Whoa, Hunter, calm down. Just trying to stop a catfight here."

Tori turned and strode purposefully into the ladies' room. Samantha followed.

"You can't keep doing this," Samantha said.

"Doing what?"

87

"Taking over. Making all the decisions. We're partners, Tori. Why the hell don't you want me going out with you?"

Tori shoved her hands into her jeans and turned to look in the mirror, meeting Samantha's eyes in the reflection.

"Because the places I'm going, I don't want you at."

"Why?"

"Because they're not . . . nice places."

"They're bars."

"Leather bars. Sex bars. Not dance clubs," Tori said.

"And you think I'll judge you?"

Tori shrugged.

"Do you frequent these places on off hours? Are you afraid someone will recognize you?"

"No, of course not."

"Then?"

Sam walked over and turned Tori to face her.

"I'm not going to judge you based on what I might see tonight, Tori. There are plenty of straight bars that I wouldn't set foot in. What's the difference?"

"We need information, Sam. If you go in, looking all wide-eyed and shocked, no one's going to talk."

"I'll be fine. And if someone hits on me, I'll trust that you'll take care of them."

Tori allowed a smile to touch her face and Sam grinned in response.

"Okay. You can go. But . . . change clothes. Jeans. We need to start about ten."

"Okay. Meet you back here?"

Tori nodded and watched her walk away. She wondered what Sam would tell Robert.


"Gay bars?"

"Yes, Robert," Samantha said. She cradled the phone as she

pulled on her jeans. "I'm sure it'll be after midnight before we're done. I'll call you tomorrow sometime."

"Why don't you just come over here when you're done?"

"Because it'll be late, Robert."

"I could wait up. It's Friday night, Samantha."

She bent her head back and stared at the ceiling. Why was he being difficult?

"Robert, please. I'm too tired to argue about this. When we're done, I'm coming home and going to bed. I'm not coming to your apartment. Now, we'll talk tomorrow."

"How will I know if you're okay?"

"Why wouldn't I be okay? We're going to some bars, asking questions. That's all."

"Samantha, anything could happen. I think you should at least call me when you get home."

"Why are you doing this?" she asked quietly.

"I just . . . worry about you. You've had this job barely a month and we've hardly seen each other. When we do, you're always tired. I just don't like what it's doing to us."

"You really want to have this conversation now?" She sat down on her bed and crossed her legs. "This is my job, Robert. Not eight to five. Just like yours is not eight to five. It's not like I'm going out for a night of fun. I'm working," she said.

"I know. I'm sorry. I know this is important to you. But . . . I want to be important to you, too."

She sighed. It shouldn't be like this. It was getting much too complicated. He was acting like she was going out on a date, for Christ's sake.

"Robert, you're blowing this out of proportion. I'm just working late. That's all. Now, I've got to go. I'm going to get a quick dinner, then head out. I'll call you tomorrow."

"Okay. I'm sorry. I love you, Samantha. Please be careful."

She squeezed her eyes shut. "I love you, too," she murmured.

She tossed her phone on the bed, staring at it. She was actually surprised by his reaction. When she was still with Assault, she'd had to go out nights on numerous occasions. She never recalled him being this upset by it. Of course, she'd never willingly gone out. She'd always wished she could stay home. With him. This time, it was her choice to go out. In fact, she'd had to practically beg to go out with Tori.

# Chapter Sixteen

Samantha walked into the squad room, finding Tori exactly where she thought she'd be. Sitting at her desk, staring at the computer.

Tori looked up, her eyes moving over Sam. Faded jeans, boots, tight T-shirt tucked inside, black belt. No bra? Well, she certainly looked the part.

"Do I pass?"

"Better than me."

Sam's eyes flicked over Tori. She had changed into black jeans and a dark shirt. She looked as powerful as always.

"I don't think so," she said. "You look nice." She sat down at her desk and opened the bag she carried. She pulled out containers of Chinese food and tossed Tori a fork. "I took a chance that you hadn't eaten." She shoved one of the boxes at her. "Shrimp and chicken, both. I wasn't sure what you'd like."

"Anything," Tori said as she took a bite. "Mmm. Thanks."

Sam smiled and opened her own. She knew Tori would not take the time for dinner. She wondered how she survived at all.

"I assume you didn't do laundry," she said. "Did you break down and go to your apartment?"

Tori nodded, still chewing.

"Where is it, anyway?"

"South."

"South of here? South of Dallas? South of the interstate?"

"What? You want an address?"

Sam shrugged. "I just would like to know where you live."

"Here, mostly."

Sam shook her head. "You know that's not healthy. You have to have some place to escape to."

"I have my boat."

"And how often do you go out there?"

"More often in the summer, and why all the questions?" she asked as she stabbed a shrimp with her fork.

Samantha shrugged. "I just don't know anything about you."

"I lead a terribly boring life. There's not really anything to know."

"All work and no play?"

"Pretty much."

Samantha knew absolutely nothing about the lesbian lifestyle, but Tori was just so attractive. She couldn't imagine why she was single. She wondered if she ever dated.

"What thoughts are running through that pretty head of yours?"

"Just . . . wondering about your love life," Sam admitted.

Tori laughed. "I'm not exactly a sociable person."

"You don't date?"

"I wouldn't call it dating," Tori said dryly.

"One-night stands?"

"I wouldn't really call it that, either."

Sam's eyes widened. "Sex for hire?"

Tori laughed again. "I've never had to pay."

92

Sam watched as Tori stabbed another shrimp and slipped it in her mouth. Yes, attractive. In fact, she was . . . well, Sam wouldn't say beautiful. Not in the normal sense. Her skin was nearly flawless and those eyelashes, God, who wouldn't kill for them? Then those eyelashes opened and dark brown eyes captured her own. Her eyes were warm, gentle. Not the angry, indifferent eyes she'd found that first day.

"Now what are you thinking?"

Sam gave her a quick smile.

"None of your business," she said and she shoved a forkful of rice into her mouth.


"Are you sure you're up for this?" Tori asked again. They were parked down the street from the most popular leather bar in the city. She'd watched as Sam's eyes widened at the sight of a woman wearing a dog collar, being led into the bar on a leash.

"Why did she have a . . . leash?"

"Dominant-submissive. It's all about control," Tori said.

"Why would she do that?"

"They're role-playing. You'll see a lot worse inside. Maybe I should just go in by myself. You can wait out here," Tori offered.

"No. I can handle this," Samantha said. *Couldn't she? God, did women really do that?*

"We'll just go in, ask a few questions, then leave. If they know we're cops, they'll never talk to us. Don't flash your badge," Tori warned.

"We're not exactly going to fit in," Samantha said. "I mean, look at us. We look normal."

"They won't all be wearing collars, Sam. In fact, some women go just to watch."

Tori opened her door and got out, waiting until Sam walked beside her.

"Stay close to me."

"Don't worry. I won't let you out of my sight," Sam said.

It was dark inside and nearly everyone wore black, she and Tori included. The music was loud, pounding, almost sinister in its sound. She tried to act casual as she looked around, but the sight of a woman bound at the hands, being forced onto the lap of another, made her eyes widen. She felt a hand take hers and she thankfully squeezed Tori's fingers with her own. She let Tori lead her to the bar without a word.

"Sit."

They sat side by side, looking around without speaking. Sam watched as the bartender came over, a tall woman with spiked hair. She wore a leather jacket, opened—and nothing else. Both her nipples were pierced, linked together by a tiny silver chain.

"Scotch," Tori said.

"And what about for your pet?"

"She'll have club soda."

Samantha was about to protest when she felt Tori's hand squeeze hers. She kept quiet.

"We're looking for a friend of ours," Tori told the bartender. "Lorraine."

The woman shook her head. "Don't know a Lorraine."

"What about Crystal?"

"Crystal? Blond?"

Tori nodded.

"Yeah. Haven't seen her in a week or so." She set their drinks on the bar. "She belongs to Johnny."

Tori raised her eyebrows.

"Down there," she pointed.

Johnny was a massive woman, sitting at the end of the bar, alone. Tori looked at Sam, then bent closer.

"Stay here," she whispered. "Don't talk to anyone."

Samantha nodded, watching only out of the corner of her eye as Tori walked away.

Tori took her drink and sat down next to Johnny. The woman finally looked at Tori, then away.

"Too butch. Not interested," she said.

Tori rolled her eyes. *As if.* But she kept her voice low. "I'm looking for Crystal."

"The bitch is gone. Not one word, just gone." Then the woman turned to Tori. "Why the hell do you want my Crystal?"

Tori discreetly pulled her badge out and flipped it at Johnny.

"What the hell?"

"I'm with Homicide. A woman was found murdered," she said quietly. "She went by Crystal on the street."

The woman stared at her for the longest time, then narrowed her eyes.

"Get the fuck out of my face."

The large woman pushed away from the bar and walked off, chains dangling from around her waist.

"Great, Hunter," she murmured. "That went well." But, at least they had a name. They could bring her in for questioning. She looked around for Sam, her eyes widening. "Oh, shit," she whispered.

"I'm with someone," Samantha said, but the woman sat down anyway.

"Don't see anyone," the woman said. Then she reached out and captured Sam's wrist, pulling Sam's hand toward her. "I'm claiming you."

"You're . . . *what?*" Sam tried to pull her hand away, but the woman wouldn't release her. "Get your hands off me."

"Dance."

"No."

"I said yes."

Sam's eyes widened.

Then Tori appeared, grasping the woman's arm and squeezing hard.

"She's mine," Tori growled. "Don't touch."

"Hey, man," the woman gasped, releasing her hold on Samantha. "The bitch was alone."

"She's not alone. She's with me."

Tori moved between them, shielding Sam. She felt Sam's hands grasp her waist urgently.

"Then she shouldn't have looked at me."

"She'll be punished, don't worry."

Samantha's hands tightened their grip, listening. Finally, the other woman shrugged.

"You better keep her on a tighter leash," she muttered as she walked away.

Tori turned, meeting Sam's eyes. She leaned forward, close to Sam.

"You okay?"

"Yes. I don't mind saying, I thought about pulling my weapon."

She heard Tori chuckle, then finally relaxed her hold on her.

"Come on. Let's get out of here."

"You don't have to ask me twice," Sam said.

Back in the car, Sam leaned her head back and sighed. She had been frightened. The woman scared her, with her spiked hair and chains. She couldn't imagine the type of people that frequented that bar on a regular basis.

"Did you get anything?" she finally asked.

"Yes."

Tori pulled out her cell phone.

"Sergeant Reynolds? This is Hunter. I need you to send out a unit and pick someone up." A pause. "Leather Girls," she said. "A woman named Johnny. She's inside. We need her for questioning. She's a large woman, military haircut, wearing a leather jacket with chains around the waist." Another pause. "Larger than that. It'll be another couple hours before we get back." Tori glanced at Sam and rolled her eyes. "Yes, I know she'll be pissed if we hold her that long. Let me worry about that." She tossed her cell phone on the seat and started the engine.

"She knew Crystal?"

"Yes, but she wouldn't talk. We'll question her later."

"Where to now?"

"Bed of Roses," Tori said. "It's a sex club."

"Sex club? What does that mean?"

96

"It means that anonymous sex is acceptable. On the premises," Tori clarified.

"Like a brothel? They have rooms and such?"

Tori grinned. "Not exactly. Just lots of nooks and crannies."

Sam's eyes widened. "In the bar?"

"Yes. It'll be dark. Women go there for sex, that's all."

"You mean, they go to meet someone and have sex?"

"More than one, most likely," Tori said.

"More than one?"

Tori laughed. "Don't stare. And certainly, don't look at anyone that's alone. They'll think you're interested."

"Is that legal?"

"No."

"You won't leave me alone, right?" Sam reached out and grasped Tori's arm. "Not for a minute?"

"No. I promise."

This time, they parked three blocks away. Sam walked silently beside Tori, glancing at her occasionally. She wondered if Tori ever frequented bars like this. She was nervous, and she shoved both hands into her pockets as their footsteps echoed on the sidewalk.

"Remember, be careful who you look at," Tori warned.

"I'll only look at you, I promise."

"You'll be fine. Just stay close."

"Don't worry," Sam murmured.

As soon as they walked inside, she was thankful when Tori again grasped her hand. The music was louder than before, if possible. Couples were everywhere, in the shadows, on the dance floor, at the bar. She stared as they passed by one couple, openly touching below the waist. Then she jumped and gasped.

"Someone just grabbed my ass," she hissed. "Please say it was you."

Tori laughed and pulled Sam closer to her as they walked to the bar.

"Not me," she said. She sat Sam down, then pulled her stool close, putting one arm behind Sam.

Despite Tori's warnings, Sam couldn't help but look around her.

Couples were locked in embraces . . . kissing and touching as if they were completely alone. Her eyes were drawn across the bar as two women sat on the same bar stool. One straddled the other's lap and Sam stared as their hips rocked together. Their mouths were joined and she watched as their tongues dueled. She felt her body respond, felt herself go warm all over as she watched them. The woman on top threw her head back, mouth open. Sam's eyes narrowed as she watched the other woman move her hand between them. The woman's scream was silent, but Sam knew she had reached orgasm. She squeezed her own legs together, uncomfortable for having stared but unable to stop herself.

"What'll it be, ladies?"

Sam pulled her attention from across the bar and glanced at the woman who approached.

"Two beers," Tori said. Then she reached into her breast pocket and pulled out the pictures of their victims. When the bartender brought their drinks, Tori laid the pictures out.

"Do you know these women?" Tori asked.

The woman stared, then raised frightened eyes to Tori.

"Jesus Christ . . . that's Angie," she said. "Who are you?"

"Homicide," Tori said quietly. "Do you know them?"

The woman pointed to Lorraine. "That's Angie."

"Angie? Got a last name?"

"No. I just know her as Angie. What happened?"

"She was found in a Dumpster a few weeks ago," Tori said. "What about the others?"

The woman shook her head. "No."

"Anybody here might know them?"

"Angie was a minor. She could only come in with a date," she said. "She's dead?"

Tori nodded.

"Damn," she whispered. Then she looked around. "She used to come with Beth."

"Is she here?"

"Only comes on Saturday. But Dana's here. She knows them both."

"Where?"

The bartender looked around, then pointed. "Over there. She's kinda . . . busy right now. The blond chick over there against the wall."

Tori and Sam glanced where she pointed to find a short blond woman locked in an embrace with a taller redhead. The blonde's shirt was gone.

Tori sighed, then glanced at Sam. Her eyes were still locked on the couple. Tori nudged her with her elbow and Sam's head snapped around.

"It's not polite to stare," she teased.

Sam blushed and grabbed the beer mug with both hands. She kept her eyes firmly focused on the foam at the top.

"I just can't believe people are actually *doing it* right here," she whispered. "Why don't they go someplace private?"

"Because they get off on this."

"What? With people watching?"

"That. And with strangers. They don't want to know names. They don't want to date them. It's just . . . sex," Tori said with a shrug.

Sam flicked her eyes at Tori, then back to her beer.

"Have you ever come here?"

Tori drank from her beer before answering. She considered lying. No telling what Sam would think if she knew that she had been one of those women a long time ago.

"Yes. I've been here a couple of times," she admitted. It was years ago, but yes, she'd come looking for a night of anonymous sex with strangers. And she didn't know their names. She didn't want to.

Sam looked around, her eyes lighting on another couple across the bar from them. She tried to imagine Tori here, with someone sitting on her lap, kissing her, touching her. She couldn't. Not with some stranger. She wanted to think of Tori with someone who loved her, cared about her. This was . . . degrading. She watched the women across from her, saw one's hand slide down the other's body and disappear between her legs. She pulled her eyes away, glancing again at Tori. Tori was watching her.

"I'm sorry," Sam whispered. "I don't like to think of you coming here."

"Then don't. I was young and foolish. And I wasn't getting off with people watching," Tori said quietly. "I just . . . needed . . . someone."

Without realizing what she was doing, Sam reached over and took Tori's hand. She drew it onto her lap.

"Have you not ever had someone, Tori? Someone to love you?"

Tori turned in her seat, her eyes sliding down to where Sam had her hand clutched between her own. Then she raised her eyes and met Sam's green ones that stared at her so expectantly.

She shook her head slowly.

"I've not ever been receptive to . . . love," Tori admitted. "I don't really have anything to offer."

Samantha wanted to disagree. She knew Tori had a lot of great qualities. And she had a sense of humor that she tried so hard to hide. Well, hide from others, not her. Samantha suspected Tori was more herself lately than she'd ever been. Unfortunately, Tori never let anyone else see this side of her. She came across as arrogant and abrasive. It was an act, Samantha now knew, to keep people at bay. It was as if Tori didn't want anyone to get close to her. It was as if she didn't want anyone to love her. Sam was about to voice her thoughts when Tori squeezed her hand.

"Come on. Before our girl finds her next partner."

The blonde was now dressed. She reached behind her for her drink, the ice long melted. She looked up as they approached.

"Wow. Two? I'm not sure I'm up to it," she drawled. "Maybe you," she said, reaching for Samantha. "I'm not sure I could handle tall, dark and dangerous there."

"Are you Dana?" Samantha asked.

The woman looked surprised.

"Do I know you?"

Tori pulled out her badge. "We have some questions," she said.

"Cops? I haven't done anything wrong."

"Do you know a girl named Angie? She comes in with Beth?"

"Hey, I know she's a minor. She's never come with me, and I've never bought her a drink."

"She's dead," Tori said. "Where can we find Beth?"

"What? Angie's dead?"

The woman sat back down, staring.

"What happened? Surely you don't think Beth had anything to do with it?"

"How well did you know Angie?"

She shrugged. "Not that well. I never saw her other than in here. She and Beth were . . . well, I don't know if you'd call it dating, but they saw each other sometimes."

"What is Beth's last name?" Sam asked.

"Perkins. But Beth wouldn't—"

"We're just trying to find out more about Angie. Did she have family?"

Dana shrugged. "I think she was a runaway."

"Where can we find Beth?" Tori asked again.

"She works nights. She's a nurse."

"Which hospital?"

"Parkland Memorial."

"Okay. Thanks."

Tori took out the other two pictures and showed them to Dana. "Do you recognize them?"

"Jesus," she whispered. "Yes. I mean, I've seen them. I don't know them. This one," she said, pointing to Crystal. "She was kinda strange. Into S&M and all that. I've seen her in here a couple of times."

"You've been a big help, Dana. Thank you."

They walked out onto the sidewalk and Sam rubbed her palms on her jeans.

"I feel like I need to wash my hands," she murmured. "Now what? You want to go see if they picked Johnny up?"

"No. Not yet. I have an idea," Tori said.

Sam followed as they walked to Tori's Explorer.

"They were all teenagers, minors. Angie was a runaway. Maybe Crystal, too."

"Yes. And?"

"And they couldn't get into a lot of the bars. At least not alone. There's a club, more of a coffeehouse than a bar, really. Belle's. Usually a younger crowd."

"Belle's? Isn't that a hostel?"

"Yes. Next door to the coffeehouse."

"So, we think our guy is targeting young lesbians. Where better to find them than at a hostel for young lesbians?"

"Maybe. Or he could be staking out the bars and watching."

It was nearly midnight as Tori drove them through downtown and on to the edge of Deep Ellum. The parking lot in front of Belle's was nearly empty. The music coming from inside was quiet, almost soothing. Nothing like they'd heard at the last two clubs.

"Not very popular tonight," Sam said.

"No. Not Friday and Saturday nights. That's when they all sneak into the bars."

Inside, the coffeehouse was well lit, with tables spaced evenly throughout. Only a handful of young women were inside.

"Well, well. Detective Hunter."

Tori and Sam turned, looking at a well-dressed woman coming from the back. Sam recognized her but couldn't place her.

"Counselor," Tori greeted.

"It's been a while. What brings you out here? Official business?"

Tori nodded.

"This is my partner, Sam Kennedy."

"It's Samantha," she said as she shook the other woman's hand.

"Anything I can help with, Detective?"

"Just want to ask a few questions," Tori said. "Do you know Belle?"

Charlotte Grayson laughed. She opened her purse and took out her keys, looking at Samantha with appraising eyes.

"Belle's my cousin," she said. "I haven't seen you around," she said to Samantha. "New in town?"

"No, she's not," Tori said.

"My, my. Possessive, aren't we, Detective?"

"We just want to ask a few questions," Tori said again.

"Well, I was just on my way out. Call me sometime, okay? I think you still owe me dinner."

"Sure."

She looked again at Samantha, then brushed past them and out the bar. Sam looked at Tori with raised eyebrows.

"Defense attorney?"

"Used to be. Works for the DA now."

"You have a history?"

Tori smiled. "It was a long time ago."

"Tell me."

"Later. Come on," she said. She walked to the small bar and sat down, then smiled at the young woman who walked up to them.

"Hello. What can I do for you?"

Tori took out her badge and the three pictures. She laid them across the bar.

"Do you know them?"

"Oh my God," she whispered. She covered her mouth with her hand. "What happened?"

"You recognize them?" Samantha asked.

"Yes. Angie, Crystal and Rachel," she said. "What happened?" she asked again.

"They were murdered, left in Dumpsters," Tori said.

Her eyes widened. "I read about that in the paper. They didn't give names."

"No. Angie and Crystal are Jane Does."

"What do you mean?"

"We can't identify them, no priors," Tori said. "We need some help. What do you know about them?"

"Maybe you should talk to Belle. She knows them," she said.

Tori nodded.

The woman left and Tori glanced at Sam.

"Maybe a break," she said.

103

"Yes. At least to their identity," Samantha said. "What is the woman's name?" she asked.

"Who?"

"You know, the attorney."

"Oh. Charlotte Grayson."

Samantha nodded. She'd heard the name before from Robert. "How do you know her?" Samantha asked.

Tori leaned her elbows on the bar and smiled. It had been years since she'd thought about it. God, she had been so young.

"It was my first year as a detective," Tori said, remembering. "She grilled the hell out of me on the stand. And she was so good, she even had time to flirt with me while she was doing it," she said. "She cornered me outside the courtroom afterward. She bet me dinner that we'd sleep together that day."

"And?"

"And I still owe her dinner," Tori said.

Samantha was about to comment when the young woman came back with an older version of Charlotte Grayson. An older, shorter, plumper version.

"I'm Belle Grayson," she said. "Catherine says you have some bad news."

"I'm Detective Hunter. This is Detective Kennedy," Tori said. "We're with Homicide."

"I see. What can I do for you?"

Tori pointed at the pictures on the bar. "You know these women?"

Belle scanned the photos, then raised her eyes to them.

"Oh my God. Yes. I know them. What happened?"

"They were murdered . . . and their bodies left in Dumpsters."

"Oh, no," she whispered. "Not Rachel, too?"

"Yes. What can you tell us about them?"

Belle looked past them to the young women in the bar, then back to Tori.

"Let's go next door to the hostel, to my office," she said quietly. "I don't want to alarm them."

A side door to the coffeehouse led them across a brick-covered walkway and onto the porch of Belle's Hostel. They both followed the older woman down a hallway.

Belle's office was sparsely decorated, an old desk and file cabinets, one bookshelf littered with pictures, not much more. Tori scanned the room, her eyes landing on the numerous doors behind Belle's desk, and she frowned slightly as she counted eight. Sam sat in the only chair and Tori stood beside her. Belle settled in behind her desk, hands folded nervously on top.

"I just can't believe this. All dead?"

"I'm sorry," Sam said sincerely.

"Angie was only seventeen. She came to me two years ago, from New Orleans. She was living with an aunt. When the aunt found out she was gay, she kicked her out. Crystal was eighteen. She'd only been around about a year. Her family is in Kansas. They kicked her out, she came here. Rachel is from Dallas. She still lived at home, although I don't think her parents were very supportive."

"Did they live here?" Sam asked.

"Angie lived here for about a year. Crystal stayed only two months. Rachel never actually lived here, although she was friends with quite a few here. She was here all the time."

"When's the last time you've seen them?" Tori asked.

"I haven't seen Angie in months. Crystal, she would come around, visit, but it's been at least a month, maybe more. Rachel, she was here this week."

"Did you know that Angie and Crystal were hookers?" Tori asked.

Belle raised her eyes to them and nodded.

"Everyone has to make a living, Detective," she said. "It's not something they were proud of, certainly."

"But they were lesbians?" Sam asked.

"Yes."

"I guess I don't understand," Samantha said, shaking her head.

"It was a job. It wasn't for pleasure, I assure you. They had turned to prostitution before I met them. I tried to talk them out of it, tried to get them a real job. But, Detective, minimum wage can't compare to what they could turn in a night."

Tori leaned her hip against the desk, one hand rubbing her eyes.

"Okay. The only connection we have is that they were lesbians and that they all have a history with Belle's. Have you noticed anyone hanging around?"

"No. We've had no problems. No one stalking."

"What about phone calls? Harassment?"

"No, none."

"Okay. Any other hangouts that they might have in common?"

"Outlaws, I suppose."

"What's that?" Samantha asked.

"It's a bar in the West End area. Wednesday nights they allow minors in. Most of the girls go there. In fact, we close up on Wednesdays for that very reason," she said.

"Is it a women's bar?" Samantha asked.

"It's mixed."

Sam glanced at Tori, who nodded.

"Thank you, Belle." Tori pushed off the desk, reaching for the older woman's hand. "We'll let you know what we find out."

"Should I warn the others? I mean, is this like a serial killer?"

"It could be, Belle," Sam said. "But it won't do any good to cause panic. Just remind them to be careful."

Tori paused at the door, turning back to Belle. She motioned to the wall behind Belle.

"Closets?"

Belle frowned. "What?"

"All the doors there."

Belle followed her gaze, then laughed. "Oh, no. Passages."

"Passages?"

"This was an old plantation house. It was moved from Louisiana in the early 1900s. They had servants' quarters in the center of the house."

"Do you still use them?" Sam asked.

Belle shook her head. "No, no. Even when I bought it, the interior of the house had been closed off. I'd thought about remodeling, making more rooms, but the expense was too much. Besides, what young girl is going to want to stay in a room without windows?"


Tori parked her Explorer in the lot, not far from Sam's car. She cut the engine and they sat quietly. It was after two.

"What about Johnny?" Samantha asked.

"I'll go talk to her. It won't take long."

"You're as tired as I am," Samantha said. "We should do it together."

"No. You go home. I'll just crash here."

"Tori, that's not fair. I should come in, too."

Tori rolled her head across the seat, meeting Sam's eyes in the lamplight.

"I doubt she'll tell us more than we already know. Go on home, Sam."

Samantha reached across the console and captured Tori's hand. She squeezed.

"Go to your boat this weekend," she said. "Relax."

Tori nodded. "And what about you? What will you do?"

Sam shrugged. "Right now, I feel like I could sleep until Sunday."

"Well, if you want to escape the city, call me. You and Robert are welcome. The boat is plenty big enough."

"Thanks. But Robert is not really . . ." *What? The boat type?* "Well, he's not much for the outdoors," she said. "But thanks for the offer." She felt Tori squeeze her hand lightly, and she returned the pressure. "Good night."

Tori watched Sam drive off, then went inside. Time to face Johnny. She doubted the large woman would be in a civil mood, considering they'd been holding her for nearly three hours.

# Chapter Seventeen

Samantha wanted to ignore the phone and let her voice mail get it again, but she knew it would be Robert. It was nearly noon. She reached a hand out from under the covers and grabbed it.

"Hello," she said, her voice still heavy with sleep.

"Samantha? Are you okay?"

"Yes, Robert. I'm in bed still."

"It's almost noon," he said. "You never sleep in."

She sat up, propping herself on the pillows and pulling the covers to her waist. She was hungry. She was tired. She didn't want to talk to Robert.

"It was nearly three before I got to bed," she said around a yawn.

"Three? What kind of bars did you go to?"

"Robert, we were working, not barhopping. We have three dead teenagers, remember?"

"Yes, I know. But still, that's so late."

She sighed. Her patience was running out. PMS? Already? She mentally counted back the weeks. No. Too early.

"I wanted to have breakfast with you, so I waited. I guess it's lunch then," he said. "You want to come over and we'll cook here? Or would you rather go out?"

She sighed again. Cook? She was in no mood to cook.

"I'm too tired to cook, Robert."

"Okay. How about the deli? We can get pasta," he suggested.

"How about the Bar and Grill?" she countered. "I could eat a greasy burger and fries."

"Samantha, you know that always upsets my stomach."

"Okay, fine. Pasta."

"Great. Now get that beautiful body of yours out of bed and come on over."

She attempted a smile as she tossed the covers off. It never quite made it to her face.

"Be right there," she said.

"And I'll make my famous omelet for you in the morning," he said. "Maybe served in bed, huh?"

She hadn't the heart to tell him she hated his omelets. He was so proud of them. So she agreed. While she showered, she wondered if Tori was out and about yet. Most likely, considering the woman hardly ever slept. She thought about calling her, to see how it went with Johnny, but then thought better of it. If something had come up, Tori would have called. She really hoped Tori went out to her boat and relaxed some. It appeared her time on her boat was the only real pleasure Tori got out of life. This thought made her sad.

Tori stripped off her shirt and sat in the sunshine in only her sports bra. It was a warm morning. Maybe spring was really here to stay this time. The marina was still quiet. Only a few boats had pulled out. Fishing, most likely. She would join them later in the day, then drop anchor and spend the night out on the water. The

109

wind was calm and there would be a full moon. Perfect for night fishing.

She reached onto the deck and picked up her glass, sipping quietly from the Bloody Mary she'd made earlier. She let her thoughts drift, going over the night before, their time in the bars, her short conversation with Johnny, not pausing over any of them long enough to matter. She was tired. She grabbed only a couple of hours' sleep on the cot, then headed out early, stopping at a grocery store for supplies. She would take Sam's advice and spend the weekend on the boat. She needed this. Her long days were catching up with her.


Samantha stared past Robert to the other couples sitting around them on the patio. They were all locked in conversations, smiling and laughing. She sighed, then brought her attention back to Robert as he continued telling her about the case he was working on. She nodded at the appropriate times, not really listening to his words but watching the animated expressions on his face. He really was a sweet man. And he cared about her, she knew that. But at this very moment, she wasn't certain what their future was. At one time, she might have thought they'd get married or at the very least, move in together. But now . . . she wasn't so certain. Their relationship had evolved into one of friendship, companionship, but not passion. On her part, anyway. Robert still seemed to enjoy their time together in bed, and she wondered if he realized how forced it had become for her. There just wasn't that excitement, that total loss of control, that burning desire to touch and be touched.

She thought back to last night and the way her body had reacted as she watched the two women across the bar. She admitted now, she had been excited. Her body had responded to what she saw and she had no explanation for that. Sitting there watching them last night, something had clicked inside of her. The looks on their faces as they touched, the natural way they moved together.

Had she ever looked like that when Robert touched her? When any man touched her? Her thoughts went to Tori, and again she tried to imagine her there. But it wasn't some stranger she saw on her lap, kissing her, touching her. She saw herself reaching out to touch Tori, to kiss her.

"Samantha?"

"Hmm?"

"Well?"

She focused on Robert and frowned.

"What?"

"Have you not been listening? I wanted your opinion."

"I'm sorry, Robert. I was lost in thought. What did you say?"

"Never mind. It wasn't important." Then he pointed to her plate. "How's your pasta?"

"It's fine." In fact, she'd barely touched it. She twirled the pasta on her fork and took a bite. She would rather have had a burger.

"You feel like seeing a movie later?" he asked. "Or maybe we could rent one and go back to my place," he suggested.

"It's so pretty out, Robert, I would hate to be inside," she said. "Why don't we go to the park?"

"The park? And do what?"

"I don't know. Sit in the sunshine? Walk around? Throw a Frisbee?"

He put his fork down and stared at her.

"Are you okay?"

"I'm fine. It's just a beautiful day. I don't want to be stuck in a dark theater."

"You want to tell me what's going on with you? You've been acting very strange for the last several weeks," he said.

She stared back at him.

"Are you suggesting that since I got transferred to Homicide, I've been different?"

He shrugged. "I think it started before that." He leaned forward. "Why was it so important for you to move to Homicide?" he asked. "That's all you focused on for months."

111

"I told you why, Robert. I didn't want to be a detective in Assault for the rest of my career. There are only two women that have made Captain. I want to be the third."

"Why?"

"Why? What kind of question is that?"

"I envision us getting married and having kids and hopefully having you home more, not less. We hardly see each other anymore, Samantha. It's like your career is more important to you than I am."

"Did you hear what you just said, Robert? Did you even listen as the words left your mouth?" she demanded.

"What?"

"You envision us getting married and having kids? So I can stay home more? So that you and the kids and the goddamn house can be more important to me than my career?" She noticed several curious stares from some of the other tables, but she hardly cared.

"Samantha, please, calm down. That's not what I meant," he said.

"What did you mean, then?"

He spread his hands and drew his eyebrows together, a gesture that Sam knew meant he was about to make a speech.

"Samantha, we've been dating for nearly two years, progressing in our relationship to an eventual joining. But both of us, me included, have been focusing on our careers and not on building a future together, a home, a family. Unless I've totally misread you, I think you want the same things I do out of life. A secure future, a nice home, kids. And eventually grandchildren coming to visit. It's a nice picture to think about, isn't it?"

Sam stared at him, wondering what she had missed. Grandchildren? They weren't even married and he's talking about *grandchildren*?

"Robert, I just turned thirty-four. I certainly don't want to talk about becoming grandparents."

He smiled. "You know what I mean. I just want us to look to the future. And base our current decisions on that."

"You know what? My current decision revolves around what to do with the rest of my weekend. And I've decided I don't want to spend it watching movies with you."

She pushed away from the table and left him staring after her. She made it to the sidewalk before he grabbed her arm.

"What the hell are you doing? Do you have any idea how embarrassing that was?"

"I don't care, Robert. Please take me to my car." She stood with her arms crossed, staring at him.

"What is wrong with you?"

"I don't know, Robert," she said honestly. "I just need some space."

"Space?"

"I just want to be alone this weekend. I'm sorry you don't understand."

"You're right. I don't understand. If something's bothering you, if I've done something to upset you, I wish you'd just tell me. Now I have to spend the rest of the weekend wondering what I've done wrong."

"You haven't done anything, Robert."

They crossed the street and got into his car. Samantha sat silently, staring out the window as he drove to his apartment.

"Are you even coming in?" he asked when they parked beside her car.

"No. I'll call you later, Robert."

With that, she slammed her door and sped away. Her grip was tight on the wheel and she finally glanced at herself in the mirror, meeting eyes that were wild with fright. She didn't understand what was happening with her. She had lashed out at Robert because he wanted to marry her and have a family. She should have told him the truth. She didn't want to marry him. She didn't want to have kids. She wondered, if they'd had this conversation a few months ago, would her reaction have been the same?

She grabbed her cell phone. She would call Amy. She would talk it out with her. But before she finished dialing, she disconnected. Amy would say she was crazy. Amy loved Robert. She stuck her hand in her purse, moving things aside until her fingers curled around the business card. She pulled it out, staring at the front before flipping it over. Then, before she could change her mind, she dialed Tori's cell phone.


The ringing woke her, and Tori lazily reached for the phone. She shielded her eyes against the sun.

"Hunter."

"Were you sleeping?"

Tori smiled at the sound of Sam's voice. She sat up, swinging her legs off the recliner and stretched.

"Just a little nap. Catching up," she said. "What about you?"

"I slept until noon. It was great." A pause. "Listen, if your invitation is still open, I would love to see your boat."

"Sure. It's great out here today. I'm still docked. I was going to take her out a little later and do some fishing."

"Do you mind company?"

"No. That'd be great."

Tori gave her quick directions, then tossed her cell phone on the recliner. She wouldn't mind Sam's company and she supposed she was about to meet Robert. She wondered what he would be like. She envisioned him tall, handsome. Dark hair. He and Sam probably made the perfect couple. She shoved her hands into the pockets of her shorts. She didn't really want to meet him, she realized. She didn't want to meet the man that Sam slept with.

Jealousy?

"Please," she murmured, disgusted with the thought. She pulled on her T-shirt and went inside, tidying the tiny kitchen. She opened the refrigerator, wondering how long they would stay. She had plenty of beer but not much food. She eyed the small package of hamburger meat that was to be her dinner. Maybe she could stretch it into three.

# Chapter Eighteen

Sam found a parking spot easily. It was so warm out, she expected the marina to be more crowded. Walking to the gate, she punched in the code that Tori had given her. She walked along the pier, looking out over Eagle Mountain Lake as the sunlight bounced off the water. It was beautiful. No wonder Tori came here to relax.

The marina itself was small, much smaller than the others Sam had passed as she made her way around Lake Worth and on to Eagle Mountain. But it suited Tori. She couldn't imagine her docked side-by-side with a hundred other boats. This marina held maybe twenty, at the most. But what surprised her was the size of the boats. Not fishing boats. Cabin cruisers. For some reason, she imagined Tori's boat as a ski boat, not like the monsters she was walking past now.

"Hey, over here."

Sam looked up at the sound of Tori's voice. She was standing at the end of the pier and lifted her hand in greeting. Sam's eyes took in the long, tanned legs and baggy shorts and T-shirt. She grinned at the smile that Tori tossed her way. She looked more relaxed than Sam had ever seen her.

"This is some place," she said when she reached Tori.

Tori shrugged. Sam followed her down one of the side piers, between the boats.

"It's quiet. Nothing fancy," Tori allowed. In fact, she was proud of her boat. It had been a major investment but was well worth every penny.

She stopped at the end and turned to Sam, pointing to her boat. "Here she is."

Sam stared at the huge cabin cruiser. *Hunter's Way* was stenciled on the back. Then under that, in smaller letters was *Emily*. Sam looked at Tori with raised eyebrows.

Tori met her gaze. "Emily was my sister," she said quietly. "She died when she was ten."

Sam drew a sharp breath, waiting for Tori to tell her more. She watched as a frown marred Tori's features, then it passed and her eyes went gentle again.

"Come on board," she said. Then she paused. "I thought you were bringing Robert."

Sam raised her eyebrows. "Why would you think that?"

Tori shrugged again. "It's the weekend. It's not like you saw him much last week. You were with me three nights," she said.

It was Sam's turn to shrug. "I had lunch with him. It was more than enough," she said evasively. "Come on. Show me around."

Tori took Sam's hand and helped her on board, then led her inside.

"The tour won't take long. Galley," she said, pointing to the small kitchen. "Down there are the cabins and head . . . or the bathroom. Go take a look. Watch your head there," she said as Sam ducked down the two steps.

Sam looked around, opening one door to a room that contained a bed, nothing else. Small shelves were built right into the wall. She opened the other door. This room was larger, but not by much. This is where Tori slept, she noted. The bed was unmade and she recognized the clothes from the previous night, thrown in a heap on the floor. The shelves contained shorts and T-shirts. Summer wear. She opened the tiny bathroom, surprised at the efficiency in the small space.

"There's a shower," she called up.

"Yep."

Sam climbed the steps and smiled.

"It's great. No wonder you come here to relax."

"I'll come out more, now that the weather has warmed up." Tori handed Sam a beer, then guided her out on deck. "Feel like a cruise?"

"Are you kidding? I'd love one."

Sam helped untie the boat, then climbed up on top with Tori, sitting beside her at the controls. Tori backed the boat out of the pier slowly, then turned it and headed out onto the open waters of the lake. She took a deep breath, letting the sunshine wash over her. It was glorious. She stretched her legs out, feeling the sun warm her skin. She smiled, looking over at Tori. She looked so comfortable, so at ease. Her feet were bare and as tanned as the rest of her. She wondered if she lived in shorts year-round.

"This is wonderful, Tori. How early can you go swimming?"

"Well, if you're brave, early to mid-May. But by Memorial Day, the water is fine."

"And do you brave it?"

"Yep. I love to swim. Part fish," she explained. "I could stay in the water for hours, I think."

"How long have you had the boat?"

"I've had this one only three years," Tori said. "The first one was only a twenty-five-footer. It was great for a day out but a little cramped if I stayed here overnight. This one is thirty-five."

"I love it. Thank you for inviting me."

"No problem. It's not often I have company," she said. In fact, Sam was the only other person to be on board. She didn't feel the need to tell Sam this. Instead, she was curious as to why she wasn't with Robert. "You want to tell me about it?"

"What?"

117

"Robert?"

Sam blushed and looked away. It seemed kinda foolish now, her outburst. Robert had meant no harm. He had just been expressing his feelings. And she expressed hers by leaving.

"We had a bit of a disagreement," she said finally. "About our future."

"Oh? You want different things?"

"Tori, he wants to get married and have kids. In fact, I think he wants to skip right over the kids and just have grandchildren. I'm only thirty-four. I can't even imagine being married, much less a house in the suburbs with kids."

"And you told him?"

"Not exactly. He said I was more interested in my career than in him. That kinda pissed me off."

"Why?"

"Because it's the truth," Sam admitted. "My career is important. So is his. But he expects me to make sacrifices, to be home more while his career continues as it is. It's not fair."

"Why can't you imagine being married?" Tori asked hesitantly.

"I don't know. I don't know if it's being married so much as being married to him," she said. "I really like him, I do. He's a very sweet man. He's very compassionate. He loves his job, he cares about the people he defends. He's a . . . nice guy."

"But?"

Sam looked away and squeezed her eyes tight. She didn't want it to be true, but it was.

"I'm not in love with him," she said quietly.

Tori nodded and waited silently for Sam to continue.

"I thought maybe I could be. Or maybe it would eventually come. And I was content going out with him and dating. But we had separate apartments. I still had my space. But now, he's ready to proceed to the next step and I know that he's not what I need in my life." She glanced quickly at Tori. "I can't believe I'm telling you all this. I usually save these conversations for Amy."

"Who's she?"

"My best friend. But she loves Robert. She thinks we're perfect together."

"Then she doesn't know you that well."

"We've known each other for ten years, but you may be right. I tend to gloss over things when it comes to Robert. It's easier that way than for her to tell me I'm crazy for not wanting him. He's really a good catch. He's just not the right one for me."

"Well, you're young," Tori said. "You've got time." What did she know about it?

Sam smiled. "Not so young anymore. How old are you? You've never said."

"I'll be thirty-seven in about a week," she said.

"A week? Why haven't you told me?"

Tori shrugged. "It's not like I celebrate," she said. In fact, the last time she remembered a birthday party, she had been twelve.

"Well, this year will be different. How about I take you out to dinner?"

"Dinner, huh? I guess I could manage that."

Sam leaned over and bumped Tori with her shoulder, then smiled. She was enjoying herself. She would worry about Robert later.

Their tour around the lake took nearly an hour. Then Tori pulled into a small cove and cut the engine. She dropped anchor, then stood and stretched. Sam watched her movements, again thinking what a contrast it was seeing Tori out here in the sunshine, in shorts and baggy T-shirt, looking so relaxed. She was very different from the woman she saw every day at work.

"You up for a little fishing? Or do you have to get back?"

"I don't have to get back. In fact, the weekend's mine. I can't remember the last time I've had a weekend to do whatever I wanted."

Soon, they were perched in lawn chairs, both with rods and reels stuck between their legs. Sam accepted Tori's offer of another beer and she sat quietly, watching the bobber as it floated slowly on the surface. She secretly hoped she didn't catch a fish. Knowing

Tori, she would expect Sam to touch it, to unhook it. She made a face. No way she was touching the slimy little things.

"What?"

"What?"

"You're making a face." Then Tori laughed. "You're imagining taking a fish off the hook, aren't you?"

"Yes I was, smart-ass."

Tori chuckled as she watched Sam. The first time she'd had company on the boat, and she was actually enjoying herself. Tori let her eyes linger, stopping when they reached her legs. Sam really had nice legs. She'd noticed that earlier at the gym. She'd noticed a lot of things at the gym. She smiled, then looked back over the lake. Yes, she was enjoying herself.

But they had no luck with the fish. Time and again, their bait was stolen, but no bites.

"How do they do that?" Sam asked.

"Probably turtles. Or perch. They're notorious for stealing bait." The sun was sinking lower and Tori suspected Sam was getting cold. She felt the chill herself. She went inside to her cabin, coming back up with a pair of sweats. She tossed them at Sam.

"Oh, thanks. How did you know?"

"Your chattering teeth gave you away." She watched as Sam pulled the pants over her shorts. "It'll be dark soon. I guess I should run you back."

"What did you have planned?" Sam asked. "I mean, if I wasn't here."

"I was going to anchor here for the night. I have stuff for burgers and a great bottle of wine. Full moon. A little night fishing." Then she grinned. "Maybe another nap."

"Oh. That sounds like fun," Sam said. "I . . . well, I wish . . ."

"You want to join me? There are two beds." Tori looked away, then back at Sam. "I mean, if you don't have to get back."

Sam met her eyes and smiled.

"I would love to. Are you sure I'm not in your way?"

"Of course not."

"And, you know, it'll give us a chance to talk about the case," Sam said, trying to find a good excuse to stay.

"No. No work. We both need to relax. There'll be plenty of time for the case next week."

Sam nodded. She was glad. She didn't really want to talk about death. Not when they were having such a good time. Well, she was, anyway. But she suspected Tori was as well. She joined Tori in the kitchen . . . galley, she silently corrected, watching as Tori took the hamburger meat out and shaped it into two extremely large patties. Seasonings followed, then Tori wrapped them and put them back in the fridge. Next, she pulled out lettuce and tomatoes and expertly sliced them. Sam would never have expected that Tori could look so at home in a kitchen. In fact, she wouldn't have been a bit surprised to learn that Tori couldn't cook at all.

"Open that cabinet above your head there." Tori motioned. "There's wine. Pinot noir? Do you like that?"

"Sure."

Sam did as she was told, finding nearly ten bottles of wine. She found the pinot noir and took it down, taking the corkscrew that Tori slid across the counter.

"How will you cook the burgers? Fry?"

"No. I've got a small grill that attaches to the side of the boat out there." She opened the cabinet under the sink and pulled out a bag of charcoal.

Sam took the sweatshirt that Tori offered and sat again in the lawn chair, watching Tori as she got the grill going. It was a gorgeous evening. They had a perfect view of the moonrise. Soon, Tori joined her, dressed now in sweatpants. Tori handed her a glass of wine and they sighed contentedly, settling back to watch the moon as it rose over the lake.

"It's so beautiful here, Tori. Thank you for sharing this with me."

"It's been my pleasure."

Sam watched her, trying to read her eyes.

"Is it safe to guess that I'm the first person you've had out here?"

Tori smiled. "Is it that obvious?"

"No. You've been a wonderful hostess. Like I said, I was just guessing."

"And like I said before, I'm not a very sociable person."

"Why is that, Tori? I mean, you're attractive. You have a wonderful sense of humor. Why is it that you don't . . . like people?"

"I haven't found a whole lot to like, I guess."

"I think it's just that you don't want anyone to like *you*," Sam said.

Tori wanted to be angry, but how could she? Sam had hit on the truth.

"You've let me see a part of you that no one else gets to see," Sam continued. "Why?"

"Are we about to have a heart-to-heart?" Tori asked.

"Yes, we are. Tell me about yourself. Tell me why you're so . . . angry, Tori."

Tori was quiet for the longest time and Sam thought she had said too much, had gone too far. They were becoming friends. Why ruin that? But finally, Tori stirred, crossing one leg across her knee, playing absently with the edge of her sweatpants.

"My father was a cop," she said quietly. "My mother stayed home, took care of us. Me and Emily and Scott and Toby. She was the best. Always had cookies or a cake or something that she'd just baked. We'd rush in after school, running to the kitchen to see what she'd whipped up that day. When my father got home, dinner was already on the table. We all ate together. Then homework. Dad would come to each of us, asking about our day, helping with our lessons. It was a happy house. We didn't fight. Not even the usual squabbles between siblings. I loved them. They loved me."

Sam stared. She knew what was coming, but she wasn't ready for it. She didn't know how she could possibly handle it. It was one thing, hearing it from Malone. It was completely different hearing it from Tori, with all the emotion of a twelve-year-old still in her voice.

"One night . . . when I was twelve, someone broke in. It had been a day much like all the others. Mom had chocolate chip cookies that day. I can still smell them. She had just taken them out of the oven when we got home. And then for dinner, she had a big roast on the table, with potatoes and carrots. It was one of our favorite meals."

Without thinking, Sam closed the short distance between their chairs, lightly clasping Tori's hand with her own.

"This man came in through the kitchen. He had a gun. Before my father could do anything, he shot him. Shot him twice. My father fell backward, knocking the chair over and he just laid there. My mother started screaming, we all did. Then he tied us up, all to our chairs. We sat around the dinner table tied to our chairs, looking at each other, all the time my father was laying there dying." Tori's voice hardened. "I was so helpless. I tried to stand up, tried to carry the chair with me. He slapped me. Emily started screaming again and he pointed the gun at her . . . and killed her. Then he went to Toby and shot him." Tori wiped at the tears that streamed down her face. "My mother went hysterical. She was screaming, she tipped her chair over. The man just laughed. Then he walked up to her and shot her, too. Then it was just me and Scott. I begged him to stop. Scott just stared at him. He was fifteen. He was a fighter. When the man walked over to him and held the gun to his head, Scott kicked him. Kicked him hard in the groin. The gun went off anyway. And then it was just me. And he held the gun to my head. I remember staring into his eyes, knowing I was next. Then I just closed my eyes. Waiting. Wanting it to be over. He just turned and walked out the kitchen the same way he'd come in, leaving me tied to that damn chair. I just wanted it to be over. But now, it'll never be over," she whispered.

Sam sat speechless, tears streaming down her own cheeks. She squeezed Tori's hand, feeling the light pressure that Tori returned. She didn't know what to say. What words could possibly console this woman?

"I'm so sorry I made you relive that," she whispered. "Please forgive me."

123

Tori turned, seeing the reflection of tears in the moonlight. She reached out, touching them with her fingers, then brushed them away from Sam's cheek.

"Don't cry for me. It's too late for that."

Sam shook her head. No wonder Tori lived as recklessly as she did. She thought she had nothing to live for.

"It's not too late. You're strong. Any twelve-year-old who lived through that must be strong," Sam insisted.

"Strong? I was practically catatonic for a year afterward. I was in and out of hospitals. No one wanted me. I couldn't blame them. Finally, an aunt took me to live with her in Houston. She was what my dad always called his 'spinster' sister. She was nearly sixty. She also wasn't a spinster. She had a lover. They took me in and made me feel welcome. And they didn't take any shit from me. They didn't tolerate my fits of silence. And they talked about my family. They kept them alive. All the others, they never even mentioned them. It was like they never existed. But Aunt Carol, she had pictures and she told stories and they were still with us in some way. Eventually, as I got older, I came to realize that what had happened wasn't just some random act of violence. It was a hit. Someone wanted my father dead. Whether the deal was for the whole family or not, I don't know. No one was ever prosecuted."

"So you became a cop to solve the case?"

"At the time, it seemed like a good idea," she said. "It wasn't like I was much help at the time. I was the only witness, yet I couldn't bring myself to talk about it for nearly two years. So, yeah, I guess originally I wanted to become a cop because of that. Aunt Carol died when I was still in college. Louise, her partner, tried to talk me out of it. She was worried I'd go off on some witch hunt and get into all sorts of trouble."

Sam smiled. It wasn't far from the truth.

"But she was there when I graduated from the Academy. She was so proud. She and Aunt Carol were so good for me. I survived. But I lost her, too, about a year later."

"And now there's no one?"

"Just me."

Tori got up and went inside and Sam let her go. She couldn't imagine the grief that Tori had endured in her lifetime. She wanted to offer some comfort, but she knew of no words that could possibly help soothe Tori's aching heart.

Tori came out a short time later. She put their patties on the grill and closed the lid.

"I'm sorry, Sam. We were having a nice evening. I didn't mean to spoil it with all that."

"You haven't spoiled anything. I just don't know what to say to you. I guess now, I understand your . . . indifference to people. But I'm so sorry, Tori."

"You have nothing to be sorry for. That was twenty-five years ago. I'd like to say that I'm over it, but I'll never be over it."

"Is that why you don't sleep much?"

"I used to have nightmares. For years, I had nightmares. I still do, sometimes. When I'm extremely tired, I still have nightmares," she said quietly. "I can close my eyes and still see his face."

"Come. Sit down." Sam refilled their wineglasses and handed Tori hers. "Let's sit and enjoy the quiet . . . and the moon. It's so peaceful out here. I can't remember the last time I've been out like this, away from the city."

"Did you grow up in Dallas?"

Sam shook her head. "In Denver. My family is still there, but we're not really close." She felt uncomfortable discussing her family in front of Tori. She wasn't close to them, but at least she had a family.

"Why not?"

"They had bigger dreams for me. A cop wasn't in their plans. In fact, a rather large wedding to the Mayor's son was."

"And you skipped town? Did you leave him at the altar?"

"Very nearly. I told him and my mother that I didn't love him and I wasn't going to marry him. They planned the wedding anyway."

"You're joking."

"I wish I was. My father had political aspirations. I was to be his stepping-stone. They haven't forgiven me yet."

"Any siblings?"

"I have an older brother. He's a priest. They're very proud."

"I take it you're not close to him, either."

"He's taken his vow of poverty very seriously. He's somewhere in South America. I exchange letters a few times a year. That's about it."

"So, holidays and such, you don't make it home?"

"No. I usually go with Amy. And, of course, the last couple of years, there's been Robert."

"Oh yes. What are you going to do about that?"

"I don't know, Tori. I would hate to hurt him. And what am I going to tell him? That I've just been hanging around the last couple of years, hoping that I'd fall hopelessly in love with him? That would hardly be fair."

"Is that what you've been doing?"

"I guess I thought what we had was enough. There was never any mind-boggling sex or passion that raged out of control, but I thought maybe it was enough."

"But it's not?"

"No," she whispered. "I *want* that mind-boggling sex. I *want* to be delirious with passion. You know what I mean?"

Tori laughed. "No, I don't. I'm sorry, but I've never come close to that."

"I know it's out there. Other people have it, don't they?"

"I think the vast majority of people settle."

"Oh, that's sad."

Tori shrugged. "Somebody is better than nobody."

"But not for you? You'd rather have nobody?"

"Like I said before, I don't really have a lot to offer anyone."

"I disagree. I doubt you've ever given anyone a chance to get to know you like you're letting me. You're so different from the person that everyone knows. I like this person better," Sam said quietly.

Tori smiled in the moonlight.

"I'll keep that in mind, Detective."

# Chapter Nineteen


Sam rushed out of the bakery, balancing two cups of coffee and the bag of muffins. She was late. Really late. In fact, she wouldn't be surprised if her cell . . .

"Rang," she murmured. "Hello?"

"Sam? Where are you?"

"Getting breakfast."

"Breakfast? Do you know what time it is?"

"Yes, I know what time it is."

"Did you at least get me a cappuccino?"

"No. You're getting too spoiled. I got you a muffin. What time do we meet with Jenkins?"

"Thirty minutes."

"Plenty of time. I'm five minutes away."

"Okay. Be careful."

"I will. See you in a bit."

She tossed her cell phone down and smiled. *Be careful?* Amazing what a couple of days on a boat together will do for you. Sam sighed. She'd had a great time. They spent most of Sunday, too, enjoying the sunshine. And they talked. God, she loved Tori's company. The more time she spent with her . . . well, the more she wanted to spend. It scared her a little. She wasn't going to deny the fact that she found Tori attractive, that she felt a tiny tug of sexual attraction when she was around her. *Tiny?* She glanced at herself in the mirror, then away. If she wasn't careful, she would get in over her head. And then what? There was still Robert to consider. It had been nearly six before she made it back to her apartment. And there were no less than twelve messages from Robert. When she finally called him back, he was so angry with her that they hardly spoke. He stayed on the line just long enough to know that she was okay. But he was coming today to take her to lunch. They were going to talk about the little fit she'd had over the weekend.

But she pushed those thoughts away. She didn't want to think about it. Lunch would come soon enough.

Tori looked up as Sam rushed into the squad room. She smiled when she saw the two cups of coffee.

"Spoiled brat," Sam murmured as she handed Tori her cappuccino.

"And what's in here?" Tori asked, tearing into the bag of muffins. She grabbed one and bit down, smiling. "Thanks. You're the best."

"Anything to make you smile."

Tori raised her eyebrows mischievously. "Anything? That could be a dangerous offer, Detective."

Sam sipped her coffee, meeting Tori's eyes but ignoring her comment. Then she smiled. Tori did the same.

"I had a wonderful time this weekend," Sam said quietly.

"Me, too. In fact, I can't remember the last time I relaxed for two whole days."

"Good."

"Detectives? In the conference room," Malone said. "Let's go over it before Jenkins and his cronies get here."

128

Tori gathered up her files and took her coffee with her. Sam grabbed the bag of muffins.

"Sit. We have twenty minutes."

Tori set her coffee on the table and opened her file. She held a muffin in one hand as she spoke.

"Lesbians. All three. Two were residents of Belle's Hostel at one time. The third, Rachel Anderson, never lived there but spent time there. As late as last week."

"Belle Grayson confirmed that Angie and Crystal were hookers. They were both runaways," Sam said.

"Angie?"

"Lorraine," Tori supplied. "Angie's her real name."

"Have we found family?"

"No. We're going to get with Grayson today and go over her records. Who knows if they gave real names? We also picked up a woman named Johnny on Friday night."

"I heard. Held her for three hours. She's threatening to sue."

"She wouldn't talk to us at the bar," Tori said. "She wouldn't talk much here, either. Crystal was her . . . plaything," she said. "They were into S&M."

"Just great. This will go over well with Jenkins."

Tori shrugged. "It's what we've got."

"Okay. Theory?"

"Perp either watches them at Belle's or some other hangout. There's a club, Outlaws, that allows minors inside on Wednesday nights. Grayson said most of the girls go there. He could watch them there. Or he could be inside and target them. It's a large dance club. He could fade into the crowd easily."

"Okay. What about the profiler?"

"He's supposed to join us with Jenkins. Then he and Sam are going to go over everything we have so far."

"Great. This will be fun," he said sarcastically. "You know how Jenkins is. He's going to flip."

"Who the hell is Jenkins?" Sam demanded. "You keep talking about him as if there's some joke between you."

"He's a prick," Tori said.

"I gathered that. What's the history with you two?"

Tori looked at Malone, who shrugged.

"He comes across as this big homophobe. Dropping his disgusting little remarks whenever I'm around. Even quotes the Bible. Well, I ran into him at a bar several years ago. He and this guy were going at it pretty good. He damn near fainted when he saw me. I never said anything to him, but whenever he sees me now, it's like he just dares me to mention it."

They all three looked up at the knock on the door and three men in suits entered.

"Malone. This is Detective Sims from CIU and Dr. Peterson, the profiler."

"You know Hunter. This is Detective Kennedy," Malone said.

"How do you do. You're Mr. Jenkins?" Samantha asked, offering him her hand.

"Yes." His eyes moved blatantly over her body, then looked to Tori. "Damn, Hunter, how'd you swing her?"

"I just made a wish, Jenkins. You ought to try it sometime."

"Can we just get on with this, please?" Malone said. "I've got another meeting in an hour."

Tori glanced briefly at her Lieutenant and nodded, knowing that he had no such meeting to attend in an hour. She gave the copies she'd made to Sam, who started passing them out.

"So, we got a few pros getting whacked, Hunter?"

"No."

"No? What? They don't match?" Jenkins demanded.

"They match, yes. But they're not getting killed because they're hookers."

"That's what I was told."

"I don't recall you asking us," Tori said. "They were killed because they're lesbians."

"What the hell? How did you come to this conclusion? You know them personally, Hunter?"

"If you'll read in the report there, Mr. Jenkins, you'll see the connection," Sam said. "We visited with Belle Grayson Friday night. She runs Belle's Hostel. It's a home for young lesbians. Runaways, mostly. Victim number one lived there about two years ago and still kept in touch with them. Victim number two lived there as recently as two months ago. Rachel Anderson, the third girl, was a weekly visitor. In fact, she had been there just last week."

"So where did the hooker thing come from? You just make that up to stall?"

"The first two, Angie and Crystal, were hookers. That was the connection between them. The third was not. We found a new connection," Tori said.

"Great. Somebody is knocking off queers. Hookers or queers, take your pick. Either way, the general public will care less. They might think someone is cleaning up the streets."

Sam felt Tori tense beside her and she quickly reached under the table and grabbed her arm, squeezing tightly. She finally felt Tori relax and she loosened her hold.

"Why don't you tell that to Rachel Anderson's parents, Jenkins? I'm sure Reverend Anderson will be thrilled at what the Mayor's office thinks. In fact, why don't you have the Mayor himself call them? That would be a nice touch," Tori quipped.

"Jenkins, we're doing fine with this case without your task force. Why don't you tell the Mayor that. We'll give you a report as soon as we have something else," Malone suggested.

"I want a daily report," Jenkins said. "Daily."

"Fine. Now, if you don't mind, we'd like to go over all of this with Dr. Peterson."

"No problem." He stood, then looked at Tori. "I know you'll work extra hard on this one, Hunter, seeing as it's so near and dear to your heart."

"Every death is near and dear to my heart, Jenkins. Even yours."

Sam stood quickly and stuck out her hand, grasping his.

"Nice to finally meet you, Mr. Jenkins. Tori has told me . . . *so very* much about you," she said sweetly. She had the pleasure of watching his eyes widen in disbelief, then he stormed from the room, with Sims at his heels.

"You always rub him the wrong way, Hunter. What's up with that?" Dr. Peterson asked.

"I rub everyone the wrong way, Peterson. Kennedy will go over this with you." She got up, lightly squeezing Sam's shoulder as she walked behind her.

"Let me know if you need anything," Lieutenant Malone said as he followed Tori. They were barely out the door before they started laughing.

"Did you see his eyes? I thought he was going to have an aneurysm right there."

"She's got balls," Malone said. "She certainly didn't score any points today."

"She scored points with me," Tori said.

Sam leaned back in the chair, rubbing her eyes. They had been at it nearly two hours. Peterson was thorough, she'd give him that.

"Okay. This is what I see with only three victims. Get me four or five and I can be more precise," he said.

"I'd rather not."

"You know what I mean, Detective. Our man is young, twenty to thirty. My guess would be Caucasian, they usually are. They also usually kill within their own ethnic group. We have one black, two white. More victims and we'll have more of a pattern. He was probably spurned by someone who was a lesbian and he didn't know it or she came out later, after they had a relationship. His victims are all young. This could be something that happened to him while he was in high school."

"Why would he now act on it?"

"Something triggered it. Or maybe he has acted on it before, he just didn't resort to killing. He was obviously a john in the first two murders. It would have been in a public place, a motel room probably. The third was abducted and killed in private. That could be why the first two weren't bloodied up. All three were placed where they would be found." He flipped through the pictures. "They were placed carefully, arms folded, legs straight. Even the third, she's laid out in much the same way. He doesn't like what he's doing."

"He left a footprint. We think it was intentional."

"Most likely. Serial killers often leave clues. It becomes a game. They taunt the police, seemingly daring us to catch him. Then there is the publicity. There wasn't much in the paper with the first two. So, a more grisly murder is sure to make headlines."

"Well, this is all great, Doctor. But, a needle in a haystack."

"Yes. Unfortunately, until you have another victim, our clues stop here."

Sam sighed. "Thanks for your time. I'll pass this on to the Lieutenant."

He helped Sam gather up the files, watching her.

"So, what's it like working with Hunter?"

Sam glanced at him, then went back to sorting the pages in order. "It's fine."

"I hear she's a real bitch. They say she practically pushed her last partner out of a three-story window."

"Is that what they say?"

"Yes."

"Well, it was a two-story window and he fell off of the fire escape," she said. "Are we done?"

"Sure. Let me know if you need anything else from me."

"I will."

Sam left him standing in the doorway as she hurried back to the squad room. Tori was perched on Ramirez's desk, smiling at something he was saying. She stopped. It was the first time she'd seen Tori interact with another detective.

"Hey, guys," she called as she tossed the file on her desk. She walked over to them. "What's got you smiling?" she asked.

"Ramirez was telling me about Adams and Donaldson's trip to the gay bar."

"The transvestite?"

"Yeah. They couldn't tell who were men and who were women. Donaldson got slapped by some chick. God, I'd have paid to see that."

"Don't say anything to them. Sikes will kill me if he knows I told you," Ramirez pleaded.

"Well, I'll keep quiet if you'll talk your mother into breakfast tomorrow," Tori said. "For both of us," she said, motioning to Sam.

"You know she would cook for you every morning if I let her," he said. "I'll bring you a couple of tacos."

"Thanks, Tony. That's sweet," Samantha said.

"Okay, what you got?" Tori asked as they walked back to their own desks.

"Not much. A young white male, twenty to thirty, who hates lesbians because he was spurned by one."

"Peterson really pulled that one out of his ass," she said.

"My thoughts exactly."

"Listen, you want to grab lunch and go pay Belle a visit? We need to go over her records."

Samantha hesitated. "I can't. Robert is coming over," she said quietly.

"Oh." Tori pushed down her disappointment. "Well, I guess you two made up, then."

"Not really. He wasn't actually speaking to me last night. He wants to do lunch and talk."

"I see. Well, I can just go over myself. You can come later if you want."

"Tori, can't we wait until one? I'd really like to go with you."

Their eyes met across the desks.

"Please? I promise I'll be back by one."

"Okay. I'll hang out here until you get back."

Samantha reached across the desk and squeezed Tori's arm. "Thanks."

Tori looked up then, watching as a tall man approached.

Handsome. Dark hair. Impeccably dressed. This would be Robert. She felt Sam's hand slip away from her and she looked up, meeting dark eyes that stared back at her.

"You're early," Samantha said to him.

"Got out of court early," he said. Then he stuck his hand out. "You must be Detective Hunter."

Tori stood and shook his hand. So, this is the man who wants to marry Sam. She could certainly do a lot worse.

"I'll be back by one, Tori. Promise."

"No problem, Sam. I'll wait."

Samantha gave her a quick smile, then walked out beside Robert. Tori sat back down in her chair, reaching purposefully for the file that she already knew by heart.


"She calls you Sam?"

"Yeah. It's kinda grown on me," Samantha admitted. They were walking down the street to the corner deli. She was starving. She would have tuna on rye, she decided. Wonder what Tori would like? Ham and cheese? No, probably turkey.

"Samantha?"

"Hmm?"

"I asked, when are you going to tell me where you were this weekend?"

"Oh." She hesitated. "Actually, I went out with Tori on her boat," she said.

He nodded. "You seem quite fond of her."

"Yes. She's grown on me, too. Remember that first week? I was ready to shoot her."

"I remember. So, what did you do?"

"On the boat? Fished, mostly."

"Fished? Do you like to fish?"

"We didn't really catch anything, Robert."

"I see you got some sun. I'm glad you weren't stuck in a dark theater," he said dryly.

"I'm sorry, Robert, but I just needed to get away. It's been a stressful couple of weeks."

"What better way to relax than being with your partner, who you were with every day last week, discussing your case some more," he said sarcastically.

"Actually, we didn't even mention the case."

"So, you just spent two whole days with a woman who is practically a stranger, and you didn't even discuss your case? What in the world did you talk about?"

"Why all the questions, Robert?"

"I just can't imagine what the two of you talked about, that's all. It's not like you have a lot in common." He paused and Sam finally glanced at him. "She's gay, you know."

"Oh, thanks Robert, for enlightening me. Of course I know she's gay. I'm wondering how on earth you know this."

"You're kidding, right? Besides the fact that it's common knowledge, just one look at her would be enough."

"Robert, I thought you wanted to have lunch to talk about us, not my partner."

"I do. I'm sorry. It's just, when you took off like that, it was so unlike you."

"I know, Robert. I'm sorry I did that."

They stood in the line that had formed and Samantha wished she had declined his offer of lunch. What they needed to discuss couldn't be done here.

"Why won't you tell me what's going on?"

"You just freaked me out when you started talking about marriage and kids and *grandchildren*, for God's sake."

"I didn't mean that we should get married next week and start having kids right away, Samantha. I just wanted you to know how I felt."

She nodded. "I know how you feel. But my career is important to me, Robert. And I'm not going to put it on hold to stay home and play mom."

"If that's how it came across, I'm sorry. I never expected you to give up your career."

"Yes, that's how it came across. You're up next," Sam said, turning him around to face the counter.

"What would you like?" he asked.

"Tuna on rye and turkey on wheat," she said.

"Two?"

"One's for Tori. She wasn't leaving for lunch." She watched as his jaw clenched, but he nodded.

"And one for your partner," he murmured.


Tori looked up as Sam walked in alone. Without conscious thought, she smiled at the other woman whose blond hair was an unruly mess around her face. Sam tried to tame it with her fingers, then she met Tori's eyes and smiled.

"Hey."

"Uh-huh."

"Lunch. Eat," she said, placing the bag on Tori's desk.

"You brought me something?" Tori tore into the bag, then grinned. "Gee, thanks, Mom," she teased.

"You do realize that the only time I see you eat is if I bring you something, don't you?"

"I recall cooking for you the other night."

Sam smiled as she sat down. "Yes, you did. And burgers, too. I had been craving a burger all day."

"So, you and Robert work things out?"

"Not really. We talked about us without really talking about us, you know?"

"Status quo?"

"I guess. But Tori, I just couldn't tell him. I didn't want to hurt him."

Tori nodded and took another bite.

"I know what you're thinking. I'm weak."

"I wasn't thinking that and it's hardly my business, anyway."

Sam picked up the thick file on Tori's desk and flipped through it. It was all in order again, with the brief notes from the profiler on top. Tori was extremely organized, she'd found out. She glanced up, watching Tori finish her sandwich. She looked adorable with mayonnaise lodged in one corner of her mouth. Then a tongue slipped out and captured the mayonnaise. Sam stared.

"Hey."

"Hmm?" Sam murmured.

"Ready?"

Sam pulled her gaze away from Tori's mouth, meeting dark eyes. She watched as one eyebrow arched.

"What?"

"Belle's?" Tori prompted.

"Oh, yeah . . . right." Sam shook herself. "Belle's."

# Chapter Twenty

"Margarita, on the rocks," Sam said. She had been waiting nearly fifteen minutes for Amy. She would start without her. But just as the waiter brought over the tall glass, Amy walked through the doors. "Hang on, my friend is here."

"Sorry I'm late. Judge Carmen was on one of his soapboxes," she explained. "Mmm, that looks good. I'll have the same." She set her purse on the corner of the table and moved her chair closer, resting her elbows on the table. Then she tilted her head, moving her red bangs out of her eyes. "You look great. You got some sun," she noted. "How did you manage to drag Robert out of the house?"

Samantha smiled and shook her head.

"I didn't. He wanted to spend Saturday afternoon in a theater, or worse, in his apartment watching movies." She shrugged. "I wanted to be outside."

"And?"

"And I went out on a boat, on a lake," she said.

"Where? Who with?"

"Out on Eagle Mountain Lake. Tori's got a cabin cruiser out there," she said as casually as she could.

"Tori? As in your partner? The psycho woman you ranted about that first week?"

"The same. Once you get to know her, she's really not all that psycho."

"So you ditched Robert and went out on a boat with her? I bet that went over well."

"We had a fight. Saturday at lunch. I left and didn't tell him. When I got back Sunday evening, he had left twelve messages."

"You spent the whole weekend with her?"

"It wasn't really planned. But I was having such a good time out there, I didn't want to come back."

"You spent the night on a boat? That does sound like fun."

"Yeah. It was. I'm not sure Robert's forgiven me yet."

"What did you fight about?"

"Grandchildren."

"As in . . . yours?"

"Yes. He started talking about getting married and having kids. He implied that my career would hinder that."

"You're joking. Robert? But he knows how important this is to you."

"I thought he did." She paused as the waiter brought Amy her drink, then continued. "He said that any decisions I make regarding my career should be based on our future together, meaning house and kids. I needed to be at home more if we were going to have kids."

"And did you tell him that maybe he shouldn't be trying so hard to make partner at his firm?"

Sam smiled at Amy. As much as she liked Robert, Amy hated any mention of double standards when it came to men and women.

"Amy, I don't think Robert's the one for me," she said quietly. "I try to picture being married to him and it doesn't feel right."

Amy reached across the table and took Samantha's hand.

"You had a disagreement about your career. Now you know how he feels and he knows how you feel. You just have to talk about it and come to an agreement that works for both of you," she said.

"Amy, it's not about that. I've been feeling this way for months, now."

"Months? But you said you loved him."

"I do love him. He's a sweet man and he'll make a good husband and father. I just don't see me in the picture."

"Maybe the whole marriage thing is scaring you."

"I'm not in love with him, Amy," she admitted. "I thought maybe I could be, eventually. But I'm not. I know that."

Amy leaned back in her chair, staring at her. "You've been going out for two years. You're just now realizing that you're not in love with him?"

"I don't need you to judge me, Amy. I just need to talk about it."

"Okay, I'm sorry. I mean, it's not a whole lot different than me and Eric. As long as we're just dating, everything will be fine. But as soon as he starts getting more serious, I know I'll bolt."

"But I doubt you'd let two years go by."

Amy leaned forward again. "What's really wrong, Samantha? I mean, you and I could always talk about anything. I get the feeling that you're skirting around the problem here, and you're afraid to talk to me."

"No. But how do you tell someone who says they love you and want to marry you that you're not in love with them?"

"I don't know. But I do know this. The longer you drag this out, letting him think that you have a future, the harder it'll be."

"I know. And last night, he cooked this wonderful meal for me, candlelight and wine."

"So you're still sleeping with him?"

"That's just it. I faked a headache and went to bed early."

"You don't even want to have sex with him?"

It was Sam's turn to lean forward. "Amy, it's gotten to where I can hardly stand his touch," she whispered.

"Well, you've got to tell him, Samantha. When's the last time you've slept together?"

Sam shrugged. "I don't know. Three weeks? A month?"

"Surely he knows something's wrong."

"Yes. I know he does. I feel like such an ass. I don't know what's wrong. Well, I do know what's wrong. My body tells me that he's not the one and I can't go through the motions anymore."

"You've been faking it?"

Samantha blushed. God, was she really having this conversation with Amy?

"I thought it would pass."

"Well, I'm not taking sides here, but you're hardly being fair to him."

"Oh, don't tell me you've never faked it."

"Of course I have. But not in a very long time and certainly not with someone I've been dating two years who wants to marry me."

"Amy, you've never dated anyone more than two months."

"And that's because when I have to start faking it, I know it's time to move on. Jesus, Samantha, this is Robert we're talking about. The guy you've been practically living with."

"You're not making this easy," she said quietly.

"I know, honey. I'm sorry." Amy squeezed her hand again. "Maybe it's just the stress of your new job. Maybe you need to give it some time, huh?"

Sam was about to protest, but she let it go. It wasn't her new job. This restlessness that she felt had been growing for months, eating at her little by little. And now, it was nearly unbearable. There was something missing—and Robert was not the answer.

# Chapter Twenty-one

The ringing pierced her sleep, and Sam reached out and punched her alarm. The ringing continued. She opened one eye.

"Four?" She grabbed the phone and pulled it under the covers with her. "Yeah?"

"Sam?"

She sat up.

"What's wrong?"

"We got another girl."

"Oh, no." Sam tossed the covers off and walked into the bathroom. "Where?"

"Downtown. You know the Starbucks on Main?"

"Yes. I'll be right there."

She splashed cold water on her face and ran wet fingers through her hair. She looked frightful but knew she had no time for a shower. She quickly pulled on jeans and a sweatshirt and hurried out. She wondered what time Tori had gotten the call. She sounded wide awake on the phone.

The streets were empty at this early hour and Sam made it to downtown in only fifteen minutes. Flashing lights of the police cruisers lit up the sky and she parked on the street, showing her badge when someone tried to stop her.

"I'm looking for Detective Hunter," she said.

"Down the alley there."

"Thanks."

She found Tori bent over the Dumpster, peering inside along with Rita Spencer from the medical examiner's office. She joined them, glancing inside.

"Jesus," she whispered.

Tori glanced at her and nodded. The condition of this body matched that of Rachel Anderson.

"Run her prints first thing, Rita. We'll be at Belle's." She nudged Sam and Sam followed her down the alley. "Got another footprint. Heel this time."

Sam looked where she pointed. Going away again.

"There's something else." Tori pointed to the side of the building.

Spray painted in black was the word *Genesis*. Sam raised her eyebrows.

"Phil Collins?"

"Your brother is a priest. You don't know?"

"Bible?"

"Yes, although I'm not exactly well versed. Rita says the story of Sodom and Gomorrah is in the book of Genesis."

"Okay, forgive my ignorance, but what does that have to do with our case?"

Tori grinned. "Sodom and Gomorrah. The alleged birthplace of homosexuality."

Samantha raised her eyes questioningly. "And?"

"You really don't have a clue, do you?"

Samantha shrugged.

"The destruction of Sodom and Gomorrah is often used as an example of the *evil* of homosexuality . . . and God's punishment."

"Ah. Well, okay then. A guy spurned by a lesbian or a guy doing the Lord's work. Either way, he's a nutcase."

"Could be both," Tori said. Then she reached out and tucked a stray hair behind Sam's ear. "Woke you out of a dead sleep, huh?"

"A margarita-induced sleep, thank you."

"Oh? Happy hour?"

"Yes. I met Amy. Happy hour turned into dinner."

"Sorry. But I thought you'd want to be here."

"Yes, I'm glad you called. You shouldn't be the only one up working at this hour." Then Sam stared at her, taking in her perfect hair and clear eyes. Even her jeans looked pressed. "How do you manage this?" she asked, pointing at her.

"What?"

"You always look so good. Don't tell me you had time for a shower?"

Tori shrugged. "I was already up."

"At four?" Sam shook her head. "Tori, what am I going to do with you?"

"Well, if you want to monitor my sleeping habits, you could always . . ."

"Detectives? We're out of here," Rita called.

Sam nodded at Rita, then grinned at Tori. "I could what?"

Tori wiggled both eyebrows mischievously, then brushed past her, jogging to catch up with Rita.

"You'll run the prints first thing?"

"First thing."

"And you'll call?"

"Immediately."

"Okay. I'll check in with Jackson later."

"I'm sure he'll be counting the minutes," Rita said as she slammed the door in Tori's face.

Sam joined her at the curb, watching the van pull away.

"Why does she always look like she's avoiding you?" Sam asked.

Tori shrugged.

"Old history?" Sam guessed.

Tori shrugged again.

"Do you . . . have feelings for her?" Sam whispered.

"Rita? No. It was a one-night mistake when we were out drinking a while back."

Sam nodded. "But she has feelings for you?"

"No," Tori scowled. "She knows me."

Sam nodded again. She hated the jealousy she suddenly felt, and she pushed it away. "Well, it's kinda early for Belle's."

"We could always go to the gym for a workout," Tori suggested.

"Are you kidding me? I was thinking breakfast."

"What? And skip your shower?"

"Oh, God. I forgot. I guess I should go home and get properly dressed, huh?"

Tori shrugged. "You look great."

"I look like I crawled out of bed at four and didn't even brush my teeth." She again ran her hands through her hair, wishing she'd taken the time yesterday for a cut. She was at least two weeks past due.

"Okay. Go home. Meet me back at the station, and we'll pick up something to eat on the way to Belle's."

"Deal."

Sam squeezed Tori's arm as she walked past and again Tori was astonished by the feelings that light touch invoked in her.

"Hunter?"

She watched as Sam drove away, then turned back to the crime scene.

"Yeah?"

"We're done here. I took a print of the bloody heel. I'll let you know if it matches the other one."

"Good. Thanks."


"I don't want pastries," Sam complained. "I want something real. Like eggs and meat."

Tori grinned. "Got a little hangover?"

"Yes. Getting up at four didn't help."

"How about McDonald's?"

Sam groaned. "Now you're just trying to punish me."

"Okay. There's a taco joint around the corner. It won't be as good as Tony's mom's stuff, but they're decent."

"Better than McDonald's."

Sam ordered two breakfast tacos and a side of hash browns, then looked guiltily at Tori. She had only a measly muffin.

"You're not hungry? Don't think you're getting any of mine," Sam said as she unwrapped her first taco.

Tori didn't comment. Frankly, she wasn't certain she could keep anything down. Sam hadn't recognized the victim, but Tori remembered her from the small group of women at Belle's Friday night. Rita had already covered most of her with a sheet. Her legs were missing below the knees.

They drove in silence, Sam happily eating and Tori wondering how to approach Belle. It was one thing to come for information. Quite another to tell her about a death.

"Hey. I guess I wasn't as hungry as I thought," Sam said. "You want this other one?"

"No, thanks."

Sam studied her, saw the lines that were etched on her beautiful face, the mouth drawn tightly in concentration.

"Tori, what's wrong?"

"I think our victim was at Belle's Friday night."

"There were only five or six girls there that night."

"Five. This one was sitting in the third chair, away from the door."

Sam stared. "Your observational skills are amazing. Maybe Saturday, I could have told you there were five and what some of them looked like. Not five days later." When Tori didn't comment, Sam touched her arm. "Are you sure?"

"Pretty sure. I'm hoping her prints will come back."

They parked in front of the hostel and Sam walked silently beside Tori as they climbed the steps of the old plantation house. Belle was perched on the sofa in the sitting room, drinking coffee and reading the morning paper.

"Detectives, good morning. Didn't think I'd see you quite so soon. Need something from the files again?"

"Belle, there was another murder last night," Samantha said quietly. "Detective Hunter thinks she recognized her as one of the young girls who was in your coffeehouse Friday night."

Belle's eyes widened.

"Do you remember the five girls who were in there when we showed up Friday night?" Tori asked.

"Yes. They're all good kids. They seldom go out to the bars. They always hang out here."

"Do they live here?"

"Yes. Four of them. The other, Sherry, she's twenty and moved to an apartment not far from here." She stood up. "Oh, my God. I just can't believe this is happening."

"Pull the files on the five of them. I need to see pictures," Tori said.

They followed her back into the office where they had spent Monday afternoon. They waited patiently as Belle pulled out five folders and handed them to Tori. The second one was their girl.

"This one," Tori said.

Belle sank into her chair. "Sue. Not Sue," she sobbed.

Sam took the file from Tori and looked at the photo. She let out a heavy breath, then flipped through the pages. She was eighteen. Freshman at one of the community colleges. Her parents lived in Amarillo.

"How long had she been with you?" Sam asked gently.

"Over a year. She's one of the few that still keeps in touch with her family. In fact, I met her mother."

"We need to see her room, Belle."

"I just can't believe it," Belle said again as she wiped at her eyes. "She and Sherry are seeing each other. They had dinner last night. Sue was so excited. She came and showed me the new outfit she bought."

Her room was impeccably neat. Bed made, no clothes lying around. Books were stacked in one corner of her desk. There was no computer. Sam walked over and picked up a framed picture of Sue and an older woman.

"Her mother," Belle said.

"Why was she here?"

"She and her mother's new husband couldn't get along. She was still sixteen when she first wrote to me, inquiring about coming here. Her mother actually drove her down here."

"We need to get in touch with Sherry," Tori said.

"I have her number. But she'll be at work."

"We need to know where they went last night. Can you call her?"

Belle left the room, and Sam and Tori stared at each other.

"I don't like this, Tori," Sam whispered.

"I know. I hope you don't have plans tonight."

"Nothing I can't get out of."

"It's Wednesday. I think we should stake out Outlaws."

Samantha nodded. Robert would kill her.

# Chapter Twenty-two

"Okay. Let's go over it again," Tori said.

They were sitting two blocks from Outlaws, parked across the street in one of the old warehouse parking lots. They'd seen two of Belle's girls go inside. So far, they had not come out.

"They had dinner at The Tavern. They walked five blocks to the bookstore. Sherry bought two books, Sue one. Then they walked to the Regency and saw a movie. It let out at midnight. They walked back to Belle's. Sherry picked up her car and Sue went inside. That was nearly one in the morning."

"They walked," Tori said. "Whoever followed them, didn't follow their car."

"Maybe he followed on foot, too. It would have been dark. There's a lot of foot traffic around there, he could have easily fit in."

"But how would he know that they would be on foot?" Tori asked.

"And, if Sherry watched Sue go inside, Sue must have come out again."

"Belle said there are no phone lines in any of the rooms and as far as we know, Sue didn't have a cell."

"Maybe she was walking inside and heard the main phone ringing and answered it?"

"We can check the logs, but that would mean our killer would have to have gotten to a phone and called at the same moment that Sue entered the building."

"He could have had a cell phone and was watching from behind them. Watched her walk in and dialed."

Tori nodded. Then she looked at Sam. The usual sparkle in her eyes was missing tonight. In fact, she hadn't been the same since her interview with Sherry.

"You never said how it went with Sherry."

Sam lowered her head and rubbed her eyes.

"It was awful, Tori. They were so young, but in love. God, it broke my heart to hear her cry."

Tori reached out and captured Sam's hand. She felt Sam's fingers tighten around hers.

"You did a good job, Sam. I could never have gotten her to tell me all the things that she told you. I don't have that . . . that compassion for people that you have."

"You would have with her, Tori. Even you would have had a hard time going up to this beautiful young woman with blue eyes and telling her that her girlfriend was dead."

"You got a lot of information out of her, considering."

"Yeah. Considering." Then Sam squeezed Tori's hand hard. "I want this bastard, Tori."

"We both do."

Sam finally released Tori's hand and reached for her bottle of water and drank. She felt like crying. She wasn't certain she could take many more days like this one.

"What plans did you have to cancel tonight?" Tori asked, changing the subject.

"God, did you have to remind me? I missed a lovely dinner party."

Tori chuckled. "I thought you'd be glad."

"Oh, I am. Of course, I had to listen to nearly thirty minutes of lecture from Robert. I finally put the phone down and let him ramble on. When I picked it up again, he had hung up. That'll be fun to explain."

"I could have done this alone, you know."

"Will you stop with that? Besides, I'd rather suffer the consequences than suffer through another dinner party."

But Tori didn't answer. She was staring in the rearview mirror.

"Give me the binoculars," she said, reaching into Sam's lap.

She turned around and faced the back, staring through the back window.

"I'll be damned," she murmured, lowering the glasses.

"What? What do you see?"

"Drug deal. Shit. Call it in," she said.

"Drug deal? How do you know?"

"Sam, call it in," Tori said patiently.

"Okay, okay." She pulled out her cell phone. "Sergeant Reynolds? Detectives Hunter and Kennedy. Possible drug deal going down. We're on Lamar, near Pacific. Warehouse district." A pause. "No, no. We're staking out a bar. Outlaws. No, no . . ."

The phone was ripped from her hands.

"Reynolds? It's Hunter. Get some goddamn units down here *now* and call Narcotics," she growled. "Idiot." She handed the phone back to Sam. "Sorry."

"No, it's fine. He wanted to chitchat with me. Now I know what tone of voice to use with him."

"Stay here. Watch for our girls," Tori said.

"What the hell are you doing?"

"There are six men. They've gone inside one of the buildings. Three are carrying large bags. This isn't just a quick sale on the street."

"No way. You're not going after them. We'll wait for backup."

"Sam, by the time backup comes, they'll already be on their

way. I'm just going to guard the door. If they try to come out, we'll have them."

"Are you insane? Six men with guns?"

"Stay here," Tori said again, already opening the door.

"I will not."

"Goddamn it, Sam. We don't have time to argue. Now watch the club."

"You're not talking your way out of this one, Hunter. I will not let you go out there alone."

"Fuck," Tori hissed. "Okay. Stay the hell behind me."

They walked quickly in the shadows, staying close to the buildings, weapons drawn. Tori pressed against the side of the building and Sam did the same.

Shouting was heard from inside, then two gunshots.

"Fuck. *Fuck*," Tori said. "Where the *hell* is backup?"

She ran for the door. It was unlocked. They crept inside the hallway. It was dark. Sam's heart pounded in her ears. Then they heard footsteps above them and they both looked up. They turned at the same time toward the stairs. Three men came running down. Tori grabbed Sam and pulled her against the wall.

"Police!" she yelled. "Stop right there, motherfuckers!"

She stepped out into the light, her gun pointed at them. They hesitated, looking from Tori to Sam, who also pointed her weapon at them.

"Drop your goddamn weapons. Now!"

They did.

"On the floor! Face down!"

Tori moved closer, still pointing her weapon at them. Sam was amazed at how easily they were being subdued. She relaxed. It was a mistake.

He came from behind them. All three men on the floor looked up. Sam saw Tori's eyes widen, then she was pushed forcibly to the floor as a gun went off. The three men on the floor got up and bolted toward the door. Finally, sirens sounded, and they heard screeching tires and shouts. Their backup.

"Have I told you that you weigh a ton?"

"Once. Are you okay?"

"Yes. You?" Tori's voice sounded strange to Sam.

Tori sat up, pulling away from Sam and reaching for her side. She felt the wet stickiness. Damn.

"We should get back." She tried to stand and fell back down on top of Sam.

"Tori!" Sam reached for her. "Oh, my God. Lie down. Where are you hit?"

"It's nothing," she murmured.

"Nothing? You're bleeding to death. Why the *hell* didn't you say something?"

"Flesh wound," she whispered.

Sam felt around her stomach, then higher, under her breasts.

"Are you feeling me up?" Tori gasped. "Now's not really a good time."

"You don't have on your goddamn vest!"

Tori reached up a hand and felt Sam's chest. "Neither do you."

"Well, *I'm* not the one who got shot, am I?"

Tori laid her head back. She felt dizzy. It was getting dark.

"Tori? Oh, please," Sam whispered. She cradled Tori's head against her lap. "Don't you even *think* about leaving me," she said into Tori's ear.

Tori took Sam's hand and pressed it to her wound at her side.

"Put pressure," she murmured.

"I've got it," Sam said, pushing hard. "Just relax."

"Easy for you to say. You're not the one bleeding . . . to . . . death," she breathed as her voice faded.

"Oh, Tori, please, stay with me," Sam whispered. "Please?" She held her hand tightly against the wound, feeling the blood still seeping through her fingers. "Help! Somebody!" she yelled. "Tori, do you hear me?" She squeezed her eyes shut, rocking Tori gently in her lap as she waited. "Don't you leave me."

It seemed like hours before someone came for them. Sam was surprised it was only ten minutes.

154

"She's going to be fine. For Hunter, that's just a scratch," one of the paramedics said.

"Sam?"

Sam stared into the eyes that slowly opened. "What is it? You shouldn't be talking."

Tori smiled. "I got dizzy because I hadn't eaten anything all day, and you didn't make me. You're slipping on your job," she whispered. "Now, go back to the club. Check on our girls."

"No. I'm coming with you," Sam said, clutching one of Tori's hands between her own.

"No. I'm fine. It's important, Sam. Check on them."

"No. I want to go with you," she said stubbornly.

"They might need you," Tori murmured.

"Okay, okay. But then I'm coming to the hospital."

"Sure. You catch up with me."

Sam watched them take Tori away, then walked slowly down the alley back to their car.

"Detective?"

She turned.

"I'm Sergeant Lewis, Narcotics. I have some questions."

"It'll have to be tomorrow. I'm kinda on a stakeout," she said.

He nodded. "How did you and Hunter, from Homicide, get here?"

"Did you get all four?"

"Yes. And two bodies on the second floor."

She nodded. "Call me tomorrow. I'll give a statement first thing."

She opened the car door and sat on the passenger side. She looked once at the empty seat, then let her tears fall. Stupid PMS, she thought.

"She could have been killed," she whispered. "*I* could have been killed." Then, "Robert's going to freak out." She wiped the tears away, staring at the club across the street. "Fuck Robert."

∾⃝∾

"What do you mean, she's gone?" Sam demanded. "She was bleeding to death."

The nurse smiled. "I assure you, a flesh wound to the side would not keep Detective Hunter in here. She left nearly an hour ago, with our blessings, I might add. That one is nothing but trouble when she's here."

Sam stormed out, speeding through town. Of all the stupid, arrogant things to do!

She found Tori exactly where she suspected she'd be—sitting at her desk.

"What the *hell* do you think you're doing?" Sam demanded as she narrowed her eyes at Tori.

Tori glanced up from the computer.

"Typing the report."

"Get up!"

"What?"

"You've been shot. You should be at the hospital! You should be in bed! Not at your goddamn desk."

"Sam, I'm fine. It just barely caught me."

"Fine? Then why do you look so pale?"

"Sam . . ."

"You simply amaze me, Tori Hunter. Now, get up. You're coming with me."

"Where?"

"To my apartment. You're going to lie down and rest. And in the morning, you're going to eat something. And then, we'll decide if you're coming to work or not."

"Sam . . ."

"Don't argue with me. I'm in no goddamn mood."

Tori sat quietly beside Sam as they drove away. Actually, she still felt dizzy, weak, but she would never tell Sam that.

"Did they give you something for pain?"

"I have a prescription, but I don't need it."

"Give it to me," Sam said, holding out her hand. "There's a twenty-four-hour pharmacy not far from my place."

"I'm not in that much pain, Sam. It'll pass."

"Bullshit. Give it to me. It'll help you sleep if nothing else."

Tori pulled out the crumpled piece of paper from her pocket and handed it to Sam. Sam glared at her.

"Sometimes, you piss me off so much, I want to shoot you myself," she said.

"So you've told me."

"Oh, God. I didn't mean that. I'm sorry," Sam said. She reached out and took Tori's hand. "I was just so scared and you were acting like it was nothing."

"I've been shot before."

"I gathered that from the nurse. Tori, why don't you wear your vest?"

"It's uncomfortable. Probably the same reason you don't wear yours."

"Maybe we should start."

Tori leaned her head back against the seat. The throbbing in her side was getting worse. Maybe she should have stayed overnight in the hospital.

"What's wrong?"

"Tired."

"You're hurting, aren't you?"

"Yes."

Sam again took her hand. "Tori, you don't have to be strong all the time. Let me take care of you. Please?"

Tori smiled, letting Sam's soft voice lull her to sleep. She felt drugged, and she supposed they had given her something in her IV. Then Sam was shaking her, touching her face.

"Come on, sweetie. I'm just on the second floor."

Tori opened her eyes. Sam was standing beside her on the passenger side, green eyes full of concern looking into her own.

Sam helped her up the stairs and Tori was embarrassed for having to lean on her. Her side was killing her and, wrapping one arm around Sam's shoulder, they managed the stairs. She walked into Sam's bedroom without protest, lying down as Sam instructed. She took the pill Sam handed her, swallowing it down with the glass of water Sam shoved in her hand. She felt her shoes being removed, felt her jeans sliding down her legs, but she couldn't open her eyes to protest.

Sam covered her lightly with the sheet, then pulled the comforter up to her waist. Without thinking, she touched Tori's face, rubbing lightly across her cheek. So soft. So peaceful looking now. She perched on the side of the bed, her hands brushing lightly across Tori's arms.

"It could have been so much worse," she whispered. "You could have been killed." She reached her hand up and stroked Tori's cheek. "I'm scared, Tori. I feel things . . . for you." She frowned, then closed her eyes. "What are you doing to me? Do you even know?"

Sam stared at her for several more minutes, then made herself leave. She closed the door quietly, taking both Tori's and her own phone from the room. She wanted Tori to sleep until morning.

Sam was too wound up to sleep. She poured Diet Coke into a glass and took a sip, then went to the cabinet and moved the few bottles of liquor around, finding the bottle of rum. She added that to her Coke and took her glass, finally settling down on the sofa. The whole night was like a whirlwind to her. One minute, they're sitting in the car discussing the case, the next, Tori is running off into a warehouse full of drug dealers. She replayed everything in her mind, knowing that if Tori hadn't pushed her out of the way, she would have been the one hit. And it wouldn't have been pretty. She was standing there, an easy target. She had frozen, she knew. She turned, saw the man . . . and stood rooted to the spot. The next thing she knew, Tori was on top of her and men were running.

"She saved my life. Two times now," she murmured. "Wonder what a whole year will bring?" she asked herself with a smile. "Won't be boring, that's for sure."

A cell phone rang and she grabbed them both, not knowing if it was hers or Tori's. It was Tori's.

"Hello?"

"Kennedy?"

"Yes, sir."

"You okay?"

"Yes, sir, I'm fine."

"I just got the call. Where's Hunter? The hospital said she went AWOL."

"She's with me, Lieutenant. She's sleeping."

"Good. Damn stubborn woman," he muttered.

"Tell me about it."

"So, went to stake out a nightclub and ended up catching drug dealers, Kennedy. Good job."

"Lieutenant, we both know that Hunter's responsible for this. I just happened to not get in the way too badly."

"Samantha, let me tell you something," he said quietly. "You know she's had six other partners before you. Each and every one of them came to me requesting a transfer. Hunter came to me within a week of each of them, *demanding* that they *be* transferred. You've lasted, what? Six weeks? She has yet to come into my office to say one derogatory thing about you. You must be doing something right."

"Lieutenant, she told me about her family," Sam said quietly. "I think it's remarkable that she's survived this long."

"Well, she's a fighter, that's for sure. I think maybe you're good for her."

"Maybe so."

"Get some sleep, Kennedy. We'll talk in the morning."

Sam tossed the phone down, staring at it. Was she good for Tori? Yes, she was. But Tori was good for her, too. She tried not to think about the growing affection she felt for Tori. If she did, it would make her crazy. Besides, she wasn't ready to analyze what she suspected the truth to be. She just couldn't go there yet.

# Chapter Twenty-three

"Will you be quiet and eat. You've done nothing but complain since you've been up."

"You drugged me. I can hardly stand."

"Good. Now eat."

Tori picked up the fork again and stabbed at the scrambled eggs. She hated plain eggs. *Toss in some chorizo and salsa, then we're talking.*

"What?"

"Nothing. It's great." She forced down another bite, then chased it with orange juice.

Sam stared at her.

Tori reached up and ran her fingers through her close crop nervously. She didn't like it when Sam stared.

"Would it do me any good at all to suggest that you stay in today and rest?"

"No."

"Would it do me any good to suggest that you sit at your desk all day, and I'll do the legwork and go over the lab results?"

"No."

"Would it do any good if I threatened you with bodily harm?" Sam asked with a grin.

"Well, now that depends. What part of my body are you talking about?"

Sam leaned her elbows on the table and looked up shyly, meeting Tori's eyes.

"That bullet was meant for me," she said quietly.

"Yes."

Sam reached across the table and took Tori's hand.

"You're the best partner ever."

Tori chuckled and Sam did the same. She finally released Tori's hand.


"Robert, now is not a good time to discuss this."

Tori looked up, then moved as if to leave. Reaching across the desk, Sam motioned for her to stay.

"Yes, I know." A pause. "I know that, too." She rolled her eyes at Tori. "Robert, please? No, I don't know if I can see you tonight. I'll call you." She looked again at Tori, meeting the dark eyes that looked back at her. "Yes, I know you do."

She put the phone down and sighed. She had to tell him. She just had to tell him and get it over with.

"Is there anything I can do?"

Sam smiled. "Will you tell him that I'm not in love with him and I'm sorry that I'm about to hurt him? Can you do that for me?"

"You must care about him a lot to not want to hurt him," Tori said.

"Yes, I do. Like I said, he's a good guy. He'll make someone very happy."

"Then you need to let him go so he can find that someone," Tori said quietly.

"The problem is, he thinks that someone is me." She pushed away from her desk and stood. "I'm going to brave the coffee. You want some?"

"No, I'm good."

"Are you feeling okay? I didn't want to say anything, but you're looking a little pale again."

"It aches a little. I'll be fine. I'm going to call the lab."

"Let me do it. You always get stressed when you call them. *Idiots*," Sam mimicked as she walked away. It was good to hear Tori laugh.


It was after six when Sam walked into her apartment. Her mind was on nothing but Tori. The woman insisted on driving herself to her apartment, insisted she would be fine. Sam made her promise she would get something to eat, at least. In fact, she'd offered for Tori to stay again with her, here. She was worried about her.

"Hello, Samantha."

"Jesus Christ!" Sam jumped, hand going to her chest. "You scared the shit out of me, Robert."

"I'm sorry, I thought you saw my car out front."

Sam shook her head, tossing her purse and keys on the bar. "No, I've just got a lot on my mind. You want a drink?"

He held up his glass. "Have one. Are you okay?"

"I'm fine."

"I mean about yesterday," he said.

"I'm fine," she said again. "As long as I don't think about it too much, I'm okay."

"Do you want to tell me why you were out chasing drug dealers?"

"We weren't chasing drug dealers. We were staking out a bar. Tori saw them, I didn't. We called for backup. We heard shots, we went in."

162

"You almost got shot," he said, his voice louder than before.

"But I didn't. My partner took the bullet for me," she said.

"It was because of her that you were even in that situation. Dammit, Samantha, what were you thinking?"

"What was I thinking? Robert, this is my *job*. I wasn't thinking," she said. She went to the fridge and pulled out the bottle of wine she'd opened the other night. She poured herself a glass, thinking she wanted something much stronger.

"I worry about you, you know that."

"I know you do."

"Samantha, maybe if we lived together, if there was some continuity in our life, maybe then it wouldn't be so bad. I mean, I'd be there when you got home, no matter what time it was. I'd know that you were safe."

She stared at him. Surely he wasn't suggesting that they move in together. Didn't he have any idea of the friction in their relationship right now?

"Let's think about it, okay?"

But she shook her head. "I don't need to think about it, Robert." She pointed to the bar stool beside her. "Sit down. We need to talk."

"Nothing good ever follows those words," he said slowly, with a hint of a smile.

"No. It doesn't, does it?" She took a quick sip of her wine, then nervously twirled the glass between her fingers. "The reason I don't want to move in with you is because I know it's the first step preceding marriage. And I don't want to marry you, Robert."

"Samantha, I know you're not ready. I don't mean for us to get married any time soon. Not even in the next year, if you're still not ready. But living together would at least give us a chance to see each other more often."

"You're not understanding me, Robert. I don't want to get married, now or next year or the year after that."

"What are you saying? You want to leave it as it is? Only seeing each other when we can snatch an evening or a weekend?"

She closed her eyes. She didn't want to hurt him. And this would hurt him. But she had no choice. She couldn't let things go on the way they were. "Robert, I don't think I'm the right one for you. I think we should . . ."

"You want to end things?"

"I'm just saying, I'm not happy like this. I know you're not happy, you've made that perfectly clear. We don't see each other much, my hours have become crazy. And I'm not willing to change that for you. That should tell us something, Robert. You were right the other day when you said that you should be more important to me than my career. And that's the problem. You're not."

"I can't believe this, Samantha. I thought we wanted the same things. To be a family, to have kids and grow old together. What happened to that?"

"That's what you wanted, Robert. I went along with it because I thought I should want those things, too. I'm sorry, but I don't. Right now, I can't think past this case. I have no idea what my life is going to be like a year from now. I don't want to settle down and have kids. I can't envision that, Robert. That's your dream. And you should have it. I just don't see it happening with me," she said softly.

"I love you, Samantha," he whispered.

"Oh, Robert." Samantha leaned forward and held him. "I'm sorry. I didn't want to hurt you."

He finally pulled away, looking her in the eyes. "Is there . . . someone else?"

"No, Robert. That's not it at all." *Was it?* Without warning, thoughts of Tori flooded her mind, and right then Sam knew she was lying. Yes, there *was* someone else.

"Then I refuse to give up on this, Samantha. I think we were meant to be together."

"No, Robert. I don't think we were."

# Chapter Twenty-four

"You're impossible, you know that?"

"Yes, I've been told."

"I'm serious," Sam said.

"So am I."

Samantha stared at Tori and narrowed her eyes. "Okay, if I let you do this, will you promise me you'll take it easy this weekend?"

Tori laughed. "If you *let* me do this?"

"You are the most stubborn woman I have *ever* met!" Sam pushed her chair back and stormed into the ladies' room. "Got shot two nights ago, big deal. We're going on another stakeout," she muttered to herself. "Arrogant . . . macho . . ."

"Who are you talking to?"

Sam whirled around, finding Tori casually leaning in the doorway. Tori shifted, crossing her legs at the ankles and shoving both hands into her slacks. Slacks? Why hadn't she noticed that before? Tori always worn jeans.

"You look nice," Sam said without thinking. She walked over, lifting up Tori's sweater at the waist. "Jeans too tight on your wound?"

Tori nodded. She nearly gasped when warm hands touched her skin.

"Tori, this is the same bandage that the hospital put on."

"I know."

"You were supposed to change it. Blood has seeped through." She looked up at Tori. "What am I going to do with you?"

Tori lifted an eyebrow. "I'm going to guess you want to change it?"

"Stay here. Don't move and I mean it."

Sam walked out to the squad room and up to Fisk's desk. "Sergeant, do we have a first aid kit?"

"Yeah. Why?"

"I need it."

He rolled his chair over to the filing cabinets behind his desk. He opened up the bottom one and pulled out an ancient first aid kit.

"That's it? It's like fifty years old," she complained. "Don't we have something from this decade, at least?"

He glared at her. "You've been working with Hunter too long. You're getting sarcastic. It's not fifty years old. They check it every other month."

"Fine. Thanks." She held out her hand. "Give it to me."

She found Tori in much the same position as she'd left her, leaning casually against the wall. She opened the antique case, surprised to find it stuffed full of medical supplies. She pulled out gauze and tape, then found a sterile bandage.

"You want to come over here or what?"

"Is it safe?"

"I won't hurt you, I promise."

Tori moved closer, meeting Sam's eyes in the mirror. She smiled. Sam did, too.

"Take it off."

"I never envisioned you saying those words to me. At least not in here, anyway," Tori teased.

166

"Oh? And where did you envision me saying them?"

Tori pulled the sweater over her head, grimacing as she stretched the stitches along her side.

Sam couldn't help but stare. The woman was . . . beautiful. She finally moved her eyes away from the sculpted shoulders, past her blue sports bra, to the small waist. She grabbed the edge of the tape and pulled it loose, slowly. She saw Tori tense her muscles, heard her quick intake of breath.

"I'm sorry," she whispered.

Tori watched her movements in the mirror. Gentle hands carefully pulled the bandage away, exposing the red, inflamed flesh.

"It still hurts, doesn't it."

"A little."

Sam took the bottle of hydrogen peroxide and dabbed a cotton ball, then wiped the dried blood away. "How long do you leave the stitches in?"

"I didn't ask."

"Tori."

"I usually take them out myself," she said.

"Usually? Does this happen often?"

"Enough."

Sam glanced up and met Tori's eyes in the mirror. "You're amazing, you know that."

"Amazing?"

"I didn't necessarily mean that as a compliment," she murmured.

Tori stood patiently while Sam cleaned the wound and put a fresh bandage on it. Tori tried unsuccessfully to ignore the warm fingers that brushed against her skin. She finally closed her eyes, relaxing as Sam continued her gentle ministrations. "There. Much better," Sam said as she straightened up.

"Thank you."

"You're welcome." Then she smiled. "Now get dressed. You're dangerous that way."

❧

"Hunter, you shouldn't even be here today," Malone said. "What makes you think I'm going to allow a stakeout?"

Tori just stared at him until he looked away.

"Okay, but Sikes and Ramirez are going with you."

"You have *got* to be joking! Sikes? At a gay bar?"

"He and Ramirez can watch the street. You two go inside. That's final."

"Lieutenant . . ."

"Take it or leave it, Hunter."

"We'll take it, Lieutenant," Sam said, glaring at Tori. She was *so* stubborn.

"Good. I have one more thing to discuss with you. Rumor has it you've been targeted. Sanchez Gomez."

"The drug bust was his?" Tori asked.

"Yes. Watch your back."

"Targeted? What are you talking about?" Sam asked.

"A hit," Tori said.

"A hit? Like . . . a *hit*? Who is Sanchez Gomez?"

"Drug dealer," Malone supplied. "He controls most of Dallas–Fort Worth. They were doing a sting the other night. They pretended to want to buy drugs from a rival. They were taking them out."

"Great," Sam murmured. "Just great."

"CIU is on top of it."

"Oh, well that makes me feel protected," Tori said.

"Just watch your back, Hunter."

"I should have stayed with Assault," Sam murmured as they walked out.

"What? And miss all this excitement?"

"You're right. What am I thinking?"

Tori chuckled, then pointed at Sikes. "You get to tell him. I'll watch."

"Again, thank you so much," Sam said, but she smiled as she walked over to Sikes.

# Chapter Twenty-five

"You got the pictures of our girls?"

"Yes, for the third time, Hunter," Sikes said.

"Ramirez?"

"We'll keep an eye out, don't worry."

"Okay." Tori turned to Sam. "You ready?"

"Ready."

They got out of the car, which Sikes had parked four blocks away, next to Tori's Explorer. They stood back as he pulled away. He was going to park across the street from the entrance to Outlaws.

"Remember, no questions tonight," Tori said. "We're just going to watch our girls and see if anyone is watching them."

"Why are you so nervous?"

"Am I?"

"Yes."

Tori shrugged. Perhaps because they were pretending to be a couple. She wondered how far Sam would be able to take their act.

They would have to dance. She rolled her eyes. Did she even remember how to dance?

"Are you okay? How is your wound?"

"It's fine. Your bandage is still in place."

When they got within a block of the club, Tori reached over and took Sam's hand. The blonde linked fingers with hers without hesitation. Maybe it would be okay, Tori thought.

Sam tried to relax and think of this as just a night out on the town. The music was loud and upbeat, the club crowded and definitely mixed. But it was a lively crowd, so different from the two bars they had visited earlier. Those bars were dark, depressing. Everyone here was talking, laughing, dancing. Just out for a good time. She waited while Tori paid their cover, tapping her foot to the music. It wouldn't be too bad. Besides, it would give them time together, time Sam desperately wanted.

"I doubt we'll get a table," Tori said, speaking loudly to be heard over the music. "Maybe we can find a place at the bar."

Sam followed Tori as she made them a path through the mass of bodies. She grasped her lightly around the waist from behind, murmuring "excuse me" to those they bumped.

They found only one empty bar stool. Tori guided Sam in to it, then leaned beside her, her back to the bar. She scanned the crowd, finding two of their three girls on the first sweep. She bent down, close to Sam's ear.

"Julie is at a table, about two o'clock. Rene is on the dance floor."

Sam nodded, then looked up and smiled at the bartender. "Two beers, draft," she said loudly over the music. She then spun around on the stool, facing the crowd the way Tori was doing. She casually glanced around the tables, finding Julie. She still hadn't found Rene.

"Five bucks."

Sam turned as their beer was placed within reach. She pulled some bills from her pocket and laid a five on the bar, shoving two single bills into the tip jar.

"Thanks."

Sam nodded at the bartender and nudged Tori. Tori reached behind her without looking, grasping one of the mugs. Sam glanced at Tori and shook her head. Always on duty. She wished she would relax a little. She reached out and tugged Tori closer.

"You look like you're a cop. Relax, will you?"

Tori smiled. "Sorry. Still looking for Annette."

Sam nodded. "Have you been in here before?"

"You mean, like on a date? I told you, I don't date."

"Yes, you told me. I don't know why. Half the women in here are checking you out."

Tori bent to her ear. "I think they may be checking you out," she teased. "You better be careful."

Sam shivered as Tori's breath tickled her ear. No, they were definitely checking Tori out. And she couldn't blame them. She was . . . magnificent. She wore the same slacks and loafers she'd had on earlier, but her sweater had been replaced with a tight shirt that was tucked neatly inside. Sam hadn't had to look twice to know that she wore no bra tonight.

"You haven't answered my question. Have you been here before?"

Tori shook her head. "No." She watched as a cute redhead walked over. She looked once at Tori, then smiled at Sam.

"You want to dance?" Then she took a step back when Tori scowled at her. "I'm sorry. Are you two together?"

Sam nearly laughed at the glare that Tori gave the woman. She reached out and grasped Tori's arm and squeezed. "Thank you, but yes, we're together."

"Okay. Sorry."

She walked away and melted into the crowd and Sam finally let out a laugh. "You practically scared the poor girl to death," she said.

"Sorry." *Damn, Hunter, relax.*

Sam slid her fingers down Tori's arm, stopping when Tori's hand captured hers. She met Tori's eyes and smiled, tugging lightly

171

on their clasped hands, bringing Tori's into her lap. "We obviously don't look like we're together."

Tori turned, moving in front of Sam. She spread Sam's legs, then stood between them. Bending down, moving her lips across Sam's cheek to her ear, she whispered, "Well, we can't have that, can we?" She pulled Sam to her feet, holding her body against her own. "Maybe we should dance?"

Sam could only manage a nod. Her heart pounded loudly in her ears and she could feel the blood as it surged through her body. She looked up, meeting Tori's eyes and seeing the teasing twinkle that danced there. Damn the woman! Tori knew exactly the effect she was having on her.

The beat was loud, fast and they moved in among the other dancers. Sam fell into step, her body moving with the music. She was surprised at how quickly Tori let go of her inhibitions. She would have expected the other woman to be stiff, stilted, but her body moved with grace, nearly floating next to Sam. Her hands reached out and clasped Sam's hips, pulling her toward her body. Sam grinned and matched Tori's rhythm, letting the music overtake her.

The music pulsed around them and Sam let go, closing her eyes as Tori's body bumped against her own. She felt—free. She opened her eyes, locking on Tori's. They danced together, eyes still locked and Sam tried to imagine what it would be like with Tori. How would it be if they were really on a date? She covered Tori's hands at her hips, holding them there as she moved her body against Tori's. Sensations completely foreign to her crawled over her, awakening feelings she never thought she could have. Blood pounded ferociously through her and she felt dizzy, drugged.

Then the music changed and the lights dimmed and she felt Tori draw her closer. Her hands slid up Tori's arms, around her shoulders without hesitation. She nearly buried her face at Tori's neck. The music was slower, sensual, her body moving with Tori's as if it were the most natural thing in the world. She didn't think it at all odd, the way her body fit with Tori's, the way their move-

172

ments mirrored each other. She stifled a moan when Tori's breasts brushed against her own. It took all of her willpower not to press her hips intimately against Tori's, and she cursed the direction her thoughts were taking. Her eyes slammed shut as Tori's arms tightened and for a brief second, she wanted to forget why they were here and simply melt into Tori.

Then Tori's mouth was at her ear, her breath echoing inside.

"There's a guy watching Julie," she said softly. "Can't take his eyes off her, in fact. I'm going to turn you around. He's at the third table. Dark hair, blue shirt."

Sam nodded, wondering how Tori could possibly be concentrating on work after that dance. But Tori turned her slowly and she opened her eyes, peering over Tori's shoulder. She found the guy. Small, thin. Odd looking. He was indeed locked on Julie.

"I see him."

"Mmm."

"Mmm?"

Tori chuckled. "Nothing." She tightened her hold on Sam.

The song ended, and Tori loosened her grip. Sam let her arms fall from Tori's shoulders and she shyly looked up, meeting her eyes.

Then Tori bent down, close to her ear. "You're a fabulous dancer."

"I think it was my partner."

Tori smiled and took her hand, pulling her back to the bar. This time, Tori sat and pulled Sam between her opened legs. They leaned back together, watching the crowd and Tori allowed her fantasy to grow as she circled Sam's waist with her arms. She closed her eyes for a second, thinking it would be so easy to pretend this was a real date. Pretend that Sam wanted to be here with her, wanted her touch. Then she sighed as Sam's hands moved over hers, resting lightly against them. Tori opened her eyes, staring at the back of Sam's neck. It would be so easy to lean forward and put her lips there. Her skin would be soft, warm.

Then Sam shifted, moving between her legs, and Tori had to

stifle a moan. She took a deep breath, trying to focus on their assignment. She let her fantasy slip away and again scanned the crowd. She finally found Annette. She was talking with an older woman, telling her something that made the other woman laugh. Annette was only eighteen. She wondered if this was the older woman that Belle said she was seeing.

Sam turned quickly, her face only inches from Tori's. Their eyes met. Tori shivered as Sam's gaze dropped to her lips. She watched Sam's lips move, trying to form words.

"Annette . . . over there," Sam murmured. *Oh God*. She raised her eyes back to Tori's. They were smoky black. She shivered. Then she felt the hands at her waist tighten. For one second, she wanted to close the gap between them. She wanted to feel Tori's lips, taste her mouth. Then she came to her senses before she did just that. She looked away from those tempting dark eyes, turning back to the dance floor and again settling between Tori's legs.

Tori leaned forward, putting her mouth at Sam's ear. "I see her. That must be her date." She felt Sam nod. "Julie's over here at the bar. So is our guy."

Sam turned her head slowly, finding Julie, trying to ignore the mouth that was still so close to her. She nodded again, unable to speak. She had a hard time focusing. She couldn't even remember why they were here anymore. All she could think of was this woman and the way her body was reacting to Tori's nearness. She finally closed her eyes and took a deep breath, forcing her mind back to the case. The guy was standing three bar stools away from Julie. He was even smaller than he had appeared at first glance. Barely five-five, Sam suspected.

"Well, well. What do we have here?"

Sam turned her head toward the voice. It was Charlotte Grayson. She stiffened, but Tori's hands kept her where she was, between her legs.

"Hello, Counselor," Tori drawled. "What brings you out slumming?"

"I was going to ask you the same thing. When you said you

were partners, I didn't think you meant *partners*," she said. "Doesn't the Department frown on these things?"

"We're working," Tori said.

"How convenient."

Tori only shrugged, looking away, dismissing the other woman.

"You really should call me sometime, Tori. Maybe we can . . . schedule something."

Tori felt Sam stiffen, saw the glare that she gave Charlotte Grayson, and Tori smiled.

"I don't think so, Charlotte. I've matured a little since the last time. I'm not quite so easy."

The other woman had the grace to blush. "Pity. Your loss."

They both watched her walk away, looking quite the executive in her business suit. She joined three other women at a table, all dressed similarly to herself.

"I don't like her," Sam hissed. "Not one bit."

Tori chuckled but agreed. Charlotte Grayson was a predator. "Don't worry about her." She looked back down the bar. Julie was gone, but their guy was still there. "Look at our guy. Who does he look like he's watching now?"

Sam casually looked down the bar, then followed the man's eyes, right to Charlotte Grayson. She looked away when she felt the man's eyes slide to her. She moved close to Tori. "Now he's looking at us," she whispered.

Tori pulled her close, as if in an embrace. "Why do you think he was watching Charlotte?"

Sam slid her arms around Tori, her mouth still pressed to Tori's ear. She forced her mind to focus on something other than the woman in her arms. "He looked like he recognized her. Maybe he's run across her in court?"

"Mmm, maybe."

Then their guy put his drink on the bar and strode quickly from the club. He looked back once, at Charlotte, then disappeared outside. Sam reluctantly let her arms fall from Tori's shoulders.

"Come on."

Sam followed closely behind Tori. When they reached the door, Tori pulled out her cell phone.

"Sikes? Follow that guy."

"What guy?"

"Short guy. Dark hair, blue shirt. He's walking south."

"I see him."

"Follow him. We're staying here with the girls. Call me back."

"Now what?" Sam asked. "I mean, he was a little weird looking, but so what?"

"Yeah, I know. But . . . something about him, the way he looked at Julie, the way he nearly freaked out when he saw Charlotte."

"Let's ask her. Maybe she recognized him," Sam suggested.

"Do we really want to go back and ask?"

"No. But it would be the wise thing to do."

"You're right. Come on."

# Chapter Twenty-six

Samantha stifled a yawn as she waited for Amy. She was already on her second cup of coffee. Staring out the window, she casually watched the passersby as she mentally went over their case. Charlotte Grayson had no idea who had been watching her, and Sam wished they had not gone back to ask. Sam didn't like the woman and admitted she felt a little threatened by her. And as far as they knew, all their girls made it home safely. Sikes and Ramirez had followed the guy they had targeted to a men's bar and stayed until it closed at two. The guy left with someone, but they didn't follow them. She and Tori had stayed until Annette and her date left at closing. They watched them get into a car together, then Tori drove them back to the station to get Sam's car. She sighed. They knew nothing more than they had before.

But Sam had definitely learned some things about herself last night. And about Tori. She closed her eyes, remembering the dances they had shared, the innocent touches that, by the end of the evening, were becoming much too instinctive, much too natural. She found her hands sought out the other woman without conscious thought. She didn't want the evening to end.

She admitted that she had been . . . aroused. On more than one occasion, she wished that Tori would just kiss her and get it over with. God, she had come so close herself. She wondered if she'd imagined the look in Tori's eyes, the dark, smoky look that hinted at desire. Sam didn't want to analyze her feelings. She was afraid of the conclusion she would come to. But Tori excited her. She couldn't deny it. It was the truth. Sam enjoyed looking at her, she enjoyed touching her. She wondered what Tori must think of her. Did she assume it had all been an act? Just part of the job? God, she wasn't that good an actress.

"Hey, morning."

Sam pushed her thoughts away and smiled at Amy. "You're late."

"Just barely. Had a late night," she explained around a yawn as she pulled out a chair.

"You and me, both. I didn't get in until after three."

"Three? Did you see Robert?"

Sam shook her head. "I was working."

"I bet that went over well. Second Friday in a row?"

"Robert and I had a talk," Sam admitted. "I . . . sort of ended things with him."

"Are you serious? I thought you were going to give it some time?" She looked up as the waitress walked over. "Coffee, please."

"I was, but he was at my apartment Thursday when I got there. He was all hysterical over the shooting."

Amy's eyes widened. "What shooting?"

"Didn't I tell you? Tori and I were staking out a club Wednesday night when she saw a drug deal going down. We . . . kinda broke it up. Well, she did, mostly. One of them got a shot off. Tori got hit." Sam looked up shyly. "It was meant for me."

"Oh my God! Is she okay? I didn't hear anything about it."

"She's fine. Wouldn't even stay at the hospital overnight. It was on her side," Sam said, pointing to her waist. "Just a flesh wound, really, but it scared the shit out of me."

"So Robert heard about it and went crazy?" Amy guessed.

"Yes. Apparently, if we lived together, it would all be better," Sam said. "I had to tell him, Amy. I told him I didn't think we wanted the same things out of life. I also told him that I wasn't going to marry him. Ever."

"Samantha, what has gotten into you? Just like that? Not let's see how it works out? You just end things? Are you sure that's what you want?"

"Amy, it's not just like that. I told you, I've been feeling this way for months."

"I bet he took it hard. Men always do."

"Yeah. Although he's convinced I'll come to my senses, so he says he's not giving up."

"He's not going to like, turn into a stalker or something, is he?"

"No. Robert is not like that. I just don't want to hurt him. I wish he would accept this and move on."

"So, you're sure this is what you want?"

Sam nodded.

"It just seems kinda sudden, Samantha." Amy watched her for a second. "You can tell me it's none of my business, but are you seeing someone else?"

Sam's eyes widened. "No, of course not. Why would you think that?"

"I don't know. You're fidgeting."

"I am not fidgeting. I've just got a lot on my mind," Sam said.

"Okay. So, you're not going out with Robert this weekend. You want to do something? I would suggest a movie, but I know your feelings on that when it's so pretty outside."

"Actually, I'm going to Tori's boat later."

"Again? Why?"

"It's her birthday today."

"She's having a party?"

"No. She doesn't really . . ." Have friends, she was going to say.

"She doesn't celebrate her birthday. She may not even remember that I know." Sam shrugged. "But I'm bringing a cake."

Amy nodded. "You've become quite fond of her, haven't you?"

"Yes, I have. Quite fond." Sam squeezed her eyes shut for a second, wondering how much to confide to Amy. "Amy, you're my best friend and you've known me for years. Can I ask you something?" she said quietly.

"Of course." Amy leaned forward. "What is it?"

"In all these years, did you ever once think that I might be . . . gay?"

"*What?* Where did that come from?" Amy shook her head. "No, of course not. Why? Is it this case? I know you've been going to lesbian bars. Did someone hit on you or something?"

"No, it's not that." Shit, she should have just kept quiet.

"Your partner? Has she hit on you?"

"No, Amy, she hasn't. But . . . I'm thinking I wouldn't mind if she did."

"*What?*" Amy gasped. She leaned forward again. "What is going on with you?"

Samantha shrugged and stared into her coffee. *Yes, what's going on with me?*

"Is this why you ended things with Robert. Because . . ."

"No, Amy." She finally raised her eyes, meeting those of her friend. "Robert doesn't . . . *move* me," she said.

"And this woman does?" Amy whispered.

"I think she could," Sam admitted. "Amy, you know as well as I do that before Robert, there really wasn't anyone. I dated, but never anything serious. None of them ignited any passion in me. I had begun to think that it just didn't exist. And Robert was handsome and nice and we got along and I thought it was enough. But it's not. I can't live the rest of my life with a man . . . that doesn't excite me."

"So who excites you? *What* excites you?" Amy asked hesitantly.

Sam squeezed her eyes shut, thinking she had said far too much already. But she so needed to talk about it, to voice her thoughts to someone.

180

"The other night when we were out, it was the first time I'd been in a gay bar. I was watching two women together, kissing and touching . . . and something happened to me," Sam whispered. "I felt a connection with what they were doing. It seemed . . . it *looked* so natural."

Amy stared. "I don't know what to say to you. You actually think you might be *gay*? You're thirty-four. Don't you think you'd have realized it before now?"

"Would I? It never occurred to me. I was brought up to look for a man to marry. I never considered I should be looking for a woman."

"Samantha, it would have come up. You would have seen some-one, made a connection before this . . . *something*. Just because you haven't met a man that excites you, doesn't mean you're gay, for God's sake!"

"Last night, Tori and I were pretending to be a couple, to fit in at the bar. We held hands, we danced . . . we touched." At Amy's gasp, Sam smiled. "Not like that, Amy. But it was so *natural* for me, you know? It should have felt odd, strange, *something*. But it didn't. I could have easily forgotten we were working and only pretending to be on a date. It could have been so real."

"What does she say about this?"

"Tori? Oh, no, I've not said a word to her. No, she's never said or done anything to make me think . . . well, other than a few teas-ing comments, but really, she's not done anything that would be considered inappropriate."

Amy shook her head. "I don't know what to say." Amy stared. "So, you're . . . attracted to her? Like . . . sexually?"

"Yes . . . like sexually."

"And you can actually see yourself touching her, letting her touch you?"

"I know you don't understand . . . but yes . . . God, yes."

"Well, you're right. I don't understand."

"I know. I'm sorry I sprung this on you like I did. And probably nothing will come of it. I mean, for one thing, we work together. And then, you know, she thinks I'm straight."

"Samantha, maybe it's just because you've been hanging out with her, working this case. You're around it more. Maybe that's all it is."

"That's what you want it to be, isn't it?"

"Yes. Is it wrong of me to want you to be normal?"

"Normal?"

"I'm sorry. You know what I mean. I've known you ten years. I can't all of a sudden think of you as . . . gay," she finished in a whisper. "I don't think you should see her this weekend," Amy said firmly. "You're not in the right frame of mind. Anything could happen."

"Amy, it's her birthday. I'm not going to attack her on her boat," Sam said with a smile.

"But she might."

"No. She won't. That's just it. No matter what happens, she would never initiate anything. I know that."

"You can't possibly know that. You've only known her two months. She might get you on that boat and God knows what might happen."

"I do know her." And as much as Sam might want Tori to do something, she knew Tori never would. "If anything comes from this, it will be my doing, not hers. Maybe that's what scares me."

"Jesus." Then Amy leaned forward, elbows on the table. "What is she like? I've never met her, but I've heard she's attractive in that lesbian sort of way."

Sam laughed. "Lesbian sort of way?"

"You know what I mean."

"She is very attractive. She's a little taller than I am, dark hair, lean, fit. She's got eyelashes you would kill for," Sam said. "Most people are intimidated by her. God knows I was that first week. But after that day in the tunnel, she's opened up to me, let me get to know her, and she's so different from what she portrays. And I am . . . attracted to her." Sam leaned forward. "Amy, last night, it was all I could do not to kiss her. God, I wanted to. I wanted to know what it would be like."

182

"Maybe you're just curious. They say a lot of straight women go through this."

"They say that, huh? Well I certainly don't want to sleep with another woman just because I'm curious."

"Oh my God. I can't believe we're sitting here talking about having sex with another woman."

Sam reached across the table and took Amy's hand. "Thank you for not freaking out about this," she said.

"You're my best friend. I'm not going to freak out. Now, Robert, that's another story. *He* will freak out."

"What makes you think I'm going to tell him?"


Sam balanced her backpack in one hand and the cake in the other. She thought it might be a bit presumptuous, but she'd packed extra clothes in case she stayed overnight. She had absolutely no illusions as to what might happen, but she didn't want to cut their boat trip short just because Tori thought she had to bring her back.

But she was nervous. Her footsteps echoed on the pier and she paused, letting an older man with three fishing poles pass by her. It was another beautiful day and the marina was busier than the last time she'd been here. Out on the water, boats were already cruising past and just as she heard the roar of a Jet Ski, she was splashed with water as they got a little too close to the pier. She laughed and waved them on when they slowed to apologize.

She found Tori sitting in a lawn chair at the end of the pier, catching the warm rays of the sun. Her breath caught. Tori was in nothing but her sports bra and shorts. She stopped, watching. Tori had her head leaned back, eyes closed, hands crossed at her stomach. She was sleeping. She looked adorable. Sam was quiet as she allowed her eyes to travel over the bare torso.

Walking over, she lightly touched Tori on the shoulder. The other woman nearly jumped out of her chair.

"Jesus Christ!"

Sam laughed. "Sorry. I didn't mean to startle you."

Tori quickly grabbed her T-shirt and slipped it over her body in one motion. She then touched her heart and grinned. "I almost had a heart attack."

"Sorry," Sam said again. She was amused at how quickly Tori covered herself. She had been enjoying the view.

"Just catching a nap." Then Tori peered in the bag that Sam held. "What you got there?"

"Birthday cake," she said.

Tori's smile faltered, then she raised her eyes to Sam. "For me?" she asked quietly.

"Of course. It's your birthday, isn't it?"

Tori clenched her jaw. She hadn't had a birthday cake since she was twelve. She had forbidden Aunt Carol to ever bake one. That was what her mother had done. Her mother was gone. So were her birthdays. But somehow, this gesture of Sam's warmed her heart more than she could have imagined. More than she could express.

"Thank you," she whispered.

"You're welcome," Sam said just as quietly. Then she handed the bag to Tori. "I brought some wine, too. And a few snacks. I didn't want to come empty-handed."

Tori still stared. "You don't know what this means to me. No one's ever done this."

"Well, it's your birthday. We're going to celebrate."

"In that case, come aboard," Tori offered.

They left the marina as soon as they had Sam's things stored inside the cabin. She again sat up top with Tori as they cruised slowly around the lake. It was a warm day, hinting at the heat that would be upon them in a few months, but Sam doubted it was ever that stifling here, out on the water. She leaned back and watched their surroundings. The trees were all leafed out again and the drab, brown landscape of winter gave way to the brilliant green colors of spring. It was rejuvenating, being outside like this. Growing up in Denver, Sam had enjoyed the outdoors, even in winter. She was no stranger to the ski slopes and she always thought that if her parents would have allowed it, she might have done quite well in competition. But her mother insisted it was no sport for a lady, especially one destined to marry the Mayor's son.

She wondered why she had gotten away from outdoor activities. College? She supposed that's when it started, but once she was working, she was often too tired. Then, Robert. He was your typical city boy. Brunch on weekends usually followed by a movie or a trip to the mall. Dinner in, which they cooked themselves, or out with a small group of friends. His friends, mostly. It wasn't that she didn't like them. In fact, she'd gotten on well with most of them. But, still, they were Robert's colleagues. And truthfully, most of the men she worked with and the few women would never have fit in with Robert's friends. But all of that left little time for play. She looked around her again, finally settling on Tori, who looked so tanned and fit and relaxed sitting up here on her boat.

"You're being quiet," Tori finally said.

Sam waved her hand, dismissing her comment. "A thousand things running through my mind," she said. "What time did you get out here?"

"About four."

"You drove up last night? You were exhausted, Tori."

"Yeah. But I'd rather be exhausted and wake up here than in my dark little apartment," she said.

Sam tried to picture what her apartment would look like. She envisioned a cramped older building with tiny, dark rooms. There would be little furniture and the blinds would always be closed. It was a sad thought, the sight in her mind. But she doubted it was far from the truth.

Tori pulled into one of the many small coves on the lake. She dropped anchor and they went below, pulling out chairs into the sun. Sam took the beer that Tori offered her and she settled back, letting her eyes close. The rocking of the boat lulled her and she felt sleep tugging. She tried to fight it off. She rolled her head to the side, watching Tori. She was sorting through fishing lures. Sam wondered if that was Tori's passion or if it was just a means to pass

185

the time when she was alone. Which was often, Sam reminded herself.

"Have you always liked to fish?" she asked.

Tori nodded. "We used to go camping all the time. Usually on a lake. In fact, we came here quite often. My dad loved to fish. I think it was therapy, you know? You just toss the line in and reel it back, over and over. It's easy to forget about . . . things." Tori stood and cast the line over the side, letting it sink, then began pulling it back in slowly. "We went up to Colorado several times, too. My dad bought an old camper," she said. "We were cramped as hell, but it was so much fun. The mountains are beautiful. You must miss that," she said.

"Yeah, sometimes I do. I always think I'll go back some summer and do some camping and hiking. But then, if I do that, I'd feel obligated to see the folks. And that just depresses me," she admitted. "So, I haven't gone up there."

"When's the last time you went to see them?"

Sam grimaced. She always hated this part. "You'll think I'm an ass," she said.

"No, I won't."

"My grandmother's funeral, six years ago."

Tori only nodded. She wasn't one to judge. Just because she'd had an ideal family growing up, didn't mean everyone had. She saw it all the time, kids running away, parents disowning their own children for whatever reason. Expectations were high, she knew. And so many parents wanted to relive their own life through their kids. To try to undo past wrongs. It seldom worked.

"Did you not have grandparents, Tori?"

"My mother's family was from Michigan. We didn't really see them much. My grandmother—my dad's mother—was alive, but not in good health. My dad's brother lived here and he was a cop, too, actually. But they never really got along, and that trickled down to the kids, so they didn't exactly welcome me with open arms. I did stay with them for a while, but they couldn't deal with it. Couldn't deal with me."

"Is your uncle still alive?"

"Yes. He retired as a Captain about six years ago."

"But you're still not close?"

Tori shrugged. "He never made it a secret he didn't like me. I never knew if it carried over from my dad, or the fact that Aunt Carol and Louise raised me. We didn't have a whole lot of run-ins, though. He was already with CIU when I moved to Homicide."

"You didn't have a lot of run-ins? Does that mean you had some?"

Tori laughed. "There was one instance when he told me I was unmanageable and out of control, and I'd be lucky if I lived to see thirty."

Sam shook her head, trying to imagine Tori as a twelve-year-old and then again as a young woman. She would have been difficult to deal with, Sam suspected. Then she smiled. Most thought she was still difficult to deal with.

They sat quietly as Tori continued to cast her line, only to reel it back in again. Conversation was sparse, but it was not an uncomfortable silence. It was companionable, relaxing. They both took turns retrieving beer and by the time the sun was sinking, Sam was feeling a buzz. A nice buzz. But she was starving. She went inside and cut up the three cheeses she had brought and piled a plate high with crackers.

"Mmm," Tori murmured with a mouthful. "I guess it is that time. I've got a couple of steaks. Is that okay?"

"That would be fabulous," Sam agreed.

"You don't need to get back, do you?"

"No. That is, if you don't mind company again."

"I don't mind yours."

Sam watched Tori walk away, back inside. She sat down, holding the plate of cheese and stared out over the water as it shimmered a rosy pink. The sun was all but gone and the lake stilled, becoming glass like in the early evening. Soon, the peeps of frogs and the answering call of the cicadas and crickets pierced the stillness. It was a beautiful spring evening. Sam couldn't think of a better place to be at that moment.

Tori came back with the bag of charcoal and two wineglasses.

Handing the wine to Sam, she poured charcoal into the grill. They sat quietly as the charcoal burned.

"Are you okay about last night?" Tori asked suddenly. She had been worried about it all day. The dances they shared last night had become intense. At least to her. By the end of the evening, she had a hard time convincing herself that they weren't on a real date. More than once, she'd had to stop herself from kissing Sam as if it were the most natural thing in the world. But they had fun. The cause for them being there in the first place was tragic, but she treasured the few hours she'd had with Sam. She found out that Sam was fun. Delightful, really. And a bit of a tease. Tori wondered if Sam was even aware of it.

"Last night? Of course. What do you mean?"

"I just . . . if I did anything to make you feel uncomfortable, I'm sorry. It wasn't intentional."

Sam smiled. "No. You didn't. In fact, I had fun. I know that sounds terrible, considering the reason we were even there. But I . . . enjoyed being with you last night."

"Good. I did, too. I mean, I don't get out much." Then she rushed on. "Not that I thought last night was anything other than work," she explained quickly, embarrassed. "It was just nice to get out and do something other than . . ."

"Be alone?" Sam guessed.

"Yeah."

Sam reached across the space between their chairs and curled her fingers around Tori's arm. "I had a good time, Tori. I'm glad you did, too."

Tori nodded, all too aware of the fingers resting warmly against her arm. Then she felt those fingers slip away and she sighed. "You haven't said anything about Robert. Is he upset that you're here?"

"He doesn't know. I haven't actually seen him since Thursday," Sam admitted. "We talked. About us, I mean. I told him that it wasn't going to work, that I didn't want to marry him."

"He took it hard?"

"He thinks that we were meant to be together, like soul mates or something," she said quietly. "But he's not my soul mate."

"Do you believe in that sort of thing?"

"I don't know. It would be nice, wouldn't it?

"Mmm."

"I feel better since I talked to Robert, though. I hurt him, I know. He doesn't really understand." She really didn't understand it herself. Six months ago, she was content in her relationship. But content wasn't the same thing as satisfied. And she knew she couldn't live her life like that. She and Robert had just been existing in their relationship. Moving along at the same steady pace as they had been for two years.

"Are you going to be able to stay friends?"

"I don't know that Robert and I were ever friends. It wasn't like I confided in him like I do Amy . . . or you. He was the guy I dated."

"Are you and I friends?" Tori asked.

"Yes. I think so. Don't you?"

Tori stared out over the water. "I don't really have . . . any," she admitted. And it was true. There was no one in her life that she would consider a friend. The closest was Malone and only because he insisted she join his family occasionally for dinner.

"Now you do," Sam said quietly.

Tori turned and met Sam's eyes. They were warm, steady—honest. "Thank you."

"Thank you for letting me see the real you, Tori. You keep this part hidden from the others. I don't know why, but you do."

Tori shrugged. It had become a habit over the years. She had lost so much. And when she allowed herself to love again, Aunt Carol and Louise had left, too. Her heart just couldn't take any more.

Sam sensed that they had talked enough. Time for the birthday party. "You want me to get the steaks?"

Tori stood up. "No, I'll get them. You can grab the wine."

Sam followed Tori inside, then went below to the cabins. She pulled her small gift from her backpack and carried it out. Tori was putting the steaks on the grill. Filling both their wineglasses, she waited for Tori to join her.

189

"Here," she said, handing Tori her gift as soon as she sat down. "Happy Birthday."

Tori took it, slowly turning over the small box in her hands. Then she looked up and smiled warmly at her friend. "Thank you."

"You haven't opened it yet," Sam teased.

It was all the invitation Tori needed. She tore into the wrapping, then fingered the long velvet case. She slowly opened the lid. A silver bracelet reflected back at her. She felt her hands tremble as she lifted it from inside. Her name was engraved across the flat surface. She looked up, cursing the tears that had formed in her eyes. "It's beautiful," she said, her voice thick with emotion.

"Turn it over," Sam said quietly.

Tori did. *The best partner ever.*

"Sam," Tori whispered. She lowered her head. She didn't know what to say.

"I mean those words. You are."

"I'll treasure it," Tori said. Then she held it out to Sam. "Will you put it on me?"

"Of course."

Sam took the bracelet and clasped it around Tori's wrist, then held her arm up to the light. It looked good on her. She had agonized over what to get her all week. She thought maybe the bracelet might be too personal. After all, they really didn't know each other all that well. But she wanted to get Tori something that conveyed what she felt. What better way than to engrave it?

"I haven't had a birthday gift . . . in forever," Tori said. "Thank you, Sam. You've made this day special."

"Thank you for letting me share it with you."

Standing, Tori made a show of turning the steaks. She was . . . touched. That first week, she had hardly made Sam feel welcome. In fact, she'd tried her best to push the younger woman away. But Sam wouldn't be pushed. And little by little, the blond woman had wormed her way into Tori's confidence, accepting her moodiness without question. They were partners, for better or worse. Tori smiled. She was definitively getting the better end of this deal.

Sam put two potatoes in the microwave and later, they sat at the small table, eating quietly, pausing occasionally to talk, but mostly eating in silence. But again, it was a comfortable silence. Sam's eyes lighted often on the bracelet. It fit Tori's personality perfectly. Sleek, strong, beautiful. Their eyes met across the table and held, the soft glow of the cabin light casting shadows across their faces.

They finished the wine outside, then retreated to their separate cabins. They were both tired. Sam fell asleep almost immediately. Tori lay awake a little longer, her fingers tracing the bracelet over and over again.

# Chapter Twenty-seven

It was later than they'd planned to stay out, but the weather was just too pretty and warm to coax them into leaving the lake and returning to the city. They enjoyed the last of the sunset as they crept back to the marina.

"I'll probably have a sunburn," Sam noted. "I can't remember the last time I've spent two full days in the sun."

"Your nose is red," Tori commented. "But you look good. Much more relaxed than when you got here."

"Maybe that's because I slept twelve hours last night."

"It's nice sleeping on the boat, isn't it?"

"Yes. Like being in a giant water bed," Sam teased, bumping Tori with her shoulder.

Tori laughed. It had been so long since she'd had this kind of interaction with someone that she still wasn't used to it. She had a flash of herself as a child—a happy, laughing child. She had lived in darkness for so many years, she was almost afraid to come out. But, little by little, Sam was drawing her out, and Tori could see glimpses of her true self, trying to break free. It surprised her. She had thought that part of her was long dead . . . just like her family.

"You know, you're welcome to come out here anytime you want," Tori offered.

"You may regret that invitation," Sam said with a laugh.

"No I won't. I've enjoyed having you here."

Their eyes met for a quick second, and they both smiled.

"Thank you. I enjoy . . . being with you," Sam admitted.

Tori slowed and expertly backed the boat into its slip. Without being told, Sam scampered down the ladder and grabbed a rope, tying it to the pier the way she'd seen Tori do last weekend. It didn't take long for them to secure the boat and they went inside to pack their things. Sam waited while Tori locked up the cabin.

Neither paid any attention to the two men leaning on the railing, fishing. It was a mistake. As they walked past, the men turned. Sam screamed as one grabbed her. Tori turned, eyes wide. She reached for Sam, then fell to her knees as a pipe smashed against her skull.

Sam stared, watching Tori fall facedown on the pier, motionless. Then she kicked out, hitting the man in the groin. She was wrapped in a bear hug from behind and she screamed again.

"Help! Help! Anybody . . . help!"

"Shut her the fuck up!"

A large hand smothered the rest of her cries for help, and her eyes widened as three more men approached them. They all were dressed like fishermen, except one. He wore a suit and tie.

"So, these are the little policewomen?" he asked. He walked to Sam, staring her in the eye. "I am Sanchez Gomez. And now I will make you sorry you ever heard my name." He motioned to one of the others, tossing him a pair of handcuffs he produced from his jacket. He pointed at Tori. "Cuff her. Then throw her in the lake."

Sam stared as they roughly pulled Tori's hands behind her back. Sam kicked again but was jerked back against the man holding her. She felt tears stream down her cheeks, and she tried to scream as they picked up Tori's limp body. Blood was dripping down her face and, without ceremony, they threw her over the pier. Sam cried out, her eyes wide as Tori's body sank from her view.

"Bring the boat. Let's go."


Tori fought against the blackness. She knew she was underwater, but she couldn't focus. As soon as she hit bottom, it was sheer instinct that caused her to use her feet to propel her upward in the twenty-foot depth. Her lungs were burning, and she kicked up, finally breaking the surface. She managed to take a breath before she sank again. She tried to clear her head, focusing all her concentration on her hands. She curled, drawing her knees to her chest, struggling to slip her hands around her feet. She was floating, her mind threatening to go blank, and she squeezed her eyes shut, trying to concentrate. She bobbed near the bottom, letting out air a few breaths at a time. Finally, her hands cleared her feet and legs and she surged again to the surface. She was able to grab the pier and hold herself up and she rested, taking several deep breaths of lifesaving air. Her head pounded and she gripped the pier tighter, afraid she was going to pass out. Finally, after a few minutes, she opened her eyes, wincing at the pain.

There was no sound, only the lapping of the waves against the posts. She struggled, finally pulling herself out of the water, lying facedown on the pier. Her face throbbed but she knew she had to move, had to get to her boat. She slowly sat up, her cuffed hands resting lightly against the gash on her forehead. It took all of her strength to stand and she grabbed the railing, steadying herself before scrambling back to her boat. Sam's backpack lay on the pier and Tori grabbed it, holding it to her as she fished her keys out of her pocket and unlocked the cabin. She fumbled with her key ring, finally finding the tiny handcuff key that she kept there. She'd never needed it before, but she remembered her father always kept one on his key chain. She was thankful now she'd followed his advice. *"Always have a spare where you can find it."*

She slipped the cuffs off her wrists and reached for her cell phone at her waist. It wasn't there.

"Fuck," she muttered. Then she tore open Sam's backpack, reaching inside, moving shorts and T-shirt out of the way, finally finding it on the bottom. She punched out Malone's number as she stumbled to her cabin, stripping off her wet clothes as she went.

"Malone? It's Hunter. They've got Kennedy, she was taken just a few minutes ago from the marina."

"What the hell are you talking about?"

"Sanchez Gomez."

"How can you be certain?"

"Who else? It wasn't kids playing a game. It wasn't random."

"Okay . . . okay. Secure the area. I'll send out a crime unit."

"Secure the area? There is no goddamn crime scene," she yelled into the phone, wincing. "They've taken her into the city. I'm on my way."

"No! Goddamn it, Hunter! I've got to call CIU. They'll want to start there at the scene."

"Call them. They can walk the pier, see my blood and nothing else. Then we'll all head back to the city anyway. I'm not staying. I'll meet you at the station."

She disconnected before he could protest further. Grabbing a towel, she dried herself and dabbed at the blood still seeping from her wound. Then she pulled on a dry pair of jeans and T-shirt and grabbed her bluejean jacket on her way out. She ran along the pier, stopping when she came to a family just tying up their boat for the weekend.

"Excuse me." She pulled out her badge, holding it up for them to see. "I'm Detective Hunter. There was a woman abducted a few minutes ago. Did you hear or see anything? There were two men."

The man nodded. "We heard some yelling down there." He pointed to where Tori had just been. "Then a boat pulled out. We just thought someone was having a fight. But there were five men in the boat," he said.

"Five? What kind of boat?"

"It was like a ski boat. Headed north around the bend there," he said slowly. "Are you okay?"

Tori swayed and grabbed the railing, shaking her head to clear it. "Yeah," she murmured. "I'll be fine." She turned away, again punching at the cell phone, calling Malone.

When the blindfold was removed, Sam looked around the dimly lit room, trying to get her bearings. Putting the vision of Tori being tossed into the lake from her mind, she tried to focus. She had to think that Tori was okay. If not, she knew she would never make it. Her gaze darted around the room nervously. There was only one door. It appeared they were in a warehouse of some kind. For a moment she panicked, thinking her best bet was to make a run for it. But the same five men stood around her. Two were talking quietly in one corner, then the man in the suit, Sanchez Gomez, turned and smiled at her.

"So, you are Detective Kennedy," he said with only a slight accent in his voice. He walked up to her. "Tell me how you and your partner, from Homicide no less, were able to bust up my little sting?"

Sam only stared at him. She was too scared to speak.

"I was told by my source in the department that it would be clear. Not only did I lose four men, but now my . . . competition knows of my little game."

Sam's eyes widened. He had someone on the inside. No wonder he was able to operate so easily in the city.

"You have someone . . . in the department?"

He laughed. "Someone? I have a Captain at my disposal. And it helps to have control of the Mayor's office."

"The Mayor?"

"He is a fool. No, I have someone much more powerful than the Mayor, Detective. But, now, obviously one of them can no longer be trusted. Which one tipped you off?"

"No one," she said.

"Why don't I believe you?" He walked closer and grabbed her chin hard, forcing her head up. "Make no mistake, we will kill you. The manner of which is entirely up to you. We can take all night. In fact, I'm sure my men would love some one-on-one time with you, *si*?"

"Fuck you."

She jerked her head away from his hand, and he slapped her quickly. She closed her eyes against the blow.

"It is imperative that I know who works against me. Now, again, who tipped you off? I doubt Jenkins would have the balls. I'm guessing it was Mabry."

Sam shook her head again. Captain Mabry was in Narcotics. And Jenkins? *Oh, my God.*

"Very well." He turned and pointed at one man. "Bring in the cot. Tie her up."


When Tori walked into the squad room, Malone was already there, along with Sikes and Ramirez.

"Goddamn it, Hunter, I've been calling your cell phone," Lieutenant Malone said as he slammed down the phone.

"Well, you won't get anyone unless some fish answers it."

"Sit down. Jesus, Hunter, you need stitches," he said, pointing at her forehead.

"It's nothing," she said, wiping at the blood that was creeping into her eye. "What does CIU say?"

"They're not convinced it was Sanchez Gomez. As you said, there was nothing at the marina. The family that saw the boat checked out. The boat was reported stolen that afternoon. They found it about a mile away from you, way the hell on the other side of the lake. They're going over it now."

"What are they doing to find Sam?"

"They're gathering evidence from the boat, trying to piece together what happened. They're sending someone over to talk to you."

Tori stood up, pacing back and forth. "Why aren't they out *looking*?" she demanded.

"Where? He's like a ghost. He has no known residence, no one even knows what he looks like. And you can't be certain that it was him."

"It was him," Tori growled. "You said yourself, we were targeted."

Malone looked up at the quick tap on his door. It was Sikes.

"Detective Travis, from CIU," he said, motioning behind him.

"Okay. Why don't you and Ramirez sit in, too."

Tori sat in the chair, leaning forward, impatiently tapping her fingers together. She tried not to think about what was happening to Sam, whether they had hurt her, whether they had killed her. She squeezed her eyes shut, silently vowing she would take out every last one of them if they hurt her.

"Detective Hunter?"

"Yeah."

"I'm Travis, from CIU. I understand you lost your partner?"

Tori stood and faced the man. He was two inches shorter than she was. "Lost?"

He smiled. "Figure of speech."

"I'm glad you're taking this so goddamn seriously," she said loudly. "She was abducted."

He looked at her, then motioned to her head. "You're injured. Sit down."

She wiped away the blood that was starting to seep again from her wound, then sat down. "Let's get this over with. What do you want to know?"

"Everything that happened," he said.

"It was almost six-thirty. We were walking down one of the side piers, past my boat."

"Where were you going?"

"Leaving the marina. There were two men, fishing. When we walked past them, one grabbed Detective Kennedy. When she screamed, I turned and the other smacked me with something, a pipe or bat or something," she said, raising her hand again to her head. "That's all. I was out. I felt them pull my arms behind me, felt them cuff me, but I couldn't open my eyes. I didn't hear anything. They threw me in the lake. When I got out, they were gone. I called my Lieutenant," she said.

"You were cuffed from behind and they threw you in the lake? How did you get out?"

Tori sighed heavily, wondering why they were wasting precious time with these insane questions. She stood up and held out her arms. "I have long arms. I curled up and brought my arms around to the front, over my legs."

"You said you were knocked out. How did you manage this?"

"Being thrown into a cold lake will do it," she said. "Why are you asking me these asinine questions?" she demanded.

"I'm just trying to find out what happened," he said.

"How I managed to get out of the fucking lake has no goddamn bearing on where they took my partner," she yelled.

"Without having any evidence as to *where* they took Detective Kennedy, we're piecing together what happened prior to. We find it hard to believe Sanchez Gomez would carry out his threat against two cops in broad daylight. It's one thing having Narcotics on his ass, completely different to have the whole goddamn department looking for him."

Tori knew in her gut that it was Sanchez Gomez and as soon as this interview was over, she was going to hit the streets, with or without Malone's permission.

"Now, can you describe the two men?"

"One was Hispanic, five-six, one-fifty. The other white, six foot, two hundred. They wore jeans. They both had on ball caps."

"Anything else you can tell me?"

"No."


Sam whimpered as her shorts were pulled off her body. Her hands were tied over her head, to the cot. Her shirt and bra had been removed earlier. She squeezed her eyes closed, silently praying that Tori was okay, praying that Tori was out looking for her.

"I ask you again, Detective. Which one is the traitor?"

She felt perspiration drip steadily down her face and she was scared. She thought briefly of just tossing out a name, but then she knew they would have no further use for her. They would kill her. So she shook her head.

"Why would you protect them? Or are they, as you say, double agents?" He laughed. "No. I don't think so. Last chance, Detective. If not, I will allow Davey here to take liberties with you. Perhaps then, you will be ready to talk, no?"

"Go to hell."

"I cannot fucking believe they are being so casual about this," Tori yelled. She paced in front of Malone's desk.

"Hunter, sit down," Malone said. "I'm not even going to suggest that you let CIU handle this. I know you won't listen. Take Sikes and Ramirez. Do what you need to do. But remember, it's their show. Listen to the radio, Hunter. Call for backup if you find anything, do you hear me?"

"I hear you," she growled.

"Tori, I mean it," he said. "You call it in if you find anything."

She turned, staring at him. "She's my partner, Lieutenant. I never really knew what that word meant before."

"Don't do anything stupid, Hunter."

Sam screamed as Davey spread her legs apart. She couldn't stop the tears that streamed from her eyes as he entered her. His heavy body pressed against her, plummeting into her, and she cried at the pain. She looked at the others, hoping someone would stop him. But they all just stared, Sanchez Gomez included.

She tried to separate herself, closing her mind to what was happening to her. She was back at the lake, sitting in the sun, enjoying the day with Tori. The sun was warm on her skin, soothing. She was safe. She wasn't lying here, being raped by this man.

*Oh, God.*

200

"Why are you going to the warehouse district, Hunter?"

"Because no one else is," she said.

"Narcotics is doing the East Dallas, CIU is doing Little Mexico. Don't you think they know something?"

"Why aren't they doing the warehouses?" she asked. She looked over at him. "I'm serious. Why not?"

"Why would he take her to the warehouses? It's too obvious. That's the first place anyone would look," Sikes said.

"If it's the first place, why hasn't anyone looked there?"

"Because he would be fucking insane to take her to the warehouses," he said.

"And maybe he took her there because he thought no one would look."

"Jesus, Hunter, you're reaching at straws here."

"You got some better place to look?"

"No. I'm sorry," he said. "I know this is hard."

She frowned. An apology from Sikes? "What the hell is wrong with you?"

"Nothing. It's just, you know, Sam is . . . something special. She's managed to put up with your sorry ass for this long, she's got to be," he said.

"Thanks a lot, Sikes."

"He's right," Tony said. "You're different around her, Tori. I think maybe . . . you know, she's good for you."

Tori shook her head, gripping the steering wheel tightly. She never thought Sikes would react this way. Ramirez, maybe. But not Sikes.

She parked across from Outlaws, not far from where they had been the night of the drug bust. They got out and walked down the alley, all three drawing their weapons as they as crept silently in the shadows.

"This would be too easy, Hunter," Sikes said. "I don't believe they'd come back here."

"You got a better idea?"

"No."

They were all pressed against the wall, listening. There was no sound. Tori reached for the door, turning the knob. It was locked.

"Ramirez?"

"I got it," he said. He walked over, pulling out a long knife. He slid it along the door, forcing the lock.

"Something I should know?" Sikes asked.

"Neighborhood thing," Ramirez said.

He pushed the door open and the rusty hinges sounded unusually loud to them. They crept inside, walking silently along the hallway. Tori glanced to the stairs, remembering the shooting. Had it only been five days ago? She looked behind them, then motioned to the stairs. They followed her, walking quietly. The stairs creaked with their weight, the sound echoing in the silent room.


"So, Detective Kennedy, are you ready to talk?"

She shook her head, biting her lip to stop herself from crying. She tasted blood. Her body felt bruised, invaded.

"I don't know why you are prolonging the inevitable, Detective. Tell me who the traitor is and this will all be over with."

"Go to hell," she hissed.

He smiled. "So, you still have some fight left. Let's see how well you fare when Rico is done with you."

Her eyes followed the large man as he walked to the foot of the cot. Behind his back, he produced a whip. Her eyes widened as he raised it. She screamed.


"Fuck!"

They ran up the stairs, following the screams. At the landing, they paused, weapons poised as they looked around. Then the screams started again, and Tori ran, Sikes and Ramirez following close behind. They surrounded the door, and Tori took a deep breath.

"On three," she whispered. She held up her fingers, silently counted down. On three, she kicked open the door.

She saw them in slow motion. Five men, all standing around a cot. A cot that held Sam, tied by all four limbs. They turned to her, startled, eyes wide with fear. She fired without thinking, emptying her gun as the men fell around her. Then there was only Sam, her screams turning to whimpers as the last man fell.

Tori ran to her, fumbling with the ropes.

"*Goddamn*, Hunter," Sikes murmured. He stared. He had not even fired his weapon.

"Call it in."

Sam opened her eyes, relief flooding them as Tori untied her arms. She had come for her.

"Oh, sweetheart, are you okay?" Tori whispered. She pulled Sam to her, wrapping both arms around her.

"You came. I thought . . . I was afraid, when they threw you in the lake . . . I thought you'd . . ."

"I'm part fish, remember?" Tori whispered.

Sam buried her face against Tori's chest, sobbing uncontrollably.

"Ramirez, there's a gym bag in my Explorer. Can you get it?"

"Sure thing."

They were left alone, and Tori pushed Sam away, just enough to untie her legs, then she again cradled Sam to her. The other woman curled up, trying to hide her nakedness.

"It's okay. I've got you. You're safe now."

Sam nodded, but her tears wouldn't stop. She knew she had been more terrified than at any other time in her life. They were going to kill her. How much time had she had left when Tori found her?

Sam finally calmed and she loosened the death grip she had on Tori. She looked up into frightened brown eyes that were brimmed with tears. She reached out and touched Tori's forehead, brushing against the wound that was again bleeding.

"You need stitches," she whispered. "What am I going to do with you?"

Tori smiled and closed her eyes. She had almost been too late. How could she have lived with herself if she'd been too late?

"I'm okay."

"You're not. You're hurt."

"Tori, here's the bag," Tony said from behind them.

"Put in on the bed, Tony. Then give us a minute."

He discreetly laid the bag on the end of the bed, then walked out into the hall, giving Sam some privacy. Tori pulled a T-shirt from her bag.

"Here, put this on," she said quietly.

Sam reached for the shirt and pulled it over her head. "Somehow, this isn't how I envisioned you seeing me naked."

Tori watched as the large shirt dropped over Sam's head, covering her small breasts. "Oh? And just what was the occasion?"

Sam blushed. *God, had she just said that?* Her legs ached and she leaned on Tori as she pulled the sweats up.

"I have socks. Do you know where your shoes are?"

Sam looked around the room for the first time. The five men lay around them, dead and bleeding. She shivered and looked up at Tori and shook her head.

"Come on. Let's get out of here."

Sam nodded, leaning into Tori as they walked from the room.

"Hunter, EMTs just pulled up," Sikes said from the bottom of the stairs. "Lieutenant's on his way. CIU's here, too."

"Great. The cavalry has arrived," she said dryly.

"I don't need an ambulance, Tori," Sam said. "I'm fine."

"Yes. You're going to the hospital."

"No. I'm fine."

Tori turned Sam to face her. "Sam, you know the procedure," she said quietly. "You were raped."

"I don't want to, Tori."

"You have to. I'll go with you, okay."

"Hunter? What the hell happened?"

"Detective Travis, I was supposed to call you, wasn't I?"

"What happened?"

She pointed at Sikes. "He can fill you in. I'm going with my partner to the hospital."

"You stay here. We need a statement."

"You'll have to get it later. I'm going to the hospital with my partner," she said again firmly. They all looked up as Malone rushed in.

"Samantha, you okay?"

"Yes, sir."

"I'm going with her to the hospital," Tori said.

"Yes, fine. I'll handle things here."

"Thank you, Stan."

"I need a statement, Hunter! From both of you!"

"You'll get your statement tomorrow, Travis. Let's just see what we've got here," Malone said, brushing past Detective Travis to join Sikes and Ramirez. "Did anyone call Narcotics?"

"Will somebody tell me what the fuck just happened here?" Detective Travis demanded.

"Well, it's like this, Travis . . ." Sikes started, motioning them up the stairs with him. "Hunter sometimes just . . . goes off, you know. She was like the Lone Ranger tonight."

# Chapter Twenty-eight

Tori stretched out and leaned her head back against the wall. She was tired. Emotionally drained. She glanced at her watch. They had been with Sam for over an hour. She tried to imagine all that had happened to Sam. She wondered if Sam would ever tell her. She closed her eyes, her fingers rubbing lightly across the bracelet that Sam had given her, and she pictured Sam as she had been on the boat, the sun shining on her face, smiling as she watched Tori fish. Yes, that's how she wanted to think of Sam. Not tied to four corners of a bed, at the mercy of five men.

"Excuse me. Detective Hunter?"

Tori opened her eyes. Robert stood next to her chair.

"Robert."

"Where is she?"

"She's in there," Tori said, motioning to the closed door.

"Is she okay?"

Tori nodded. "She appeared to be, yes."

"She was . . . raped?"

"Yes."

He clutched his fists. "If I find the bastards, I'll kill them," he growled.

"You're too late for that."

"What happened? Amy said she was taken from your marina," he said.

"Yes."

"How could you let that happen?" he demanded.

Tori narrowed her eyes, piercing him with a glare that caused him to take a step back. "Let it happen?" she repeated quietly. "I did everything in my power to find her."

He ran both hands through his neat hair. In fact, he was impeccably dressed. No doubt, he'd taken time for a shower. Amazing.

"I'm sorry, this just freaks me out," he said. "Ever since she transferred to Homicide, it's been one problem after another."

"Problem? She's a cop. This is what we do."

"She's been trapped in a tunnel, shot at, mixed up in that drug bust that was all your doing and now this. It keeps coming back to you," he spat.

Tori's reply was cut short when a nurse opened the door. She smiled at Tori and nodded.

"She's fine. She's asking for you."

"Wait. I'm her fiancé. I need to see her," Robert said, walking toward the nurse.

*Fiancé?* Tori sighed.

"I'm sorry, sir. She only asked me to send Detective Hunter in."

"Will you just tell her I'm here? I'm sure she'll want to see me."

"Of course." She held the door open for Tori, then followed her inside, closing the door firmly in Robert's face.

"Hey," Tori said. She was greeted with a hesitant smile, then Sam patted the bed for her to come closer. She was on top of the sheet, still wearing the sweats that Tori had found for her.

"Thank you for staying. I know it's been a long night."

"I wouldn't think of leaving you," Tori said honestly, perching on the edge of the bed.

"Detective Kennedy? There's a gentleman outside. He says he's your fiancé," the nurse told her.

"Robert," Sam murmured. "How did he hear about it?"

"I . . . used your cell and called Amy. I thought you would want someone to know," Tori said.

Sam nodded. "Tell him it'll just be a second."

"I should probably go," Tori said. "I'm sure you'd rather have him here."

"I would rather you stay, Tori. They said I can go home, but . . ." She didn't want to be alone. But she couldn't deal with Robert right now.

"Okay. You want me to . . . take you home? I can stay with you tonight," Tori offered. "Or maybe Robert should."

Sam reached out and grasped Tori's hand. She looked pale. She looked more tired than Sam had ever seen her. "I want you to stay with me," she said quietly. "Please?"

Tori nodded.

"Why don't you have someone look at your head? I can't believe you've been here this long and didn't grab a nurse."

"Grab a nurse, huh?"

Sam smiled. "You know what I mean."

"Okay." She stood, then looked down at their clasped hands. She squeezed. "Is everything . . . all right with you?"

"A few bruises."

Tori reached out and brushed Sam's cheek. It was swollen.

"You'll need to make sure they check the victims for . . . HIV," Sam said with difficulty.

Tori nodded. "All of them?"

"Just two," Sam whispered and felt tears gather again.

Tori nodded again. "I'm so sorry, Sam."

"It's not your fault. It was just . . . the job," she said. "I have to look at it that way, Tori. Like when you got shot. It was the job."

"Have they set you up with a psychologist?"

"Yes. I spoke briefly with Doctor MacIntyre. I'm going to see her in a couple of days."

"Good."

"Go have someone take a look at you, Tori. And send Robert in, okay? I might as well get it over with."

"Yeah. I'll be waiting out there whenever you're ready to leave."

Sam took a deep breath, then released Tori's hand. "Thank you for staying."

"It's the only way I'm assured of getting my clothes back," Tori teased. At the door, she paused, looking back. Sam met her eyes for a long moment. Then Tori nodded and opened the door. Robert was waiting. "She'll talk to you now," Tori said.

"Thank you, Detective, but I can handle it from here. I know you must be tired."

"Whatever you say. I'll just be . . ."

Robert closed the door on her reply, moving instead to Samantha's side.

"Samantha, God, look at you," he said. He clasped her hands, bringing them to his lips. "You could have been hurt."

"Hurt? I am hurt, Robert," she said quietly.

"You know what I mean, Samantha. They could have killed you."

"Yeah, that was the plan. Thank God Tori found me in time."

"I want you to transfer out of Homicide. After this, I doubt anyone would object. You can go back to Assault," he said.

"Are you listening to what you're saying, Robert?"

"Samantha, you could have been hurt," he said again. "Now, when can you leave? I'm taking you home with me."

"No, Robert. I'm not going with you."

"Of course you are, Samantha. You can't go to your apartment alone. I'll call Amy and see if she can stay with you tomorrow."

"Will you stop? You don't . . . control me, Robert. I am going to my apartment but I won't be alone. Tori is going with me."

"Tori? After what she did to you, you want her to be with you?"

"What she did to me? She saved my life, Robert. CIU wasn't around, just Tori. She found me." Sam softened her words by taking his hand. "Robert, I thought we'd talked about us. I thought you understood."

"I love you, Samantha. I want to be with you," he said sadly.

209

"I'm sorry, Robert. I'm not going to lie to you. I care about you, I really do. But I'm not . . . in love with you," she whispered. "We can't go on like we were, pretending that we have a future together. That's not fair to you, Robert."

"Samantha, we can work through this. We're good together, you know we are."

"No, Robert. I'm sorry."

"I'm not giving up on us, Samantha. You're everything I want in a woman, I won't give this up."

"I'm not everything you want, Robert. You want me to transfer out of here because this isn't what you want. Don't you see? This is what *I* want."

He stood, pulling away. "Why, Samantha? Why would you want this? Look what it's done to us."

"Yes. It's made me realize that we don't belong together. I need a partner that will support me, Robert. Not want me to change."

They were interrupted by a quick knock on the door and the nurse entered. She smiled, holding up a chart. "I've got your release, Detective Kennedy. Whenever you're ready to go," she said.

"Thank you."

Sam swung her legs off the bed, grimacing at the pain. "Is Detective Hunter outside?"

"No. She's getting a few stitches. That one is a big baby," the nurse said with a laugh.

Sam smiled. No doubt. She could take a blow to the head but ran scared when it came to doctors.

"Samantha, please, let me take you home," Robert said again.

"No, Robert. But thank you for coming up here. I'll call you tomorrow and let you know how I'm doing."

He finally nodded, then walked to her and kissed her cheek. She tried not to flinch, but she did.

"I'm sorry. I guess . . ."

"It's okay, Robert. I'll call you."

The nurse watched him leave, then shook her head. "Men, they don't understand," she said quietly. "He's your fiancé?"

"No."

"I didn't think so."

Sam frowned. "What do you mean?"

The nurse shrugged. "You seemed much more pleased to see your partner out there than him."

"Yes."

"I can tell these things," she said. "He doesn't know, does he?"

"No. Neither does she."

The nurse smiled and patted her hand. "Oh, I think she knows, Detective."

# Chapter Twenty-nine

"Are you hungry?" Tori asked when she locked the door.

"No. I'm just . . . exhausted." Then Sam turned, still clad in the borrowed sweats and T-shirt. "Are you?"

"No."

Sam nodded. "I want to take another shower."

"I understand. Go ahead. I'll flip through the channels."

"Tori, will you sleep with me tonight?"

Their eyes met across the room. "If you want me to, of course," Tori said quietly.

"I don't . . . I don't want to be alone," she whispered.

Tori walked over, wrapping long arms around her. Sam clung to her and cried.

"It's okay," Tori murmured. "Shhh."

"I was so scared."

"I know. I was scared, too."

Sam pulled out of her arms, wiping at her tears. "I'm sorry. I'm just so tired."

"Go take a shower. Maybe we'll have a glass of wine? It'll help you sleep."

Sam nodded. "There's another shower, in the small bathroom there," she said, pointing. "I have some shorts you can borrow."

"I have some in my bag," Tori said. "Go on. Don't worry about me."

Tori waited until she heard the water running before stripping off her own clothes. She stood under the hot spray, trying to wash away the last ten hours. Sam was being so brave about the whole thing. It hadn't hit her yet, Tori knew. Tomorrow, probably, in the light of day. She wished she could stay with her, but she knew that was impossible. She had statements to give and she had their own case to think about. She had hardly given it a thought over the weekend. Her only consolation was that their killer had taken the weekend off, too.

She found Sam sitting on the sofa, holding a glass of wine. Another sat on the low table in front of her.

"Feel better?" she asked. Tori stood in her shorts and bare feet, staring at Sam.

"Better. You?"

"Yes."

Tori joined her on the sofa and they both put their feet up. Sam had nice feet, Tori noted. Then she saw the light bruises around her ankles. Again, she couldn't imagine what Sam had gone through.

"Do you want to talk about what happened?"

Sam shook her head. "No."

Tori nodded. She understood. "Was Robert . . . upset?"

"He seemed to be more upset that I wouldn't go home with him than he did by this whole ordeal," Sam said.

"Men, sometimes, don't know how to handle this," Tori said diplomatically. "It's hard for them to . . . relate, I guess."

"Yes, I guess. But he, he never really asked how I was, you know? He wanted me to transfer out of Homicide and go some-place safe, like to his apartment."

"I'm sure he's just looking out for you, Sam."

Sam turned her head and met Tori's eyes. "I think in his own way, yes, he was. I think he saw this as an opportunity to mend our relationship. He's having a hard time accepting that it's over."

"And you're certain you want it to be?"

Sam nodded. "Yes. I'm not in love with him, Tori. He's not who I want to spend the rest of my life with."

They sat quietly, both sipping their wine. So many thoughts running through Sam's mind, she didn't know where to start. But one thing was certain, she was so very thankful that Tori was the one who looked for her tonight. She was certain CIU would never have found her in time.

"I'm really tired, Tori. Can we go to bed?"

Tori sat up immediately. "Of course."

Sam put the lamp on beside her bed and Tori stood in the doorway, looking around the room. It was neat, no clutter. It matched Sam. She pulled the covers back, revealing dark blue sheets.

"Come on. I won't bite," Sam said.

Smiling slightly, Tori walked into the room. She slipped off her shorts, dutifully leaving her T-shirt on. She pulled the covers over them both, then waited as Sam turned off the lamp. They both lay in silence, then Sam sighed.

"Will you hold me?" she whispered.

Tori turned and drew Sam into her arms, pulling her close against her. Sam snuggled into her warmth, breathing in the scent that she had come to recognize. She couldn't think of a time in her life that she felt safer than she did right at that moment. Then Tori slowly moved her hand, rubbing lightly on her back.

"Tori?"

"Hmm?"

"You do know, you're just a teddy bear, don't you?"

"A teddy bear?"

"Yes. You pretend to be this great big grizzly bear with everyone else, but with me, you're a teddy bear," Sam murmured.

"Only with you," Tori whispered. And she knew it was true.

214

Her arms tightened and she closed her eyes. She couldn't remember the last time she'd slept with someone. This was nice.

"Tori?"

"Hmm?"

"Thank you for finding me."

Tori smiled. "You're welcome."

"Remind me to tell you something in the morning. Something he said to me," she murmured tiredly.

"Sanchez Gomez?"

"Yes."

"Okay. Now, close your eyes."

"They are closed."

Tori chuckled, then bent and lightly kissed Sam's forehead. "Sleep."

Sam sighed and burrowed deeper against Tori. She was soft. The arm circling Tori's waist tightened. As she fell asleep, she was dimly aware that she was using Tori's breast as a pillow. It was nice.

# Chapter Thirty

The banging on the door roused Tori, and she forced her eyes open. Sunlight streamed in from the blinds, and she closed her eyes again. They were in much the same position as when they had fallen asleep, only Sam had thrown one leg over Tori's and that leg was nestled firmly between her thighs.

Tori groaned, giving her fantasy full rein as she pulled Sam closer against her. The other woman tightened her arms but didn't wake. But the pounding on the door wouldn't stop. Tori finally moved away from Sam, smiling as Sam whimpered at the loss of contact. Tori pulled the covers around her again, then padded quietly from the room, her bare feet silent on the carpeted floor.

"Who is it?" she asked at the door.

"Amy."

Tori nodded, then unlocked the door, holding it open. Amy stared at her, roving over her scantily clad body slowly. She raised her eyebrows.

"Her partner?"

"Yes. Tori Hunter."

"Is she okay?"

"Yes. She's still asleep."

"I'm sorry, but it's nearly ten. I didn't know when to come over."

Tori shrugged. "Let me get dressed."

Amy watched her walk off . . . to the bedroom. *The bedroom?* Good God, *this* was her partner? She was . . . stunning. No wonder Sam wouldn't mind if this woman hit on her. Amy wasn't sure she would mind, either. Then she shook her head, moving into the kitchen to start coffee.

Tori stood at the edge of the bed, watching Sam. She looked peaceful. Tori hated to wake her. She pulled the covers back and sat down next to her, lightly rubbing Sam's shoulder until she groaned. Sam finally rolled onto her back, releasing Tori's pillow that she had been clutching. Sam's eyes opened slowly, finding hers.

"Hey."

"Mmm," Sam sighed as she stretched.

"Amy is here."

Sam closed her eyes again. For one second, she had forgotten why Tori was here, in her bedroom. But reality suddenly hit. She liked her dreams much better. She reached out and grasped Tori's hand, pulling it under the covers with her.

"I don't think I woke up once during the night. Thank you for staying with me."

Tori nodded and leaned down on her elbow. "I can't remember the last time I slept this long. Maybe I should be thanking you."

When their eyes locked, Sam tightened her grip on Tori's hand. Whatever fantasies she had been having about this woman, she knew at that very moment that she wanted them all to come true. She shivered as her eyes dropped briefly to Tori's lips. Then she closed her eyes, relaxing back against the pillow.

"You're leaving?"

217

"Yes. I need to go in. They're going to want a statement. Amy will be here with you."

Sam nodded, but she still held Tori's hand captive. She didn't want her to leave. She finally loosened her grip, feeling Tori's hand slip away from her own. She watched as Tori stood, pulling shorts over long legs. Then Tori straightened up, watching her.

"You were going to tell me something?"

Sam nodded. Reality. It sucked.

"He's got two guys on the inside," Sam said. "Captain Mabry."

"In Narcotics? Captain Mabry? No wonder the guy just slips through the cracks."

"He also said he had someone in the Mayor's office. Jenkins."

"Holy shit! You're fucking me."

Sam smiled. "No."

"Jenkins?"

"He felt that the bust we did, one of them set him up. He kept calling them a traitor and he wanted to know which one had tipped us off."

"So he was . . . trying to get you to talk?"

Sam nodded.

"I'm sorry. If I'd never seen that damn thing going down, none of this would have happened."

"Tori, it's our job. You didn't do anything wrong."

"I feel like I'm to blame," she said, voicing her thoughts for the first time. Robert had implied as much last night.

"You listen to me, I don't blame you for anything. If it was left up to CIU, I'd probably be dead. I owe you so much, Tori. Don't you dare blame yourself."

"They're probably going to send someone over for a statement. Especially when I tell them this," Tori warned.

"I'll be fine. Amy will stay with me today."

"Okay. I should probably get going."

"Will you come back?"

"Yes."

"Will you . . . will you stay with me again tonight?"

"Of course. If you want me to."

Sam nodded.

"Okay. I'm going to grab a shower and head out. I'll call you if I learn anything."

Sam nodded again. Tori paused at the door then walked back to Sam, sitting beside her again. She pulled Sam into her arms and held her, feeling the other woman cling to her.

"It'll be okay, Sam. We'll get through this."

"Thank you for . . . everything." Sam pulled away, but she couldn't resist smoothing the hair over Tori's ear. Their eyes locked for a moment and Sam let her hand fall away. Tori leaned forward and lightly brushed her lips across Sam's cheek, then stood and walked purposefully from the room.

Sam sat staring, her hand going slowly to her cheek, touching where Tori's lips had rested.

# Chapter Thirty-one

Tori strolled into the squad room, not at all surprised to see Detective Travis waiting for her. Sikes and Ramirez both looked up, then Sikes walked over.

"How you doing?" he asked quietly.

"Better."

"How's Sam?"

"She's going to be okay." Tori touched his arm briefly. "Listen, thanks for being there last night, John."

"No problem."

"Detective Hunter, glad you could grace us with your presence. You're quite the hero this morning, aren't you?"

"What are you talking about?"

"Well, in one night, you managed to do what Narcotics has been unable to do in three years—take Sanchez Gomez out," Travis said.

"Yeah. About that . . . I need to speak to my Lieutenant."

"I need a statement, Hunter."

"Yeah, I know. Hang on a second, would you?"

Lieutenant Malone stood in his doorway, watching. He motioned for Tori. "How is she?" he asked quietly.

"She'll be fine. She's got a friend staying with her today."

"Good. Did you stay last night?"

"Yes."

"Good. Now talk. Travis has been browbeating me all morning to call you. The guy hasn't even been home yet."

"Sanchez Gomez had two on the inside," she said.

"Dirty cops?"

"Captain Mabry in Narcotics and Jenkins in the Mayor's office."

Malone sat back, speechless. "You have *got* to be kidding."

"Can we trust Travis with this?"

"Yes, of course. I've known Travis for years. He's by the book." Tori nodded. "Okay. Then let's do it."

"You know they're going to want to talk to Sam about this."

"Yeah, I told her. She'll be okay."

Malone stared at her for a long moment. "How are you holding up, Tori?"

"I'm fine."

"I mean, with the shooting."

"What about it?"

"Five men, Hunter," he said.

"Are you asking if I feel remorse? Should I?"

"You know the procedure, Tori."

"I don't need to talk to a goddamn shrink about this, Lieutenant."

"Well, you have to. Get it over with and make it good. I don't need you on desk duty for a week."

Malone got up and opened his door, motioning for Detective Travis to join them. They all sat, then Malone looked at Tori and nodded.

"Last night, I was really surprised that no one was checking out the warehouse district. Narcotics was in East Dallas and CIU was asking around Little Mexico. But no one bothered to check where the bust had gone down. I mean, obviously they knew the area enough to know which ones were vacant. They had keys to this one. When we went inside, we heard her screaming." Tori shrugged. "You know the rest."

"Yes. You're damn lucky they all carried pieces or you'd have Internal Affairs all over your ass."

"Like I stopped long enough to ask."

"I know. Anyway, it'll go down as a clean shoot. Don't worry about that. I'm more interested in how you managed to find them and Narcotics didn't. It just doesn't make sense."

"Actually, it makes perfect sense," Tori said. "Sanchez Gomez felt he was set up. The drug sting was supposed to go unobserved. He'd been told as much."

"What the hell are you suggesting?"

"Detective Kennedy said that Sanchez Gomez had two men on the inside. He felt one had betrayed his trust. He wanted to know which of the two tipped us off."

"Come on, Hunter. You want me to believe he had men on the inside that could keep him so well informed that he's managed to avoid Narcotics for three goddamn years?"

"Yes, I do. When you've got the lead investigator on your payroll, that wouldn't be hard. Toss in someone in the Mayor's office and you've got it made."

Travis leaned forward. "You've got names?"

"Yes. Mabry and Jenkins."

"*Captain* Mabry?"

"Yes."

"Goddamn pansy-assed Jenkins?"

Tori allowed a hint of a smile. "Yes."

"Shit. And Kennedy will confirm this?"

"Yes. She told me that Sanchez Gomez referred to one of them as a traitor, and he wanted to know which one had tipped us off."

Travis shook his head. "Well, I've got to notify Internal Affairs about this." He started to rise, but Tori grabbed his arm.

"Wait a minute. Don't you think we need to get some evidence before you notify the brass and everybody starts covering their ass?"

"This is the procedure, Hunter. I'm fairly certain you don't know the meaning of that word."

"Fuck the procedure. Don't you think the Mayor's office will be the first one notified? Jenkins will be covering his ass so deep we'll never dig him out."

Travis looked to Malone, then back to Hunter. "Who else knows about this?"

"Just us and Kennedy."

Detective Travis stared at her for the longest moment, then down at his notes. "This goes against my better judgment, Hunter, but you may be right. The problem is, how do we investigate someone as high up as Captain Mabry without arousing suspicion? Jesus, not to mention Jenkins."

"What about the DA's office?"

"Not without Internal Affairs being involved."

"Then CIU has to do it. You guys have the power, right? That's what you keep telling us anyway," Tori said.

"I'll see what I can do. But Jenkins has his hand in CIU. It'll have to be very discreet," he said. "I'm going to need a statement from Kennedy. Is she up to it?"

"Yes."

"Okay. God, I hate days like this." He stood. "My Captain is going to have my ass if nothing checks out."


"How are you holding up?" Amy asked.

"Surprisingly, I feel okay," Samantha said. She left the window and sat beside Amy on the sofa. It had been easier giving her statement than she would have thought. The nightmare was fading somewhat and if not for the bruises and her aching muscles, she

223

could almost think it was all a bad dream. But it wasn't. She had been kidnapped, assaulted and . . . raped. She didn't want it to be true, but it was. But she felt so disconnected from the person who had been tied to that bed. She kept telling herself that it wasn't a sexual rape. They had only wanted information from her. They were simply using a form of torture on her. And she had survived it. They hadn't. Thanks to Tori.

"You know, you've got to talk to Robert sometime. He's called three times."

"Why is he doing this, Amy?"

"Because he cares about you."

"Technically, I broke up with him. Why does he act like we're still a couple?"

"What do you want me to say? He loves you and he still wants you to be a couple. I guess he doesn't believe that you really want to end things. Hell, I don't know. It's not like I'm an expert in relationships."

"If I tell you something, you won't freak out?"

Amy's eyes widened. "Oh my God. You slept with her?"

Sam smiled. "Well, yes, we slept together, Amy."

"You know what I mean. On the boat?"

"No." Sam wrapped her arms around herself and looked away. "Last night, when she was holding me, for the first time, I fell asleep with someone *not* wishing I was alone."

"What do you mean?"

"With others, with Robert, sleeping was always so . . . personal. I didn't want to share that with them. I actually hated sharing my bed with him. That sounds so awful, but I always wished I were alone. I didn't want to wake up with him."

"You were practically living together."

"No, not really. Weekends, sure. I didn't really have a reason not to stay with him. I could never understand why I felt that way, Amy. But last night, when she was holding me . . . and this morning . . . I'm sorry, I know you don't want to hear this."

"Samantha, I do want to hear it. I want to understand what you feel for this woman."

"When I'm with her, I feel . . . happy. It's like, there's this light that goes on inside me when she's around."

"Are you . . . are you falling in love with her?"

"I think I may be," Sam whispered, meeting Amy's eyes.

"But you still haven't talked to her about this?"

"No."

Amy reached out and took her hand. "Are you sure about this, Samantha? I mean, maybe . . ."

"I know you don't understand this, Amy. I told you, I'm not sure I understand it myself."

"Well, she's definitely attractive. I mean, that body, God. I nearly fainted when she stood there in nothing but her T-shirt."

"Try sleeping next to that body," Sam said quietly. She wouldn't admit this to Amy, but Tori's body excited her more than anyone she'd ever met. She was powerful, yet soft. Muscular, yet feminine. Then she smiled. Tori would probably be offended by that description.

"Samantha, you should tell Robert. Until you do, he's going to continue thinking that he has a chance."

"I can't tell him that, Amy. He would never understand. He wouldn't believe me. I mean, after two years, he's not going to believe that I'm gay."

"Do you really think you are?"

Sam stared at Amy, unafraid to meet her eyes. "Yes, I do. I *want* her, Amy."

"Okay. But just promise me one thing. Before you do anything, say anything, please be certain of that. I don't want you to rush into anything just because she's . . . attractive to you. Don't screw up your life if it's not for certain, Samantha."

"I know, Amy."

"And like you said, you've not even talked to her about this."

"No." But there was something about the way Tori looked at

her. Her eyes were always so gentle on her, so different than they were with anyone else.

There was a light tapping on the door and they both looked up.

"It's going to be Robert," Amy warned. "You want me to leave?"

"Are you kidding? No, don't you dare."

Amy got up, opening the door to a smiling Robert. He greeted Amy with a quick hug, then walked into the room, bending to kiss Samantha's cheek.

"Are you feeling better?"

"I've not been sick, Robert," she said lightly. "I feel fine."

"Well, I've come to take you to dinner. I'm sure you're sick of being stuck inside all day."

Sam met Amy's eyes across the room. He just didn't have a clue.

"Robert, I don't feel up to going out."

"Samantha, you need to get out. You can't hide in here forever."

Sam stared at him, speechless. It was Amy who spoke up.

"Robert, you're out of line. She was assaulted, just yesterday. I doubt she feels like mingling with people."

"I'm just trying to help. It won't do her any good to stay closed up in here. The sooner she gets back out there, the better it'll be."

"Why are you speaking as if I'm not in the room?" Sam asked. "I'm not going out to dinner, Robert. In fact, why are you here?"

"I care about you. I'm trying to help you."

"Robert, please, I don't want this kind of help from you."

He shoved his hands in his pockets, looking from Samantha to Amy. "What do you want me to do? Just stay away? Just pretend that I don't love you? Pretend that we've not been a couple for two goddamn years?"

"Why does this have to be about you, Robert? What about what I want?"

Amy shifted uncomfortably, then retreated to the kitchen to give them some privacy.

"I can't just shut it off like you can, Samantha. I'm sorry. This is such a shock, you know. One minute we're fine, and the next, you tell me that you don't want me in your life anymore. How the hell am I supposed to act?"

"I don't know, Robert. I only know how I feel. And you've got to stop this. Give it some time, Robert."

"Time? You think that's going to make me feel better?"

"What do you want me to say to you, Robert? I'm truly sorry, I am."

He stared at her for the longest moment, then turned away. "Okay. I'm sorry, Samantha. I've been acting like a lovesick teenager, I guess. You're right. I need to give it some time. I just wanted to make sure you were okay," he said.

"I'm going to be fine, Robert. And thank you for caring."

He nodded. "Okay. Will you promise you'll call me and let me know how you are? I mean, maybe we could get dinner one night."

"I'll call you, Robert. I promise."

He nodded again. "Well, tell Amy I'll see her around, okay?"

"I will."

He hesitated, taking one step toward her, and Sam was afraid he was going to kiss her. But he finally turned and left without another word. When the door closed, Sam glanced toward the kitchen.

"You can come out now, Amy. I think it's safe," she called.

The swinging door to the kitchen popped open and Amy stuck her head out, looking around.

"What did he say?"

Sam smiled. "As if you weren't listening at the door the whole time."

"I was not. Do you want something to drink? Are you hungry?"

"I think . . . a beer," she said. "I am hungry, but I want to wait until Tori gets here."

"Are you sure she's coming? I mean, she hasn't called at all today," Amy reminded her.

No, she hadn't called. Sam wondered what she'd been up to all day. But she would come, Sam didn't doubt that. "She'll be here. She told me she would."

Amy had just handed Sam her beer when a loud banging sounded on the door.

"Hey guys, it's me."

Sam smiled, but it was Amy who opened the door. Tori stood there with two boxes of pizza and a six-pack of beer.

"Thanks." She walked in and smiled at Sam. "Hungry?"

"Very."

"Good." She handed the beer to Amy and placed the pizzas on the low table in front of the sofa. Then she squatted down next to Sam. "How was it today?"

"Okay. They came and took a statement."

"Yeah. Travis freaked out when I told him." At Sam's raised eyebrows, she explained. "Detective Travis from CIU. He was the guy that showed up late, wanting a statement."

"I remember." Sam reached out and lifted the hair away from Tori's forehead, looking at her stitches. "Still hurt?"

"No."

Then Sam frowned. "What about the ones on your side? I forgot about them."

Tori stood up. "The damn nurse poked around them last night. She said to leave them in another couple of days. Apparently, my swim yesterday didn't do them much good."

"About that, how did you get out? And don't say you're part fish," Sam teased.

Amy watched them from the kitchen, smiling at their interaction. It was so different from what she'd seen with Robert in the past. There was a playfulness between them that never had been there with Robert.

"I have long arms."

"And?"

Tori put her arms behind her back, demonstrating much as she had done with Travis. "I pulled my knees to my chest, slipped my hands under my feet and brought them to the front."

"And all without drowning. My, you are good."

"I'm very good," Tori said and raised her eyebrows mischievously.

Sam laughed, then turned serious as Tori stared at her. "What?"

"It's so good to hear you laugh," Tori said quietly. She walked over and sat down, taking Sam's hand. "You're going to be okay, right?"

"It might take me a little while to get back to normal, but I'm going to be fine, Tori."

"Yes, I think you will. Because you're strong that way. I tried to imagine how I would be reacting if it were me, and I don't think I could hold up like this. I think I would . . ."

"Retreat again?" Sam guessed.

"Maybe. Probably."

"No, you wouldn't. Because I wouldn't let you."

Tori squeezed Sam's hand. "I've got some really good news. Lab results came back on their blood tests."

Sam smiled. "Yeah? Negative?"

"Negative. No HIV."

"Thank God." She reached out and hugged Tori. "That's fabulous."

"Yeah, it is."

Amy finally pushed away from the door, walking over with a beer for Tori and a handful of napkins. "I should probably be going," she said.

"No. You haven't eaten," Sam said.

"Please stay, Amy," Tori offered.

"Depends. What kind you got?" she asked with a smile.

"Two of everything. Pick off what you don't like and put it on mine."

Tori sat down on the floor and opened both boxes. They all grabbed a piece, groaning at the first bite. It was the only thing any of them had eaten all day.

"I've heard a lot about you, Detective," Amy said around a mouthful.

"Oh? From Sam? Or nasty rumors?"

Amy grinned. "Samantha too, but mostly nasty rumors," she admitted.

"Well, they're mostly true."

229

"They are not, and you know it," Sam said. "Even Dr. Peterson, the profiler, asked me if it was true that you'd *pushed* your partner out of a *three*-story window. And he works for the department."

Tori only shrugged. "Rumors are rumors. And it's not like I have a lot of friends on the force who can vouch for me."

"Is it true you punched out a Captain for botching up a warrant that caused someone to walk?" Amy asked.

"No, of course not. It was a Lieutenant."

"Are you serious?" Sam asked. "And you still had a job?"

"I got suspended for a week."

"You are amazing," Sam murmured. "And again, that's not a compliment."

"Oh, Sam, I'm much better now. I've been told you're a good influence on me. Even Sikes said I was nearly bearable."

"He said that?"

"That I was bearable?"

"That I was a good influence on you," Sam said.

"Yeah, he did."

"Hmm, imagine that. What are we going to do if people actually start liking you?"

Tori smiled. "I have no idea."

Amy drank from her beer, watching as they watched each other. Maybe they hadn't talked about it, but there was some very real chemistry going on here. Again, she noticed how different the interaction was with Tori as compared to Robert. She had been out with Samantha and Robert on numerous occasions, and she never once witnessed the teasing banter between them that Samantha seemed to enjoy with Tori. And Samantha had been right. It was almost as if a lightbulb had gone on as soon as Tori walked in the room.

"Listen, you guys, I'm going to call it a night," Amy said. "Thank you for the pizza, Tori. It was nice to finally meet you."

"No problem. Nice to meet you, too."

Sam walked with Amy to the door and hugged her. "Thank you for staying with me today. I really needed that, Amy. I appreciate it."

"What about tomorrow?"

"I'll be okay. I've got an appointment, anyway."

"The shrink?"

"Yeah."

Amy motioned to Tori, who was still eating. "She's staying, right?"

"Yes."

"She's cute as hell," Amy whispered.

Sam blushed. "Yes, I know."

"Not at all like I imagined."

Sam rolled her eyes.

"Call me tomorrow, okay?"

"I will. Drive carefully."

Sam closed and locked the door, then turned to Tori. She was still on the floor, leaning back against the sofa. A beer bottle was shoved between her legs. Sam pulled her eyes away, resuming her position on the sofa, not far from Tori.

"She's nice."

"Yes, she is."

"So what were you whispering about?"

Sam blushed. "She said you were cute as hell."

Tori grinned. "She did, huh?"

"Don't get a big head."

"I wouldn't dream of it." Then Tori raised an eyebrow. "So, how are you really?"

"If I don't think about it, I'm fine," Sam admitted. "It seems almost like a dream." Sam looked away. "But I know it's not."

"You have an appointment tomorrow, right? You want me to take you?"

"Thank you, but I think I need to be able to do this by myself. If I can't leave the house without being afraid, I won't be much use to you out on the street."

Tori nodded. "You know Malone won't let you back until she clears you."

"I know. That's why I want to go alone. I don't want to be out long. Besides, we've got a case."

"Yeah. About that, they got a match on the shoe prints. Size seven."

"Seven? That's small. Could be a woman. We haven't even thought our guy could be a woman," Sam said.

"Not a woman. Remember the semen match from the first two," Tori said.

"Oh, right. I'm sorry. I'm not thinking clearly."

"Don't be sorry. I thought the same thing."

"Wait a minute. What about the guy at the bar? He was small."

"Yeah. But we don't know who he is. I thought maybe tomorrow night I might go back there and see if he shows."

"You shouldn't go alone."

"I'm thinking I might recruit Sikes and Ramirez. Get them to play a couple. Wouldn't that be fun?"

Sam grinned. "I'd pay to see that."

They sat quietly for a moment, then Tori reached up and tugged at Sam's jeans. "You tired?"

"Yeah, I am. It's been stressful. CIU stayed an hour and a half. They're thorough, that's for sure. Then Robert showed up," she said.

"Oh yeah? How did that go?"

"Not good," she said quietly. "He's trying to help, but . . . we just end up arguing about our relationship. He actually showed up announcing that he was taking me out to dinner. He said I couldn't hide in here forever."

"Jesus Christ," Tori muttered. "Does he not understand what happened to you?"

"You know, I'm not really certain that he does. He asked me if I was feeling better, as if I'd been down with the flu or something."

"Maybe he just doesn't want to admit what happened," Tori suggested. "If he doesn't talk about it, then it's not true."

"You're probably right."

Tori stood up. "Come on. Let's get this cleaned up. A good night's sleep would do us both good."

They put the leftover pizza in the fridge, then Tori went to the spare bathroom to shower. Sam brushed her teeth, getting ready for bed. She wondered if Tori would sleep in here again tonight or if she would prefer the sofa. Sam hadn't considered that maybe

Tori was uncomfortable sleeping with her. She met her own eyes in the mirror, remembering the way Tori had held her. She really wanted Tori to hold her again tonight. But she would offer the sofa, just in case.

She was again sitting in the living room with a glass of wine when Tori walked out of the shower, clad as before in shorts and a T-shirt with her feet bare. She walked over and took the glass of wine that Sam had poured for her. They sat much as they had the night before, with feet propped on the table.

"I appreciate you staying with me, Tori. I know you're used to being alone," Sam said.

"This is nice. Much better than my apartment and a hell of a lot better than the cot in the locker room," she said.

"Why do you stay there so much? And don't say because you work late and it's easier than driving to your apartment."

"My apartment is just an apartment. Just a place to sleep. It's not really a home," Tori said quietly. "I have a bed and a recliner and a TV. That's about it."

"Your boat is home," Sam said.

"Yeah, it is. But now, every time I go out there, I'll think about what happened to you."

"No. What happened to us," Sam corrected.

"I think maybe I'll move her to another marina," Tori said. "There are a couple of other small ones out there. I want you to be able to come out, you know."

Sam reached over and took Tori's hand. "Thank you. And you're right. It would be tough going back. Right now, anyway. Maybe in a few weeks . . ."

Tori watched as their fingers entwined. It was so easy to be with Sam. So natural to touch her like this. She raised her eyes, meeting the gentle green ones that looked back at her. It occurred to her then how it had become between them. The quiet teasing, the innocent touches, the shyness that she saw in Sam's eyes sometimes. What was she thinking? What was she feeling? Was it anything like the thoughts Tori had been having lately?

"Bed?"

"Mmm."

"Do you want me . . . I mean, would you rather I slept out here?" She felt Sam's hand tighten, then release.

"No. I mean, would you rather sleep out here?"

Tori smiled. "Let's see. A bed or a sofa? That is a tough choice," she teased.

Sam stood and pulled Tori to her feet. "Bed."

Tori slipped out of her shorts and crawled under the covers, again waiting until Sam turned out the lamp. In the darkness, she felt Sam shift, felt her move until they were almost touching. Then Tori slowly reached for her and pulled Sam into her arms. Sam snuggled against her immediately, her arm folding across Tori's waist like before.

Sam took a deep breath and released it. Tori's arms tightened around her and Sam felt . . . heard Tori's rapid heartbeat. Her hand rested along Tori's hip and without really thinking, she moved it under Tori's T-shirt, wanting to touch warm flesh. She felt Tori tremble, heard her quiet intake of breath. She closed her eyes, fighting off the feelings that were threatening to consume her. But God, she so wanted to touch her.

Tori fought to squelch the desire that had settled firmly over her like a heavy blanket, nearly choking her. Sam wasn't making it easy. In fact, she wondered if Sam had any idea what she was doing to her. And if she had any sense at all, Tori would remove Sam's hand from under her shirt. But she was powerless to do any such thing. Sam's hand was warm, soft upon her. And it had been so long since anyone had touched her. At that moment, all she wanted to do was pull Sam on top of her, feel her weight as it pressed down against her . . . and kiss her. She closed her eyes and wondered what Sam's reaction would be. Would she be shocked, angry? Or would she feel Tori's desire and match it?

Desire? Yes. And Tori hated herself for what she was feeling. The thoughts running through her mind were totally inappropriate. Sam had just been assaulted . . . raped. She was seeking comfort, protection. Nothing more. She moved, finally capturing Sam's hand and stopping its slow movements against her skin. She sighed, trying to relax.

"Tori?"

"Hmm?"

"Thank you for staying with me again," Sam whispered.

"It's no problem."

Sam closed her eyes, her grip tightening momentarily around Tori, then relaxing. Again, she thought how nice it felt to be sleeping with Tori, like this. She moved her head, resting it lightly against Tori's breast. Under her cheek, she felt Tori's nipple harden and she trembled. So close . . . oh, God . . . she could almost feel it, taste it in her mouth. She moaned.

*I'm dying here*, Tori thought. She squeezed her legs together, wondering how long she could hold out before she did something really stupid. She tried to ignore her feelings, ignore the fact that Sam was nestled against her breast, ignore the quiet moan she'd heard. She wondered if Sam could hear her thundering heartbeat.

*What would Tori's reaction be if I just raised up and kissed her*, Sam thought. *Would she think I'd lost my mind? Or would she welcome it?* But she would never know. Tori's hand came out and brushed against her hair lightly.

"Go to sleep," she murmured.

Sam nodded. It was the only sensible thing to do.

# Chapter Thirty-two

The ringing penetrated her brain, and Tori forced her eyes open. They had changed positions. Tori was now the one curled at Sam's side, face pressed against her neck. Sam stirred, moving in Tori's arms, rolling toward her. Their arms and legs were tangled and then the ringing stopped.

"Hello," Sam murmured.

"Samantha, it's Sikes. I'm sorry to call so early, but we can't find Hunter. Malone thought she might be with you."

"Sikes?" Sam opened her eyes. She was on top of Tori and their eyes met. Her own slid to Tori's lips, only inches away. She became aware of their bare legs entwined, of the thigh that was pressed against her. She felt the phone fall from her fingers as her lower body moved instinctively against that thigh. Sam gasped as, for one brief second, she felt Tori move against her. She was powerless to stop the moan that escaped and she watched as Tori's eyes slid shut, heard the quiet moan as Tori's hands gripped her tighter. Then

Tori reached between them, searching for the phone, and Sam rolled over, moving away from Tori, embarrassed beyond belief over what had just happened.

Tori held the phone to her chest, clearing her throat before speaking. "Sikes? It's Hunter."

"Listen, they found another body. North Dallas this time. The guy's got balls. It's at a goddamn mall."

"Okay. I'll be right there."

"What is it?" Sam asked. "Another girl?"

"Yes." Tori hesitated. "Listen, I'm sorry . . . about . . . well, earlier when . . . *shit*," she murmured, turning away.

Sam grabbed her arm. "Stop it. It was . . . me and we both know it. I don't know . . . what came over me."

Tori swallowed with difficulty and sat up. "I should get going."

Sam did the same. "I'm coming with you."

"No, you're not." Tori reached for Sam and pulled her back down, wrapping the comforter around her again. "It's four. You stay under the covers, okay? I'll come back as soon as we're done."

"No. It's okay, Tori. You don't have to. I've got that appointment at ten anyway. I'll be okay here."

"Are you sure?"

"Yes. But please be careful," she said quietly.

"I will. I promise. Will you call after your appointment? If I'm not at the station, call my cell. I should have my new phone this morning." Tori grabbed her shorts off of the floor and stood staring at Sam. "Are you sure you'll be okay?"

"I'm sure. I need to be able do this."

"Okay. I'll lock the door when I leave."

Sam lay awake long after Tori had left. She finally grabbed the pillow Tori had used and pulled it to her, trying to make sense out of what she was feeling, but there was really only one answer. She was attracted to Tori on several levels, but the sexual attraction she felt was threatening to overtake her, control her. Last night, as Tori held her, she'd felt desire she'd never experienced before. And earlier, as Tori's thigh was pressed against her center, as her hips instinctively moved against that thigh, she knew with clarity what a burning desire felt like. She tried to remember the first time she and Robert had made love. Had she wanted him that much? Had she *ever* really wanted him? Or was it just what was expected?

"Oh God," she whispered. She was too old to be discovering these feelings. Amy was right. Why hadn't she ever met a woman before that she was attracted to? She wanted to say that it was because she never considered that she might be gay and the female friendships in her life were just that: friendships. But there was Lori, in college. They had been nearly inseparable. Was it only friendship that she felt? She remembered not being at all shocked when Lori told her she had met someone, a woman. They had remained friends for a while, then had just drifted apart. And then when she was in the Academy, several of the female recruits were lesbians, but none really attracted her. Did they? Jesus, not like this. Not the way Tori did.

She finally drifted off, Tori's pillow still clutched to her chest . . . unanswered questions still running through her mind.

"Oh my God," Tori whispered.

"You know her?" Rita asked.

"Julie Barnes. She's a resident at Belle's. Just like the others."

"Why do you think he only cut the legs off of one?" Rita asked. "The only thing consistent in this case is the way they're laid out in Dumpsters. Makes no sense."

"You bagged her hands? She fought back?"

"Yes. We'll get a skin sample, I'm sure of it. Hands and feet were bound. The bruising around the neck is consistent."

Tori rubbed her face with both hands and sighed. "Okay, tell Jackson I'll be calling."

She walked around the Dumpster to where Sikes was talking to the manager of the cleaning crew. "Anything?"

"She was put here sometime after three. They dumped the first load then. When they came back, they found her." He looked at his notes. "Three thirty-five."

"So, lucky break for him or he knew the routine. And why here where it's so public?"

"He's getting bold," Sikes said. "They didn't find any shoe prints this time, by the way."

"You know what I think? I want to find that guy you and Ramirez followed the other night from the bar."

"How do you propose we find him? With Sam out, are you going to go in and play the field, Hunter? You might get side-tracked with all those women in there."

Tori smiled. "Actually, it's a mixed bar. I'm thinking you and Ramirez get to be the couple this time."

"Oh, now you're just out of your fucking mind!"

# Chapter Thirty-three

"You're looking much better, Detective," Dr. MacIntyre said.

"It's amazing what a few days will do," Sam replied.

"I understand from looking at your file that before Homicide, you worked in Assault. I'm sure you saw your share of this type of abuse."

"I did. But I don't consider myself abused, Doctor. I wasn't picked off the street at random. I wasn't date-raped. No one broke into my home. I was doing my job, and that job comes with risks."

"This wasn't simply doing your job, Samantha. You were raped."

"Is that any different than if I'd been shot? I wasn't raped because someone wanted sexual favors. I was raped because they wanted information. If I were a man, I would have been beaten or tortured until I talked. But because I'm a woman, what better way than to rape?"

"I must admit, you're being very calm about this. Reasonable in your deduction, even. But before you can go back to work, my job is to make sure you are handling this emotionally, Detective. Can you go back on the street and not be afraid that someone is going to attack you again? Will you be overly aggressive now that this has happened?"

Sam leaned forward. "Would you be asking me these questions if I were a man? Or if I had been shot? Would you be concerned that I couldn't go back on the street because someone might shoot me?"

"Have you accepted what's happened to you or have you just pushed it away, pretending that it was just part of the job? Detective, being physically and sexually violated is so very different than being shot."

"When I was tied to that bed, I was scared. I was afraid that I wouldn't be able to hold out and that I would tell them what they wanted to know. Then they would kill me. So I lay there and took it, knowing that if I could just hold out a little longer, someone would come for me. And they did." Sam met Dr. MacIntyre's eyes across the desk. "I know I was raped, Doctor. And when I left the hospital that night, I was afraid to be alone. And the next day, I had a friend stay with me because I was afraid to be alone. Then I realized I wasn't afraid to be alone because someone might come and hurt me again. I was afraid to be alone because I didn't want to think about it."

"And . . . have you thought about it?"

"I've thought about it so much, I can remember every detail. I think I should be angry, and I suppose I am. But they're not going to hurt me anymore, are they?"

"No, they're not. Does that make you angry that they're gone and you can't confront them?"

"No. I survived this. They didn't."

# Chapter Thirty-four

Tori stood at the door a long time before knocking. She was nervous and didn't know why. Well, she knew why, didn't she? All day long, she couldn't put her finger on it, but suddenly, it hit her. The innocent touches, Sam wanting to spend time with her, Sam's wide eyes at the gay bars. Then the night they had posed as a couple, the dances they shared, the way Sam looked at her. And the last few nights, sleeping together. The way Sam wrapped around her. And God, this morning. She closed her eyes and leaned her head back against the wall. Sam was feeling the same desire that she was. Sam, who was straight. Then she sighed. Sam, who thought she was straight. Tori wondered what was going through the other woman's mind. Was she frightened by what she was feeling? Was she trying to fight it, too?

They were partners, for God's sake! This couldn't happen. If Tori let it happen, she would lose the only partner she'd ever felt comfortable with. The only partner she'd ever become friends with. Hell, Sam was the only friend, period. And if she let this happen, Sam would run. She would transfer out, and Tori would be alone again.

No, she couldn't let it happen.

Tori finally pushed off the wall and knocked, then waited.

"Is that you?"

Tori couldn't help but grin. "You, who?"

Sam opened the door, matching Tori's smile. "Hi."

Tori held up a bag. "Chinese?"

"I'm starved. Thanks," Sam said, pulling Tori inside.

Tori watched Sam walk away. She stood at the door, wondering how she was going to get through the night sleeping with Sam again.

Sam stopped and looked back. "What's wrong?"

Tori shook her head. "Nothing."

"Are you sure?"

Tori nodded and smiled, finally following Sam into the kitchen.

Sam took down two plates and dished out the food on both. "There's wine in the fridge," she said.

Tori brought the bottle and two glasses and they settled at the table, both eating immediately.

"You haven't eaten today, I take it," Sam finally said.

Tori shook her head. "You?"

"No."

"So, are you sure you're ready to come back, Sam? I mean, it's only been three days."

"I'm sure. I'll go crazy if I'm stuck here much longer." She stabbed a shrimp off of Tori's plate and grinned at Tori's raised eyebrows. "Besides, do you really think you can get Sikes into a gay bar?"

"No."

"How did Belle take the news?"

"Not well. I think she's ready to close up the hostel. A lot of the girls are actually starting to move out. But I didn't go over. I only talked to her on the phone. In the morning, we should get the lab reports back. We can go over there, then."

243

Sam nodded. "Does Malone know I'm coming back?"

"Yes. He wasn't happy. He thinks it's too soon. In fact, I think he called your Dr. MacIntyre."

"He thinks I'm not ready?"

"He doesn't want you to rush things," Tori said.

"What do you think?"

"I don't want you to rush things, either, Sam. But you know better than anyone how you feel. If you're ready, then you're ready."

"Thank you."

"For what?"

"Thank you for not insisting that I stay away, and thank you for letting me decide on my own. If I stay here another day or two, what good would that do? I would just have more time to think about it. And I don't want to sit and relive it over and over again. For me, what I need is to get back out there and put some normalcy back in my life."

Tori nodded. "I understand. And maybe I'm being selfish," she said. "Maybe I want you to come back because I missed you being around."

"And maybe you're ready for me to come back because you're tired of babysitting me at night."

"I would hardly call it babysitting." Her eyes turned serious as she met Sam's. "Actually, I can't remember when I've slept so well. I think maybe I've needed this, too."

Sam reached across the table and captured Tori's hand. Their fingers entwined immediately. "Can I tell you something?"

Tori nodded, her eyes lingering on their clasped hands.

"I've never felt safer . . . or more protected than I have the last couple of nights with you lying next to me. I slept as if there wasn't a care in the world, just because you were holding me."

Their eyes were locked across the table, as were their hands. Tori wondered what Sam saw in her eyes. Could she see the desire that Tori was trying to hide? Did she have any idea that Tori was being completely selfish by volunteering to stay with her?

"I'll stay as long as you need me to, Sam," Tori said quietly.

Sam smiled. "You may regret that offer."

The phone interrupted Tori's response and Sam went into the living room to get it.

"Hello?" Sam glanced at Tori. "I'm fine, Robert." She listened and shook her head. "No, I'm not alone. Tori's here."

Tori got up, pointing to the bathroom. Sam nodded and sat down on the sofa.

"No, I'm going back to work tomorrow."

"Tomorrow? Samantha, that's too soon. I think you should at least stay out the rest of the week," he said.

Sam heard the water running and she imagined Tori standing under the spray, naked.

"And do what, Robert? Hang out here at the apartment?"

"You need to rest."

"I've been resting. I'm fine, Robert. You're the one who said I needed to get out and not hide in here," she reminded him.

"I didn't mean go back to work, Samantha."

Sam sighed. "Why are you calling, Robert? Just to lecture to me?"

"I'm calling to check on you. You said you'd call."

"I'm sorry."

"I just don't understand, Samantha. Why would you rather have her there with you than me? I should be the one you reach out to, Samantha. Not her."

"Why not her? She's my partner," Sam said.

"I'm your *boyfriend*."

"Robert . . . you're not. Please, let's don't get into this again. Not now."

"Samantha, I can't take this. Please, you've got to tell me what's going on. You can't just end our relationship like this and not tell me why."

She grabbed the bridge of her nose and squeezed. "I told you why, Robert. You want to get married and have kids. I don't. You need to find someone that wants the same things you do. I need to do the same," she said.

"Why don't you want to get married and have kids?"

"I just don't, Robert. I can't tell you why. It's just how I feel."
She heard the water turn off and she closed her eyes. Tori would be
out soon. "I've got to go, Robert. Please, don't keep calling. In a
few weeks, we can talk, okay?"

"You know I'm going to call, Samantha. Like I said before, I
can't just turn off my feelings like they were never there. I love
you, Samantha."

"Why are you making this so hard, Robert?"

"Because love is hard, Samantha."

She listened to the dial tone for a second, then tossed the phone
on the sofa. She never thought Robert would be like this. In fact,
when she thought about their relationship, it was always so controlled and orderly. No fights, no arguing . . . no passion. She actually found it hard to believe that he was all that much in love with
her. He was more likely in love with just the idea of getting married and starting a family.

"Everything okay?"

Sam looked up. Tori's hair was still damp. She wore flannel
boxers tonight and a white T-shirt. She looked so . . . sexy. God,
did she ever think she would find flannel boxers sexy on a woman?

"He's . . . having a hard time with this," she said. Then she
stood up. "I want to grab a shower, too. Do you mind?"

"Of course not. I'll clean up dinner."

Sam slipped out of her jeans, then stood looking at herself in
the mirror. She tucked her hair behind her ears and stared, the
bruise on her thigh beginning to fade as was the bite mark on her
breast. Her eyes followed the length of her body in the mirror. She
was probably too thin, she thought. Her breasts were small.
Robert had always teased her about them. She wondered if Tori
even found her attractive. Wouldn't that be just her luck? Here she
was, about to combust any time she was around Tori. How ironic
it would be if Tori had no such feelings. She met her eyes in the
mirror. But Tori did, didn't she? She hadn't mistaken Tori's reaction last night, she hadn't imagined the thundering heartbeat
below her ear. And she certainly hadn't imagined that little scene
that took place early this morning. No, Tori appeared to be in the

same shape she was. Both struggling with their feelings, both fighting against the desire that was creeping closer and closer.

She met her eyes in the mirror. She didn't want to fight it. She wanted to embrace it. She knew in her very soul that this was meant to be. And knowing that, it frightened her a little. She could very well have denied it. She could have continued to plug along in her relationship with Robert, only wondering what might have been. As she'd told Amy before, Tori would never be the one to initiate anything between them. Even now, Tori'd been the one to keep her distance, the one strong enough to keep their relationship on a friendly level. Then she laughed quietly. Friendly? How many female friends would she hold hands with? Snuggle up with at night? No, they were past that. And if it went any further, Sam would have to be the one to do it. Tori never would.

She finally walked into the shower, scrubbing herself. She wondered how long she would be compelled to take three showers a day, as if she could wash herself clean. She hadn't mentioned that to Dr. MacIntyre. She assumed that would only ensure her another visit with the good doctor.

When she walked out, Tori was in the bedroom, pulling the covers back. Their eyes met.

"I figured you wanted me to sleep in here again," Tori said shyly. "I mean, if you want me to take the sofa, I can."

Sam smiled. "You know very well I don't want you on the sofa."

"Okay. I just wanted to be sure."

Tori crawled under the covers, extremely aware of how nervous she was. What if tonight, she couldn't control it? What if she gave in to what she was feeling? Then what? Maybe Sam was better tonight. Maybe she wouldn't want to sleep in Tori's arms again. But that thought caused a deep ache in her chest.

Sam turned off the lamp and lay on her back, much as Tori was doing. She wanted to be in her arms and she was nearly frightened by the need she had. Did Tori have any idea how she was feeling? Yes, certainly she did. But she made herself stay where she was, hoping sleep would claim her. It didn't.

"Tori?"

"Hmm?"

Sam took a deep breath. "Would you hold me again?" she whispered.

Tori's resistance melted at those softly whispered words. "Come here." She pulled Sam to her, slipping one arm around her back and cradling Sam to her side. She shivered as Sam slipped an arm around her waist, fitting her body next to Tori's.

"Thank you," Sam murmured.

"Mmm." It was glorious, the way Sam felt in her arms. She reached out a hand and brushed lightly at the hair on Sam's forehead, moving it away from her face. Sam's arm tightened around her waist. Then Tori gasped as Sam's hand slid under her shirt, rubbing lightly against her skin.

Sam trembled as her hand moved across smooth, soft skin. It would be so easy, so easy to slide it higher. She wondered what Tori's breast would feel like. Soft, like the skin under her hand now? She ached to know how it would feel and she lost what little control she had left. She slid her hand higher, across Tori's ribs, feeling the swell of breast just under her fingers.

Tori couldn't stifle the moan that escaped. She tried, but it was out before she could stop it. She slid her hand to Sam's, stopping her movements. "Sam, I'm dying here," she whispered. "Please stop."

"I can't." She lifted her head, her mouth just inches from Tori's. "When are you going to kiss me? You must know how much I want you to," she whispered.

"Oh Sam, don't do this to me."

"I you want to. Please don't fight this, Tori."

Their eyes met in the darkness, so close that they breathed the same air. Tori tried to fight it, she did. But her arms tightened, bringing Sam even closer to her. Then, against her better judgment, she gave in, taking what was offered. Their kiss wasn't gentle. Sam's mouth opened under hers, meeting Tori's tongue wildly.

Sam thought she might very well faint. She moaned, her hand

finally moving the last few inches to Tori's breast. It was soft and firm beneath her hand, the nipple hardening immediately against her palm. She heard the groan that escaped Tori, felt Tori press hard against her hand. Then Tori pulled her on top, opening her legs, and Sam settled between them. She pulled her mouth from Tori's, breathing hard as she felt Tori's hands grip her hips, pulling her firmly against her.

"Oh God," she whispered. Desire swept over her body, taking complete control. Her hips rocked against Tori as her mouth was captured once again. Then Tori's hands were at her face, her kiss gentle now, lips moving lightly against her own, then stopping.

"Sam, we can't," she whispered.

Sam groaned. "I want you. God, I want your touch. We *can*."

"No."

Sam nearly sobbed. She laid her head against Tori's chest, hearing the pounding of her heart, her rapid gasps for air. All these years, she thought, wasted. Right here, right now. This is what she wanted . . . what she *needed*.

"Sam . . . listen to me," Tori said. "I want to make love to you. God, I do. But you're not ready for this."

"I've been waiting for you my whole life," Sam whispered. "Please, Tori, don't do this. Don't push me away."

Tori squeezed her eyes shut and held Sam tightly to her. "It's not because I'm a woman that you're not ready, Sam. You know that. I won't do that to you."

Sam let her head fall back to Tori's chest. "I know." Then the tears came without warning, sobs that shook her. She clutched at Tori.

"Talk to me. Please," Tori whispered in her ear. "Tell me what happened."

Sam cried harder. "They hurt me. They . . . hurt me," she cried.

"I know, sweetheart." Tori cradled Sam to her, rocking her in her arms. "Tell me how they hurt you."

"I tried to fight them, Tori, I did. I screamed and I begged and I cried. But they wouldn't stop . . . they just wouldn't stop. And the rest, they just . . . watched. And laughed." She cried as she'd never cried before, nearly wailing as Tori held her. "They wouldn't stop. They tied me to the bed and took my clothes off . . . I was so help-less."

Tori's heart was breaking as Sam wept. Her own tears streamed down her face, and she gathered Sam more firmly against her.

"I kept hoping that you would come for me," Sam whispered. "I tried not to think about how they'd hurt you, how they . . . dumped you in the lake. But I was so afraid. I was afraid that you were dead," she cried. "And there was nothing I could do. So I just closed everything out. I was back on your boat, it was sunny and warm. You were fishing. You looked so relaxed. You looked so happy. That's all I thought about. I didn't feel them anymore. I wasn't there. I was with you."

"I'm so sorry," Tori said softly. "I'm sorry I wasn't there for you. I'm sorry I didn't find you sooner."

"No. It's not your fault. And you were there for me, Tori. Only you. I never gave a thought to anyone else. Not Robert, not Amy . . . just you. Somehow, I knew you would come for me."

It was Tori's turn to cry and Sam pulled Tori to her, wiping at the tears on her face. "Don't cry. Please. Don't cry." For some reason, Sam didn't want Tori to ever cry again. She'd had so much pain in her life and so little love. Sam couldn't stand for her to cry.

They lay quietly together, still wrapped in each other's arms. No more words were spoken. They fell asleep listening to each other's heartbeat.

# Chapter Thirty-five

Tori knocked, then waited, looking quickly at Sam. Her eyes were still puffy, but she looked better than she had earlier. Last night had been so hard, but she knew that Sam needed to get it out. She knew that Sam had not cried before. Had not really accepted what had happened to her.

"You okay?"

Sam smiled. "For the third time, yes." Then she reached out and squeezed Tori's arm. "Thank you. And we haven't really talked about . . . what else happened."

"I know."

The door opened and Belle greeted them.

"Good morning, Detectives. Please tell me you're not here with more bad news."

"No." Tori held up a piece of paper. "We have a warrant. We're going to need all your records on current and past residents," Tori said.

"You didn't need a warrant, Detective Hunter. I would have gladly given you anything. I want this to stop as much as you do."

"I know. It's just procedure."

"Come in. You know where the office is."

Tori and Sam followed the older woman inside. It was early and quiet. Either the residents of the hostel weren't up yet or they hadn't spent last night there. Belle opened the door to the office and motioned for Tori and Sam to enter.

"I was just about to get coffee. Would you like some?"

"That would be nice, thank you," Sam said.

"I'll be right back."

Tori walked to the file cabinet and opened a drawer, leafing through the files inside, stopping when she came to Julie Barnes.

Sam walked around the room, glancing at the pictures on the shelves, many of young women posing with Belle. She recognized Rachel Anderson in one. She picked it up, her brows drawn as she remembered the young girl who was left in a Dumpster. When she moved to put it back, she saw another photo on the shelf. A photo of a young man, probably a high school picture. She picked it up and stared.

"Tori."

"Hmm?"

"Look at this," she said. She held the framed photo to Tori.

"Shit," Tori murmured. "It's him."

Sam quickly put the photo back as Belle approached.

"Here you go," Belle said, carrying a tray with three cups, along with sugar and cream. She set the tray on her desk, then offered a cup to Sam.

"I never noticed all your pictures before, Belle," Sam said. "They must go back quite a ways."

"Yes. Over the years, so many young girls have come to stay here. I watched them grow up and then leave. These are some of my favorites."

"You have one of a young man here," Tori said. "Did he stay with you?"

252

"Oh, you mean Ricky. No, that's my son."

"Your son? I didn't know you had children," Tori said casually as she took the cup of coffee Sam offered.

"Just the one." Belle sat down and smiled, looking at the photo on the shelf. "When I was your age, it wasn't quite as easy to be gay as it is today," she said. "My family was having a very hard time with it, in fact. I was thirty and at a crossroads. I thought if I had a child, my family would accept me, would accept him. And they did. For a while. But then I met someone. A woman. And none of it mattered to them. I was still a lesbian." She sighed. "But I had Ricky. He was a good kid."

"Where is he now?" Sam asked.

"Oh, he's in college. Oklahoma."

Tori smiled. "That must be hard. Living in Texas and having a son that's a Sooner?"

"Oh, no. Now that wouldn't be allowed. He's at Oklahoma State. That I can tolerate."

Tori glanced at Sam, then moved to the file cabinets. "Well, we shouldn't keep you. I want to take your current files with us. We'll send someone over to get the rest."

"I'll help in any way I can, Detective Hunter, you know that."


"Her son? Are you sure it's the same guy?"

"We're sure, Lieutenant."

"Then maybe she's in on it," Malone said.

"No way," Tori said. "These are her girls. She loves them as her own."

"Okay. Sikes, get on the phone to Oklahoma State. Find out if he's still there. Ramirez, call the PD up there in Stillwater. See if they have any murders similar to ours. If it's him, maybe he's done it before."

"He has to be living here now," Tori said. "We saw him on a Wednesday."

"Why wouldn't Belle know if he was living here?"

"Maybe he doesn't want her to know," Sam said.

"And you're positive it's the same guy?"

"Positive."

"Well, it's all we've got. Let's pull the whole team in on this one. Get Adams and Donaldson up to speed."

Tori was about to protest, but Sam nodded. "I'll brief them."

"Hunter," Malone called as they were about to walk out. "A word."

She sat back down, looking at him expectantly.

"Is she okay to be here? It's only been four days."

"She was cleared, Stan."

"I know. I'm asking your opinion," he said.

"She'll be fine."

He nodded. "Are you still staying with her?"

Tori hesitated, then nodded.

"You're doing a good thing, Tori. Taking her under your wing like you have. That first week, I didn't know if she could take it, you know."

Tori nodded. If he only knew, she thought.

"You watch her, okay?"

"Don't worry. I'll take care of her."

Sam was standing beside Adams and Donaldson, file in her hand as she went over the events of the last two months. Donaldson was taking notes and even Adams appeared to be listening. They all liked Sam, Tori knew. How could they not? At first, they steered clear of her simply because she was Tori's partner. But it was hard to resist that friendly smile and those green eyes. God knew Tori had tried. And last night, she had failed.

She sat down, her eyes again going to Sam. Her hands moved as she talked and both Adams and Donaldson watched her intently. Sam was dressed nearly identical to Tori today. Jeans with a long-sleeved shirt tucked in. Brown leather boots took the place of Tori's sneakers, and Sam had a soft blue blazer over her shirt. She moved the blazer now and tucked both hands in her pockets. Tori's eyes lighted where her shirt was pulled tight across her breasts.

254

Then she closed her eyes, remembering Sam's hand as she'd cupped Tori's breast last night. They had been so close.

And this morning, they had both been shy as they showered and dressed, neither discussing the events of last night. In fact, they both acted as if it didn't happen. As if they hadn't been kissing and touching and on the verge of making love.

"Hey, you daydreaming?"

Tori looked up, right into the green eyes she had been thinking of. Then Sam's eyes darkened and Tori knew that Sam was remembering last night, too.

"Yes, I was."

Sam sat down, still holding Tori's eyes captive. "Should we talk about it?" she asked quietly.

"No. I'm afraid to talk about it," Tori admitted. "Should I say I'm sorry?"

Sam raised her eyebrows. "Are you sorry?"

"No." Then she smiled. "Should I be?"

Sam leaned forward. "Maybe I should say I'm sorry. I started it. I'm the one who wanted . . . to make love last night," she whispered.

"I wanted that, too. But . . ."

Sikes slammed his phone down and walked over. "You're not going to believe this. Richard Grayson hasn't been enrolled at OSU in two semesters. Last known address is listed here, at Belle's."

Malone walked out of his office. "Ramirez? You got anything?"

He was still on the phone, and he shook his head.

"Okay. Hunter? How do you want to play this? You want to bring in Belle Grayson and question her?"

"No. We don't really have anything. Other than the fact he was seen at the bar watching Julie."

"Besides, if Belle does know anything, she may tip off her son," Sam said.

"What about getting a court order for DNA?" Sikes suggested.

"On what grounds?" Malone asked. "No. We've got to get more."

"It's Wednesday. Let's do the bar again. Maybe he'll show."

Malone nodded. "Okay. But I want two groups inside. Sikes, you and Ramirez just got married."

"No way. I'm not doing it," Sikes said. "I can't."

"And why not? Half the department thinks you're gay, anyway."

His eyes widened. "What the hell are you talking about?"

"I told you, it's the way you dress," Sam said.

"What's wrong with the way I dress?"

"You're all coordinated, pressed, starched. You never wear anything out of season."

"So I have a fashion sense—that makes me gay? Should I dress like Hunter here? Jeans and sneakers?"

"You'd rather dress like a lesbian than a gay man?" Tori asked with a smile.

"Bite me. I'm not doing it."

"You *are* doing it," Malone said. "Adams, Donaldson, you'll be out front in the car."

"We go in separately," Hunter said. "No contact once we're inside. We find our guy, we watch him. When he leaves, we follow. Even if he goes to another bar, we follow. We've got to find out where he lives," she said.

"If we get an address, I'll call the DA and see about getting a warrant for a search," Malone said.

"We need to be inside by nine," Tori said. "Let's meet back here no later than eight."

"You owe me big for this, Hunter," Sikes said.

"John, wear black slacks and a tight black T-shirt. You'll look more like you're cruising that way," Sam said. "We don't want our guy getting nervous if you're watching him. Tony? You don't really look the part. Sorry. What are you going to wear?"

"I know what to wear. Don't worry."

"And how do you know what gay guys look like when they're cruising?" Tori asked when they were alone.

Sam shrugged. "I'm not quite as innocent as I appear, Detective Hunter."

"Is that right? And what do women wear when they're cruising?"

Sam smiled. "I don't know. I won't be cruising. I already have a date."

Their eyes met, and Tori felt her heart catch at Sam's teasing words. "Yes, you do."

Sam pushed away from her desk. "I better go home and change. What about you?"

"Yeah. I'll swing by my apartment and see what's left. I can't remember the last time I did laundry."

"You can always do it at my place," Sam offered.

"I may take you up on that."

"You want to get dinner? Or I can pick up some burgers and bring them back here."

"That's probably better." Tori hesitated. "Will you be okay? Do you want me to go with you?"

Sam shook her head. "I'll be okay. I need to do this."

"Okay. Then I'll meet you back here."

"See you soon."

Sam turned, then paused, her eyes finding Tori's again. What she saw in Tori's eyes in that brief glance caused her heart to race.

# Chapter Thirty-six

Tori watched Sam walk into the squad room, and her heart stopped. She looked stunning. Tight-fitting jeans and black boots, snug shirt tucked inside, black belt. Tori's eyes stopped at her breasts, watching her nipples as they strained against the fabric.

"You're staring," Sam said lightly. "I guess I pass."

Tori blushed. "Sorry. You look . . . great," she murmured.

"So do you. As always."

Tori blushed again, then cleared her throat. "What you got there?"

"Burgers. No onions."

"No onions?"

Sam smiled. "No onions." She handed Tori one and sat down at her desk. "Heard from the guys?"

"No. I wouldn't be a bit surprised if Sikes chickened out," Tori said. "Mmm," she murmured as she took a bite. They had missed lunch again.

"He'll show. I think he's secretly intrigued by the whole thing.

I wouldn't put it past him to try to pick up some guy, just to see if he could," Sam said.

"You know, he's so homophobic, almost too much. You don't suppose he's been suppressing it, do you?"

Sam laughed. "If he heard you say that, he would just die."

"Say what?" Sikes asked as he and Ramirez walked in.

Tori was speechless. John Sikes was the poster child of gay men. Black slacks, tight black T-shirt, both of which were pressed. Cell phone clipped neatly to his belt. He looked . . . handsome.

"Well?" He spread his arms. "Do I pass?"

"John, you look great," Sam said. Then she looked at Tony. "Damn, where'd you get the duds?"

"My cousin." Tony grinned. "He gave me pointers." Then he walked over. "Smell me. He said I'd have to beat them off."

Tori and Sam laughed. Even Sikes loosened up and joined in.

"If you guys go home with anybody tonight, you're both fired," Tori teased. "We're working, don't forget that."

"As if," John said. "If anyone asks me to dance, I might very well deck them."

"Sikes, you've got to fit in. Please don't cause a scene," Tori warned. "Maybe you and Ramirez could get out and dance, huh?"

"Fast songs," Sam added at John's panicked look.

Sikes pointed his finger at them all. "If you tell *anyone* about what happens tonight, I'll make your life hell," he threatened.

"Like you don't already," Tori drawled, drawing laughs from the others.

"What's so funny?" Donaldson asked as he walked in.

"Nothing," Sikes said. "Where's Adams?"

"He's waiting out front. Are we ready?"

Tori stood, grabbing the photo of Richard Grayson they'd had faxed over from OSU. "Here. Make sure Adams takes a look at this. Everybody's got their cell, right? Donaldson, you guys park across the street. Sam and I'll be in my Explorer. Sikes, you taking your car?"

"Yeah." Then he looked at Tony. "That okay?"

"Sure."

"Okay. Sam and I will go in first. You guys wait about fifteen minutes, then come in. We'll try and get a table. You sit at the bar. Remember, no contact. We see our guy, we watch. If he shows, he might not stay long. I doubt any of Belle's girls will show up. They're all pretty spooked by all this. If there is no one there, he might just split."

"And if he leaves, we're to follow?" Donaldson asked.

"Yes. But we'll be right behind you. We can't lose him." She looked at them all. "Any questions?" She glanced at Sam. "Okay, let's roll."


Tori and Sam sat quietly, watching the entrance. Sam glanced at her watch. It was almost nine.

"About time," she said.

"Yes." Then Tori leaned back, glancing at Sam. "You okay?"

"I'm fine." Then she shrugged. "Maybe a little nervous. But you'll be there. I'm not worried about anything."

"Yes, I'll be there."

"I'm more worried about dancing with you, actually," Sam admitted.

"Why is that?"

"You know very well why. Wouldn't Sikes get a kick out of that," she said.

"Don't worry about them. We're working. It's all just an act," Tori said.

"Is it? Is that all it is?"

Tori reached over and took Sam's hand, letting their fingers entwine. "That's all they need to know, Sam. Whatever is happening between us, it's just between us."

Sam nodded and squeezed her hand. "Tori, I wanted to thank you for last night," Sam said quietly. "It was the first time I'd . . . let it out. I had been suppressing everything. I told everyone I was fine, that it hadn't really affected me. But it did."

"I know, sweetheart," Tori whispered.

"It's something I'll never forget, something that will always be at the back of my mind." Sam cleared her throat. "I was *raped*."

Tori sat silently, her fingers still entwined with Sam's.

"I feel better today, though. Every day is a little better, you know."

"I know."

Sam paused. "We haven't . . . talked about . . . what else happened," she said vaguely.

"Yes. But we don't have to talk about it, Sam. It's just . . . there."

Sam nodded. "Have I told you that you're the best partner anyone could have?"

Tori grinned. "You even had it engraved. But I think there are several men that might disagree with you."

Sam touched Tori's bracelet, running her fingers over the smooth surface. "I meant it then. I certainly mean it now."

"Thank you. But I happen to think that you hold that title," Tori said softly.

"Maybe we're just good together."

"Maybe so." Then she squeezed Sam's hand. "Come on. Let's go inside."

The music was loud as soon as the door opened, and Sam reached for Tori's hand, following her inside. She was a little nervous, she admitted. It was the first time she'd been around this many people since . . . well, since it happened. But Tori wouldn't let anything happen to her, she knew that. They walked into the bar. It wasn't crowded yet, and they found a table easily.

"Stay here," Tori said. "I'll get us a beer."

Sam nodded, watching her walk away. She scanned the crowd, looking for familiar faces. She found none. But it was still early. Then Tori came back, motioning behind her. "Annette is here. She must have come early."

"Where?"

"She was at the bar. Her girlfriend was buying them drinks."

"Why the hell would she come here? Surely she knows what's going on?"

"Yes. Belle said she talked with all of them."

"I don't understand, Tori. Why would they put themselves in danger?"

"She's young. They all are. I doubt they think anything could happen to them." Then Tori glanced at the door. "Sikes and Ramirez just walked in." She smiled. "Sikes looks like he's scared to death."

"I know this is awful, but I really hope someone hits on him," Sam said with a laugh. "That would be priceless."

Tori watched as they made their way to the bar, then looked back at Sam. "We've got some time. You want to dance?"

"Dance?"

Tori blushed slightly. "It's a totally selfish request," she admitted quietly.

"I would love to dance with you."

Tori stood and held out her hand, which Sam took immediately. She led her to the dance floor, then released her, letting the music wash over her. Sam moved around her, grabbing her waist as she twirled around her. Tori grinned, her body moving with the music and Sam. For a moment, she forgot about the case. It was just the two of them. Their eyes held as they moved around each other, lightly touching. Then the music changed, slower now, and Sam moved into her arms, wrapping her own around Tori's neck. Tori pulled her close, fitting Sam's body against her own. Memories from last night crowded in, as she knew they would, and her body responded immediately to the woman she held against her.

Sam brought her mouth to Tori's ear. "I wish we weren't working," she whispered. "I wish this was for real."

Tori tightened her arms around Sam. "This is for real."

Their bodies moved together, like a magnet, and Sam heard Tori moan. She closed her eyes, her lips moving along Tori's cheek until she found her mouth. It was a hungry kiss, and Sam groaned as Tori's tongue found its way into her mouth. Her legs nearly gave way, and she clutched Tori tighter, her hips pressing tightly against Tori's.

"Oh, God, Sam," Tori whispered. "You don't know how much I want you."

Sam wanted to disagree. She knew exactly how much Tori wanted her, and if it was even half as much as Sam's want, they were

262

going to be in for a very long night. Sam brought her mouth back to Tori's, moaning as Tori pulled her tightly against her breasts. She felt Tori's hand slid up her side, resting just beneath her breast.

"I swear to God, if you touch me now, I'll not be responsible for my actions," Sam warned.

"I can't help it," Tori murmured against her lips. She moved her hand between them, cupping Sam's breast.

"God, why aren't we alone?" Sam whispered as her body moved against Tori. She felt Tori's fingers caress her nipple and she moaned, feeling the heat spread down her body. Her hips jerked instinctively, moving against Tori. She felt moisture between her thighs, and, for a moment, she lost all sense of reality. In the dim light of the dance floor, her mouth found Tori's again. She kissed her hard, hearing Tori's quiet moan as she slipped her tongue inside Tori's mouth. The hand on her breast tightened, and she moved into it. At that moment, she wanted nothing more than to take that hand and slip it between her thighs.

Tori finally loosened her grip on Sam, slipping away from her breast, her eyes wild as she looked into Sam's. "I'm sorry. God, I'm sorry." She pushed Sam farther away from her, trying to regain her focus. They were working, for God's sake.

Sam took deep breaths, trying in vain to control the desire that was surging through her. "You're dangerous, Detective," she murmured. She glanced past Tori's shoulder, praying that Sikes and Ramirez had not seen them. How would they ever explain this?

The music faded, only to be replaced with another fast song, and Tori stopped, taking Sam's trembling hand and leading her back to their table. They sat back down, both trying to read the other's eyes.

Tori finally looked away. "I was out of line," she said. "I'm so sorry."

Sam leaned her elbows on the table. "Tori, you must know how much I want you. If last night didn't tell you anything, then that dance must have."

"Why, Sam?"

"Why?"

Tori looked away. This wasn't the time. They were working. But Sam took her hand, pulling her back toward her.

"Why what?" Sam asked.

"Why me? Why now? You've been with Robert for a while," Tori said. "Why now?"

Sam released Tori's hand and looked away. She didn't have an answer. Why Tori? Why now? God, she had asked herself that question a thousand times.

"I don't know," she answered honestly. "Don't you think I've asked myself that same question? I'm not in love with Robert. And before him, there was never anyone serious. When I'm with you . . . when I'm near you, I feel all the things that I ever imagined I'd feel. I don't know *why*, Tori."

"Sam, don't do this if you're not sure. Please don't do that to me."

"I don't ever want to hurt you, Tori. Not ever." Sam reached across the table and took Tori's hand again. "Please don't hurt *me*."

Tori didn't know what to say. She wished, oh, she wished that they could have some time together. But they didn't. Not now. She released Sam's hand and reached for her beer, looking around. Sikes and Ramirez were still sitting at the bar, staring at two women kissing. She shook her head.

"Tori."

"Hmm?"

"It's him."

"Where?"

"Behind you, walking around the back side of the dance floor."

"Come on." She stood, taking Sam's hand and leading her to the floor. They faded into the crowd, turning until they found him. He walked toward the back, leaning against the wall, watching.

Tori pulled Sam against her, speaking into her ear. "He's watching Annette."

Sam nodded, moving away from Tori again. They waited until the song ended, then casually walked back to their table. Richard Grayson had not moved.

264

Tori pulled out her cell phone, keeping one eye on their guy. "Sikes, he's here."

"Where?"

"Far corner across from the bar. Blue shirt. He's leaning against the wall."

"Got him."

Tori put her phone away, then looked at Sam. "Are you okay?"

"I'm fine. My body is still on fire, but I'm fine."

Tori smiled. "Mine, too."

"Good. I'd hate to be the only one in this condition."

Tori leaned back, her eyes moving over Sam, resting at her breasts for a moment. She could still feel Sam's nipple against her fingers. Her tongue came out and wet her suddenly dry lips. In her mind, she could imagine taking Sam's shirt off, imagine her hands moving over soft flesh, imagine her mouth at Sam's breast.

"Detective, if you don't stop looking at me that way, I might very well come across this table and do something that will embarrass us both."

Their eyes met, and Sam nearly melted from the fire she saw in Tori's dark eyes. She didn't know how they were going to make it through the rest of the night. Right now, right this minute, all she wanted was Tori's hands on her. And if that meant out on the dance floor for anyone to see, she no longer cared.

"I'm thinking we should stick to fast songs," Tori said with a smile.

"You may be right."

And they did. Occasionally. Mostly, they sat and talked and watched Richard Grayson. He moved from the wall only once, to make a quick trip to the bar. He talked to no one. He only stood and watched Annette Tippet.

Finally, at nearly midnight, he left. Sam called Donaldson immediately.

"We see him. He's walking north."

"If he gets in a car, run the plates," she said. "We're right behind you." She looked at Sam. "Go tell Sikes. I'm going to call

Sergeant Reynolds and get a unit over here to follow Annette home."

"If he stays in much longer, we're going to have to send Sikes and Ramirez in," Tori said.

They were parked a block away from a men's bathhouse. Grayson had entered alone nearly an hour before. He hadn't been seen since.

"In fact, I think that's a good idea. What if he saw us tail him? He may have slipped out the back," Tori said.

"His car is still here," Sam said. "Do you really think Sikes could pull it off in there? I mean, I'm only speculating, but I can imagine what is going on in that place."

Tori laughed. "You're right. Sikes would pull his weapon and pop the first person who touched him."

Sam grabbed her arm. "There. He's coming out."

Tori speed-dialed, and Sikes picked up.

"We got him," Sikes said. "Thank God. I just knew you would want us to go in after him."

"That was the plan, Sikes. Okay, don't lose him," she said. She waited until Grayson got in his car, then she pulled out onto the street. They followed him, staying several car lengths back until he reached a residential area. She slowed, allowing him to get ahead of them. There were no other cars on the street. Finally, he pulled into a duplex and she drove past, watching in the mirror as he went to the front door.

"This is only a few blocks from Belle's," Sam said.

"Yeah. I can't believe he's living here and Belle doesn't know."

"Do you think she does?"

"No. She didn't even blink when we asked about him." Tori slowed to a crawl, watching for Sikes in the mirror. "Why don't you give Reynolds a call, have him send some units out to watch Grayson tonight."

"Okay."

266

Tori parked on the street two blocks away and waited until Sikes pulled past her. She called him.

"You and Ramirez call it a night, Sikes. We'll hang out for a few minutes until we can get a couple of units to watch him overnight."

"Okay, Hunter. It's been a real pleasure playing with you girls tonight."

"Sorry you didn't get lucky, man," she teased.

"Oh, I don't know. I had a couple of phone numbers passed my way."

She laughed. "See you tomorrow, John." She disconnected, then dialed Donaldson. "Did you run the plates?"

"Yeah. Came back to Belle Grayson," he said.

"Okay. Call it a night. We'll see if we can get a warrant. Thanks, Donaldson."

Tori clipped the phone back on her waist, then glanced at Sam. "Reynolds?"

"He's sending two units, going to leave one at each end of the street."

Tori nodded. "Good." A pause. "You tired?"

"Yeah."

"Me, too." She pulled out on the street, driving slowly past the duplex. The lights were out. "There's one now," she said, pointing to the patrol car easing to a stop a block away.

Sam leaned back against the seat and closed her eyes. Then she reached blindly across the console and laid her hand on Tori's thigh. "Come home with me tonight?" she asked quietly.

"Are you sure?"

"Yes. I'm sure." She turned her head, meeting Tori's eyes for a brief second. "Please?"

With that one whispered word, Tori knew everything was about to change. They would crawl into Sam's bed together, and there would be no more barriers. Was she ready? Was Sam ready?

# Chapter Thirty-seven

Tori closed the door behind them, then stood nervously as Sam walked into the apartment.

"I feel like a shower," Sam said. "I smell like smoke."

"Okay." She stood rooted by the door.

Sam turned around, then walked back toward her. "Tori? It's late and we're both tired." She took Tori's hand and smiled. "Don't look so scared."

"Do I?" She smiled, too.

"Yes. Terrified. Now, go take a shower," Sam said, pulling Tori after her, then giving her a gentle push toward the bathroom.

As Sam stripped off her clothes, she nearly laughed. The look on Tori's face was pure terror. This strong, beautiful woman was afraid to make love to her. She was afraid of risking her heart. Sam met her own eyes in the mirror. Was she sure of this? Then she remembered their dance, the kisses that controlled them, the feel of Tori's hand at her breast. She touched her breast now, feeling her nipples against her palm, and nodded. Yes, she was sure. Robert—in fact, no man—had ever driven her so close to the edge with only a kiss. But Tori, oh God, Sam had wanted to forget they were in a public place and just finish what they had started. She wanted her touch. She wanted Tori's touch more than she'd ever wanted anything.

She pulled a T-shirt over her naked body and brushed at her damp hair. She had taken only a moment to blow-dry it. She met her own eyes again. Now who was scared?

Tori was already in bed when she walked out. But she wasn't asleep. Their eyes met and held. Sam took a deep breath, then moved to the bed. She turned off the lamp before pulling back the covers, then she slid between the sheets, her bare thigh lightly touching Tori's.

Tori wished she could say she was tired, but the blood pumping through her veins had her wide awake. She rolled her head slightly, watching the rapid rise and fall of Sam's chest. It matched her own. She could feel the heat radiating from Sam's body and she was drawn to it. She knew it was wise not to touch Sam, but she was powerless to stop her hand from moving between them, linking fingers with Sam. She felt the gentle squeeze. Then Sam turned on her side, facing Tori.

"If you don't kiss me soon, I will combust right here before your eyes," she whispered. She lifted her head, her mouth only inches from Tori's. "I want you to make love to me." She closed the distance, kissing Tori softly, lightly. Lips moved against lips, meltingly slow. She closed her eyes, hearing Tori's quiet moan. Then she felt Tori shift, felt the hand that slid up her thigh, resting at her hip. Tori pulled her closer until their bodies touched. Sam could stand it no longer. She opened her mouth, letting Tori inside. She groaned as Tori's tongue explored her mouth, and she met it with her own. Then Tori rolled over, leaning over Sam. One thigh slipped between Sam's legs and they opened for her. She pressed her hot center hard against Tori.

"Oh, God," Sam murmured. She pulled Tori tight against her,

feeling her weight as Tori settled on top of her. Her body had a mind of its own as it strove to touch Tori. Her hands moved over Tori's back, feeling muscles contract under her fingertips.

Then Tori's mouth was back, kissing her tenderly, sucking Sam's lower lip into her mouth. "You have no idea how much I want you," Tori whispered against her mouth.

"Yes, I have a very good idea."

"Please tell me if I hurt you."

"You won't hurt me."

Tori sat up, slowly pulling Sam's T-shirt over her head. She gasped as Sam's breasts were revealed to her in the dim light of the bedroom. She pulled her own shirt off, leaving both of them nearly naked. With a trembling hand, she reached out to touch Sam. Small breasts, but so responsive, her nipples hardened immediately at Tori's touch.

"So . . . beautiful," Tori breathed. Her fingers raked lightly across them, then she lowered her head, her tongue tracing the rigid peak, teasing, before taking it inside. Their moans mingled as Tori suckled her breast, feasting upon her.

Sam leaned her head back and closed her eyes, her mouth parting to draw breath. So gentle, so loving was Tori's touch. She thought she would be afraid the first time they made love. Afraid she wouldn't know how to respond, afraid she wouldn't know how to touch. But, God, it was the most natural thing in the world to have Tori's mouth on her. Her hands came out and burrowed into Tori's short hair, holding her firmly against her breast when Tori would have pulled away. At last she released Tori, pulling her back to her mouth, kissing her lips, memorizing them with her tongue.

Tori slid her hand along Sam's side, past her ribs to her waist. Her flesh was smooth, hot. She slipped under the waistband of her panties, moving over her hips. She heard Sam gasp, felt Sam's hips as they rose up.

"If you want me to stop, just say so," Tori whispered. "I don't want to hurt you," she said again.

"I may very well hurt *you* if you stop," Sam murmured.

Tori smiled as she peeled Sam's panties down her hips. The scent of her drifted to Tori and it was all she could do not to bury her head between Sam's thighs.

"Take yours off," Sam pleaded. "I want to feel your skin against me."

Tori did, laying her naked body on top of Sam, fitting between Sam's opened legs.

"I knew it would be like this with you," Sam whispered. "So soft. So gentle. I knew you would love me this way."

Tori groaned as their hips met, thrusting together. She lowered her head, capturing a breast with her mouth.

"God, I've dreamed of your mouth on me. I tried to imagine what it would feel like," Sam murmured, holding Tori tight to her breast.

"Did you imagine my mouth everywhere on you?"

"Yes," Sam hissed. Her legs opened wider as she felt Tori's hand move between them. Then gentle fingers moved through her wetness, sliding through her folds to touch her swollen clit. Her hips bucked and she groaned a low growl that came from deep in her chest. "Oh, Tori. *God* . . ."

Tori's patience faded the moment her fingers touched Sam. So wet, so ready. She had to have her mouth there. She moved lower, spreading Sam's legs. Her tongue replaced her fingers, entering Sam slowly. She heard the younger woman gasp, felt hands move through her hair. Her tongue licked at her, tasting her, then her lips closed over her clit, suckling it.

"*Jesus*," Sam whispered. Only in her most vivid dreams did she think it could be like this—gentle lovemaking that shook her to her very core. With fists clenched at her sides, head thrown back, she lost all control of her thoughts, her feelings. Her eyes squeezed closed as she felt her body respond to Tori, felt her orgasm build and build until she couldn't hold it, until she simply exploded with it. Her hips rose off the bed, pressing hard against Tori's mouth. But Tori didn't stop. Her tongue moved through her again, slipping inside her before circling her clit. Again her mouth closed

271

over her, sucking her hard. Sam trembled, shook uncontrollably as Tori took her over the edge again. She cried out, a primal scream that left her breathless, spent. She collapsed against the bed, her hands slipping away from Tori as she tried to catch her breath.

Tori kissed her lightly, moving across her legs, wetting a path over her stomach to her breasts, finally stopping when she reached her lips.

"Okay?"

"More than okay," Sam murmured as she tasted herself on Tori's lips. She gathered Tori in her arms and held her. "I knew it would be like that with you." Sam kissed her lightly, eyes still closed. "I want so badly to touch you, but I can't seem to move."

Tori lay back and pulled Sam into her arms, cradling her. "Rest. We've got plenty of time."

But Sam didn't answer. She was already asleep. Tori smiled, gently moving the hair off Sam's forehead. She was falling in love with her, and she was powerless to stop it. She bent her head, kissing her briefly. She felt Sam's arm tighten across her waist, and she closed her eyes.

So, this was what falling in love feels like. It was nice. But it was scary as hell.

# Chapter Thirty-eight

Sam opened her eyes, watching Tori as she slept. The soft light of dawn surrounded them, and the transformation was enormous. Tori looked almost like a child, so innocent, so peaceful. Sam shifted slowly, stretching her legs. She smiled and closed her eyes, allowing herself to relive the precious moments when Tori had made love to her. It was everything she thought it would be and so much more. Tori had been so incredibly gentle with her, she didn't think it possible. This strong, tough detective who had instilled such fear in her that first week, had made love to her in the most tender way possible.

"A teddy bear," she whispered.

She slid her hand under the covers, moving over smooth skin until she reached Tori's breast. Her hand curled around it, feeling the nipple harden against her palm. She circled it with her fingers, wondering how it would feel in her mouth. She closed her eyes. Tori had made love to her last night. Sam had not even touched Tori.

She slowly moved the covers off Tori, feeling the other woman stir but not wake. Her greedy eyes took in the beautiful sight before her. Perfect breasts greeted her. Her eyes moved over Tori's torso, so firm, yet soft. Then she glanced at her wound, noting absently that the stitches needed to come out. She bent her head, kissing lightly around the now-healed injury. Then she moved higher, finding the breasts that she had been dreaming of for weeks. Shyly, her tongue circled the hard nipple and she moaned, then closed her mouth over it, sucking it gently inside. She heard Tori's answering moan, felt her stir under her mouth, felt hands move into her hair. She slipped one thigh between Tori's legs and felt the other woman rise to meet it.

Pulling her mouth from Tori's breast, Sam met her smoky eyes. Then, without a word, Sam moved her hand across Tori's skin, lingering over her hip before slipping down between her legs. She heard Tori's quick intake of breath, saw her eyes close as Sam moved into her wetness. Her own eyes closed as fingers slid into the velvety warmth.

Gently reaching out, Tori covered Sam's hand, holding her firmly against her. Then her hips moved and she opened her legs. "Please, go inside me," Tori whispered.

Sam watched Tori's face as she slid two fingers inside her, and she groaned as she felt muscles contract against her fingers. So wet, so warm . . . so incredibly intimate.

She closed her eyes, moving again to kiss Tori when the phone made her jerk. "Oh, God, please not now," she murmured. "Not now."

Tori groaned, then pulled Sam's fingers from her. "It's okay. Answer it," she said quietly.

Sam reached over Tori for the phone, cradling it against her shoulder as her hands again went to Tori.

"Hello?"

"Kennedy? It's Malone."

Sam sat up, away from Tori. "Yes, sir?"

"I can't reach Hunter. Is she there?"

"Ah . . . yes, sir. She is." Sam glanced at Tori and grinned.

"Okay. I got the DA up at the crack of dawn. We should get a warrant first thing this morning. I know you had a late night, but I thought you'd want to get here early. I've been in contact with the two units watching the house. He's not left."

"Yes, sir. Okay, I'll tell her. We'll be in as soon as we can."

She disconnected, then tossed the phone on the bed. "Malone. We've got a warrant."

"Good," Tori said quietly. She sat up and ran her hands through her hair. Then she glanced at Sam. The sheet was bunched around her waist and Tori's eyes landed on her exposed breasts. Then she raised them, meeting Sam's emerald eyes. "I'm sorry."

"Why are you sorry?"

Tori shrugged. It seemed like the proper thing to say. It wasn't like she had a lot of experience in mornings after.

"I'm not sorry, Tori." Then she smiled. "Well, I'm sorry he interrupted just now." Sam moved closer, touching Tori's lips with her own. "But I'm not sorry for last night. I only wish we had time now. I so want to touch you, to make love to you."

"I don't know how I'm supposed to act this morning," Tori admitted.

"You don't have to act, Tori. Last night was just about us, remember?"

Tori was about to answer when the phone rang again. Sam snatched it up, frowning as she listened.

"I'm fine, Robert," she murmured. She glanced at Tori, saw the uncertainty on her face, in her eyes. Then she watched as Tori tossed the covers off of her naked body and walked from the room. *Damn.*

"I wanted to catch you before you left for work," he said. "Do you think we could have dinner tonight?"

She pulled her knees to her chest and closed her eyes. "No, Robert. Tonight is not good. I worked late last night, well, this morning, actually."

"We can do an early dinner," he offered.

"No, Robert. We can't. I'm tired." Then she sighed. "Please don't call me," she said quietly. "In a few weeks, maybe we can get together."

"Samantha, I just want to have dinner and visit. That's all."

"Fine. In a few weeks."

"Samantha, please . . ."

"No, Robert. I've got to go. A few weeks, okay?"

"No. I'll call you this weekend. I've got to see you."

"Whatever," she murmured and disconnected. She stared at the door, wanting to go to Tori. But there wasn't time. She flung the covers off and hurried into the shower. They would have to talk later.

Tori knocked loudly on the door and waited. Then she knocked again.

"Richard Grayson? Police," she called loudly. Still nothing. She nodded to the two uniforms standing beside her. "Break it," she said.

They walked into the dark house, weapons drawn. It was quiet inside. Too quiet. The living room held only one chair and a small table. Nothing else. No TV, no stereo. Tori glanced around the room. There were no pictures, no personal things. It was more stark than a motel room.

"You sure you got the right place?" one of the uniforms asked.

"We're sure. His car's outside," Sam said quietly.

"Check all the rooms. Let's secure it," Tori said. They moved slowly down the short hallway. The bedroom door was ajar and Tori slowly opened it with her foot, weapon held out in front as she entered. "Holy shit," she murmured.

A single mattress lay on the floor. Dirty sheets were bunched together and thrown on top. It smelled rank. Empty take-out containers littered the floor, weeks' worth, she suspected. But where the walls were bare in the rest of the house, these walls were covered with photos. Photos of young girls. Tori pointed at one and motioned for Sam.

276

"Rachel Anderson," Sam murmured. "There's Julie. Crystal."

Some were photographs snapped around the city as the girls went about their daily lives. Others, they recognized as copies from Belle's files.

"Detective? Take a look."

Tori turned, following Officer Spaten. Behind the door was a chart. Twenty-two names were listed. The first name on the list was Angie. A red line was drawn through it. Crystal followed. Then Rachel Anderson. Sue and then Julie Barnes. Annette was next.

"Sam. Call in a crime unit. We need to get all of this to the lab." She turned to Officer Spaten. "Secure the place."

"Yes, ma'am."

"Detectives? I think we found the murder scene," Officer Tate called from the laundry room.

They followed his voice, all peering through the door into the laundry room.

"Oh my God," Sam whispered.

The kitchen table was wedged into one corner. It was covered in dried blood, as was the floor.

"Jesus," he murmured. "Are those legs?"

"Don't fucking touch anything," Tori instructed. She turned again to Sam, who was ghostly white. "Call it in, Sam," she said again. Tori took out her own phone, calling Malone.

"He's not here. Are we sure Annette is safe?"

"They followed her to her girlfriend's. She's not left."

"Have them pick her up," Tori said. "He's got a . . . shrine here. There was a list of names. Annette is next. It's a fucking mess here."

"How the hell did he slip away?" Malone demanded.

"On foot, I guess. His car is still here."

"Okay. It's time you let Belle Grayson in on this."

"We'll go there now."

She folded her phone up, then looked at Sam. "Are you thinking what I'm thinking?"

"Belle's is only a few blocks from here," Sam agreed.

Tori raised her hand to knock, then Sam grabbed it, stopping her. "Maybe we shouldn't knock," she said quietly.

Tori raised her eyebrows.

"If he's here, do we really want to give him a chance to run?" she asked reasonably.

"We have no warrant," Tori reminded her. "What's our probable cause?"

"*Now* you decide to start following rules?"

"You're right. What was I thinking?"

But there was no need to break in. The door was unlocked. They crept in silently, then both pulled their weapons when they reached Belle's office door. It was ajar, the light on. Tori motioned Sam to one side of the door, then quickly pushed the door open.

Belle was tied to her chair, blood coming from her mouth, her lifeless eyes staring right at them.

"Oh God," Sam gasped. She would have rushed forward, but Tori put an arm out, stopping her.

"It's too late for her," she said quietly. "Let's secure the house."

Sam paled but nodded, then watched as Tori pulled her cell phone out and dialed, all the while scanning the room.

"Malone? Send a wagon and a crime unit. Belle's been hit. We're going to check the rest of the house."

"Wait for backup, Hunter."

They both looked up at the sound of boards creaking overhead and soft footsteps running.

"No time, Malone. I think he's still in the house."

"Goddammit, Hunter. Just this once, will you listen to me?"

"Tell them to hurry, Lieutenant." She disconnected, then grabbed Sam's arm. "Slow and careful," she said quietly.

Sam nodded and followed Tori up the stairs. The old boards shifted and moaned with their every step, making it impossible to sneak up to the second floor. Tori moved against the wall, eyes glued to the landing as she blindly crept up the staircase.

"Shhh," Sam hissed. She cocked her head, listening. Footsteps again. Tori nodded and motioned for Sam to follow. They stopped again as the screaming of door hinges echoed in the silent house. Tori pointed down the hall to the left. Sam nodded.

She swallowed with difficulty. Sam didn't mind admitting that she was scared. Her palms were sweaty, and her weapon seemed to weigh a ton in her hand. Her only comfort was that she'd insisted they both wear their vests today.

They stood at the landing, staring down the long hall. There were six rooms. Sam watched as Tori silently lay flat on her stomach, cheek pressed to the floor as she looked under each door. At the fourth door, she nodded. She pulled herself back up, motioning to Sam, who nodded.

Tori raised one finger, then two, then three. One powerful leg came out and kicked the door in. They entered, weapons swinging from side to side as screaming assailed them.

Wide, frantic eyes stared at them as the young girl crouched in the corner, a baseball bat held over her head. Tori lowered her weapon and held up her hand.

"Police . . . it's okay," she said. She pulled out her badge, showing it to the girl, who finally quieted, her screams turning to sobs as she let the bat fall beside her.

Sam went to her, gently taking her in her arms as they heard sirens approaching. Finally.

Tori watched them for a moment, again amazed at the compassion Sam could offer a complete stranger. Then she turned away and walked into the hall, her thumb already punching out a number on her cell phone.

"Yes, this is Detective Hunter. I need to speak with Charlotte Grayson." Tori closed her eyes. "It's urgent."

# Chapter Thirty-nine

"Will you hold still?"

"I'm used to doing this myself," Tori said. "You're going to hurt me."

"You are such a baby. You didn't whine this much when you got shot."

Tori looked in the mirror, watching Sam as she cut through the stitches at her waist. They should have been taken out days ago. She'd be lucky if it wasn't infected.

"I don't know why you won't just go to the doctor for this," Sam said. She pulled another one out and felt Tori jump. "I'm sorry. Did that hurt?"

"Yes," Tori hissed. Then she took a breath as Sam put her lips there, kissing her lightly.

"Better?"

Tori smiled. "You know, the nurses never do that."

"Well, you need better nurses, then."

Sam finished, dabbing at the scabs with peroxide from the first aid kit she'd taken from Sergeant Fisk again. The scar was red, but she didn't think it was infected. She pulled Tori's shirt down, just barely avoiding caressing her smooth skin.

Tori stood back. "Thanks."

"My pleasure. Now, what about these?" she asked, touching the wound on Tori's forehead.

"Not yet."

They stood facing each other, eyes locked.

"Do you . . . do you have plans tonight?" Tori finally asked.

"Plans?"

Tori looked away. "Well, I know Robert called this morning."

Ah. Robert. Sam was wondering when Tori would bring up the phone call. She watched the flicker of uncertainty cross Tori's face. For such a strong woman, she was sometimes so vulnerable.

"Actually, I did have plans," Sam said. "I was planning on inviting you out to an early dinner. Then afterward, I was hoping you'd come home with me."

"What about Robert?"

"What about him?" Sam moved closer, grasping Tori's arms. "Tori, I'd like to say that Robert called only to check on me. It's not true. He wants to see me. I don't want to see him. I don't feel anything for him, Tori. He doesn't really believe that, though. So, he keeps calling."

Tori looked into her eyes, trying desperately to read them. "I don't know what you want from me," Tori whispered.

Sam closed her eyes. God, this was not the time or place to have this conversation. "You want to talk about us *here*, Tori? In the ladies' room?"

"I just . . ."

"I know. Let's go home, okay? We'll talk there."

Home? Did she have a home? Sam's apartment was starting to feel that way. It scared her. For the first time in her life, she was wishing for something she had thought she'd never have. And she was frightened by that.

"Actually, I think I'll stay here. I haven't . . . worked out in forever," Tori said. "After today, I need it."

Sam tried to capture her eyes, but Tori looked away. "You want to go to the *gym*?"

"Yeah."

"I see." Sam took a step back, watching Tori. She caught a glimpse of sadness in her eyes before Tori hid it. "Well, you know what? No, you're not."

Tori looked up. "What?"

Sam walked up to her, stopping only when their bodies were nearly touching. "You're coming home with me. I'm not going to let you run from this. We're going to talk about it." Sam's voice softened. "Then I'm going to finish what I started this morning."

"Sam . . ."

"Don't run from this, Tori. Please."

"Don't . . . hurt me," Tori whispered.

"Sweetheart, I don't ever want to hurt you." She took her hand. "Come on. We need to be alone."

Tori nodded and followed Sam, releasing her hand as they walked back into the squad room.

# Chapter Forty

Sam locked the door behind them, then stood watching Tori. She had been mostly silent during the drive over, and Sam wondered what thoughts were running through her mind. One thing was for certain, she knew Tori wasn't used to talking about her feelings. She was so used to keeping everything inside, hidden from others, only dealing with it internally. Well, that was about to change.

"Shower?"

Tori nodded.

Sam smiled. "Want to share?" Sam took Tori's bag from her, then grabbed her hand with the other. "Come on. Don't be afraid." Sam shook her head. A few hours ago, Tori was so strong and in control, leading them fearlessly up the stairs to God knew what. Now, she nearly trembled with fear.

Tori stood by mutely as Sam undressed. She watched each piece of clothing fall from her body and she stared, only dimly aware that she wasn't breathing.

"Need some help?" Sam asked.

"Hmm?"

"With your clothes?"

"Oh, sorry," Tori murmured. She quickly undressed, then stepped into the shower with Sam. Soapy hands came to her, moving over her skin, teasing her. She stood still as Sam washed her, their eyes meeting in the warm mist. She was afraid, but the desire in Sam's eyes was enough to smother that fear. She stepped closer, pulling Sam to her. Their wet bodies slid together. Tori lowered her head, finding Sam's mouth. Their kiss was slow, gentle, unhurried. Then Sam pulled away and shoved the bar of soap into her hands.

Tori rubbed the soap lightly across Sam's breasts, watching in fascination as her nipples hardened. She saw Sam's chest rise and fall with each increasing breath, then slipped her hands lower. She heard the soft moan as she moved between Sam's legs, and the soap fell from her hands. Whatever emotions were warring within her, desire won. She gripped Sam's hips hard and pulled her flush against her own body. Their kiss was no longer gentle. Hungry mouths fought for control, and she moaned as Sam slipped her tongue inside her mouth. Under the spray of water they stood, kissing and touching until they were out of breath.

"Make love to me," Sam pleaded. Her body was on fire and she pulled Tori's hand to her, pressing it firmly against her. "Please . . . make love to me."

Tori's hand trembled as she reached around Sam and turned the water off. Without a word, she led Sam from the shower, wrapping a thick towel around her. They dried each other, their eyes meeting often. It was Sam who led them into the bedroom, Sam who lay down and pulled Tori with her. She groaned as Tori's weight settled over her. Their mouths met again, slower now.

Sam moved her hands between them, cupping both of Tori's breasts, urging her up higher. Tori lifted, offering her breasts to Sam. Sam moaned as her mouth closed around her nipple. She felt Tori straddle her thigh, felt her wetness as she moved against her.

Tori was throbbing, on the verge of exploding just from the gentle pressure of Sam's mouth at her breast. She moved against Sam's thigh, wanting release. Then Sam's hand found her, and she groaned. Her legs opened wider, and she sought Sam's fingers, grinding hard against them.

"No," Sam whispered.

"No?" Tori bent down and captured Sam's mouth, her tongue tracing her lips. "Yes."

"Not yet. Not like this." She pulled her hand away, ignoring Tori's protest. She rolled them over, fitting between Tori's legs as her mouth went back to Tori's breast.

"Sam, please," Tori begged. "I'm dying." She grabbed Sam's hips and pulled her hard against her, her own lifting off the bed to meet her.

"Oh, God . . . you're not making this easy," Sam murmured as her hips undulated against Tori's. She wanted to let go, to give Tori the release she craved. But not like this. She pulled away, finding Tori's mouth. "I want to make love to you," she whispered. "I want to know what it's like. I want to know how you taste. I want my mouth on you . . . I want my tongue inside you."

Tori closed her eyes and groaned. God, she was so close. One touch and she'd be gone. She gasped as she felt Sam move down her body, felt her tongue as it traced a wet path across her breasts and stomach. Not once, in all her life, had she wanted someone to make love to her the way she now wanted Sam . . . wanted Sam's mouth on her.

Sam trembled as she spread Tori's legs apart. She wanted so badly to please Tori, to bring her to the heights that she had experienced last night. It was with a hungry mouth that she found Tori, wet and ready for her. She let instinct take over as her tongue moved through her wetness and she moaned at the first taste of her. Tori's hips bucked against her face and she held them down, slipping her tongue deep inside her.

"Sam . . . *God*," Tori moaned.

Sam's tongue licked at her, finally settling over her swollen clit

285

and sucking it hard into her mouth. She heard Tori scream, felt her press up, felt the hands that gripped her head so firmly. Against her tongue, she felt Tori throb, nearly felt the explosion that penetrated Tori's body. She shuddered, trembled under her. Sam refused to stop. She'd not had nearly enough. She suckled her, feeling Tori respond again, feeling her wetness as it coated her face, her cheeks. Then Tori's hips rocked against her mouth, faster. Sam groaned as she felt Tori's thighs tighten around her head, then Tori lifted them both off the bed as another orgasm shook her.

Sam finally released her, and she rested her face against Tori's flat stomach. Never had she experienced something so . . . intimate. She closed her eyes as she felt Tori's hand lightly brushing at her hair. She kissed Tori's stomach lightly, then raised her head. Tori's eyes were closed, then they opened, meeting hers. Sam frowned at the misting of tears there.

"What's wrong?" She crawled up beside Tori, touching her face. "Why do you look so sad?" she whispered.

"I'm scared," Tori admitted.

Their eyes locked and Sam understood. Tori was afraid to love, afraid of being left behind again.

"Oh, no . . . no. Don't be scared," Sam said softly. She ran her hands through Tori's short hair, smoothing it. Then she wrapped her arms around Tori and held her. "I've been waiting . . . my whole life, it seems like . . . to feel . . . this connection that I feel with you. Oh, Tori, I look into your eyes and I see such strength, such passion . . . oh, God, and such sadness sometimes." She cupped Tori's face and forced her to look at her. "But mostly, I see . . . I see love. When you look at me, I want you to see that, too. I want you to believe that."

Tori stared into her eyes, feeling tears gather before she could stop them. She tried to look away, but Sam held her.

"Oh, sweetheart, it's okay to cry."

Tori felt a lifetime of heartache melting away. She looked into Sam's eyes and she so wanted to believe her.

"Why won't you tell me how you feel?"

Tori lowered her eyes. "I'm not . . . I'm not good at this," Tori admitted. "I don't know how."

Sam nodded. "Okay." She wouldn't push. Tori was obviously uncomfortable, as Sam knew she would be. But, now, Sam was the one scared by what she was feeling. What if Tori wasn't ready for this? What if Tori didn't want this?

Tori saw a flash of hurt cross Sam's face that she tried to hide. When Sam would have pulled away, Tori stopped her. "I . . . feel . . ."

"Tell me, Tori."

"I feel safe with you. But I'm scared to death," she whispered.

Sam's eyes softened as she stared into Tori's. Her sweet Tori, so scared of what she felt. Sam reached for Tori's hand and brought it to her lips, kissing it softly.

"I won't hurt you. You know that, don't you?"

Tori bent her head to her chest and did something she hadn't done since she was twelve. She cried. She buried her face against Sam as she felt arms go around her and hold her.

Sam felt her heart breaking at the sobs that came from Tori. For years and years, this woman had been alone, with no one to love her. Sam felt her own tears escape her eyes. This proud woman trusted her enough to let go. Sam's arms tightened, vowing silently that she would never, ever hurt her—no matter what.

It was a long time later before they recovered enough to get out of bed and dress. Tori opened the wine and sat quietly at the table while Sam fixed them something to eat. Sam glanced at her often, seeing the thoughtful expression on her face. She wondered again what Tori was thinking. Then she stopped what she was doing and walked over, bending to kiss Tori lightly on the lips.

"Please trust me, okay?"

"I do."

# Chapter Forty-one

"How well do you know him?"

Charlotte Grayson shook her head, eyes moving from Tori to Sam and back again. She folded her hands together nervously.

"I've known him since he was a baby," she said quietly. "I was only fifteen when he was born. He was always quiet, withdrawn." Then she looked up with tear-filled eyes. "I just can't believe he killed his own mother," she whispered.

Tori shifted uncomfortably. She watched as Sam reached out a hand and lightly touched Charlotte's arm.

"We know this is hard, Ms. Grayson. But we've got to find him before he does this again."

"What about the hostel? What about the girls? It was . . . Belle's whole life," she cried.

"The girls are gone. Some left without a trace, others are staying with friends. Those that we know about, we're watching." Tori pulled out a chair and sat down. "The note he left next to Belle, it mentioned you. He seemed nearly as angry with you as he did his mother. Why?"

Charlotte shook her head. "I don't know. I rarely saw him, not since he went off to college. Belle and I were more like friends than cousins. We spent a lot of time together when he was younger, but I don't remember there being any problems. He was—like I said, quiet. He and Belle weren't extremely close. You would think that they would be, both ostracized by the family, but . . . there wasn't much affection between them."

"Belle seemed very proud of him," Sam said. "She told us a little about him once."

"Yes. She was just thankful he got into college. In high school, he was always in trouble. He was suspended at least once that I know of. She couldn't do anything with him."

"Did you know he was gay?" Tori asked.

"Gay? No, I didn't. Belle never said. But then, he never dated in school. In fact, I don't remember him having any friends, male or female."

"Maybe he was embarrassed about his mother and the hostel?" Sam suggested.

"I think he was jealous," Charlotte said. "Belle doted over the girls."

"Was she ever involved with any of them?"

"What? Belle? No. They were like her own children. She would have done anything for them."

"Something had to have triggered this," Tori said. She rubbed both eyes with one hand. They had nothing. He had simply disappeared.

"Is there a family member, perhaps, that he would have confided in?" Sam asked.

"Are you kidding? Her parents wouldn't give either of them the time of day."

"Cousins?"

"No. They had no contact with them."

Sam sat back and sighed, watching Tori as she continued to rub her eyes in frustration.

"Okay." Tori finally stood up. "Protective custody."

"For me? No way," Charlotte said.

"You don't have a choice. He threatened to kill you in the note."

"I don't give a shit. I have a very busy life, Detective. I don't need the police tagging after me everywhere I go."

"Like I said, you don't have a choice. Until we find him, you're not safe, Charlotte. You've been in the business long enough to know that."

Sam watched the exchange, eyes moving from one woman to the other. Then Charlotte smiled.

"Will you be assigned to protect me? I might be persuaded, if that's the case."

Tori lifted one corner of her mouth but shook her head. "Uniforms. Two shifts. One at the office, one at the house."

"And what if I decide to go to the bar?"

"Then Detective Kennedy and I might tag along."



"What did you get?"

"Nothing."

"Nothing? You were in there over an hour," Malone said, his voice rising.

"And we still got nothing."

"Hunter, the goddamn Mayor called me. He wants answers."

"I can't snap my fingers and miraculously produce him, now can I?"

"Have you read the paper?"

"I don't read the paper, and you damn well know it."

Sam was watching the exchange silently, as were the other detectives.

"We're getting dragged through the mud, Hunter. Six dead."

"Don't you think I know that? I've been at the scene of every one of them," Tori yelled. "I goddamn know every detail of their deaths. What do you want me to do?"

It was Sikes who intervened.

"Lieutenant Malone, Hunter—calm down. This is solving nothing. The Mayor can call all he wants, and the paper can write what they want, but we still have a job to do. Come on, guys." He spread his arms, a charming smile on his face. "Let's go over it all again and we'll solve it like any other case."

Sam hid a smile behind her hand. Oh, when had they turned into one big, happy family?

"I'm sorry, Hunter," Malone finally said. "It's just . . . the brass is coming down on me."

"They're coming down on you for appearance's sake. But this is personal for us."

"We'll get the bastard, Lieutenant," Sikes said. "If I have to stake out a damn men's bar, I will."

There was silence in the room as they all stared at Sikes. He looked around. "What?"

"You haven't been calling those phone numbers that got shoved at you the other night, have you?"

"Very funny, Hunter."

She laughed and walked up to him, playfully patting his cheek. "Thanks, John."

He nearly blushed and Sam smiled, walking over to him, too. "Thank you for stepping in there," she said quietly.

"Yeah. No problem."

Malone stared at his detectives. For the first time ever, they seemed to be a unit. Even Adams. Damn, who would have thought? Then his eyes slid to Kennedy as she walked up to Hunter. He saw the brief caress as Samantha touched Tori's back, watched as their eyes locked together.

"I'll be damned," he muttered. He cleared his throat. "Kennedy? A word?"

Sam looked at Malone and nodded, turning to meet Tori's eyes for a second. She closed the door behind her.

"What's up, Lieutenant?"

"Nothing. We haven't visited in a while now. Just checking on you."

"I'm fine."

"Everything okay since . . . you know."

"Yes, sir. I'm fine."

"You're sure you're okay? I know Hunter's been staying with you. That's probably put a crimp in your personal life. Not that I'm prying, but I know you've got a boyfriend," he said. "How's he handling all this?"

Sam leaned her head back and stared at the ceiling. *Yes, how was Robert handling all of this?* She took the easy way out. "He understands," she said.

"So he's okay with Tori staying with you?"

Sam looked at him. "What are you saying?"

"Well, it's no secret that Tori's . . . gay. I just, well, if it were me, I'm not sure how I would handle it," he admitted. "Not that I think Tori would ever . . . you know."

Sam smiled, then chuckled. It was all so comical. He was worried about Tori. He never once thought to be worried that Sam would be the one to cross over that line.

"Lieutenant, if you're worried about Tori, please put your mind at ease. We've become friends."

"Good . . . good. I had hoped that she might be able to let you in. She's let so few people get close to her. None that I know of, in fact." He leaned back and smiled. "What happened out there today, I never would have thought possible. Sikes taking up for Hunter. Wonders never cease."

"I think John has warmed up to her."

"Yes, you may be right." Then he leaned forward. "But I think you're responsible for that. Tori's changed. She's more human, if that's a good word to use. You've been very good for her, Kennedy. I hope you can make this partnership last."

"So do I, Lieutenant. So do I."


"Are you okay?"

Tori nodded but kept her eyes on the traffic.

"Everyone's a little stressed," Sam said vaguely.

At this, Tori smiled. "You think?"

"I can't believe Sikes. He surprised me."

"Yeah. I know what you mean."

"Tori, the Lieutenant didn't mean anything. It's not your fault."

"I know, Sam. Like you said, everyone's a little stressed out."

Sam sat back in her seat, still watching Tori. Lines of worry were etched across her face and Sam knew that a small part of Tori did blame herself. Sam wondered how she would be handling this if Sam wasn't around, if Sam hadn't come into her life. Would she be sleeping at all? Or would she be up at all hours, only snatching a few hours each night on the cot in the locker room? The cot, most likely. And this case would eat at her until Tori either solved it or—broke.

"What are you thinking?"

Sam looked up, unaware she had been staring. She reached over and captured Tori's hand. "I was thinking about you, actually."

Tori squeezed her fingers, then pulled Sam's hand into her lap. "I'm okay, Sam. Having you with me . . . it makes it . . . bearable."

Sam nodded. "You never asked what Malone said to me."

"Oh, yeah. What was that about?"

"He was just making sure I was okay. You know, with you staying with me and all."

"Oh?"

"He was making sure that I knew you were gay and . . ."

"And making sure I was behaving myself?"

"Something like that."

Tori smiled, but her mind was reeling. If Lieutenant Malone had any idea how far their relationship had escalated, he would put an end to their partnership immediately. And, of course, she understood the department's rules. But of all the partners she'd had, she trusted Sam completely to watch her back. And not just because they had become lovers. Sam was smart, and she wouldn't take unnecessary chances. There was no competition between them.

"What are you thinking?"

"I'm thinking we've got to be careful," Tori said.

"Careful?"

"About us. I kinda like you as a partner. I'd hate to be paired up with Adams and if Malone finds out, that's what'll happen. Or worse, he'll transfer you out."

"Because we're . . . lovers?"

"Yes."

Sam considered this, then squeezed Tori's hand. "I don't want another partner."

"Maybe I don't need to stay with you tonight," Tori said quietly. "I'm sure everyone's already wondering about that anyway."

But Sam shook her head. "If we have to take separate cars and both leave our cell phones by the bed, that's fine. But I'm not going to just steal a few moments here and there, Tori. God, I hope that's not what you want. I love having you in my bed. I love waking up with you," she said quietly.

Tori glanced at her briefly as she pulled up to the old red-brick school. Richard Grayson's former high school. She cut the engine, then sat silently staring ahead.

"I hate . . . I really hate having to hide this, Sam," she whispered. "We've just got to be careful."

"I can be careful."

"Okay. Let's just see what happens. You may be begging me to stay at my own apartment before long anyway."

"You don't really believe that?"

"I don't want to believe that, no."

"Because I . . ." *Because I love you*, she longed to say. "Because that will never happen, Tori."

Tori sighed, then squeezed Sam's hand one more time. "Come on. Let's go see what we can dig up. Maybe there's some juicy details in Grayson's records."

The bell sounded just as they opened the doors and students materialized in droves, all talking at once. They sidestepped the crowd, making their way to the offices. The noise was only slightly less deafening in there.

"May I help you?" the receptionist asked.

Tori held out her badge. "We'd like to speak to the principal, please."

Sam checked her notes. "Mr. Dreyfus." Then she smiled. "This

294

is Detective Hunter. I'm Detective Kennedy. We just have some questions regarding a former student."

"Is he expecting you?" she asked nervously.

"No."

"Okay. Let me see if he's available."

She left and Tori rolled her eyes, glancing at Sam. "The badge always scares them."

"Can you blame her? She's not even eighteen."

Tori paced while Sam waited patiently. She finally grabbed Tori's arm on her fourth pass by the desk.

"Will you stop? You're making me dizzy."

"How long can it take to announce us? Jesus!"

The office door opened and they both looked up expectantly as a gray-haired man approached.

"Detectives, I'm Howard Dreyfus. What can I do for you?"

Sam stepped forward, shaking his hand and smiling. "We just have a few questions. May we go into your office?"

"Of course, of course. Right this way."

They followed him inside, then Tori shut the door firmly behind her. "I'm Detective Hunter. This is Detective Kennedy. Homicide. We have a subpoena for the records of Richard L. Grayson. He would have graduated in . . ." She turned to Sam with eyebrows raised.

Sam smiled only slightly. She knew very well that Tori had all this information on the tip of her tongue, but she dutifully glanced to her notes.

"Two thousand and one."

"Very well. If I may ask, what is this in regards to?"

"A homicide investigation." Tori laid the subpoena on his desk and pulled out a chair. "We're in a hurry," she said pointedly.

"Of course." He lifted his phone and waited. "Steph, please pull the records on Richard L. Grayson, class of two thousand and one."

"Did you know him?" Sam asked when he hung up.

"I recognize the name."

"A school this size, I'm surprised you remember the students that pass through here," Tori said.

"Unfortunately, I tend to remember the very good students . . . and the most difficult."

"And what can you tell us about Grayson?"

"I wouldn't have called him a troublemaker, if that's what you mean. He was far too quiet in class for that, and it's not like he had a group that he hung out with. But he seldom did assignments, never participated in class. I still find it amazing that he was able to graduate. No, the incidents I remember him for were destructive. Little things at first, spray-painting the girls' locker room, locking Mrs. Stephens in her lab with the snakes, switching the music at the school play, things like that."

A quick knock on the door interrupted him and the receptionist, Steph, Tori presumed, walked in with a file.

"Thank you, Steph." He glanced through it briefly before handing it to Tori. "Grayson? That was his mother who was killed the other day?"

"Yes."

"I met her only once that I recall," he said. "Richard had been suspended. He poisoned the aquarium in the science lab. She seemed genuinely concerned, not like some parents."

"This was . . . his last year here?" Tori asked, flipping through the file.

"Yes."

"Is there anyone that you know of—teachers, students—that might have kept in touch with him?"

He shook his head. "Like I said, he didn't have a group that he hung out with. And the teachers, well, he wasn't exactly a model student. Most were just glad to be rid of him."

Tori and Sam exchanged glances, then Sam stood, reaching across the desk to shake hands again. "Thank you, Mr. Dreyfus. We appreciate your time."

"No problem. If I can help in any way . . ."

Tori paused at the door, eyes still glued to the file. "Says here he poisoned the fish with something from the janitor's closet. That's how he was caught. A Mr. Guerrero turned him in."

"Yes."

"Is he still employed here? I think maybe we'd like to speak with him."

"I'm sorry. Mr. Guerrero . . . was killed that very summer."

"Killed?" They both turned back and took their seats again. "Murdered?"

"Yes. He was found here at the school."

"What happened?" Sam asked.

"I'm surprised you don't remember. It was quite gruesome, actually."

"His head was cut off and he was left in the Dumpster," Tori murmured, remembering the case. It had been Adams and Donaldson's case, one they never solved.

"Yes."

"Jesus," Sam whispered.

Tori stood quickly. "Thank you. You've been a big help."

"Surely, you don't think . . . that Richard did that?"

"That's premature, Mr. Dreyfus. I'm sure we'll be in touch." She motioned to the door. "Sam?"

"Holy fucking shit," Sam murmured as they walked down the silent hall. "Can you believe that?"

"Adams and Donaldson had that one. Let's go pull their file."

"God, I hope it's clean. I hope they didn't fuck it up."

Tori smiled. "Detective Kennedy. Your language."

"I'm sorry. But if this was right in front of their noses, and all those girls died because of it—"

"Sam, it's easy to second-guess now. We may not be the best of buddies, but they're good cops."

"I know. You're right. I'm overreacting."


Malone stared at them, then tossed his glasses on his cluttered desk. "Pull the file. Adams is going to have a coronary if Grayson was the perp all along." He shook his head. "Christ! I hate days like this."

"Lieutenant, it might be better if you're the one to pull the file and not us," Tori suggested.

"Hell, Hunter, since when have you been afraid to step on toes?"

Sam cleared her throat. "Lieutenant, it's just that . . . everyone is . . . getting along. We're like a team."

"A team? Damn, who would have thought?" He rubbed his eyes. "Okay. I'll get Fisk to pull it. The only saving grace is that everyone's caseload is thin right now. This is top priority. I know it's your case, but I want everyone in on it."

"Yes, sir."

Malone stared. Just a few months ago, Tori would have been screaming at him if he'd suggested that she needed help with a case.

"What?"

He shook his head. "Nothing. You might want to bring Sikes and Ramirez up to speed, though."

"Yes, sir. I'll do it," Sam said.

They got up to leave, but Malone called to Tori.

"Hunter. A word?"

She nodded, with only a quick glance at Sam. She crossed her legs, waiting.

"Everything okay?"

"Fine."

He leaned back in his chair and watched her. "I've never seen you this way."

"What way?"

"You know what the hell I'm talking about, don't play games with me."

"I'm just . . . trying to get along with everyone."

"Why?"

"*Why?*"

"Tori, I've known you seven years. In the last couple of months, you're like a different person." He leaned forward. "Kennedy?"

"She seems to have a calming effect on me," Tori said vaguely.

He smiled. "So, best move I ever made, huh?"

"What do you mean?"

"The Captain wanted to pair you with Adams. Hell, it's no secret he and Donaldson are like oil and water."

"You said it wasn't your idea to put me with Kennedy," she reminded him.

"I lied."

She lifted one corner of her mouth in a smile and nodded. "Best move you ever made. Adams would be dead by now."

He laughed, leaning forward to face Tori. "You seem . . . happy, Tori. I don't know that I would ever have used that word to describe you before."

She considered his statement, then nodded. "I'm as happy as I can ever remember being, Lieutenant."

"Are we talking work here, Tori? Or personally?"

She stiffened. "Work, of course."

He stared at her for the longest moment, then nodded. "Okay. I guess I was hoping it was personal, too."

Their eyes locked across the desk.

"Because I'd like . . . for you to have someone . . . in your life," he continued.

Tori shrugged. "Rules and all."

He smiled. "Since when do you follow the rules?"

"Stan . . ."

"I'm not blind, Tori. It's just . . . hell, I thought she had a boyfriend."

Tori smiled. "She did."

He smiled, too. "Just keep it quiet, Tori."

"Stan, I don't know what to say."

"Tori Hunter, at a loss for words. Damn, this place just keeps getting crazier by the day. Now, get out of here. We've got work to do."

"Yes, sir." She paused at the door. "Lieutenant, thank you for understanding."

He nodded, then shoved on his glasses, dismissing her.

# Chapter Forty-two

It was late, and Sam was tired. She eyed the coffee suspiciously, then thought better of it. Actually, she wanted a glass of wine. And she wanted that glass of wine curled on her sofa eating take-out with Tori, of course.

Walking back to her desk, she found Tori in much the same position she'd been for the last few hours—staring at her computer screen, a frown on her face.

"Hey," she said quietly.

"Hmm?"

"It's late, Tori."

Tori sat back, noticing the empty squad room. She glanced at the clock, surprised that it was nearly seven.

"I'm sorry. I . . ."

"Lost track of time?" Sam walked behind her and lightly squeezed her shoulders, smiling at the low moan that Tori let escape. "You must be starving. I know I am."

"Is that a hint?"

"Yes, that's a hint." She gave Tori's shoulder one last squeeze, then urged her up. "Let's call it a night. Please? It's Friday, and you know as well as I do that we'll be up here all weekend."

Tori looked back at her computer. There was still so much to do. The Guerrero case had holes in it a mile wide. In the old days, she wouldn't have thought about leaving. She would be poring over the case until midnight, at least. But that was then. She never had a reason to stop before. It wasn't like she had a life outside of this department. Now she knew why the others left at normal hours. They all had someone to go home to. She looked up and met gentle green eyes, green eyes that promised so much. She shut her computer down.

"Pizza?"

Sam smiled as she grabbed her purse. "I don't care, as long as it can be eaten while I'm lounging on my sofa."

"Oh yeah? Are you planning on being alone while you lounge?"

"I plan on being curled next to a very warm body." Her voice softened. "Yours, in fact. Then, if I still have any energy left, I'm going to make love to you."

Tori stopped, her heart tumbling in her chest, all from those simple words spoken so quietly in the empty room. Sam paused at the door, her eyes questioning.

What did I do to deserve this? Tori thought. She never would have believed that someone like Sam would want her. But she did. It was there, splashed across her face, her eyes, for all to see.

"What?"

Tori shrugged. "Nothing."

"You sure?"

"Sure. Come on. There's a sofa calling our names."

Sam used her cell phone to call in the pizza, and they stopped on their way to her apartment, using the drive-through instead of getting out. But as soon as the door was closed behind them, Sam took the pizza and blindly laid it on the counter, her arms wrapping around Tori immediately. She held her, face pressed snugly against her neck.

"Shower first?" she murmured.

"Mmm."

Sam raised her head, her lips moving slowly across Tori's cheek to her lips. Their kiss was light, gentle. Anything more and their pizza would be forgotten. She pulled away before her desire took over completely.

"Shower," she said again.

Tori put the pizza in the oven to keep warm and Sam punched her answering machine as she walked past.

*"Hey, it's Amy. Just checking on you, kid. I need an update and not just on your health, if you know what I mean."*

Sam blushed as her eyes met Tori's across the room.

*"And how is that cute-as-hell partner of yours? Have you told her yet? I want details!"*

Sam rolled her eyes, and Tori chuckled.

*"Call me."*

"Sorry," Sam murmured. Tori just smiled and walked to the spare bathroom. After the beep, Robert's voice sounded in the quiet apartment and Tori stopped.

*"Samantha, it's me. I've got to talk to you. I need to see you. I can't take this any longer. I love you, you must know that. I want to marry you, for God's sake! Please, call me and let's talk about this. Please?"*

Sam watched the uncertainty cross Tori's face, and she silently cursed Robert. Why couldn't he just let it go?

"I'm sorry."

Tori shrugged. "Not your fault. You can't help it . . . if someone loves you. Besides, you've got a lot of history with him." Tori felt the emptiness settle over her, nearly choking her. What was she doing here? Did she really think that Sam would find this relationship satisfying? After a few months, maybe even weeks, Sam would grow tired of this, would come to her senses and finally call Robert and tell him she'd made a mistake. Then what? Tori would have lost the only friend, the only person important to her in her solitary life.

Sam's heart broke as she watched the sadness settle over Tori.

She walked closer, seeing the doubt in Tori's eyes. She reached out, gently touching Tori's cheek.

"You can't keep doing this, Tori," she whispered.

"What?"

"Doubting this . . . this thing between us. I wish I could explain to you exactly how I feel. My whole life, it seems, I've been looking for something but I didn't know what. No one touched me. No one ever got inside me. I kept looking, finally settling, thinking I would never find it." She let her hand slip into Tori's. "But you let me see a part of you . . . that . . . I love, Tori. You *touch* me, you *move* me. I can't explain why, Tori. What I feel for you, it's what I've always imagined . . . dreamed it would be like when I fell in love."

"Sam," Tori breathed.

"Please don't doubt this. Don't doubt what I feel for you." She squeezed Tori's hand. "Because I can see in your eyes how you feel about me. You don't have to say the words, honey."

Tori felt a lone tear escape and fall helplessly down her cheek.

"I . . . I love you, Tori. I feel that . . . I *know* that. Please believe me when I tell you. Don't fight this, Tori."

"I'm so scared, Sam."

"I know, sweetheart. I know you are." Sam gathered Tori in her arms and held her. She was such a strong woman on the outside but so vulnerable on the inside. Her big macho cop was not afraid to face a gun but was terrified at the prospect of giving away her heart. "I promise I won't hurt you," she whispered. "Trust me." Her lips lightly brushed Tori's. "Please?"

# Chapter Forty-three

Sam looked at her tired eyes in the mirror, then bent and splashed cold water on her face. They'd only had Sunday to themselves and they'd spent most of that time in bed. She was exhausted, but, God, it had been worth it. She could still feel Tori's hands moving across her body. Closing her eyes, she shuddered as she remembered Tori's mouth coming to her again and again, bringing her to heights she'd never thought possible. Her body felt nearly numb but even early this morning, she had still responded to Tori's touch, still craved the release that only Tori could give her. They had slept only a few hours, but still, she'd pulled Tori to her, had welcomed her weight as she'd settled between her legs again this morning. Sam smiled at her reflection, wondering if she should be embarrassed by the nearly insatiable woman she had become.

All these years, pretending, just going through the motions. Now? She met her eyes in the mirror and smiled. Now she knew what it was like to be madly, hopelessly in love. And Tori, oh she couldn't bring herself to say the words, but that hardly mattered. Her touch, the look in her eyes as she made love to Sam said more than any words ever could.

She finally moved away from the mirror, grabbing a couple of paper towels to dry her face. She opened the door, watching the activity in the squad room. Sikes and Ramirez were huddled around Tori, peering at her computer screen as she talked. Adams and Donaldson were in Malone's office, no doubt going over the old case. Adams had bristled when the Lieutenant pulled the file. They'd all gone over it and even she could see the many leads that pointed to Grayson, but neither Adams nor Donaldson had followed through on them. She had been angry at first, but Tori had reminded them all that it was easy to second-guess now that they had all the facts in front of them.

Tori's phone rang and Sam smiled as Tori blindly reached for it, still pointing to her computer. Then her face changed and Sam walked over, listening.

*"You're never going to find me, bitch cop."*

Tori felt the hairs on the back of her neck stand out. "Who is this?"

*"You know who I am,"* came the quiet response.

Tori grabbed Sikes's arm and squeezed until he met her eyes.

"Ricky? Is that you? We've been looking all over for you, man."

*"Have you seen Aunt Charlotte lately?"*

Tori shivered at the quiet laugh that came from the phone. She pulled up a blank screen on her computer and typed quickly.

RAMIREZ: CHECK ON CHARLOTTE GRAYSON. SIKES: FIND OUT WHERE THE HELL THIS CALL ORIGINATED.

Sam read the screen, then ran to Malone's office. She opened the door without knocking.

"Lieutenant, I think Grayson's on the phone."

"What the hell?" His chair nearly fell over in his haste to follow Sam.

305

They all huddled around Tori, and Sam could see the tension in her body, on her face.

"Where are you, Richard? Let's end this. There's no need for anyone else to get hurt."

*"You're too late, Detective. And be very careful. I've been watching you. I've been watching you and . . . your partner. I know where she lives."*

Tori gasped as the line went dead. The phone slipped from her fingers as her eyes met Sam's.

"What the hell's going on, Hunter?"

Tori turned to Malone, then looked expectantly at Ramirez as he shook his head.

"Nothing. They're not answering the call," he said.

"We just have the one unit there?" Malone asked.

"Yes, just the one." Tori looked at John. "Sikes?"

He hung up and looked at his notes. "Twelve eighty-seven Whispering Oaks Circle," he said and shrugged.

Tori closed her eyes and Sam reached for their file, flipping through it.

"Jesus Christ," she murmured. "That's Charlotte Grayson's address."

"And he's got her."

"What the fuck? She's under round-the-clock surveillance," Malone yelled. "Try raising the unit again!"

"They're not picking up, Lieutenant," Ramirez said again.

"Get out there now! Fisk?" Malone yelled. "Get some units out there. Now!" He watched everyone run, his eyes wide. Then he rubbed his bald head, reaching for the phone. "This is Malone. Is the Captain in?"


Tori sped through the city, glancing occasionally in the mirror to see Sikes and Ramirez trying to keep up. Sam had one hand clutched on the dash, the other pressed tightly against Tori's leg.

"What did he say?" Sam finally asked.

"Not much."

"Bullshit. I saw your face. Tell me."

Tori clutched the steering wheel hard as she sped through the traffic light, ignoring the blasting of horns behind her.

"He's been watching us. He knows where you live."

"What? Why would he care?"

"Because it's our case, Sam. And because he's got a thing about lesbians."

"So? He's going to add us to his hit list?"

"He might. But the bastard won't get the chance." Tori slammed on her brakes as a car pulled out in front of them. She laid on her horn, then passed them.

"If you don't slow down, you'll save him the bother of trying to kill us."

Tori smiled, then chuckled. Trust Sam not to make a big deal out of it.

"I'm serious. Whatever happened at Charlotte Grayson's house has already happened."

"I know. I just . . . God, I don't want to find her. She was right. We should have been the ones watching out for her."

"Tori, even you can't be everywhere at once."

"I can fucking try."

Sam shook her head. God, she loved this woman. So fearless, so in control. She got a rush just being around her when she was like this. She kept quiet as Tori safely maneuvered them through traffic, finally slowing when they reached the residential district.

"One more block," Sam said, pointing.

They found the squad car parked in the driveway. It was empty. Tori pulled behind it and got out, just seconds before Sikes pulled to a screeching halt on the street. In the distance, they heard sirens. Backup.

"Take the back door, Sikes," Tori called. They watched Sikes and Ramirez round the corner of the house, weapons drawn, then proceeded to the front door. It was wide open.

Tori looked at Sam, then nodded. They walked slowly into the hall, Tori's gut telling her no one was inside. At least, no one alive.

They found them in the living room.

"Oh my God," Sam whispered. Tori grabbed her before Sam could enter.

"Secure the premises first, Sam."

Sam nodded, but she still stared at the two officers lying on the carpeted floor. They had been decapitated. She finally pulled her eyes away, moving silently with Tori as they went to the back of the house. The bedrooms were empty; nothing looked disturbed. They both jumped when Sikes and Ramirez walked up behind them.

"Anything?"

"No. You?"

"Clean."

"Sam, call Jackson. Get a crime unit out here," she said calmly. When Sam walked away, Tori turned and put her fist through the wall.

"Jesus Christ, Hunter!"

"Goddammit!" she yelled. "That sonofabitch!"

Sikes grabbed her arm. "It's not your fault."

Tori clenched her fists, then relaxed as Sam ran back in.

"What happened?" she demanded as she disconnected her phone.

"Nothing."

Sam's eyes slid past her to the hole in the wall, then she motioned for Sikes and Ramirez to leave. When they were alone, she walked to Tori and took her hands, rubbing against the already reddening knuckle with her thumb.

"Stop it," she said softly. "Stop it right now. This is not your fault and you damn well know it. We've got a job to do. We've got two officers down and a missing woman to find."

"I'm sorry."

"We all need you to be strong, Tori. I need you to be strong."

"Oh, Sam. You know he's killed her."

"We don't know that. And we're going to find her." She brushed Tori's face and met her eyes. "Now, focus."

"Yes. I will."

"Good. Because I kinda need your hands. No more punching the walls."

She turned before Tori could respond but not before she saw the ghost of a smile touch her face.

"Sam."

Sam looked back, meeting Tori's eyes. The intensity of her stare took her breath away.

"Sam, I . . . I . . ." Shit. Just say it, her mind begged, but her mouth clamped shut and she let out her breath.

Sam wanted to tell her she didn't have to say the words. My God, the look in her eyes nearly brought her to her knees. What would actual words do to her?

Walking closer, Sam stopped only when their thighs brushed. She closed her eyes, her mouth moving to Tori's ear.

"I love you, too."

Tori let out her breath as the other woman walked away, her heart still clutching, almost painfully, in her chest.

"Okay, focus, Hunter," she whispered. "Focus." She took a deep breath, then walked into the chaos of the living room. The two bodies were still uncovered and she looked away from the severed heads. One was Sanchez, the young cop who was always so polite to Sam. The other, she couldn't place.

"Hunter, over here," Sikes called.

She sidestepped the crime unit and nodded a curt hello to Rita Spencer, who was bent over the bodies.

There on the wall, above the dining room table, were words dripping in blood . . . words that made her skin crawl.

*Genesis*

And below that:

*Have you found the others? Adams knows . . .*

"What the fuck do you make of that?"

Tori frowned. "Adams knows? He's playing with us. Adams knows jack."

"Maybe. But Grayson's bound to know Adams was on the old case."

"Missing Persons?"

"That's what I'm thinking."

"Tori?"

She and Sikes both looked up as Sam hurried over, glancing only once into the living room.

"Her car is still in the garage. And, you know, we impounded Grayson's green Chevy."

"Great." Tori ran one hand through her hair, then called to Ramirez. "Tony, we're looking for a stolen car. Probably grabbed this morning."

"I'm on it."

Tori turned to Sam, her eyes softening. "Sam, why don't you ride back with John. I'm going to stick around here for a while."

"Why? The crime unit's going over everything. Mac promised a rush on the reports."

"Yeah, good. But I want to talk to Rita when she's done. You can help John. I want to go over old Missing Persons reports, see if we can find a link, a pattern or something."

"But I could stay and help. Talk to the neighbors . . ."

"That's being handled. Come on, Sam. I won't be long."

She paused. "Okay, then. If that's what you want."

She squeezed Tori's arm as she walked away, but Tori could tell she was upset. She wanted to call her back, take Sam in her arms and tell her everything would be okay. But she didn't.

"You think we should check with Fort Worth, too?"

"Wouldn't hurt."

"I've got a buddy over in Homicide there. I'll give him a call."

"Good. Thanks, John."

"Sure." He turned back, then followed her eyes to the two fallen officers, now thankfully covered.

"You really going to stick around and talk to the ME or are you just trying to get Sam out of here?"

Her retort died on her lips. The old Tori would have told him to mind his own fucking business. But that person was long gone, she knew that. She shrugged.

310

"I knew one of them. His name was Sanchez. Who was the other?"

"Rogers. First year on the force."

"Damn."

"Yeah. It sucks big-time. But it's not your fault, Tori."

"Right now, it feels like my fault."

"Let it go. Tonight, you and Sam can go home and . . . talk about it."

Surprised, she met his eyes.

He just shrugged and smiled. "Not blind, Hunter. You two can't hide it for shit."

She didn't know what to say, so she said nothing.

"Meet you back at the office, huh?"

"Yeah."

When she was alone, she turned back to the wall, staring at the words, wondering what they meant. A clue? Or was he just fucking with them? And what the hell could Adams possibly know?

"Turner? Make sure you get this," she said, motioning to the wall.

The photographer nodded. "Yes ma'am, don't worry."

Tori made herself walk into the living room, waiting patiently as Rita Spencer finished up. It was a mess. She couldn't imagine how a little fuckup like Richard Grayson had subdued two officers . . . and done *this* to them.

"You have anything or do we need to wait?" she asked when Rita stood up.

"Damn, Hunter, in all my years . . ."

"I know."

"Their heads were severed postmortem. There are no other obvious wounds. They may have been injected with something, I don't know yet. I'm guessing, with the amount of blood, that he slit their throats first."

"The only blood is here?"

"They found traces in the sink where he must have washed up. They're going over the two bathrooms right now, but the scene appears to be right here. The officers were obviously incapacitated somehow. Laid out, then . . ."

"Yeah. What did he use, do you think?"

"The flesh is jagged. I'd say a large serrated knife to start. He may have finished with that or used a hacksaw to finish. I'm just guessing."

"Remember Rachel Anderson? Jackson said he used a serrated kitchen knife or maybe a bread knife."

"Yes. We'll match the cuts."

"Crime unit picked up knives at his place."

"Don't worry, Hunter. We'll go over everything. I'll assist Jackson with the post. We'll get to them immediately."

"Okay. Thanks, Rita."

Rita started to walk away, then paused. "I don't envy you this case, Hunter. It's blown out at the seams."

"Tell me about it," she murmured.

Tori walked into the kitchen, watching as Mac, from the crime unit, was still testing for blood. Her eyes went to the wall where a beautiful knife set hung. She moved closer, staring at the handles. Beautiful wood, hand carved.

"Mac?"

"Yeah?"

"Did you test these for traces?"

"No, not yet. I'll do them next. These in the drawer are clean."

She nodded, her eyes still glued to the shiny serrated edges of the seldom-used knives.


"It goddamn makes no sense," Malone said.

"He said there were others."

"What others? We don't have any unsolved cases where young girls were killed. Shit! And Missing Persons? Hell, most of them are runaways and we'll never find them. We're wasting our time with this."

He paced across the room, glancing occasionally at both Sikes and Kennedy as they flipped through the database.

"Waste of goddamn time," he said again.

Ramirez sidestepped Malone and laid a paper on Sikes's desk. "We've got two cars stolen this morning in the area of Belle's Hostel and one taken within a mile of Charlotte Grayson's place. Last night, the only one in the area reported stolen was six blocks from Belle's."

"He would have been on foot. It has to be one of those taken from Belle's area," Sam said. She glanced at the door again, wishing Tori was here.

"Okay. Put all four on APB. We might get lucky," Malone said. Then he turned to Sam. "Where the hell is Hunter?"

"She stayed behind at the scene."

"We need her here. Call her."

"Yes, sir."

"Lieutenant?"

"What?" he snapped.

"I think your blood pressure is . . . maybe off the scale," Sikes said quietly. "We're doing everything we can."

"Well, it's not enough! I've been on the phone all morning with the Captain, the Mayor and the goddamn Chief! Charlotte Grayson works for the DA's office, for Christ's sake!"

They all looked up as Tori walked calmly into the room, meeting first Sam's eyes, then Malone's.

"You look like you're about to have a stroke, Lieutenant. Can I have a word?"

"Shit, Hunter. Where the hell have you been?"

She only raised an eyebrow, and he looked away.

"Okay. I'm sorry. In my office."

She followed him, then turned back.

"Ramirez? Anything?"

"We got four possibilities."

"Good."

She shut the door and watched as Malone took out a bottle of antacids from his drawer and tossed four into his mouth. His face was red, and she noticed the perspiration on his bald head.

"Are you okay?"

"I've got to meet with the Chief this afternoon. How the hell do you think I am?"

"I suppose they told you about the message on the wall?"

"Yeah. Missing Persons, Hunter? What the hell are you thinking?"

"'*There are others. Adams knows,*'" she said quietly, quoting the words left behind. "The only link we know of with Adams is the old case. But then, I remembered their case about a month or so ago. Donaldson asked me for some information on gay bars. They had a guy that had been decapitated . . . a transvestite, Donaldson said."

"I remember. It went nowhere."

"Yeah. It went nowhere. Why is that?"

"What are you getting at, Hunter?"

"Is it just coincidence that he was decapitated, and Adams had the case? Coincidence that Grayson did that to two officers and left us that message?"

"You think he killed the transvestite, too?"

"You're a serial killer and you kill, but it's not credited to you. Would that piss you off?"

"He was killing young women from Belle's. Not cross-dressers," Malone said.

"What if he was doing both? We assumed he was gay, because he hung out at gay bars. Outlaws, obviously, he was there stalking our girls. But we followed him to other bars, bars that cater to men. We assumed he was gay but maybe he's not. Maybe he was staking out potential victims there, too."

"And we've not found bodies, so Missing Persons?"

"It's a theory. What the hell else do we have?"

Malone finally sat down and held his head in his hands. "Fuck, Hunter. Adams is already up in arms about us pulling the old case. Now, you want to pull this one, too?"

"Yes, I do."

Malone nodded. "Okay. You're right. It's a theory, at least." He leaned back, watching her. "You okay?"

"Hanging in there."

"I know it's been tough, Hunter. It's gotten personal."

"Yeah. But I don't think he's killed her yet. I don't think he wants to. He's leaving clues. He's giving us a chance."

"But why?"

"I don't know, Stan." She paused, then finally decided to confide in him. "He told me something on the phone. He said he's been watching us . . . me and Sam. He said he knows where she lives. I think . . . he wants us."

"Jesus Christ, Hunter. Have you told her?"

"Yes."

"Okay. You want to put a unit at her place?"

"No. We've already lost one today. We can handle it."

"The hell you can," he yelled. "I won't take that chance."

"We won't be at her place, Lieutenant. I've got my apartment, you know."

"You don't think he knows about that? Hell, Hunter, what are you thinking? You've been targeted, just like Charlotte Grayson. You think I'm going to leave you unprotected?"

"Maybe this is what we need, Stan. Someone to draw him out."

"Are you out of your mind? He's killed nine people that we know of."

"And he'll kill more if we don't fucking stop him," she yelled.

"Well, I won't allow you to be bait! And you can argue that all you want," he yelled just as loudly.

"Do you seriously think I'd put Sam's life in jeopardy? I'm not talking bait, Lieutenant, but I don't see any reason to park a unit on my street where they might be in danger. We've seen what he can do."

They stared at each other, both breathing hard. He finally looked away. "Okay, Hunter. I'm going to trust you on this one. How do you want to play it?"

"I think it's up to him. He'll contact us again, I'm sure. In fact, I wouldn't doubt if he called before we leave today. But tonight, we'll take an unmarked car to my apartment. I'm on the fourth floor. There's only one entrance. He won't get in."

"He could be waiting. He'll know you won't go back to her place."

"He doesn't know about my apartment, Stan." She shoved her hands in her pockets. "It's not in my name. I got it when I moved back here, all those years ago. I didn't want . . . anyone to know I was here. Louise put it in her name when I was at the Academy. So he won't know about the apartment." She shrugged. "It's not like he could have followed me there recently, anyway."

"Are you sure about this?"

"Yeah. But let me talk to Sikes. I think maybe he and Ramirez might want to watch Sam's place. Just in case."

"Okay. But shit, I don't like this one bit."

"You think I do?"

"No. I'm sorry." He stood. "Let's pull the file, see what they missed."

"They're yelling," Sikes said.

"Yeah."

"Wonder what she found out?"

"We'll know soon enough," Sam said. She watched through the glass as Tori paced in front of the Lieutenant's desk. Malone didn't look happy. For that matter, neither did Tori.

"Sam?"

"Hmm?" She pulled her eyes away from a pacing Tori and looked at Sikes.

"Can I ask you a personal question?"

She raised her eyebrows and nodded.

"How long have you and Tori . . . been, well . . . more than just partners?" he asked quietly.

"What?" she whispered. "What makes you think . . . ?"

He smiled. "Come on. I've known Hunter a lot of years and I've never seen her go ballistic like she did when you were abducted and she couldn't find you." He lowered his voice. "You're in love with her, right?"

Sam closed her eyes. *Damn.*

"I think it's . . . great, Sam. I really do."

"You do?"

"Yeah. Tori's been so different. You've brought out a side of her that none of us even knew existed. I mean, hell, I even find myself liking her."

"She's the most dynamic person I've ever met . . . and yes, I'm in love with her."

"If Malone finds out . . ."

"I know. Please, John, keep this to yourself."

"What about . . . I mean, you had a boyfriend and all. What does he think about it?"

Sam sighed. "I ended things with him before . . . well, before Tori and I became involved."

"So you're . . . bisexual?"

She smiled. "Why are we having this conversation?"

"I'm just trying to understand."

"Please tell me you're not imagining us in bed together."

He had the grace to blush, then laughed. "Well, I am a guy."

She reached across the desk and squeezed his arm. "And I'm not bisexual."

He nodded, and she looked back into the Lieutenant's office, meeting Tori's eyes through the glass. They softened immediately, and Sam gave her a slight smile, then dutifully returned to the database.

# Chapter Forty-four

"Are you okay with this?" Tori asked for the second time as she drove them to Oak Cliff.

"Tori, if you think it's the best thing, yes. I wish I had a change of clothes, though." Sam reached across the seat and squeezed Tori's thigh. "I'll admit, I am curious about where you live."

"It's not . . . home, you know. It's just a place where I can crash sometimes. Your place, it's a home. It's warm. It's . . . you." Actually, Tori was embarrassed for Sam to see the tiny apartment. It was dark, sterile. Much the way her life had been for so long. Before Sam. And she really didn't want her to see it now.

"We should probably pick up something for dinner," Sam suggested.

"Yeah. I know for a fact there's not a thing at my place."

"I could really go for a burger."

"Oh, yeah? There's a great place close by that delivers. We could do that."

"Good."

Sam watched her as she drove, not missing the frown that Tori had been wearing most of the day. They'd not really had a chance to talk all afternoon, and she had no idea what her conversation with Malone was all about. But it could wait. They needed some time alone, away from the case. Or at least, she did. She knew Tori's mind was still reeling. They had spent the afternoon going over missing persons reports, trying to weed out the ones who might have been gay or lesbian. It was a tedious process, and she had been shocked at the vast numbers of missing and assumed runaways from the Dallas–Fort Worth area.

She pulled her attention from Tori and watched the shabby buildings flash by. They were definitely in an older, well-worn area of the city. In fact, when she worked in Assault, she could remember numerous calls to this area. It was a poor part of the city. For the life of her, she couldn't imagine why Tori kept an apartment here.

Tori found a spot on the street and parallel parked without incident. When she cut the engine, she glanced first at the old building, then at Sam.

"This is it."

Sam ducked her head, peering out the window at the dilapidated building. There were several broken windows that had been taped up and a couple that were simply boarded up with plywood. She was amazed that the building hadn't been condemned.

"Uh-huh," she murmured.

"We could always just get a room somewhere," Tori suggested. In fact, she didn't know why she hadn't thought of that before.

"No, this will be fine." Then Sam grabbed Tori's hand and squeezed. "Why, Tori?"

"Why? Why here? Why this apartment?"

"Yes."

Tori shrugged. How did she explain to Sam why she hung on to this?

"We lived here for three years when I was five," she said quietly.

319

"When I moved back, I had Louise get the apartment in her name. It wasn't like this when we lived here. Even when I moved back, it was shabby, but not like this. But it was the only place . . . where I could go that was familiar."

"I'm sorry."

"Don't be sorry. It's silly to have it, I know. And it's not like I live here anyway."

Sam brought Tori's hand to her lips and kissed it. "It's not silly. If it's what you needed, then it's not silly at all."

Tori turned in the seat and faced Sam, meeting her eyes in the dusky glow of the streetlights. "I don't know that I need it anymore," she admitted. "It was a lifeline of sorts, I guess. But I don't feel like I'm in that dark place anymore."

"I'm glad."

"And I have you to thank for that."

Sam smiled and leaned across the console and kissed Tori gently. "You're welcome."

"Come on. Let's order some dinner. I'm bushed."

"Me, too."


The ringing penetrated her sleepy haze, and Tori untangled herself from Sam to grab her cell phone.

"Hunter," she murmured.

"It's me. The goddamn bastard was here," Sikes said.

Tori sat up. "At Sam's?"

"Yes. I've got an APB out on the car. It's a match for the stolen Honda."

"Why the hell didn't you follow him?" she demanded.

"You think we didn't try? The bastard is smart. He took us to the Deep Ellum bar district and faded into the traffic."

"Christ, Sikes."

"I know. We had him. But I didn't think you'd want me plowing down drunken pedestrians to catch him."

"You're right. I'm sorry." She ran her hand through her short hair, then sighed as she felt Sam's hand moving soothingly across her naked back. "It's two, Sikes. Get some sleep. Maybe we'll get lucky and some cruiser will spot the car."

"Yeah. I'm sorry, Tori. We had the little prick."

"It's not your fault, John. Tomorrow is another day. We'll get him. Go home."

She lay back down, and Sam immediately curled against her. Tori kissed her forehead lightly and gathered her closer.

"He was there?" Sam finally whispered.

"Yeah."

Sam was quiet for a moment, then her hand moved lazily to Tori's breast. Her nipple responded, and Sam rubbed against it with her palm, content to just feel Tori under her hand. They were both too tired for more, especially since their nearly sleepless night the day before. But it was nice, this touching. She closed her eyes and sighed, feeling Tori's arms tighten around her.

"He's getting very bold," she murmured.

Tori nodded. Yes, he was. She wondered where he was hiding, where he was keeping Charlotte and whether she was alive or not. She suspected he would already have displayed the body if he'd killed her. He'd want them to know that he'd won again.

"Tori?"

"Hmm?"

"You know I feel completely safe with you, don't you?"

"I hope so."

"And I don't just mean about him. It's . . . everything. I'm with you and my life feels . . . complete, you know," she whispered.

"Yes."

"Do you feel that way, too?"

Tori hesitated. How did she tell Sam all she felt? How could words convey what she felt in her heart?

"Sam, for the first time in my adult life, I feel . . . happy, content. I don't feel like I'm running away anymore. I don't feel like I need to hide from anything." She tightened her arms. "You make *me* feel safe."

"I'm so glad, Tori. When this case is over, I hope we have some normal time together. I think we need that. I wish we could spend a few days alone on the boat, just us. Where we can be ourselves and talk . . . and make love," she whispered. "I love how you touch me, Tori. You bring all my senses alive, and it's like I can't get enough of you."

Tori closed her eyes, letting Sam's words wash over her and settle into her heart. She didn't know why, but Sam loved her. She wouldn't question it, she wouldn't fight it. She couldn't. But still, the words she longed to say to Sam wouldn't come. Yes, she knew she was in love with her. Tori had no doubt about her own feelings. She had never given her love to anyone. She hadn't thought she had any to give. Even now, she found it amazing that Sam had been able to find the light within her after she'd spent so very many years in darkness.

"Tori?"

"Hmm?"

"I'm not going to leave, you know. I know you still have doubts about this, about me."

"Sam . . ."

"You do, Tori. I don't blame you, really. But I know how much I love you. And someday, you'll know it, too. You'll believe me."

Tori didn't know what to say. She pulled Sam to her, finding her mouth in the darkness.

# Chapter Forty-five

"Christ, Donaldson. You talk to a few people at the bar, you find no prints at the scene, and you deem it unsolvable?" Tori tossed the file on her desk and stared at Donaldson, waiting.

"What did you expect us to do? We had nothing and nobody would talk to us. When your first girl was killed, you didn't have shit either," he reminded her.

"But I didn't close the goddamn case." She picked it up again, reading the medical examiner's report. A serrated knife was used. She picked up the phone, waiting impatiently until it was answered on the third ring. "Sara, it's Hunter. I need you to have Jackson look at something. The knife wounds on our two cops, have him pull the report on Jason Branson, the transvestite who was murdered last month. Spencer did the post. She reported a serrated knife was used in that decapitation. See if we've got a match."

"Rita has already pulled the file, Hunter."

"Good, good. Okay, let me know."

323

Tori nodded as she hung up the phone. Rita Spencer was smart and thorough. Tori should have known she would remember the case. She looked back at Donaldson. "We need to go back over this case, Donaldson. Who did Branson leave with? Who was he talking to? Surely, someone saw something. He was a regular there." She looked back to the file. "You say the only one who remembered him being there that night was a bartender. That's all you got? What did the bartender say?"

"He didn't say anything, Hunter. He said he saw *her* there, that *she* was called *Lisa*. What the hell were we supposed to do with that?"

"You were supposed to put your goddamn prejudice aside and work the case. I can just imagine the two of you in that bar. You probably asked a couple of questions and got the hell out. Christ!"

"It was a dead end."

"Dead end, my ass. When I talk to the bartender, if he gives me any information that points to Grayson, you and Adams will have hell to pay."

"You're not my fucking Lieutenant, Hunter. Don't threaten me."

Malone was listening to the exchange from his doorway. He should have pulled the case from Adams and given it to Hunter in the first place. He knew they'd hardly probed the surface. But Hunter was overloaded as it was. They had no way of knowing the two cases were connected. But still, he should at least have run it by Hunter. But, you have a transvestite with no family badgering them to find the murderer, it was easy to let it slip through.

"Donaldson?"

He and Tori both looked up.

"What Hunter says on this goes. No questions. Do as she says. We have nine victims, possibly ten if your case checks out. Hunter is in charge of this. Clear?"

He nodded slowly. "Yes, sir."

Malone scanned the empty squad room. "Where the hell is Adams?"

"He is . . . he called and said he had a doctor's appointment."

"If he's gone much longer, he better hope they admitted him to the goddamn hospital. We need everyone here. We don't have time for fucking doctor's appointments!"

"Yes, sir."

"Hunter? I need a word."

Tori sighed and shoved away from her desk. *Now what?*

"Close the door. Sit down."

"What's going on?"

"CIU is coming aboard."

"What the hell for?"

"Two officers murdered, that's what the hell for."

"Lieutenant . . ."

But he held up his hand to stop her. "You can complain all you want, but it's a done deal. I requested that Travis head it up. At least we know we can work with him."

"Christ! CIU! I'm surprised Jenkins hasn't been around yet."

"Yeah. But I think he's been keeping a low profile since the Gomez incident. I got a call from Travis yesterday about it. Both Jenkins and Mabry have bank accounts that have had large cash deposits in the last two years. You'd think they'd be smarter than that. Idiots."

Tori shook her head. She hadn't given much thought to Jenkins and Mabry. Politics being what it was, she could imagine the two of them weaseling their way out of this.

"Okay, enough of that. Let's get up to speed on this. You sent Kennedy and Sikes to Fort Worth. What you got?"

"About six months ago, they found a gay man beaten, with his throat slit. He was left in a Dumpster in an alley about three blocks from a gay bar. It went down as a gay bashing. No suspects. They're talking to the detectives who worked the case and then the ME. I'd like to get the report to Jackson to see if he can find a match on anything. Maybe he used the same knife."

"Okay, good. What about missing persons?"

"We have three possibilities. A nineteen-year-old girl was

reported missing last year by her grandmother. She was a lesbian and had been living with her grandmother for the last two years, ever since her family told her to get lost," Tori said with just a hint of bitterness. "The grandmother said she'd often talked about moving to California. When she disappeared"—Tori shrugged—"they figured that's where she'd headed and let it drop." She flipped open her notes. "Two men disappeared within a week of each other last November. Both were reported missing by their lovers. There was no connection between them and not a trace ever found. That case is also dead."

Malone nodded. "What about Ramirez?"

"Tony's at the lab. I want him there when they go over the stolen Honda, maybe find a clue as to where he's been hiding."

"What about the Branson case? I heard a little of your conversation with Donaldson."

"The Branson case was barely worked, Lieutenant. Why did you let them shelve it?"

"Because they had no leads—"

"No leads?" she asked, her voice rising. "I guess not. They talked to one person, the bartender."

"It's my fault. I shouldn't have given them the case to begin with. I should have put you on it, but your case was taking off. I just didn't want you to take time away from it. Not with the brass coming down on us like they were."

"I'm going to talk to the bartender again, see if he can still remember anything. Shit, whatever leads there may have been will be long cold by now. Christ, Lieutenant, I can't believe how they handled it. I thought they were good detectives. Hell, someone fresh out of the Academy could have done a better job than this."

"I know, Hunter. Again, it's my fault. Let's just open it up again and go from there."

"I'm going back to the bar, see if someone will talk to me."

"You want to take Donaldson with you?"

"Are you kidding? No way."

"Okay. Travis is coming over at three. Make sure you're back. We need to brief him."

"Yes, sir."


The Pink Lagoon was still closed, but Tori saw activity inside. She knocked several times and waited.

"Police," she called, tapping again on the glass, harder this time. "Open the goddamn door."

Finally, someone came over, and they stared at each other through the glass. The door was opened, and a young man peered out at her.

"What?"

She held up her badge. "I'm Detective Hunter." She pushed past the man and walked into the empty bar. It smelled of stale cigarette smoke and beer. "I'm looking for one of your bartenders. Marty Stevens."

"What for?"

Tori turned to face the young man, piercing him with a stare. "I have some questions regarding a homicide. Is he here?"

The man swallowed nervously, then tucked his long hair behind both ears. "I'm Marty," he finally said.

Tori relaxed, then smiled. "Great. Is there somewhere we can talk?"


"Damn, Sikes. What happened to Ramirez? This one's a hell of a lot cuter."

John smiled apologetically at Sam, then pointed to his old friend Danny Gardner.

"This is Detective Kennedy, Danny. She's just my partner for the day. Ramirez is still around."

"Sorry to hear that, man." Danny stuck out his hand and shook Sam's. "Nice to meet you. John says ya'll want to dig up an old case of mine." He shook his head as he walked away, and John and Sam followed. "Been reading about it in the paper. Damn glad it's in Dallas and not Fort Worth."

They followed him into an empty conference room where he handed them each a folder.

"I made copies of what we got. It's not much. Our guy was last seen leaving the bar about one-thirty. He was alone. He didn't talk to one particular guy, didn't dance with one particular guy. There was no one inside that raised suspicions. He was a regular."

Sam scanned the file, noting that they had talked to at least a dozen people from the bar, not including friends and relatives.

"He had no enemies that anyone knew of, no threats, nothing. It appeared to be random. Thus, we labeled it gay bashing. But we still got shit."

"You still have the case open?" Sam asked.

"Yeah. But it's not like we're working it. There're no leads."

John flipped to the back of the file and the Medical Examiner's report, struggling through the medical jargon, trying to find something similar to their case. His fingers followed the words, stopping when he read a serrated knife was used on the neck.

"You had anything similar since? Or before?" John asked.

"No, Sikes. You know, the queers hang out more in Dallas. I think Fort Worth is a little too redneck for them."

John felt Sam stiffen beside him, and he reached under the table and grabbed her arm, squeezing gently.

"Danny, we appreciate you sharing the file. I don't suppose your ME could shed any more light, do you?"

"She might. Rumor has it, this one was close to home for her, if you know what I mean. She badgered us about this case for weeks afterward," he said, grabbing a cup next to him and spitting tobacco juice into it. "But it wasn't like it was the salt of the earth that was killed, you know?"

Sam stood, her disgust for this man growing with each passing second. "Thanks, Detective Gardner. If we find anything, we'll be sure to let you know."

"No problem, ma'am."

John hurried after Sam, finally catching up to her just before she burst through the double doors.

"Christ, Sikes! He's your *friend*?"

"Oh, calm down, Sam. Hell, he's a cop. In Fort Worth. It's not exactly the gay-friendly capital of the world, you know."

"I don't know why I'm complaining. They did a better job of investigating the murder than Adams and Donaldson would have."

"Yeah. But, it's also personal for you now, you know."

Sam stopped. Yes, it was. "I'm sorry, John. It is personal. A month ago, I don't know what my reaction would have been. I hope it would have been the same."

"Can I tell you something, Sam? I'm sorry to say, I was much like Danny there. Queers, faggots. I didn't understand. It wasn't about relationships and love. It was just about sex. Hunter, for instance. She's a damn attractive woman. I couldn't for the life of me figure out why she would rather be with another woman than a man. It made no sense. But the night we were in that bar with you guys, I saw women together and I saw men together and they were looking at each other . . . with affection and with love. It wasn't just about deviant sex, you know? It opened my eyes."

Sam reached out and squeezed his arm. "We're all just people, John. We can't control who we fall in love with."

He smiled. "Yeah, I know. I also saw you two dancing and . . . well, kissing."

Sam turned scarlet, remembering the way she and Tori had touched.

John laughed, then grabbed Sam's arm and guided her to the car. "Come on. Let's go look up the ME."


Tori sipped from her Coke and studied the young man who stood across the bar from her. He absently wiped the already clean bar top with a wet rag.

"I understand you remember Jason Branson being here at the bar the night he died. He went by Lisa?"

"Yes. She preferred to be called Lisa."

329

"Okay. Did she come here alone?"

"Yes."

Tori flipped open her notes. "And she left alone?"

"Yes."

"In between? Did she talk to anyone in particular?"

Marty stared at her for the longest time, finally leaning his elbows on the counter. "Why are you just now asking? It's been well over a month."

"I know. The other two detectives assigned to the case . . . well, it's been transferred to me."

"I'm not surprised. The old guy almost shit in his pants when I saw him."

Tori frowned. "What do you mean?"

"He comes in every Saturday night. Sits down there." He pointed. "Always drinks Jack Daniel's straight up."

"Adams?"

"I don't remember what he said his name was. He goes by Carl. He was here the night Lisa died."

Tori stared, dumbfounded. Part of her wanted to laugh hysterically, but she managed to control the impulse.

"Let me get this straight. Detective Adams, Carl, comes in every Saturday night, sits right down there, and drinks Jack Daniel's?"

"Yep."

"Does he . . . you know, dance and stuff?"

"Yeah. He likes them blond. Lisa was blond, if you get my drift."

Tori rubbed both eyes with her thumb and forefinger, wondering where in the *hell* this was going. "Okay, let's get back to the case. They came in asking about Jason. There's not a whole lot in the report other than you knew him as Lisa."

"I guess not. That's about all they asked. The black cop wanted to ask more, but Carl pulled him out. I haven't heard from them since. In fact, Carl hasn't been in here since then, either."

330

"Okay. Let's forget about them. Let's talk about Lisa. Was anyone harassing her, that you knew about? Any threats?"

"No. The only one harassing her was some dude she didn't want to have anything to do with. He would come in here, watch her dance, offer to buy her drinks, but Lisa didn't want no part of him."

"Why not?"

"Lisa said the guy was straight and was just fucking with her. He was a little squirrelly guy. Came in every weekend for a while."

"Can you describe him?"

"Little short guy, kinda weird looking. Dark hair."

Tori opened up the file folder she was carrying, pulled out a picture of Richard Grayson and slid it across the bar.

"Jesus! That's him."

"Has he been in since?"

"No, I don't think so."

"Okay." Tori took the picture and slipped it back inside the folder. "Marty, you've been a big help. If you happen to see him around, you'll call me, right?" She handed over her card.

"Of course. Do you think he was the one?"

Tori scratched the back of her neck and nodded. "He's wanted in a similar crime."

"Bastard."

"That he is."


"Doctor Ferguson? I'm Detective Kennedy, this is Detective Sikes. We're with Dallas PD. Homicide."

The petite woman removed her wire-rimmed glasses and pointed to two chairs. "Sit down. I understand you have some questions about an old case."

"Yes. Thank you for taking the time to see us on such short notice," John said. He flashed one of his most charming smiles, noting with dismay that Dr. Ferguson had slid her eyes back to

Sam, dismissing him. He shrugged. Apparently Gardner was right. He sat quietly, waiting for Sam to take the lead.

"About six months ago, a Patrick Colley was found beaten and left in a Dumpster. The police labeled it a gay bashing."

She nodded. "Yes. Although *beaten* doesn't nearly describe what happened to this young man. His face was so badly disfigured, he was hardly recognizable. He was sodomized with a wooden object, his penis and testicles were smashed and cut and he'd been stabbed twelve times. And just in case that wasn't enough, he was decapitated for good measure." Dr. Ferguson flicked her glance to Sikes. "So when the police labeled him as beaten, I took offense. This man was brutalized. Detective Gardner brushed it off as gay-bashing and simply in the wrong place at the wrong time. They spent maybe a week on it, and it barely made the paper."

"I'm sorry, Doctor Ferguson," Sam said. "We have a similar case in Dallas. We were hoping you would provide us a copy of your report. We want to have our ME take a look at it for similarities."

"I know Jackson. We get along well. Of course I'll provide any help that I can. Nobody deserves to die this way and have it simply dismissed in less than a week. I'll fax over the report immediately."

Sam stood and offered her hand, noting the firm handshake the doctor gave her. "Thank you so much for your time, Doctor Ferguson. We really appreciate it."

"No problem, Detective. It was a pleasure meeting you."

Her gaze moved briefly to John and she nodded in his direction. He forced a smile to his face, then quickly followed Sam from the office.

"Damn, talk about cold as ice," he said quietly.

"You think so? I thought she was very helpful."

John laughed. "You have no clue, do you?"

"What are you talking about?"

"She was checking you out from the moment we walked in the room, and she barely gave me a glance, that's what I'm talking about."

Sam stopped. "She was not checking me out. Women don't . . . check me out."

John laughed again. "God, you are so naïve. No wonder it's taken you this long to figure out you're gay."

"I think I should be offended," she said. "Shouldn't I?"

John placed one hand on her back and gallantly opened the door for her. "No, you should not be offended. I think it's rather sweet, how innocent you are."

# Chapter Forty-six

Tori heard the door open and looked up, seeing Sam's reflection in the mirror. She grabbed a couple of paper towels and turned, drying her hands as a slow smile appeared on her face.

"Hey."

"Hey yourself," Sam said. She moved closer, stopping only when their bodies nearly brushed. "I missed you," she said quietly.

"Yeah? No fun hanging out with Sikes?"

"John has proven to be quite fun to work with, but I want my partner back."

"Good." Tori's eyes softened and she dropped them briefly to Sam's lips. "I missed you, too."

Sam reached out one hand, lightly grasping Tori's arm. "Please say we can make an early night of it. I so want to be alone with you, Tori," she whispered.

"Me, too. But I don't know about an early night. CIU is coming aboard. We're supposed to meet with them at three. We need to get everyone together and go over what we got."

"Okay. We met with Dr. Ferguson today. She told us much more about the case in Fort Worth than Detective Gardner did."

"Oh?"

"It was brutal. She's going to fax her report to Jackson. John called and briefed him."

"Good." Tori hesitated, wondering if she should tell Sam about Adams. Hell, she had to tell someone. "I talked to the bartender at The Pink Lagoon. About Jason Branson, the case that Adams and Donaldson had, the transvestite."

"How did it go?"

"He fingered Grayson. But there was something else. I'm not sure that it merits mentioning in front of the others, though. He knows Adams. He knows him as Carl," she said.

"What do you mean?"

"He said Adams comes in every Saturday night."

"You're joking."

"I'm not."

"Adams goes to a gay bar?"

"Not just any gay bar. One that caters to the transgendered crowd."

"Carl?"

Tori shrugged. "If this is just something personal with Adams, then it's not any of our business. But if it has anything to do with this case—"

"You've got to tell Malone," Sam said. "It's too much of a coincidence. Maybe that's why he didn't follow through with the investigation."

"Yes, I'm sure of it. He didn't want to be found out. But still, we hadn't fingered Grayson. He would have been just a description that would have gone nowhere."

"You still need to tell Malone."

"Yeah, I know. But shit, Adams? He's like Mr. Homophobe. I can't believe it."

"This is so weird, Tori. What if Grayson's message was for real? What if Adams does know more?"

"Then he's fucked."

"Come on. Let's get it over with. We only have thirty minutes before CIU shows up."

The squad room was quiet. Sikes and Ramirez were both staring at their computers, John occasionally interjecting something. Donaldson was sitting alone, absently tapping a pencil on his desk.

"Where's Adams?" Sam whispered.

Tori shrugged. "Had a doctor's appointment this morning but I've not seen him all day."

Malone stuck his head out of his office. "We need to meet, people. In the conference room. CIU will be here at three."

"Lieutenant, can I have a word?" Tori glanced around her. "In private?"

He nodded, then stood back to allow her into his office. "Kennedy, make sure you have enough copies of the file. Travis is bringing two other detectives with him."

"Yes, sir."

Malone shut his door and watched Tori as she fidgeted with the silver bracelet around her wrist. He studied it, wondering when she'd gotten it. He'd not noticed it before. Then he smiled. Kennedy, no doubt.

"What's up, Hunter? Something you don't want to share with the team?"

"Yeah. It may have a bearing on the case, may not. It might just be delving into someone's personal life, which I hate."

"Spill it. We don't have time for niceties."

"I saw the bartender. He described Grayson, then fingered him when I showed him the picture."

"Good. But that's not why you're here. Out with it, Hunter."

"Adams goes there. Every Saturday night. They know him as Carl."

"What the fuck?" Malone leaned forward. "Are you shitting me?"

"No, sir. Marty, that's the bartender, said when Adams and Donaldson came in asking questions, that Adams was extremely

336

nervous. They asked a couple of questions, then left. He said Adams was there the night Branson was killed. He indicated that Branson and Adams may have had contact."

"Contact? What the hell do you mean?"

"He said that Adams . . . Carl liked blondes. Lisa was a blonde."

"Jesus Christ," he murmured. "You don't think Adams whacked him, do you?"

"No. But I think they may have been involved . . . physically, at some point. It's none of our business what Adams does with his free time, but in this case, he let a murder investigation go down the drain because of it." Tori leaned forward too. "Lieutenant, what if they could have fingered Grayson then? How many lives could have been saved, not to mention two police officers?"

"Fuck, Tori. Since the bartender fingered Grayson, Travis and his crew will be going over the case with a microscope. Adams and Donaldson will get their asses busted. We've got to come clean with Travis. He's got to know everything. I'm not going to let them bring down our whole team just because Adams screwed up."

"I agree. But this is not going to be pretty."

"Adams hasn't shown up today. I'm going to have Donaldson call his house. Let me talk to Travis in private. It might help some. Send Donaldson in, then go brief the others."

"Yes, sir."

When Tori was at the door, Malone called her back.

"Tori, thanks, you did a good job. Let's hope we can put an end to this soon."


Tori took a seat next to Sam and across from Sikes and Ramirez, who were both reading through the report that Sam had given them. Tori flipped to the end, noting that Sam had added their notes from the Fort Worth case. Absent was any mention of the Branson case.

"Detective Travis will be here with CIU in a few minutes.

They're going to . . . assist us. But it's still our show. Malone says they are making all their resources available to us, so I know you all feel better about that."

"Yeah, right," Sikes said with a laugh.

"I got some news today that I wanted to share with you before CIU gets here."

"Where's Donaldson and Adams?" Ramirez asked. "Are they still on the team?"

"Adams AWOL," Tori said with a shrug. "The Lieutenant was having Donaldson try to get in touch with him."

"AWOL?"

"Look, let's just go over this quickly. When Malone gets here, we can discuss the case." Tori cleared her throat, then looked at Sam, who offered a slight smile. "I opened up the Branson case. That was the transvestite that Adams and Donaldson had a month or so ago. I went back to the bar today and spoke with Marty Stevens, the bartender. Good news is he remembers Grayson being at the bar the same Saturday night that Branson was killed. He also said that Grayson had been harassing Branson. Branson, by the way, was transgendered and went by *Lisa*." She looked at Sikes, who snorted. "I knew I could count on you for adolescent background noises, John."

"It's not that. I can just imagine Adams questioning this guy."

Tori nodded. "Which brings me to the next thing. If you'll look at the file on this case, you'll see that they questioned only the bartender and only then, a few questions at best. Reason being, Adams was a regular at the bar."

"What the hell? Adams at a gay bar?"

"He went by *Carl*."

They all stared in silence, then John broke out into a smile. "I'll be goddamned."

Tori nodded, then grinned. Soon, chuckles replaced smiles and then laughter rang out.

"It's not really funny," Sam said. "But Jesus . . . *Carl*?"

"So, was he like . . ."

338

"I don't know," Tori said. "I don't even want to think about it. It's not any of our business other than the investigation was compromised. Which brings us back to why we're here in the first place. Where the hell is Grayson? Where's he hiding? We can most likely pin this murder on him. Hopefully, the one in Fort Worth, too. But still, where the hell is he, and how do we find him?"

A quick knock on the door and Malone preceded Travis and two other detectives inside.

"You all know Detective Travis. This is Morris and Fields."

"Hunter, good to see you again," Travis said. "Kennedy."

"Hello, Detective Travis." She stood and offered her hand to both Morris and Fields, then pointed at the others. "Sikes and Ramirez."

"First of all, the Chief requested CIU to assist in your investigation. It's still your investigation. We have a serial killer, and they want a task force. However, I spoke with my Captain and everyone is in agreement that the more hands you have involved, the messier it gets. So, for now, it's just us." He looked at Hunter, who nodded. "Your Lieutenant has filled me in on the latest . . . development. While it obviously affected the investigation of the Branson case, it doesn't change the fact that we are still looking for Grayson. Any misconduct will be investigated by Internal Affairs, not us. So let's move on to Grayson. Right now, he's holding an assistant DA and it's our job to find her. When we find Grayson, if he's still alive, then we'll put our case together." He flipped open the file, then looked at Hunter. "With that said, how do we find him?"

"He stakes out his victims at gay bars, other than the ones he had access to from Belle's Hostel. You would think he would lay low for a while, especially if he's keeping Charlotte Grayson alive. And I think she's still alive. If he'd killed her, he would have displayed the body somewhere. He'd want us to know that he'd killed her. I'm no profiler, but I've been on the streets long enough to know that he'll kill again. He has to. That's his only reason for existing."

"Where does he get his money from?" Sam asked.

"Good question. He has no job that we know of."

"Bank accounts?" Travis asked.

"None."

"What about his mother?"

"She may have given him some, but she wasn't exactly wealthy. And, of course now, her assets are frozen."

"I'll have our guys do a thorough check on his financial background. There has to be something."

"Okay, good." Tori flipped through the file, stopping at the list of gay bars they'd checked out. "Page twelve lists possible targets. We've staked out Outlaws in the past, mostly because that's where the girls from Belle's went. It was where we first spotted him. We also tailed him to a men's bar called The Brickyard. We know he was at The Pink Lagoon. If we're going to stake out bars, obviously it'll have to be men's bars or Outlaws, that's the only mixed bar."

"He knows we're looking for him," Morris said. "Do you really think he's foolish enough to go out to a bar looking for his next victim?"

"Yes, I do. And right now, that's all we've got."

"And there's been no contact with him, other than the one phone call?" Travis asked.

"No. I really thought, well, I thought he'd try to contact us again. I think he gets off on it," Tori said.

A knock on the door interrupted them and Donaldson stuck his head in.

"Lieutenant?"

Malone stared. "Adams?"

"No. His wife said he left like usual this morning."

"And his cell?"

"Still no answer."

"Shit," Malone murmured.

"He may pose a problem, Lieutenant," Travis said. "I think maybe we should go to your Captain with this and see about bringing him in."

"I'd really like to talk to him before this all gets out. It would . . . ruin him."

"It's most likely going to anyway."

"What are you talking about?" Donaldson asked. "What will ruin him?"

They were saved answering by Tori's cell phone. She moved away from the table.

"Hunter."

*"Detective? It's Marty . . . from the bar."*

"Yes. What is it, Marty?" She flicked her eyes to Sam, then Malone.

*"Carl was here. He pretty much went berserk when I told him you'd been in asking about Lisa. He . . . well, he kinda trashed the place . . . broken chairs and tables. I was afraid he was going to shoot me."*

"Are you okay, Marty?"

*"Yeah, sure. He pushed me around a little, but he left. The manager already called the cops, but I thought I should let you know."*

"You did good, Marty. Hang tight. I'll be right over."

*"Okay, I'll be here."*

Tori stared around the table, then finally looked at Malone. "Adams showed up at The Pink Lagoon. That was the bartender I spoke with earlier."

"What happened?"

"Nothing. He apparently lost it when Marty told him I'd been in asking questions. He tore up the place, then left." She cleared her throat, then continued. "I think we need to go out there and see if maybe there's more going on with Adams than just this." She looked at Travis. "Maybe do a little background," she suggested. He nodded.

"What the hell are you talking about?" Donaldson demanded. "Adams isn't involved in any of this."

"Donaldson, Adams is running and we need to find him. He knows something," Tori said.

"Knows something about what? This case?"

Tori looked helplessly to Malone.

"Donaldson, let's talk in my office. Hunter, you and Sam head out there. Travis?"

"We'll do a background and run the financials on Grayson and see what hits. Let's meet again in the morning."

Tori walked over to Sikes and grasped his arm. "John, you mind coming, too?"

"Of course not. What about Tony?"

"I think maybe Donaldson might need someone here. Tony, that okay with you?"

"Sure. Just keep me posted."

# Chapter Forty-seven

"You know, I just can't wrap my mind around all this," Sikes said as they walked to the bar. "Adams? Hell, he's a grandfather."

"John, you've been a cop long enough to have pretty much seen it all," Sam said.

"Yeah, on the streets, maybe. But not in my own department. And not somebody as uptight and conservative as Richard Adams. It just doesn't make sense."

"This whole fucking case doesn't make sense," Tori said as she held the door open for them. "Marty? You here?"

A head popped up from behind the bar. "Over here, Detective." He stood up, a broom and dust pan in his hand. "Just cleaning up a bit."

They all looked around them. Smashed chairs littered the floor, and the mirror behind the bar was shattered.

"Jesus," John murmured.

"Marty, this is Detective Kennedy and Detective Sikes," she

said, pointing at her two partners. "Just tell us everything that happened."

"Okay. Maybe I should get the manager."

"No. Let's talk first." Tori picked up a fallen bar stool and sat, motioning for the others to do the same. "What time did Adams come in?"

"Carl? He came in right after three."

"Was the front door locked?"

"No. We open at three."

"Anyone else here?"

"No. Just me and the manager."

"Okay. What happened?"


"No way, Lieutenant. No way Adams was involved."

"Donaldson, I'm not saying he was involved in the murders. But your investigation was compromised on the Branson case." Malone stood, pacing behind his desk. "Didn't you think it strange Adams wanted to close the case?"

"We didn't have anything to go on."

"I guess not! You didn't fucking investigate it!" He turned on him then, pointing his finger. "And it's my ass, too. I let it go down as a dead end. I didn't check to make sure you'd covered all your bases. Hell, Donaldson, we have a serial killer to worry about. I'd like to think my detectives are professional enough to do their job without me going over every detail of every fucking case you're working on!" Malone stared, feeling the blood pounding in his head. He jerked open his desk, pulling out his nearly empty bottle of antacids.

"I was just—"

"Following his lead, I know." Malone sat back down, chewing the three tablets quickly. "Where is he, Donaldson?"

"I don't know, Lieutenant. It's not like we were close, you know."

Malone shook his head. "Fucking makes no sense. If we don't

344

find him, you're going to be left to take the blame, Donaldson." He sighed. "You and me."

They both looked up as Ramirez tapped on the glass. Malone motioned for him to enter.

"Sikes is on the line, Lieutenant."

"Thanks. Tony, why don't you get Donaldson up to speed on everything, huh?" Malone suggested, dismissing them as he reached for the phone. "We need all hands on deck for this one." He waited until his door was closed before picking up.

"Yeah, Sikes. What you got?"

"Not much. Adams turned psycho and trashed the place pretty good. The manager called it in as a disgruntled customer. Apparently, Marty the bartender has a crush on Hunter or something. He's not said a word about knowing *Carl* is really a cop."

"I hope we can keep it that way for a while. The last thing we need is for this to hit the paper. We've got to find Adams, Sikes."

"Yeah, I know. But we didn't get shit. We're heading back."

Malone sighed, then reached for his bottle of aspirin, tossing three into his mouth before picking up the phone again.

"It's Malone in Homicide. Detective Travis in?"


"Hey, why don't we grab Tony and go get a drink or something?" Sikes suggested. "It's been a hell of a long day."

Tori was caught off guard. It occurred to her that in all her years on the force, this was the first time anyone had included her in their invitation for after-hours drinks. She was speechless.

Sam noticed her hesitation and was about to decline when Tori found her voice. "That's a great idea, John. Thanks. I think we could all use a drink."

Sam tried to hide her smile, but looked sideways at Tori, noticing her normal frown missing. She made a mental note to thank John later.

Sam was the one who felt they would be leaving Donaldson out if they didn't invite him, but he declined, saying his wife was expecting him for dinner.

"But maybe next time, guys."

"Sure, man." Sikes shook his head as they walked to their cars. "One big happy family. Damn, Kennedy, see what you did."

"Me?"

Their one drink turned into two with appetizers. There was little talk of the case, and Sam suspected they all were glad to push it to the back burner, if only for a few hours. She was amazed at the change in everyone. A few short months ago, Sikes and Hunter could hardly stand to be in the same room. Now, teasing as if they were best buddies. Sam had never seen Tori open up this much, show her true self to anyone else. It pleased her so to think that Tori was finally out of the darkness that had followed her for so many years.

When they were leaving, Sam pulled John aside.

"Thanks, John. This was a wonderful idea. Tori is finally . . . letting you in. Thanks for being open to that."

"Like I said, she's a different person. Hell, I like her."

Sam laughed. "Yeah, she can have that effect on people."

They smiled at each other silently as Tori and Ramirez walked over. Tori stared, a slow smile forming.

"What are you two whispering about?"

"Nothing," Sam said quickly.

"Uh-huh."

"Where are you guys staying tonight? Your apartment again?"

Tori shook her head. "No. I don't know how Sam feels about it, but it's depressing as hell there. We got a room."

"Oh? Something fancy?"

"Fancy?" Sam laughed. "If you call the Dallas Inn fancy."

"Well, be careful. You never know about this guy," Sikes said. "Maybe you should take Malone up on his offer. It wouldn't hurt to have a unit follow you around."

"Worried about us, Sikes? Damn, you never used to be concerned about me," Tori teased.

"Hell, Hunter. Not you. It's Sam I'm worried about."

Sam squeezed his arm affectionately. "Thanks, but we'll be okay. Tomorrow we'll hit the ground running."

"Yeah we will. Okay, we'll see you in the morning. Come on, Tony. Let's let these two start their evening," John said with a wink at Sam.

Tori stared as John's laugh faded away. She turned to Sam and smiled.

"I guess we're not being too subtle, huh?"

Sam laughed, linking arms with Tori as they walked across the street to Tori's Explorer.

"Not too subtle, no. John and I had a little talk, actually. He's . . . he's okay, Tori."

"Yeah, he is. Amazing."

# Chapter Forty-eight

Tori tossed both their bags on the bed and dutifully locked the door as Sam inspected the room.

"This is nice."

"Yeah. Better."

"Your apartment wasn't bad, Tori. At least it was clean."

"That's because I'm never there to dirty it. But it's dark. And sparse."

"Yeah. It wasn't really you."

"You don't think?"

Sam walked over, wrapping both arms around Tori and pulling her close.

"No. I don't see you like that. You're all sunshine and freshness."

Tori laughed. "Sunshine, huh?"

Sam turned serious as her hand brushed Tori's cheek. "You're my sunshine," she said softly. "Don't ever forget it."

Tori's heart skipped a beat at the love she found in Sam's eyes. She would be so glad when this was all over and they could have some real time together. She bent her head to kiss her when Sam's cell rang.

"Perfect timing, as always," Sam murmured, pulling away. She checked caller ID, then groaned. "Robert."

Tori raised her eyebrows, then moved away, but Sam pulled her back, letting it go to voice mail.

"I'd rather have a shower. Share?"

"Absolutely."

Tori let out a satisfied moan as she lifted her face into the warm spray, closing her eyes as Sam's soapy hands moved lightly over her back, then gasped as those same hands slipped around her and cupped her breasts. She felt Sam move close behind her, pressing her body intimately against her own. She covered Sam's hands, holding them tight against her breasts as her eyes closed.

"Let me make love to you," Sam whispered into her ear.

Tori groaned again as Sam slid one hand lower, pausing briefly at her belly before moving into damp curls. Tori's legs parted and she jerked involuntarily as Sam's fingers found her.

"I want you to come for me, Tori. Right here," she murmured.

Tori was powerless to resist. Sam was pressed tightly against her buttocks, the warm water cascading over them both. One hand still held her breast captive and Tori moved against the other, trying to match the rhythm Sam had set. She finally moved her arms, bracing against the shower wall as Sam stroked her, feeling Sam grind into her from behind.

"Oh, God, Tori," Sam murmured. Her hips had a will of their own as she pressed her hot center against Tori's firm backside.

Tori was gasping now, feeling her own wetness mix with the warm mist around her, feeling Sam's fingers as they moved quickly over her swollen clit, feeling Sam press harder and harder against her. She squeezed her eyes shut, drawing in a quick breath as her orgasm hit without warning, nearly buckling her knees. She turned, her hand going immediately to Sam, slipping between her legs, giving her the release she craved. Her mouth covered Sam's, catching her scream as Sam's hips finally stilled.

They stood together, arms wrapped tightly around each other as they caught their breath.

"I love you," Sam murmured. "It's never been like this for me, Tori."

"Sam," Tori breathed, unable to voice her feelings. Her heart nearly stopped every time Sam said those words, so afraid it would be the last time she heard them.

"I know, sweetheart. I know." Sam pulled away, meeting Tori's smoky eyes. She reached out and brushed the water away from Tori's face. "I know."

Tori only nodded, bending slowly to capture Sam's lips.

"Come on. Bed."

They were both tired, but as soon as Sam wound herself around Tori, her insatiable desire stirred. Her hands moved freely across Tori's smooth skin, and she moaned as Tori found her mouth.

"I just can't get enough of you."

Tori wanted to tell her that it was she who couldn't get enough, but her words died as Sam's tongue found its way into her mouth. She rolled them over, pinning Sam with her weight as her mouth captured Sam's breast. Sam's moan was music to her ears, and she slipped a hand between them, searching for the wetness she knew she'd find.

"Please . . . I want your mouth on me," Sam whispered.

"Yes, sweetheart, I want that, too."

Tori moved lower, her mouth wetting a path across Sam's stomach. Sam's hands were urgent as they wound their way through her hair, urging her downward. She settled between Sam's legs, one hand pushing her thighs apart. But just as her mouth found her, just as her tongue moved through her wetness, just as Sam's hips rose to meet her, her cell rang.

"*Jesus*," Sam hissed. "Not now."

Tori groaned, but moved away from Sam, reaching blindly for her phone.

"Hunter."

*"I hope I'm not interrupting anything, bitch cop."*

Tori sat up, motioning quickly at Sam, pointing at her own cell.

"Ricky? Is that you? Damn, your timing sucks, man."

*"I knew it. You're just like all the others . . . just like her."*

"Where are you, Ricky?" Tori watched as Sam punched out Sikes's number, waiting.

*"You'll never find me."*

"Okay. Then where's Charlotte?"

*"You won't find her either. But I did leave a present for you, Detective. Just for you."*

Tori glanced once at Sam, listening as she whispered into her phone.

"You didn't have to give me a present, Ricky. I think you've done enough." His quiet laugh sent chills down her spine.

*"Check the alley behind The Brickyard. And Detective, don't think you can hide at the Dallas Inn again tomorrow."*

Tori tossed her cell down, then grabbed Sam's.

"Sikes?"

"I'm here."

"The alley behind The Brickyard. We'll meet you there."

"Okay, I'm on it."

Tori was nearly shaking as she disconnected. She reached for Sam, embracing her.

"He's knows we're here," she said quietly. "We've got to be careful. He may be watching."

"Shit. What did he say?"

"He said he left me a present in the alley behind The Brickyard. And he said we shouldn't hide here again tomorrow."

"That son of a bitch!" Sam pulled away, pacing naked across the floor. "If I see the bastard, I'll shoot him myself!"

Tori stared, a smile forming before she laughed outright. Sam stared at her.

"What?"

"You're adorable."

351

Sam put her hands on her hips, head cocked sideways as she watched Tori. Only then did it dawn on her that they were both completely naked. She blushed.

"Jesus, look at us."

"Yeah, look at us." Tori reached for her jeans. "Come on, Sam. We'll call it in on the way."


The flashing lights of a police unit guided them into the alley and Tori parked, looking for Sikes's car.

"I don't think he's here yet," Sam said.

"No. He lives in North Dallas."

They both pulled out their shields, walking to the Dumpster that the two uniforms were gathered around.

"What we got?" Tori asked.

"Male victim. He's . . . fuck, he's decapitated."

"Son of a bitch," Sam whispered. "Did you call it in?"

"Yes ma'am. ME's on the way."

Tori peered into the Dumpster, her gasp bringing Sam to her side.

"Oh my God."

"Jesus fucking Christ," Tori murmured.

"You know him?"

Tori looked up, meeting the eyes of one of the officers. She nodded.

Blood covered his naked body. His stomach had been ripped opened, much like Rachel Anderson's. His severed head was placed carefully on his torso.

"Jesus Christ," she whispered again. She reached for her cell, finally turning away. "Sam?"

Sam still stared at the body, her head shaking slowly back and forth.

"Sam?"

She finally looked up, her eyes wild with fright.

"Secure the area," Tori said.

Sam nodded. "Right . . . okay, sure. Secure the area."

Tori moved away as Sam began giving instructions. She punched out a number, waiting nearly five rings before it was answered.

"Lieutenant . . . it's Hunter. We've got another body." She could hear him sitting up, hear covers moving.

"Charlotte Grayson?"

"No, sir. I think you want to get down here for this one." She looked up as Sikes rushed into the alley. "It's Jenkins."

"What the fuck?"

Tori pointed to the Dumpster as Sikes approached, then looked around for Sam. "Yes, sir. Jenkins. He's much like the others."

"Holy shit."

"ME's on the way." She paused. "Grayson called me tonight on my cell. He told me he'd left a present for me in the alley behind The Brickyard." She could hear Malone dressing, hear his wife whispering to him. She closed her eyes, wondering when this madness would end.

"How the hell did he get your cell number?"

"I don't know, Lieutenant."

"Charlotte Grayson?"

"No, she wouldn't have it."

"Shit, shit, shit. Okay, Hunter. I'll call Travis on my way in. After you're done there, we'll meet at the station. Has anyone called Sikes? Ramirez?"

"Sikes is here."

"Okay. Let's keep it together." He paused. "I need to call the Captain."

"Yes, sir."

"Hunter? You okay?"

"No. It's getting too fucking personal." Sikes walked over, meeting her eyes. "We'll meet you there, Lieutenant."

She disconnected, still staring at John.

"You okay?"

"No. Shit, John, he killed him because of *me*."

"What the hell are you talking about?"

"Me and Jenkins . . . hell, we never got along. Ever since that time I saw him at the bar, you know."

"What bar?"

Tori closed her eyes, forgetting that she and John had never shared things, had never communicated.

"A few years ago, I saw him and another guy . . . getting it on at a bar. Ever since then—"

"Hell . . . *Jenkins?*"

"Yeah. And somehow, Grayson knew that. He said he left me a present."

"That doesn't mean shit."

"He killed him for me."

"Fuck that. He's just jacking with you, Tori."

"What? You think it's a coincidence?" she yelled. "Random? And it happens to be Jenkins?"

Sam walked over, her gaze moving between the two of them.

"Stop it," she said forcibly. She grabbed Tori's arm, feeling the tension that flowed through her. "Jenkins is not dead because of you."

"Sam—"

"No. You listen. If he wanted to get to you, he'd go after me, Tori. He knows Jenkins from somewhere else. There's some other connection. And he said it was a present because it's another killing. That's what he does. He kills."

Tori finally let her breath out, meeting first Sam's eyes, then John's. "I'm sorry, man. It's just . . ."

"No problem. Hell, if the guy was calling me on my cell, I'd be freaked, too."

They all looked up as more vehicles approached, lights flashing. Rita Spencer stepped out of the van, bag in hand.

"Hunter? Another one?"

"Yeah. Another one."

# Chapter Forty-nine

"Where the hell is he hiding?" Tori asked again as she drove through the empty streets.

"Some obscure motel?"

"No. He's got Charlotte forcibly restrained. It'd have to be someplace more private."

"Maybe he's got a friend somewhere?"

"No, Sam. He's a loner. He lives alone, he kills alone."

"Yeah. Well, maybe CIU will dig up something tomorrow."

"No job, no money," Tori murmured. "And he's hiding . . . somewhere. Somewhere where he won't be noticed."

"Jesus, you don't think Adams is in on it and is hiding him?"

Tori shook her head. "Adams may have fallen off the deep end, but I doubt that far."

"Maybe an abandoned house or a condemned building?"

Tori shrugged. If that were the case, they would never find him. Her mind reeled as she tried to put herself in his place, tried to imagine where she'd feel safe. Then her eyes widened and she slammed on her brakes, making an illegal turn on the deserted street.

"What the hell are you doing?" Sam asked as she grabbed the dash.

"I know where he is."

"*What?*"

Tori was already punching out Sikes's number on her cell as she drove with one hand.

"Hey, it's me. Are you at the station yet?"

"Just drove up. Where are you?"

"We're going to check something out, John. Stay close to the phone, okay?"

"Where are you going, Hunter? You need backup."

"If my guess is right, we can't go charging in with backup. We're just going to check things out first. Don't worry, I'm not crazy enough to go busting in alone."

"Right. Who are you kidding?"

"We'll call, John. Promise."

She tossed the phone on her console, then grinned at Sam. "Where would you go to feel safe? Somewhere where nobody lives, where nobody comes in and out, where a yellow crime scene tape deters even vandals."

"Jesus Christ . . . *Belle's?*"

"Exactly."

"Oh, Tori. That would just be crazy. Investigators could drop by anytime looking for evidence. That would be too risky."

"He could be perfectly safe there until it sold. He grew up there, Sam. He knows all the secret places."

"What are you talking about?"

"The passages, Sam. The servants' quarters. Remember, the interior of the house is closed off."

"Holy shit. And you think . . . damn, talk about balls."

"Yes. He's been sitting right under our noses, so close no one would dream of looking there."

Sam reached out and squeezed Tori's thigh. "We shouldn't do this alone, Tori. Let's call John, get some backup."

"We will. Let's check it out first. I could be way off base." But in her gut, she knew she wasn't. The bastard was there. She could feel it.

The traffic was sparse at this time of the morning. She slowed and turned off her lights as they approached Belle's. The yellow crime scene tape glowed under the streetlights. A few cars lined the street, but all was quiet. Tori parked a block away and they sat and stared.

"I've got a bad feeling, Tori," Sam whispered.

"You feel it, too, don't you? He's in there."

"Yeah."

"Procedure states we call in a tactical unit and flush him out."

"But?"

"But I don't think Charlotte Grayson would survive it." She reached for her phone again. Sikes answered on the first ring.

"Hang on. The Lieutenant's about to have a stroke," John said, handing the phone over.

"Hunter? What the hell are you doing?" he demanded.

"Checking out a hunch, Lieutenant."

"Yeah, well check it out with fucking backup! You were supposed to come here first. Travis is here. The fucking Mayor has already been called. It's two o'clock in the morning and the goddamn paper has already called. Get your ass over here!" he demanded.

"We're at Belle's. I think he may be hiding inside."

"What the fuck? Hunter, have you lost your mind? It's a goddamn crime scene. Even he's not crazy enough to hole up there."

"Not crazy. Smart. It's an old plantation house. The interior has rooms that have been closed off for years."

"You're reaching here, Hunter. You know that, don't you?"

"I don't think so. I just want to check it out."

"Shit." A pause, then, "Okay, check it out. Don't fucking go inside until some units get there. You hear me?"

"Don't send the troops with horns blasting, Lieutenant. If he's here—"

"Just stay put. We're on our way."

"Yes, sir."

"Okay. Good. You're listening to reason. There's a first time for everything, Hunter."

Tori glanced at Sam and shrugged. "They're on their way, but he thinks it's a dead end."

"Good."

Tori squeezed her hand. "We're going to be fine. Now turn off the ringer on your phone."

"What for?"

"Because we don't want it to ring while we're snooping around."

"Backup?"

"Yeah. We won't go inside. I just want to look around."

Sam stared, hating the look in Tori's eyes. It was fierce, and it sent chills over her. But she nodded. "Okay. I trust you."

Tori's eyes softened. "Sam, I promise, I won't let anything happen to you."

"I'm more worried about you, actually."

"We're just going to look around," she said again.

They shut the doors quietly, then faded into the shadows, Sam following closely behind Tori. When the dark, hulking shape of the house covered them, Tori pulled out her weapon, and Sam did the same. They stayed close to the shrubs, listening for any sound from inside. The old brick wall that served as a fence blocked their way, and Tori pulled herself up, swinging her leg over and landing quietly on the wet grass on the other side.

"Sam," she whispered. "Come on."

"Shit," Sam murmured. She looked for a foothold, struggling to pull herself up. She managed to get one leg over, then Tori was there, pulling her down beside her. A rustling in the bushes beside them startled Sam, and Tori clamped a hand over her mouth.

"Cat," she whispered.

Sam let out her breath and nodded. They walked on, crouched low to the ground. The windows were shuttered on this side of the house. Sam assumed these were Belle's quarters. There was a small brick patio, but the blinds were pulled over the door. Tori motioned for her to stop and she did, watching as Tori crept up on the patio, head cocked, listening. She held her breath as Tori reached for the knob, silently thankful that it didn't turn.

They both jumped when they heard glass breaking from inside. Murmurs and a muffled scream, then silence.

"Oh shit," she whispered, seeing the expression on Tori's face. "No! We wait for backup."

"Goddammit, Sam . . . she's still alive."

"Tori . . ." But Tori had started running back to the brick fence. "Fuck," she muttered, following. She found Tori crawling through a window on the front porch. "Stubborn, macho . . ."

"Shhh."

"You are pissing me off," Sam hissed.

"Fine. Stay out there and keep a lookout then."

"Like hell I will!"

Their eyes met, both fierce as they stared.

"Sam . . ."

"What?"

"I love you."

Sam's breath left her, and she leaned against the wall to steady herself. She opened her mouth to speak, but no words would come.

"I just . . . wanted to make sure you knew that."

"Tori . . . damn, your timing sucks, sweetheart."

Tori shrugged. "Kinda new at this," she whispered. "Come on."

They crept into the entryway, going immediately to Belle's office. The door was closed but unlocked. They both cringed as the hinges screamed a warning, then silence.

Tori stared at the doors, five of them. Which one? She looked at Sam who only shrugged. Tori walked to the first one and turned the knob. It opened. Again, the old hinges moaned. Inside was nothing but darkness. Tori's small flashlight was no help. The long hallway seemed endless as Tori stepped inside, Sam following close behind. Thirty feet later, they came to another door. Tori pressed her ear against it, listening.

"Nothing," she whispered. "Maybe we should try another."

Sam was about to answer when loud banging on the front door made her jump. They both turned, eyes wide.

*"Grayson! Let me in!"*

Sam whipped around, meeting Tori's eyes in the shadows.

"Is that . . ."

Running footsteps sounded through the walls, and Tori reached for Sam, pushing her against the wall. They heard a door open in Belle's office, and Tori quickly made her way back the way they'd come.

*"Let me in!"*

*"Shut the fuck up! What the hell are you doing here?"*

Sam glanced once at Tori. "Adams?"

"Yeah. Come on!"

Sam's heart was pounding so loudly that she could hardly make out the yelling. She saw Tori at the door. She wanted to call to her, to tell her not to go out, but Tori had the door open, weapon held out in front of her.

Gunfire sounded and Sam hit the floor.

"Tori!"

She got up, running blindly through the door, only to collide with Richard Grayson. He grabbed her easily, and she felt the cold metal of his gun touch her cheek.

"Gotcha."

Wild eyes looked for Tori and she stared into the barrel of Tori's gun as it was pointed at both her and Grayson.

"Drop your goddamn gun, Grayson. We are *not* going to do this," Tori said calmly.

"Bitch cop, you're not going to shoot me. We both know that." He laughed. "You're going to end up like Carl over there," he said, motioning with his head.

Sam's eyes slid to Adams, staring as he lay in a pool of his own blood.

"Then it'll just be me and her," he threatened.

Sam squeezed her eyes shut as his grip tightened.

"And you know what I'm going to do to her? I'm going to do it like a man. Like a *man*!" he yelled. "Like it's supposed to be!"

Sam nearly trembled at his words and she shook herself, memories of the warehouse crowding in, taking over, threatening to overwhelm her senses. She would die before she let this man touch her.

"Oh, no you're not," Tori nearly whispered. She stepped closer, moving into the center of the room. "You're not going to *touch* her, you little faggot."

"I'm in control. Not you. Not ever you. I have the power. Just like I had over Adams. He was a naughty boy. Very naughty." He laughed as he followed Tori's movements, pulling Sam along with him. "He gave me everything I wanted, just because he didn't want his family to find out. Stupid bastard."

"Stop this right now, Grayson. Backup will be here any minute. You're done. Now let her go before I blow your fucking brains out."

Tori's eyes widened as his index finger tightened on the trigger. "I'll shoot her so fast you won't have time to blink. So, drop *your* fucking gun, Detective."

Tori's eyes locked with his, and she felt her pulse pounding in her temples at the darkness she saw there. She slid her glance to Sam, seeing fear in her eyes.

"Do it now!"

"Okay . . . okay. Calm down, Grayson." Tori lowered her weapon, hands outstretched. "Look, I'm putting it down. Don't hurt her."

"No, Tori. Don't . . . please," Sam whispered.

"Shut up!"

Grayson pulled Sam roughly against him, his eyes never leaving Tori as she bent and laid her weapon on the wooden floor.

He grinned, loosening his hold on Sam. "Stupid bitch." He raised his gun, pointing it at Tori. "Say good-bye."

Sam screamed at the sound of gunfire, then hit the floor as Grayson was knocked back against the wall, his hand going to his shoulder as blood seeped through his fingers. Tori dove for her gun, dropping it once as it slid from her sweaty hands. Adams fired again, his shot missing badly as he collapsed. Grayson raised his gun just as Tori found hers. She fired four times, each shot jerking Grayson's body as he was slammed against the wall. His eyes finally went blank as he slid unceremoniously to the floor.

"Tori?"

"I'm okay. You?"

"Yeah."

Tori stared, meeting her eyes, and nodded. She was shaking so badly, her weapon fell from her hands. Then Sam was there, warm hands stroking her face, arms pulling her close.

"I was afraid," Tori whispered. "I was afraid he was going to hurt you."

"I know. I know, sweetheart. It's over."

Tori closed her eyes for a second, chasing out old memories. When she opened them, Sam was still there, love and compassion looking back at her.

"Hell of a day," Tori murmured.

"Yes. Hell of a day." Sam squeezed her arm, thankful to finally hear cars approaching, doors slamming, feet running. "Backup."

Tori nodded. "Adams?"

Sam shook her head. "No."

Tori finally looked at Adams, his lifeless eyes staring past them. Then Sikes was there, bending to Adams, fingers held against his neck, searching for a pulse. He stood up slowly, his eyes finding Tori's. Then he smiled.

"Just checking out a hunch, huh?"

Tori shrugged. "I hate it when I'm right."

"Sure you do."

# Chapter Fifty

Sam lazily rolled her head, her eyes adjusting to the bright sunshine. She must have fallen asleep again. The rocking of the boat did that to her. She shielded her eyes, looking for Tori. What she saw stole her breath away. Tori was standing in only a sports bra and shorts, the sun nearly swallowing her as she casually tossed in her line then absently reeled it back again.

As if sensing her watching, Tori turned her head slowly, a smile slashing across her features.

"How was your nap?"

Sam sat up and stretched. "My third nap of the day was great, thanks." She walked over, slipping her arms around Tori's bare torso. "You've been doing this all day. Catch dinner yet?"

Tori laughed. "No. It's too hot to catch anything. You'll have to settle for burgers."

Ah. The fishing was just therapy. Sam nodded, understanding. They had two days to themselves, two days to recover. Then, interviews scheduled with Internal Affairs. They weren't worried. It was just a formality, Detective Travis had assured them. Just putting all the pieces in place so they could close the case. She didn't want to think about it, but Charlotte Grayson's face kept creeping into her mind. She'd looked so helpless, so frightened when they'd found her chained to the bed right next to three other bodies. Sam knew it would take years for Charlotte Grayson to recover, if she ever did.

The ringing of her cell phone interrupted her thoughts and she moved back to her lounge chair, lazily reached for the phone, frowning slightly when she saw caller ID. Robert. She thought of just letting it go to voice mail. It would be easier. But this had to end. She answered as businesslike as possible.

"Kennedy."

"*Samantha?*"

She rolled her eyes. "Yes, Robert." Her eyes flicked to Tori, noticing the slight straightening of her shoulders, but nothing else to indicate that she was listening. Sam smiled, knowing without a doubt that Tori hung on her every word.

"*Are you okay? I heard there was a shooting.*"

"Yes. But I'm fine."

"*I've been worried. You haven't called. I was thinking maybe we could get dinner,*" he said hopefully.

"Robert, no. I'm not going to have dinner with you." She rubbed her eyes, slowly shaking her head.

"*But Samantha, you—*"

"Robert, listen to me. It's over. Why can't you accept that?"

"*I love you. Why can't you accept that?*"

"Oh, Robert. I don't want to hurt you. I really don't." *Shit.* "But . . . there's someone else in my life. Someone that I've fallen in love with. I know you won't understand, but you've got to accept this."

"*What are you saying?*"

Sam glanced at Tori, meeting her eyes. "Tori . . . Tori and I have . . . well . . . we've . . ."

"*Tori? Your partner? You're not . . . oh my God.*"

"Yes."

"*Samantha, please, you can't be serious. She's a fucking dyke, for God's sake!*"

"I'm in love with her, Robert. I'm sorry. I know you don't understand this. But she's what I want. She's who I want to spend the rest of my life with."

"*I can't believe this! What the hell happened?*"

"Robert, it wasn't good with us and you know it. I didn't know why, not until I met Tori. I've been living a lie for so long. I won't live like that any longer. I know who I am and who I love," she said quietly, her eyes never leaving Tori's. "You've got to let this go, Robert."

"*You expect me to believe that you're . . . a fucking dyke?*"

Sam bristled. "You know what? I don't really care what you believe. Let it go, Robert. It's over."

"*But . . . no, I don't believe that. Samantha, please, come to your senses. What has she done to you? You can't possibly—*"

Sam tilted her head, then pulled the phone away from her ear, staring at it as his monologue continued. Without warning, she leaned back, tossing the phone overboard, listening with pleasure at the splash it created in the lake.

Tori lifted an eyebrow, then turned back to her fishing, tossing the line into the lake once again.

Sam nearly laughed at Tori's indifference. No doubt Tori had been listening to all she said. She got up, walking slowly to Tori, slipping her arms around her from behind. She kissed Tori's back, squeezing gently. Right now, she didn't want to think about Robert . . . or the case. It was their time. Right now, she just wanted to think about *them*.

Tori turned in her arms, bringing Sam close, burying her head at Sam's neck. Sam sighed, loving the sensations that washed over her each and every time Tori touched her. She felt the familiar stirrings of desire, desire that ignited with just the lightest of touches.

Tori squeezed her eyes shut, wondering again, for the hundredth time, what she'd done to deserve this. This beautiful woman loved her, cared about her. This woman, who brought so much joy into her life—really, really loved her.

"Sam?"

"Hmm?"

"Can we make love?" Tori whispered. "I . . . I need that right now."

Sam shivered, Tori's breath tickling her ear. She pulled back, gently placing her lips against Tori's. The woman had been so quiet, ever since the shooting at Belle's. She knew that Adams's death affected Tori more than she let on. She was blaming herself, Sam knew.

"We can make love all day, all night," Sam murmured. "It would never be enough."

Tori captured her hands, bringing them up to Tori's breast, holding them there. Her eyes turned serious and Sam waited, wondering at the sadness in them.

"Sam . . . Sam, I want to give you something."

Sam nodded. "Okay."

"But you have to promise me something first."

Sam nodded again.

"You have to be gentle with it. It's very . . . it's very fragile, but it's a gift I've never given anyone before."

Sam felt tears gather as she saw the love in Tori's eyes. She nodded.

"I want you to have . . . my heart, Sam. I . . . I love you. You're my light in this dark world, you make everything seem okay, no matter what." Then Tori tilted her head, smiling slightly at the tears she saw. "Oh, Sam. Don't cry."

"I'm sorry." Sam wound her arms tight around Tori. "It's just . . . God, I love you so much. I sometimes feel like I'm just going to explode with it."

Tori nodded. "I know . . . me, too. So, back to my original question."

Sam grinned and pulled Tori with her into the cabin.

"Yes."

## About the Author

Gerri lives in the Piney Woods of East Texas with her partner, Diane, and their two labs, Zach and Max. The resident cats Sierra, Tori and now Jordan round out the household. Hobbies include any outdoor activity, from tending the orchard and vegetable garden to hiking in the woods with camera and binoculars. For more, visit Gerri's Web site at: www.gerrihill.com.

LOVE ON THE LINE by Laura DeHart Young. 240 pp. Kay leaves a younger woman behind to go on a mission to Alaska . . . will she regret it?     ISBN 1-59493-008-2   $12.95

UNDER THE SOUTHERN CROSS by Claire McNab. 200 pp. Lee, an American travel agent, goes down under and meets Australian Alex, and the sparks fly under the Southern Cross.     ISBN 1-59493-029-5   $12.95

SUGAR by Karin Kallmaker. 240 pp. Three women want sugar from Sugar, who can't make up her mind.     ISBN 1-59493-001-5   $12.95

FALL GUY by Claire McNab. 200 pp. 16th Detective Inspector Carol Ashton Mystery.     ISBN 1-59493-000-7   $12.95

ONE SUMMER NIGHT by Gerri Hill. 232 pp. Johanna swore to never fall in love again—but then she met the charming Kelly . . .     ISBN 1-59493-007-4   $12.95

TALK OF THE TOWN TOO by Saxon Bennett. 181 pp. Second in the series about wild and fun loving friends.     ISBN 1-931513-77-5   $12.95

LOVE SPEAKS HER NAME by Laura DeHart Young. 170 pp. Love and friendship, desire and intrigue, spark this exciting sequel to *Forever and the Night*.     ISBN 1-59493-002-3   $12.95

TO HAVE AND TO HOLD by Peggy J. Herring. 184 pp. By finally letting down her defenses, will Dorian be opening herself to a devastating betrayal?     ISBN 1-59493-005-8   $12.95

WILD THINGS by Karin Kallmaker. 228 pp. Dutiful daughter Faith has met the perfect man. There's just one problem: she's in love with his sister.     ISBN 1-931513-64-3   $12.95

SHARED WINDS by Kenna White. 216 pp. Can Emma rebuild more than just Lanny's marina?     ISBN 1-59493-006-6   $12.95

THE UNKNOWN MILE by Jaime Clevenger. 253 pp. Kelly's world is getting more and more complicated every moment.     ISBN 1-931513-57-0   $12.95

TREASURED PAST by Linda Hill. 189 pp. A shared passion for antiques leads to love.     ISBN 1-59493-003-1   $12.95

SIERRA CITY by Gerri Hill. 284 pp. Chris and Jesse cannot deny their growing attraction . . .     ISBN 1-931513-98-8   $12.95

ALL THE WRONG PLACES by Karin Kallmaker. 174 pp. Sex and the single girl—Brandy is looking for love and usually she finds it. Karin Kallmaker's first *After Dark* erotic novel.     ISBN 1-931513-76-7   $12.95

WHEN THE CORPSE LIES A Motor City Thriller by Therese Szymanski. 328 pp. Butch bad-girl Brett Higgins is used to waking up next to beautiful women she hardly knows. Problem is, this one's dead.     ISBN 1-931513-74-0   $12.95

GUARDED HEARTS by Hannah Rickard. 240 pp. Someone's reminding Alyssa about her secret past, and then she becomes the suspect in a series of burglaries.     ISBN 1-931513-99-6   $12.95

ONCE MORE WITH FEELING by Peggy J. Herring. 184 pp. Lighthearted, loving, romantic adventure.     ISBN 1-931513-60-0   $12.95

TANGLED AND DARK A Brenda Strange Mystery by Patty G. Henderson. 240 pp. When investigating a local death, Brenda finds two possible killers—one diagnosed with Multiple Personality Disorder.     ISBN 1-931513-75-9   $12.95

WHITE LACE AND PROMISES by Peggy J. Herring. 240 pp. Maxine and Betina realize sex may not be the most important thing in their lives. ISBN 1-931513-73-2 $12.95

UNFORGETTABLE by Karin Kallmaker. 288 pp. Can Rett find love with the cheerleader who broke her heart so many years ago? ISBN 1-931513-63-5 $12.95

HIGHER GROUND by Saxon Bennett. 280 pp. A delightfully complex reflection of the successful, high society lives of a small group of women. ISBN 1-931513-69-4 $12.95

LAST CALL A Detective Franco Mystery by Baxter Clare. 240 pp. Frank overlooks all else to try to solve a cold case of two murdered children . . . ISBN 1-931513-70-8 $12.95

ONCE UPON A DYKE: NEW EXPLOITS OF FAIRY-TALE LESBIANS by Karin Kallmaker, Julia Watts, Barbara Johnson & Therese Szymanski. 320 pp. You've never read fairy tales like these before! From Bella After Dark. ISBN 1-931513-71-6 $14.95

FINEST KIND OF LOVE by Diana Tremain Braund. 224 pp. Can Molly and Carolyn stop clashing long enough to see beyond their differences? ISBN 1-931513-68-6 $12.95

DREAM LOVER by Lyn Denison. 188 pp. A soft, sensuous, romantic fantasy. ISBN 1-931513-96-1 $12.95

NEVER SAY NEVER by Linda Hill. 224 pp. A classic love story . . . where rules aren't the only things broken. ISBN 1-931513-67-8 $12.95

PAINTED MOON by Karin Kallmaker. 214 pp. Stranded together in a snowbound cabin, Jackie and Leah's lives will never be the same. ISBN 1-931513-53-8 $12.95

WIZARD OF ISIS by Jean Stewart. 240 pp. Fifth in the exciting Isis series. ISBN 1-931513-71-4 $12.95

WOMAN IN THE MIRROR by Jackie Calhoun. 216 pp. Josey learns to love again, while her niece is learning to love women for the first time. ISBN 1-931513-78-3 $12.95

SUBSTITUTE FOR LOVE by Karin Kallmaker. 200 pp. When Holly and Reyna meet the combination adds up to pure passion. But what about tomorrow? ISBN 1-931513-62-7 $12.95

GULF BREEZE by Gerri Hill. 288 pp. Could Carly really be the woman Pat has always been searching for? ISBN 1-931513-97-X $12.95

THE TOMSTOWN INCIDENT by Penny Hayes. 184 pp. Caught between two worlds, Eloise must make a decision that will change her life forever. ISBN 1-931513-56-2 $12.95

MAKING UP FOR LOST TIME by Karin Kallmaker. 240 pp. Discover delicious recipes for romance by the undisputed mistress. ISBN 1-931513-61-9 $12.95

THE WAY LIFE SHOULD BE by Diana Tremain Braund. 173 pp. With which woman will Jennifer find the true meaning of love? ISBN 1-931513-66-X $12.95

BACK TO BASICS: A BUTCH/FEMME ANTHOLOGY edited by Therese Szymanski—from Bella After Dark. 324 pp. ISBN 1-931513-35-X $14.95

SURVIVAL OF LOVE by Frankie J. Jones. 236 pp. What will Jody do when she falls in love with her best friend's daughter? ISBN 1-931513-55-4 $12.95

LESSONS IN MURDER by Claire McNab. 184 pp. 1st Detective Inspector Carol Ashton Mystery. ISBN 1-931513-65-1 $12.95

DEATH BY DEATH by Claire McNab. 167 pp. 5th Denise Cleever Thriller. ISBN 1-931513-34-1 $12.95

CAUGHT IN THE NET by Jessica Thomas. 188 pp. A wickedly observant story of mystery, danger, and love in Provincetown. ISBN 1-931513-54-6 $12.95

DREAMS FOUND by Lyn Denison. Australian Riley embarks on a journey to meet her birth mother . . . and gains not just a family, but the love of her life. ISBN 1-931513-58-9 $12.95

A MOMENT'S INDISCRETION by Peggy J. Herring. 154 pp. Jackie is torn between her better judgment and the overwhelming attraction she feels for Valerie.
ISBN 1-931513-59-7 $12.95

IN EVERY PORT by Karin Kallmaker. 224 pp. Jessica has a woman in every port. Will meeting Cat change all that? ISBN 1-931513-36-8 $12.95

TOUCHWOOD by Karin Kallmaker. 240 pp. Rayann loves Louisa. Louisa loves Rayann. Can the decades between their ages keep them apart? ISBN 1-931513-37-6 $12.95

WATERMARK by Karin Kallmaker. 248 pp. Teresa wants a future with a woman whose heart has been frozen by loss. Sequel to *Touchwood*. ISBN 1-931513-38-4 $12.95

EMBRACE IN MOTION by Karin Kallmaker. 240 pp. Has Sarah found lust or love?
ISBN 1-931513-39-2 $12.95

ONE DEGREE OF SEPARATION by Karin Kallmaker. 232 pp. Sizzling small town romance between Marian, the town librarian, and the new girl from the big city.
ISBN 1-931513-30-9 $12.95

CRY HAVOC A Detective Franco Mystery by Baxter Clare. 240 pp. A dead hustler with a headless rooster in his lap sends Lt. L.A. Franco headfirst against Mother Love.
ISBN 1-931513931-7 $12.95

DISTANT THUNDER by Peggy J. Herring. 294 pp. Bankrobbing drifter Cordy awakens strange new feelings in Leo in this romantic tale set in the Old West.
ISBN 1-931513-28-7 $12.95

COP OUT by Claire McNab. 216 pp. 4th Detective Inspector Carol Ashton Mystery.
ISBN 1-931513-29-5 $12.95

BLOOD LINK by Claire McNab. 159 pp. 15th Detective Inspector Carol Ashton Mystery. Is Carol unwittingly playing into a deadly plan? ISBN 1-931513-27-9 $12.95

TALK OF THE TOWN by Saxon Bennett. 239 pp. With enough beer, barbecue and B.S., anything is possible! ISBN 1-931513-18-X $12.95

MAYBE NEXT TIME by Karin Kallmaker. 256 pp. Sabrina has everything she ever wanted—except Jorie. ISBN 1-931513-26-0 $12.95

WHEN GOOD GIRLS GO BAD: A Motor City Thriller by Therese Szymanski. 230 pp. Brett, Randi, and Allie join forces to stop a serial killer. ISBN 1-931513-11-2 $12.95

A DAY TOO LONG: A Helen Black Mystery by Pat Welch. 328 pp. This time Helen's fate is in her own hands. ISBN 1-931513-22-8 $12.95

THE RED LINE OF YARMALD by Diana Rivers. 256 pp. The Hadra's only hope lies in a magical red line . . . climactic sequel to *Clouds of War*. ISBN 1-931513-23-6 $12.95

OUTSIDE THE FLOCK by Jackie Calhoun. 224 pp. Jo embraces her new love and life.
ISBN 1-931513-13-9 $12.95

LEGACY OF LOVE by Marianne K. Martin. 224 pp. Read the whole Sage Bristo story.
ISBN 1-931513-15-5 $12.95

STREET RULES: A Detective Franco Mystery by Baxter Clare. 304 pp. Gritty, fast-paced mystery with compelling Detective L.A. Franco. ISBN 1-931513-14-7 $12.95

RECOGNITION FACTOR: 4th Denise Cleever Thriller by Claire McNab. 176 pp. Denise Cleever tracks a notorious terrorist to America. ISBN 1-931513-24-4 $12.95

NORA AND LIZ by Nancy Garden. 296 pp. Lesbian romance by the author of *Annie on My Mind*.　　　　　　　　　　　　　　　ISBN 1931513-20-1　$12.95

MIDAS TOUCH by Frankie J. Jones. 208 pp. Sandra had everything but love.
　　　　　　　　　　　　　　　　　　　ISBN 1-931513-21-X　$12.95

BEYOND ALL REASON by Peggy J. Herring. 240 pp. A romance hotter than Texas.
　　　　　　　　　　　　　　　　　　　ISBN 1-9513-25-2　　$12.95

ACCIDENTAL MURDER: 14th Detective Inspector Carol Ashton Mystery by Claire McNab. 208 pp. Carol Ashton tracks an elusive killer.　　ISBN 1-931513-16-3　$12.95

SEEDS OF FIRE: Tunnel of Light Trilogy, Book 2 by Karin Kallmaker writing as Laura Adams. 274 pp. In Autumn's dreams no one is who they seem.　ISBN 1-931513-19-8　$12.95

DRIFTING AT THE BOTTOM OF THE WORLD by Auden Bailey. 288 pp. Beautifully written first novel set in Antarctica.　　　　　　ISBN 1-931513-17-1　$12.95

CLOUDS OF WAR by Diana Rivers. 288 pp. Women unite to defend Zelindar!
　　　　　　　　　　　　　　　　　　　ISBN 1-931513-12-0　$12.95

DEATHS OF JOCASTA: 2nd Micky Knight Mystery by J.M. Redmann. 408 pp. Sexy and intriguing Lambda Literary Award–nominated mystery.　ISBN 1-931513-10-4　$12.95

LOVE IN THE BALANCE by Marianne K. Martin. 256 pp. The classic lesbian love story, back in print!　　　　　　　　　　　　ISBN 1-931513-08-2　$12.95

THE COMFORT OF STRANGERS by Peggy J. Herring. 272 pp. Lela's work was her passion . . . until now.　　　　　　　　　　ISBN 1-931513-09-0　$12.95

WHEN EVIL CHANGES FACE: A Motor City Thriller by Therese Szymanski. 240 pp. Brett Higgins is back in another heart-pounding thriller.　ISBN 0-9677753-3-7　$11.95

CHICKEN by Paula Martinac. 208 pp. Lynn finds that the only thing harder than being in a lesbian relationship is ending one.　　　ISBN 1-931513-07-4　$11.95

TAMARACK CREEK by Jackie Calhoun. 208 pp. An intriguing story of love and danger.
　　　　　　　　　　　　　　　　　　　ISBN 1-931513-06-6　$11.95

DEATH BY THE RIVERSIDE: 1st Micky Knight Mystery by J.M. Redmann. 320 pp. Finally back in print, the book that launched the Lambda Literary Award–winning Micky Knight mystery series.　　　　　　　　ISBN 1-931513-05-8　$11.95

EIGHTH DAY: A Cassidy James Mystery by Kate Calloway. 272 pp. In the eighth installment of the Cassidy James mystery series, Cassidy goes undercover at a camp for troubled teens.　　　　　　　　　　　　　　ISBN 1-931513-04-X　$11.95

MIRRORS by Marianne K. Martin. 208 pp. Jean Carson and Shayna Bradley fight for a future together.　　　　　　　　　　ISBN 1-931513-02-3　$11.95

THE ULTIMATE EXIT STRATEGY: A Virginia Kelly Mystery by Nikki Baker. 240 pp. The long-awaited return of the wickedly observant Virginia Kelly.
　　　　　　　　　　　　　　　　　　　ISBN 1-931513-03-1　$11.95

FOREVER AND THE NIGHT by Laura DeHart Young. 224 pp. Desire and passion ignite the frozen Arctic in this exciting sequel to the classic romantic adventure *Love on the Line*.
ISBN 0-931513-00-7　　　　　　　　　　　$11.95

WINGED ISIS by Jean Stewart. 240 pp. The long-awaited sequel to *Warriors of Isis* and the fourth in the exciting Isis series.　　　　ISBN 1-931513-01-5　$11.95

ROOM FOR LOVE by Frankie J. Jones. 192 pp. Jo and Beth must overcome the past in order to have a future together.　　　　ISBN 0-9677753-9-6　$11.95